Ready to Die

In the picture she was beautiful.

Without a trace of her usual cynicism or caustic wit, she had been a gorgeous woman. No more. Tossing his hunting knife in the air and catching it deftly, he smiled as he plunged its sharp tip into the space between his victim's eyes. So much for beauty, he thought as he sliced the photograph.

"Bitch," he muttered under his breath.

Turning his attention to the remaining five photographs, he felt his insides begin to curdle. God, he hated them all. They would have to pay; each and every one of them. But who would be next?

His gaze settled on one face: Stern. Brooding. Contemplative. With a hard jaw and deepset eyes. In that instant, he knew who his next target would be. Dan Grayson.

Make that *Sheriff* Dan Grayson.

Ready to Die

Lisa Jackson

HODDER

First published in Great Britain in 2013 by Hodder & Stoughton
An Hachette UK company
First published in the United States of America by Kensington Publishing Corp.

1

A CIP catalogue record for this title is available from the British Library

B format paperback ISBN 978 1 444 76477 2
A format paperback 978 1 444 76476 5

Printed and bound by CPI Group (UK) Ltd, Croydon, CR0 4YY

Hodder & Stoughton policy is to use papers that are natural, renewable
and recyclable products and made from wood grown in sustainable forests.
The logging and manufacturing processes are expected to conform to the
environmental regulations of the country of origin.

Hodder & Stoughton Ltd
338 Euston Road
London NW1 3BH

www.hodder.co.uk

READY
TO DIE

CHAPTER 1

Tick. Tick. Tick.

He was losing time.

Losing daylight.

The sun, threatening to set early this time of year, was disappearing behind a mountain ridge, the last cold shafts of light a brilliant blaze filtering through the gathering clouds and skeletal branches of the surrounding trees.

He felt the seconds clicking past. Far too quickly.

Tick. Tick. Tick.

By rote, with the precision he'd learned years before in the military, he set up his shot, in an open area that would allow a clean, neat shot.

Not that the bitch deserved the quick death he planned to mete. He would prefer she suffer. But there was no time for waiting. His patience was stretched thin, his skin starting to itch in anticipation.

He knew her routine.

Sighting through his scope one last time, he waited, breath fogging in the air, muscles tense, a drip of sweat collecting under his ski mask despite the frigid temperatures.

Come on, come on, he thought and felt a moment of panic. What if today she changed her mind? What if, for some unknown reason—a phone call, or a visit, or a migraine—she abandoned her yearly ritual? What if, God forbid, this was all for naught, that he'd planned and plotted for a year and by some freak decision she wasn't coming?

No! That's impossible. Stay steady. Be patient. Trust your instincts. Don't give into the doubts. You know what you have to do.

Slowly, he counted to ten, then to twenty, decelerating his heart-beat, calming his mind, clearing his focus. A bird flapped to his right, landing on a snow-covered branch, clumps of white powder falling to the ground. He barely glanced over his shoulder, so intent was he on the area he'd decided would be his killing ground, where the little-used cross-country ski trail veered away from the lake, angling inward through the wintery vegetation.

This would be the place she would die.

His finger tightened over the trigger, just a bit.

Tick. Tick. Tick.

And then he saw her. From the corner of his eye, a tall, slim figure glided easily on her skis.

Good.

Reddish hair poked out from beneath her ski cap as she skied, ever faster. Recklessly. Dangerously. Tall, rangy, and athletic, she wound her way closer. She'd been called "bullheaded" and "tenacious," as well as "determined." Like a dog with a bone, she never gave up, was always ready to fight.

Well, no more. He licked his lips, barely noticing how dry they were. A hum filled his mind, the familiar sound he always heard before a kill.

Just a couple more seconds . . .

Every nerve ending taut, he waited until she broke from the trees. His shot was clear. She glanced in his direction, those glacial bluish eyes searching the forest, that strong chin set.

As if she sensed him, she slowed, squinting.

He pulled the trigger.

Craaaack!

With an ear-splitting report, the rifle kicked hard and familiar against his shoulder.

Her head snapped backward. She spun, skis cutting the air like out-of-kilter chopper blades.

She dropped dead in her tracks.

"Bingo," he whispered, thrilled that he'd brought her down, one of the most newsworthy women in all of Grizzly County. "And then there were five."

Just as the first few flakes of snow began to fall, he shoved hard on his own ski poles, driving them deep into the snow, pushing himself forward. In easy, long strides, he took off through the trees, a phantom slicing a private path into the undergrowth deep within the Bitterroot Mountains. He'd lived here most of his life and knew this back hill country as well as his own name. Down a steep hollow, along a creek and over a small footbridge, he skied. The air was crisp, snow falling more steadily, covering his tracks. He startled a rabbit a good two miles from the kill site and it hopped away through icy brambles, disappearing into the wintry woods.

Darkness was thick by the time he reached the wide spot in the road where he'd parked his van. All in all, he'd traveled five miles and was slightly out of breath. But his blood was on fire, adrenaline rushing through his veins, the thought of what he'd accomplished warming him from the inside out.

How long he'd waited to see her fall!

Stepping out of his skis, he carefully placed them inside the back of his van with his rifle, then tore off his white outer clothing. Ski mask, ski jacket, and winter camouflage pants, insulated against the stinging cold, were replaced quickly with thermal underwear, jeans, flannel shirt, padded jacket, and a Stetson—his usual wear.

After locking the back of the van, he slid into the vehicle's freezing interior and fired up the engine. The old Ford started smoothly, and soon he was driving toward the main road, where, he knew, because of the holidays and impending storm, traffic would be lighter than usual. Only a few hearty souls would be spending Christmas in this remote part of the wilderness where electricity and running water were luxuries. Most of the cabins in this neck of the woods were bare-bones essentials for hunters, some without the basics of electricity or running water, so few people spent the holidays here.

Which was perfect.

At the county road, he turned uphill, heading to his own cabin, snow churning under the van's tires, spying only one set of headlights before he turned off again and into the lane where the snow was piling in the ruts he'd made earlier. Yes, he should be safe here. He'd ditch this van for his Jeep, but not until he'd celebrated a little.

Half a mile in, he rounded an outcropping of boulders and saw the cabin, a dilapidated A-frame most people in the family had long forgotten. It was dark, of course; he'd left it two hours earlier while there was still daylight. After pulling into a rustic garage, he killed the engine, then let out his breath.

He'd made it.

No one had seen.

No one would know . . . yet. Until the time was right. Carrying all of his equipment into the house, he then closed the garage door, listening as the wind moaned through the trees and echoed in this particular canyon.

In the light from his lantern, he hung his ski clothing on pegs near the door, cleaned his rifle, then again, as the cabin warmed, undressed. Once he was naked, he started his workout, stretching his muscles, silently counting, breaking a sweat to a routine he'd learned years ago in the army. This austerity was in counterbalance to the good life he led, the one far from this tiny cabin. His routine worked; it kept him in shape, and he never let a day go by without the satisfaction of exercising as well as he had the day before.

Only then did he clean himself with water cold enough to make him suck his breath in through his teeth. This, too, was part of the ritual, to remind him not to get too soft, to always excel, always push himself. He demanded perfection for himself and expected it of others.

As his body air-dried, he poured himself a glass of whiskey and walked to the hand-hewn desk attached to the wall near his bunk. Pictures were strewn across the desktop, all head shots, faces looking directly at the camera . . . his camera, he thought with more than a grain of pleasure.

He found the photograph of the woman he'd just sent to St. Peter, and in the picture she was beautiful. Without a trace of her usual cynicism, or caustic wit, she had been a gorgeous woman.

No more. Tossing his hunting knife in the air and catching it deftly, he smiled as he plunged its sharp tip into the space between his victim's eyes. So much for beauty, he thought as he sliced the photograph. Staring at its marred surface, he rattled the ice in his drink and swept in a long swallow.

"Bitch," he muttered under his breath.

Turning his attention to the remaining five photographs, he felt his insides begin to curdle. God, he hated them all. They would have to pay; each and every one of them. But who would be next?

Sipping from his glass, he pointed at the first with the tip of his knife and moved it to the others. "Eeny, meeny, miney, mo . . ." But before he could continue and make his selection, his gaze settled on one face: Stern. Brooding. Contemplative. With a hard jaw and deep-set eyes. In that instant, he knew who his next target would be.

Dan Grayson.

Make that *Sheriff* Dan Grayson.

"Merry Christmas," he said to the photograph as the wind picked up and rattled the panes of the old building. With his new target in mind, he took the last swallow from his glass and felt the whiskey warm him from the inside out. Deep in his heart he'd known all along that Grayson would be next.

He hoped the bastard was ready to die.

Grayson snapped off the lights of his office and whistled to his dog, a black Lab who had been with him for years. "Come on, boy." With a groan Sturgis climbed to his feet and, tail wagging slowly, followed Grayson through the hallways of the Pinewood Sheriff's Department.

The cubicles and desks were gratefully quiet tonight, the staff composed of a few volunteers like him, who had elected not to celebrate with their families so others could be with their loved ones.

"You outta here?" Detective Selena Alvarez asked. She was huddled over her desk, computer monitor glowing, a cup of tea cooling near her in-basket.

"Yeah." He glanced at the clock. It was ten minutes after midnight and already a few of those who had either agreed to or who had drawn the short straw were arriving. "What about you?"

"Hmm. Soon." She threw a glance over her shoulder and he noticed how her black hair shined under the fluorescents suspended overhead. As smart and dedicated as anyone in the department, Alvarez had proved herself time and time again on the field of duty, yet he knew little more about her than what was listed on her résumé.

He'd been sure to keep it that way. She had a haunted, secretive demeanor about her, and he'd been tempted to dig a little deeper into what made her tick, then had thought better of it. She'd been interested in him; he wasn't so unaware not to recognize chemistry and attraction when it snuck up on him, and he'd considered returning the favor but had stopped himself. Business and pleasure didn't mix, and he wasn't ready to start a serious relationship again, even though his most recent divorce had been years earlier. But the sting of Cara's betrayal had cut deep and now, with Alvarez, the opportunity had passed. His second marriage had barely lasted a year, again because Cara had never really been out of the picture, and though Alvarez may have thought she was falling in love with him, it was probably just a bit of hero worship on her part, unfounded, of course. He'd certainly felt her heightened interest, but before he'd reciprocated, she'd become involved with someone else, which was, he knew, best for all.

Still . . .

"Merry Christmas," he said and sketched a wave.

"You too." Her smile, so rare as to be almost nonexistent, touched a private spot in his heart. With a nod, he turned away. His dog at his heels, he flipped up his collar, yanked on his gloves, and walked the length of a long hall decorated with twinkling lights and silvery snowflakes, compliments of an overzealous secretary who took the holidays seriously.

Grayson barely noticed. His thoughts were still muddled and dark, all knotted up with images of Alvarez huddled over her desk. Silently, he wondered if he'd made a big mistake; the kind that could alter a man's life. She'd almost died recently and he was just grateful that she was alive.

His steps slowed and he looked back down the hall. Maybe this was the moment to take that extra step and learn what she was about, see if there really was something smoldering there . . . maybe . . .

He caught himself and resumed walking, his footsteps sharper.

"Stupid," he muttered under his breath, giving himself a quick mental shake as he shouldered open the exterior door and stepped into the cold Montana night.

Aside for a few hours with his ex-sister-in-law and his nieces, he'd spend Christmas alone, he thought with a grimace.

It wasn't the first time.

And probably wouldn't be the last.

CHAPTER 2

"I said, 'I want for us to be together. Forever.' "

Standing in front of the woodstove in his old cabin, Nate Santana reached into the front pocket of his jeans and withdrew a small, velvet box.

"Oh, Jesus." Regan Pescoli stared at the tiny box as if it were pure poison. She even took a step backward, but it didn't stop him from dropping down onto one knee, opening the box, and holding it in his palm, the diamond ring within winking against white satin. Tears filled her eyes, burning, and reminding her of the sappy fool she was just under the surface of her crusty exterior. "You don't . . . I mean, I can't . . . Oh, Jesus."

"Regan Pescoli, will you marry me?"

He looked up at her and her heart melted. Snow drifted against the windows, a storm brewing outside, but in this hundred-year-old cabin, it was just the two of them and Santana's husky, who was sleeping on a rug in the corner of the room. "I guess I should have done this before I told you that I wanted you to marry me."

"You mean, asked me first?"

"Yeah."

"That would have been nice." She tried to sound tough, to not allow him to see just how he'd touched her.

"You haven't answered my question."

"I know, I know . . ." She bit her tongue. The simple answer would be: "Yes, yes, a thousand times yes!" before throwing her arms around him and crying happily as he placed the ring on her finger, then carried her into his tiny bedroom where they would make love all night long.

She blinked back that particular fantasy. Her life wasn't simple. And this wasn't a fairy tale. She was a woman, no, make that a detective, with two nearly grown children and two marriages in her wake. Her first husband, Joe Strand, also a cop, had died in the line of duty. They'd been college sweethearts and she'd gotten pregnant, hence the hasty, often-rocky marriage and her son Jeremy, as bullheaded and handsome as his father. Then there had been marriage number two to Luke "Lucky" Pescoli, a truck driver who was as charming as he was good-looking and with whom both kids were spending Christmas Eve this year. That marriage hadn't lasted long either, but the result was worth it: her daughter, pretty, smart, back-talking Bianca who, at sixteen, still believed the world revolved around her.

Two strikes.

Could she take another?

"For the love of God, Santana," she said, clasping his hand and hauling him to his feet. "I'm not ready for this. You *know* that. What the hell are you doing?"

"Proposing," he said dryly.

"Yeah, yeah, I get it, but . . ."

"But what?" he asked, and his eyes were sparkling a bit. Was it the reflection of the Christmas lights, a single strand he'd hung over the front room window, or her imagination that he might actually be *amused* at her confounded response?

"We've been over this before. I thought you understood. It's not that I don't love you—you know that I do—but me and marriage . . . it's just never worked out."

"Because you were always with the wrong guy."

"Or they were with the wrong woman," she said. When she saw that he was about to argue with her, she put out a hand to stop whatever arguments he came up with. "You know I don't believe any one person is the blame of a marriage cracking or rotting. It takes two people to work really hard and . . ." She sat down on the old ottoman, so that now she was the one looking up, the one pleading, "Frankly, I just don't know if I'm up to it."

"It could be fun."

"And it could be a disaster. My kids—"

"Will get used to the idea. You can't live your life for them, you know. This is for you."

"I know, but . . ."

"But what?" His playful attitude seemed to shift. "Either you want to get married or you don't."

"Oh, sure. If it were just that simple."

"It's as simple as you want it to be." He arched a dark eyebrow and she felt her heart melt. In beat-up jeans, a dark T-shirt, and an open flannel shirt with the sleeves pushed to his elbows, he was earthy and male, whip-smart and cocky, a cowboy type with a murky past who had appealed to her from the moment their gazes first clashed.

It had always been that way with Santana. One look and he could turn her inside out. She was a strong, no-nonsense woman who couldn't be bullied into anything, a hard-nosed detective who had been accused more often than not of being stubborn to the point of mule-headed. She'd never been the wishy-washy sort.

Except when it came to the subject of Santana and marriage.

She shouldn't have been so floored. She'd seen this coming for a long time; a bullet she couldn't dodge. She didn't know if she was ready and truth be told, she wasn't sure she ever would be.

"Come on, Pescoli," he said with the slightest bit of irritation beneath his cajoling. "Is it that hard to say 'yes'?"

She shook her head. "No, that part would be easy, it's the rest. The believing it will work out, that we'll always love each other, that it won't turn into something ugly where all we do is try to get even."

"That won't happen," he said, and for a second she believed him. "Not with us."

"I think that's what everyone who stands before God and family or a justice of the peace believes."

For a second he didn't say anything; then he snapped the box closed and set it on a table. "Tell ya what. It's Christmas Eve. You've got one week."

"You're giving me an ultimatum?" She couldn't believe her ears.

"You *are* a brilliant detective," he said and smiled faintly as he leaned over to stoke the fire. Not bothering with gloves, he tossed a couple of chunks of pine into already-glowing embers, then stood and dusted his hands. All the while she'd noticed the way his battered Levi's had stretched over his buttocks, and when she realized that she'd been staring, even fantasizing, she was annoyed at herself even further.

"I'm not going to be backed into a corner and forced to make a decision."

"That's not what I'm doing."

"Yeah?"

"Okay. Fine. Think of it that way, then." He shrugged as the fire popped behind him. "I'm not going to bug you about it. In fact, I'm going to stay out of your way; I'm not coming over to your house tomorrow. You have your time with your kids alone. But on New Year's Day, I expect to hear that you're ready to plan a future, that you and your kids are going to move into the new house with me, or . . . you're not. If you can't commit, then I think we'd better take a good, hard look at what we've got here."

"And?"

"And if it's not working out, then we'd better face it, don't you think?"

"What I think is that we have a damned good thing going and even if it's not . . . conventional . . . or even expected, it kind of works for us. No rules. You do your thing and I do mine. Everyone's happy."

His look called her a liar. "Then you're not hearing me. What I'm saying is that I want to make you my wife. I want us to be a family. We've had our . . . fling." She nodded, remembering their hot affair and how it had started, purely physically. "And it matured into this"—he motioned back and forth between them with one hand—"relationship that we've got now." Her throat was tight, but she couldn't help but agree. "And you're right, it's been great."

"*Really* great." Not only the best sex of her life, but a feeling of belonging, of trust, of letting this man see all the complex sides to her and loving him despite his flaws.

"So, now I want to take what we've got to the next level. Do you?"

The room seemed to shrink, to the point that it was just the two of them alone in the universe, which was just plain ridiculous because she was still a mother. Letting her breath out slowly, she said, "It's not about want or desire. It's not about not having dreams of us being together forever. It's about being practical."

He had the nerve to smile, that same slow, crooked slash of white that she'd found so impossibly sexy. "It's about fear," he countered, clasping her hands and pulling her to her feet. "*Your* fear."

"Bullshit."

"You know I'm right."

She felt suddenly close to tears. Stupid tears. *Woman* tears. "I just don't want you to end up hating me."

He half-laughed and wrapped his arms around her. "Do you really think that's possible?"

"Yes."

"Then you really don't know me, now, darlin', do you?" Before she could answer, he drew her close and kissed her forehead, a soft brush of his lips against her skin. His breath was warm, his arms strong, and she felt the urge to melt into them. "It's Christmas. Let's not argue."

"Is that possible?"

"Probably not." When she tilted her face upward to stare into his eyes, she saw a spark of mirth, and deeper in those dark depths, something more, something that he quickly hid. She realized she should resist, that they needed to work this marriage thing out, but she was tired of arguing and besides, it would serve no purpose. And he was right: It was Christmas.

His lips found hers and as he kissed her, he swept her into his arms. "Wait . . ." she said, but Nate paid no heed as he carried her into the bedroom and dropped her unceremoniously onto his bed. "You're presuming a lot, mister," she pointed out, fighting her own smile.

"You bet I am." He was already falling onto the old mattress with her and starting to unzip the front opening of her sweater.

"You know you're a bastard, Santana."

"Yep, and you love me for it."

"Probably."

"No probably about it, Detective." He yanked both of his shirts over his head and tossed them into the corner. "And I think I'm going to prove it to you."

She laughed. "That's way too corny."

"Yeah, I know." Nuzzling her neck, he rolled atop her and, nose-to-nose, said, "I've got to find a way to convince you to marry me."

"Good luck with that."

"Is that a challenge?"

"What do you think?"

His hands, large and warm, pushed aside her sweater. "Good," he murmured across the top of her breasts, "Because, darlin', I'm definitely up for one."

"You're bad," she said, holding her breath as her blood began to heat.

"The worst." He kissed one of her nipples and looked up at her, his eyes glistening in the half-light.

Regan sighed, slowly sinking into sweet capitulation, at least in this.

"Hey, Alvarez! Give it a rest." Pete Watershed's voice nearly echoed through the quiet offices of the sheriff's department. He'd been striding past her open doorway, the scent of tobacco smoke clinging to him, but he'd stopped and backtracked to her when he'd noticed her still at her desk, her computer monitor glowing with images of the victims of the latest serial killer to make Grizzly Falls his personal killing grounds as recently as two weeks before. He'd been dubbed the Ice Mummy Killer by the press and the name had stuck.

"Got any idea what time it is?" Watershed asked. A lanky road deputy with a perpetual scowl and propensity for crude jokes, he, too, had volunteered to work the night shift. She didn't much like him, but he was a decent enough cop, and willing to give up his Christmas Eve so another deputy with a family could spend the night at home.

"A vague idea."

"Yeah? So what're you tryin' to do, make the rest of us look bad?" He chuckled and his laughter turned into a cough, the result of a two-pack-a-day habit.

"Yeah, that's it: My ultimate plan," she said, and he laughed even more. "Fortunately with you, I don't have to try very hard." She half-smiled.

"Well, that was uncalled for." The coughing attack slowly subsided.

"Actually, I'm packing it in." Gathering up her keys and purse, Alvarez pushed her chair away from the desk. Her leg, from her most recent injury, pained a little, but she fought through it, barely wincing. Though she hated to admit it, Watershed was right, the digital readout on her computer monitor registered 1:16 a.m. She should have left the office over an hour earlier, but, of course, she'd put off going home. Again. A habit she'd tried hard to break. For years her job had been her life, and she'd seen nothing wrong with being known as a workaholic. It had suited her just fine until Dylan O'Keefe had barreled back into her life a little over a month ago. They'd been together ever since, and though their relationship was far from smooth, she was hopeful that it could develop into something permanent. Tonight, O'Keefe was with his family in Helena, so she was alone.

"Good, because I'm already on overtime and the department can't afford us both."

He wasn't kidding. The sheriff's department's budget was stretched to the max. In early December there had been an intense, seemingly unending blizzard that had required extra man hours for road closures, electrical outages, and evacuations of the elderly. The recent serial killer's rampage had added an extra strain to the resources of the department.

"If you're so worried about the budget, why're you still here?"

"Finishing up a report." His eyes darkened a bit and he rubbed the beard stubble evident on his jaw. "Single-car accident out by Horsebrier Ridge." Shaking his head, he added, "Nineteen-year-old kid."

"Dead?" She felt a sudden chill deep inside.

"Nearly. Helluva thing for his parents to hear on Christmas Eve."

"Or anytime," she said, thinking of her own son in Helena, a boy being raised by another family as she'd given him up for adoption at his birth. Her heart twisted a little when she thought of Gabriel, the sixteen-year-old who had so recently come bursting back into her life.

Watershed asked, "So why are you still here?"

Slipping into her jacket, she decided to duck the question; the answer was just too personal. Since O'Keefe wasn't returning to Grizzly Falls until the morning, she was avoiding her town house and all the ghosts of Christmases past. "Just tying up some loose ends."

"On Christmas Eve?"

With a shrug, she wrapped a scarf around her neck and pocketed her keys.

"I thought you were on restricted hours or half time, or something." He pointed at her leg.

At the thought of her struggle, how she'd nearly lost her life during her encounter with Grizzly Falls's latest serial killer, she shuddered inwardly but forced a smile she didn't feel. "The doc says I'm good to go."

"And the sheriff?"

"Grayson knows."

"Sure." Obviously he thought her explanation was bogus, but he didn't press it. "Okay, I gotta run. So, Merry Christmas, Alvarez. Have a good one, well, what's left of it."

"Got a whole day, Watershed. Or at least twenty-three hours left." And it was going to feel like forever. She already wished the holiday was over.

Watershed didn't hear her remark as he was already walking toward the area of the offices where the restrooms were located.

Usually the department was a bustle of activity, phones jangling, footsteps in the hallways, voices of officers and witnesses, keyboards clicking, the occasional burst of laughter or clink of chains on shackles, but tonight, with most of the lights dimmed and only a skeleton crew tucked inside, the offices were eerily quiet.

"Silent night," she muttered under her breath as she slid her pistol into her holster and snapped off the lights.

Quickly, she zipped her jacket and headed toward the back of the building. Hopefully she wouldn't meet anyone else and have to again dodge why she was here so late, why she had such an aversion to the holidays.

For the first half of her life, growing up in Woodburn, Oregon, in a large Hispanic family, she'd felt that special electricity that seemed to surround Christmas. Midnight mass with her family, the smell of tamales her grandmother created, the laughter and anticipation of her siblings as they decorated the tree, the anticipation of Christmas morning; it had been a magical, special time in an outgoing girl's life.

And it had been stolen from her in an instant.

Her stomach soured when she thought of her cousin and how she'd been violated, how her innocence had been stripped from her.

"Get over it," she whispered under her breath as she walked through the deserted lunchroom, but she knew she never would. There weren't enough psychologists or antidepressants or kind, consoling thoughts to erase that particular pain. It would always be there, a scar that was just only lightly healed.

But she'd learned to deal and cope and now . . . even love again.

Maybe.

In contrast to the muted lights of the offices, the lunchroom was ablaze, fluorescent bulbs burning brightly overhead, while white Formica-topped tables seemed to reflect that very light. And everywhere, of course, shiny, silver snowflakes and gold wreaths, suspended from the ceiling and plastered to the walls, created weird mirrors.

Joelle Fisher, the department's receptionist, was an *uber* Christmas enthusiast. Well, make that any holiday. She was up for celebrating all of the majors, like the Fourth of July and Christmas, as well as the minors, like Arbor Day and Flag Day. It seemed to be Joelle's mission to find even the most obscure holiday and find a way to celebrate it here at the office. Joelle was never more in her element than around the end of the year when the biggies came: Halloween, Thanksgiving, and Christmas. Bang, bang, bang! From mid-September through February fifteenth, Joelle's personal mission was to spread the cheer.

Ad nauseum.

Joelle's idea of celebration meant decorating the office in the brightest, most glittery, and sometimes gaudiest decorations available. Somehow Alvarez didn't think that tinsel and colored lights blinking rapidly enough to bring on seizures were exactly how God thought the world should celebrate the holy day, but then, what did she know? And she wasn't one to complain, not like Pescoli, her partner.

A few reindeer cookies remained on a plastic platter cut into the shape of a snowflake. Alvarez resisted, as she was determined to return to her normal diet and exercise regimen. As she stepped outside, the nagging pain in her leg reminded her once more of her last struggle with a madman. She actively ignored it, concentrating instead on how much better her life was now. If she let it, the magic of Christmas might just steal into her heart and touch her soul.

Maybe.

The jury was still out on that one.

CHAPTER 3

Pescoli floored it.

Though it was snowing and the roads were dicey at best, she hit the gas and her Jeep sprang forward, following the snaking road through steep canyons and sheer mountains. The forest was silent, aside from the rumble of the Jeep's engine, the stands of pine and hemlock blanketed in three inches of fresh, pristine snow. Picture-postcard perfect, but she barely noticed. She was tired as all get-out from a sleepless night of tossing and turning and inwardly fretting. After making love to Santana until nearly two a.m., she'd tried to fall asleep, but her churning thoughts had kept her awake for hours. Should she accept his proposal? Could she give up her independence? What would happen to her kids? Her job? The life she had worked so hard to carve out for herself after her divorce from Lucky?

Marrying Santana seemed like a no-brainer, and, she supposed in the warmth of her SUV, if she hadn't been down the slippery slope of marriage before, she would have leaped at the chance to become his wife. But she had already suffered through two messy marriages and though she was leaning toward saying yes, it pissed her off to be put on the spot, be given a deadline.

Shifting down for a corner, she told herself how ridiculous that sounded. He had the right to move on if the relationship didn't develop the way he wanted. Still, she was bugged.

She flipped her wipers onto a faster rhythm, the blades scraping away snow from her windshield as the engine purred and the tires whined. The police band crackled a bit, and she turned on the radio straight to Burl Ives singing "Have a Holly Jolly Christmas" for about the three millionth time this Christmas season. Quickly, she punched in another station that was all talk radio and the news.

Her kids were coming over this morning, well, make that the afternoon as Jeremy had trouble getting his butt out of bed before eleven these days, so she didn't have much time. She hated the fact that she had to share them both, especially during the holidays, but couldn't argue the fact. Luke, a louse of a husband while they'd been married, was slightly better as a stepfather and father, though she wasn't that crazy about his wife. Still south of thirty, Michelle had a killer figure, and despite the dumb-blond routine was, Pescoli estimated, at least a little smarter than she let on.

Now, because of Santana's proposal, she was on her way to see her boss. It might not be a good idea to bust in on him on Christmas morning, but Grayson was of the mind-set that he *always* had time for his employees, day or night. He'd said as much as recently as last week, so Pescoli intended to take him at his word. She needed advice and with one week to make up her mind, she wanted to know if working part-time was an option, or if there was some way to adjust her hours. Though Jeremy was about out of the house, Bianca, still in high school, could use her around more. If there were anything about her job Pescoli regretted, it was how much time it took her away from the kids, and her dedication to her work was certainly one factor in the erosion of both of her marriages.

Not that she'd ever give it up. Hell no. She loved being a detective and was a damned good one. Recently, while Alvarez recuperated, she'd been teamed with Brett Gage who, although capable enough, didn't really click with her. Everything had felt awkward and out of sync at the station. However, now that Alvarez was back on the job, things were humming again.

Maybe she could cut down her time away from home, she mused, and if that didn't work, she could maybe play around with the idea of going private. O'Keefe had mentioned something about it, and the idea was attractive. Sort of. The plain hard truth of it was that she loved her job; not quite as much as she loved her kids, of course, but right up there.

How about Santana? Do you love him more than working for the Pinewood Sheriff's Department?

"Apples and oranges," she told herself as the weather report came on the radio. "Apples and oranges."

A fresh pot of coffee was brewing, filling his kitchen with that warm, heady aroma Grayson looked forward to from the minute he opened his eyes. He was a morning person, always had been, despite the years he'd been forced to work swing or graveyard when he'd first become a road deputy. His wife hadn't much liked the late nights either, but back then, he'd taken whatever shift was offered and had let Cara's complaints slide off him just like water on a duck's back.

Of course, his refusing to engage in an argument about his work, about his "putting his job before his wife" had no doubt helped contribute to the death of an already deteriorating marriage.

Now, he poured himself a cup and checked his phone again where a text message from Regan Pescoli announced that she was on her way to see him. "Wonder what that's all about?" he said to his dog. Sturgis, his black Lab who'd been eagerly lapping water from his bowl near the back door, looked over his shoulder and wagged his tail.

Why the hell would Pescoli be making a run to his house on Christmas morning? Probably not with good news or a damned fruit-cake considering how she felt about all of Joelle's Christmas machinations at the office. Pescoli, though not a traditionalist, always spent what time she could with her kids over the holidays. No way would she be heading to his house unless it was important. "Guess we'll find out when we find out," he said and glanced out the window over his sink.

A new layer of snow had fallen overnight, probably four inches if the accumulation on his deck railing was accurate. He was isolated up here, a two-bedroom cabin that he'd been working on for years in his spare time. So far he'd added a second bathroom, fixed up the first and was contemplating gutting the kitchen. But that would be a while. As it was, the old wooden, sloped counters and solid cupboards suited him just fine. For now. For his bachelor lifestyle.

Sturgis looked up again, water dripping from his mouth to the old wood floor. "You know you've got a drinking problem, don't you?"

Again, he was rewarded with a tail wag. Smiling, Grayson scratched his dog's ears and set his half-drunk cup on the scarred counter. "Merry Christmas, fella," he said and thought of the day ahead. He'd been invited to his ex-sister-in-law's house for dinner. Hattie, who had been married to his brother, Bart, had always included him in her holiday plans and he'd usually accepted her invitations, even though it was complicated. *Very* complicated. Hattie was a local girl who had, in her youth, dated three out of four of the Grayson brothers, including Dan.

So that was tricky to begin with.

She'd ended up marrying Bart, had twin girls, and when the marriage unraveled, moved off the ranch. The divorce had been bitter, and Bart, despondent, had ended up committing suicide by hanging himself in the barn.

Ugly all the way around. And that didn't include another slightly incestuous twist. Hattie was his ex-wife Cara's younger sister . . . make that estranged younger half sister. Yeah, things with Hattie were complicated, the kind of intertwined relationship that bred in a town the size of Grizzly Falls.

Of course, Hattie had felt terrible ever since Bart's death, even going so far as to insist that he would never kill himself. The evidence was the evidence, however; she just chose to ignore it. But whenever she was with the Grayson family, which was often as she'd seemed to dedicate herself to the Grayson family more and more after Bart's death, she would bring it up again, that Bart would never take his own life. She also explained hanging around more because she wanted the girls to know their father's kin. Maybe that was true, but Dan's brothers, Cade and Big Zed, weren't convinced that her motives were so pure. They'd both vociferously declared that she was just interested in the ranch and the family money.

"Jesus, Dan, how can you be so naive?" Cade had demanded the last time he'd been at the ranch. "You should know better. You dated her!" He and his two brothers had been leaning over the rails near the barn, watching the cattle gather under the overhang, red and black coats shaggy with the harsh winter, their breaths coming out in clouds as the animals lowed and filed inside for feed.

"Ancient history," Dan had replied. "And besides—"

"Yeah, yeah. I know, all right? I did too." Cade scowled darkly at the memory while Big Zed, three inches taller than his brothers and fifty pounds heavier, eyed them both narrowly. Cade continued, "The difference is that I got smarter for the experience!"

"Kinda," Big Zed said. The oldest of the Grayson brothers, he was usually quieter than Cade, who was known to be explosive, or Dan, who didn't run on Cade's hot emotions but always had his say.

"What's that supposed to mean?" Cade demanded.

"Just what I said. You kinda got over her." Zed shrugged a brawny shoulder. "And you kind of didn't."

"Shitfire, what do you know?" Cade grumbled, then kicked at a dirt clod that had stuck out of the snow. "I'm just saying you, brother"— he pointed a gloved finger at Dan—"better tread carefully."

Of course Dan hadn't taken any bit of his brothers' advice. It didn't really matter what Hattie's motives were. It was the twins, McKenzie and Mallory, who were important. He'd never had any kids himself, and those two energetic eight-year-olds had burrowed deep into his heart.

So he'd agreed to the dinner. He'd even managed to buy some girl-type games at a toy store in Missoula and put them into red bags filled with green tissue paper and tied with gold ribbons. As was his usual routine, he'd included a check for each of Bart's daughters in the cards he'd added to the bags. For college. He figured it was the least he could do.

He only hoped Hattie would keep her feelings about Bart's suicide to herself, though he suspected that was wishful thinking because as recently as two weeks ago, she'd brought up the subject.

"Think about it," she'd said to him. "Do you really think your brother would hang himself? That just wasn't Bart's style!" Her eyes narrowed on a distant point. "If someone had said he'd ridden a horse up to Cougar Ridge and used his own gun . . . then maybe I could buy it. *Maybe*. But that's still a big if."

"Hattie, the man was depressed."

"Lots of people are," she flung back at him, her eyes snapping fire. "That's what Prozac is for!"

"Well, Prozac wasn't exactly Bart's style either," he reasoned and she had suspended the argument. But it was going to be resurrected; he could feel it. His ex-sister-in-law was nothing if not dogged.

Glancing at his watch now, he scowled. Pescoli, and whatever it was that was so damned important that it had to be dealt with this morning, would be here soon and the fire in the woodstove needed stoking.

"We'd better get to it," he said to the dog, then slipped on the boots he'd left near the back door. As soon as he opened the door, a cold wind swirled inside. Sturgis sprang onto the porch and, paws scraping loudly, took off like a streak. Squaring a Stetson onto his head, Grayson strode outside, his boots ringing across the porch. "Okay," he muttered under his breath, eyeing the small stack of firewood near the door. Fair enough. He'd split some more.

After all, a little exercise sure wouldn't kill him.

Tick. Tick. Tick.

Time was passing. Too fast. He didn't have all day. It was Christmas morning. He had places to be, alibis to create.

And yet he waited.

Perched on the steep rise above Grayson's cabin, watching smoke curl from the ancient chimney that was missing more than a few bricks, he bided his time. Impatiently. His gloved hands nearly caressed his rifle's barrel as his gaze fastened on the ice-glazed windows where he'd seen the sheriff's distorted silhouette pass by, though never linger.

Snow was falling more rapidly. Big, fat flakes nearly obscured his view, drifting with the wind. The snowfall was an impediment, yes, but also a cover.

He resisted the urge to look at his watch.

Dawn had broken, so he was already running late.

For crying out loud, would the man ever quit moving? Take a stand by one of the windows that faced this direction?

Okay, you bastard, come to Papa!

As if on cue, the back door to the cabin opened and Grayson's black Lab shot across the porch, leaping over the steps into the snow.

The killer's gut tightened a bit. The dog could be a problem. If the hound caught his scent and sent up a ruckus or even came over to investigate, Grayson would be warned and there was no shooting the animal. Yet. Gritting his teeth behind the rotting stump where he'd sought cover, he settled his rifle atop the uneven surface, sighted through it, and waited as the seconds ticked by.

Come on, come on . . .

The door slammed shut and footsteps echoed across the porch.

Good.

The killer smiled, trained his rifle on the porch.

Tick. Tick. Tick.

He needed a clean shot. Then he'd squeeze the trigger and send Dan Grayson to his maker. The thought was like warm honey that balmed his soul, sweet and thick, calming. Oh, what perfect revenge this would be. But he was getting ahead of himself. As much as he felt the zing of anticipation through his blood, he couldn't play into it. Not yet. Carefully, he steadied his accelerating heartbeat as well as his hand. Sighting through the crosshairs of his scope, he aimed, watching as the big man strode down two steps, ax in hand. The stupid dog was running back and forth, a distraction, but so far hadn't noticed that Grayson was being stalked.

Good boy. Just continue to be an idiot.

Grayson crossed the driveway, making tracks in the new snow, to the other side of the garage where he'd stacked big chunks of wood. He didn't hesitate; he found a couple of pieces and split them neatly, the wood cracking as kindling split off and flew to the ground.

He itched to pull the trigger, but a tree was in the way, so he held tight. Beneath his ski mask, sweat began to pepper his brow as he thought of how long he'd waited for just this moment, this instant in time when he could finally get rid of Grayson forever.

Payback's a bitch.

Craaack! Another piece split. Then another.

Come on, come on. How much kindling do you really need?

The answer, of course, was none.

Finally, Grayson bent over, picked up an armload of kindling, and stepped from under the overhang.

He trained his sight on the now-moving target . . . aiming . . . aiming . . . centering the crosshairs so there was no slipup. His finger started to squeeze.

Woof! Woof!

Sharp barks rang through the canyon.

The dog! Where the hell is the damned dog?

Without moving his head, his hands still steady on the rifle stock, he glanced to one side. In his peripheral vision, he saw a flash of black dashing through the trees.

Damned mutt! Go away!

Nerves jangled slightly, he reminded himself that he was upwind. No way could the dog—

"Sturgis!" Grayson's voice boomed, seeming loud enough to cause an avalanche.

He froze.

"Come!" Grayson commanded, squinting into the growing light, scouring the woods for his stupid mutt.

Oh, hell!

His heart began to jackhammer, his nerves stretched tight as crossbow strings.

Concentrate, don't be distracted. You can do this . . . Again he focused on his target. Grayson had rotated slightly and stood facing his direction. *Perfect.*

He started to squeeze.

Another sharp, warning bark.

Shit!

Grayson started walking away from the house, disappearing behind a copse of saplings. *Son of a bitch!* The killer needed to finish this, get a clean shot and pull the damned trigger.

A familiar hum filled his head and he licked his lips. From the corner of his eye, he noted that the dog wasn't far off.

"Sturgis, come!" Grayson ordered, then looked directly toward the stump that offered him some cover

The dog stopped dead in his tracks, nose lifted to the wind.

Stiff as a statue, ears pricked forward, the black Lab stared directly at him. Not obeying Grayson, but not bounding and barking either. Just watching.

Not good.

A shiver ran up his spine and he thought he'd have to take the dog out too. Fair enough.

Grayson stopped. Cocked his head. As if he'd suddenly sensed that he was being stalked.

The killer ignored the dog. Focused again on his mission.

Tick. Tick. Tick.

The hum grew to a rumble. Loud. Roaring.

Now!

The humming in his brain increased. Louder and louder.

This time, he moved the rifle's muzzle a fraction, just enough to get Grayson in his crosshairs once more.

Finally, he got a bead on the man just as the humming became a roar and he realized the sound wasn't internal. The grinding noise was from an approaching car or, more likely, a truck, its engine whining as it climbed a steep hill.

A visitor?

To Grayson's remote cabin on Christmas morning?

There was no other cabin nearby.

The engine's growl increased, seeming to thunder in the killer's head.

No, no, no! This is not *part of the plan. An intrusion could ruin everything.*

Tick. Tick. Tick.

Through the veil of snow, he spied Grayson, still carrying his armload of kindling. The sheriff took a step toward the house, into the clearing, where he paused, as he, too, apparently had finally heard the approaching vehicle.

Ignore it! Focus!

A hundred yards away, the Jeep swung into view.

Now!

He pulled the trigger.

Blam! His rifle kicked back hard. The shot was off.

Grayson's body jerked violently, snapping backward, his arms flailing crazily, his head spinning. Kindling went flying in all directions, bouncing and burying in the snow. His hat flew off his head, then skittered away, but the son of a bitch was still standing, facing away. Staggering, starting to drop. Not good enough!

Sighting quickly, he squeezed the trigger once more. His rifle blasted. Grayson jerked again like a marionette; then he fell, half rotating from the blast, blood blooming on his chest and upward through his collar, staining the pristine blanket a deep, beautiful red.

"Die, bastard," he whispered just as twin beams from headlights flashed in the early-morning light.

Damn!

The beams glowed brighter, splashing on the cabin's wall despite the veil of snowflakes. He saw that they were from a fast-approaching Jeep. The driver was pushing it, as if he knew that there was danger.

He had to leave. Now. No time to waste.

The damned dog let out a bone-chilling howl. In frustration, he trained the barrel of his rifle toward the animal, sighting the beast just as the Jeep slid to a stop.

No time.

Despite the clean shot, he stopped himself.

He would show his hand if he killed the damned dog. Whoever was driving the Jeep would be certain to see him. It would be lucky if the driver hadn't seen the flash of his barrel as it was. He couldn't take a chance.

Unless he took the Jeep's owner out too.

The driver's side door burst open. A woman with reddish hair threw herself out of her county-issue vehicle.

His heart nearly stopped as he recognized her: *Detective Regan Pescoli of the Pinewood Sheriff's Department, and a Bitch on Wheels.*

Wouldn't you know?

For half a second, he considered shooting her too. A two-for-one. Why not?

He hesitated but couldn't get a clean shot. Besides, she would be armed, and the dog was already looking in his direction, starting to move toward the rise where he'd taken cover. No, he couldn't take the risk. Couldn't get caught. There was too much to do, and it had to be done precisely. No mistakes. According to plan.

Heart hammering, he backed away from the stump and into the cover of the frigid forest. Quickly, he slid his rifle into its case, strapped over his back, and plunged his ski poles into the snow. He took off like the bullet that had dropped the sheriff. Running late, but not about to be caught by the damned mutt or ID'd by the detective. Tucking his body tight, he sped down the steep trail, shooting between the trees and jumping over exposed boulders as he heard the chilling howl of Grayson's dog reverberating down the ravine.

But the animal would never catch him.

And then there were four.

That was, if his shot was true, if Grayson was really dead. For now, he decided, he'd assume the best. Behind his mask he smiled a skeleton's grin.

Sayonara, sucker. You got what you damned well deserved.

CHAPTER 4

Blam!
Pescoli watched in horror as Grayson's body jerked spasmodically, then spun, his Stetson flung off his head, the pieces of wood that had been in his arms flying into the air to land in the snow. "No!"

Blam! Another shot blasted through the valley, this time as he was falling. His head snapped forward as he fell, reeling.

"No, no! Oh, God, no!" Horrified, Pescoli gunned her rig to the parking area, then slammed on the brakes, so that the Jeep skidded to a stop between Grayson and the area from which she thought the shots originated.

Keeping low, she moved over the center console and across the seat, to open the far door and drop to the ground next to Grayson as the engine continued to run, the wipers still scraping snow from the windshield. Automatically dialing her cell for assistance, with one hand, she yanked her sidearm from its holster and scanned the terrain. Watching Grayson's dog take off like a black bullet through the snow, she screamed into her phone, "Officer down!" as the emergency operator answered. *What the hell happened here?* Moving instinctively, her gaze scouring the thickly forested terrain, she identified herself and the victim. "I'm at Sheriff Dan Grayson's cabin up on Spangler Lane," she stated, then rattled off the nearest cross street. Half expecting another rifle shot, with all her senses on high alert, she fell to her knees at Grayson's side.

Oh, God, he looked bad.

So gray. Barely breathing.

She wondered if the assailant was still nearby, if, even now, he was aiming his weapon again. Or had he done what he intended and taken off. From the sound of it, Grayson's dog was giving chase to something, most likely the would-be assassin.

Get him, Sturgis. Run that bastard to the ground and rip his frickin' throat out.

Her thoughts were brutal as she turned her full attention to the sheriff. His face was ashen, blood turning the snow an ominous red. "Sweet Jesus." Was he dead? For the love of God . . . Fully dressed, he lay on the snow, bareheaded, his gaze fixed to the sky, blood pumping from beneath his collar to drizzle down his neck to the icy ground. "Grayson? Can you hear me?" she said loudly. *Oh, Jesus, please respond. Come on, Grayson. Don't die . . . don't you dare die . . . you just can't.* Dropping her sidearm, still on the phone, Pescoli found the pulse at his neck, beneath the trickle of red. "He's got a pulse," she said to the operator, hope rising a bit. "Not strong, but a pulse." To the sheriff, she added, "Dan! Stay with me! Can you hear me? Sheriff!"

Who would do this? Who would gun down a good man like Grayson. *Far too many. He's a lawman. A target.*

"Detective?"

"Yeah, I'm here."

"Can you give me vitals?"

"Of course not! He's alive, but just barely. Two wounds. Head and chest! Get me help! Now!" With her free hand she unzipped his jacket, felt the warmth and stickiness of his blood . . . so damned much blood. Beneath his shirt was the wound . . . dear God. Raw and gaping, bloody flesh beneath a torn mat of skin and chest hair. "Help me," she whispered to a deity she rarely invoked.

"Detective?"

"I'm here. It's bad. Chest wound, possibly heart or lung, or artery. Lots of blood loss. And the head wound, left side, above the temple . . . maybe through and through, I can't tell. Look, we don't have much time!"

"Officers and paramedics have been dispatched."

"Tell them to get here fast!" She had to staunch the flow of blood and then . . . what? Her first-aid training took over and she tore off her own jacket, pulled the lining free, and used the interior side to press against his chest. "Get me on the line with a paramedic," she ordered.

"They'll be there in fifteen minutes."

"That's thirteen minutes too late!" she yelled in frustration. "For the love of God, get me help NOW!"

"Detective, stay calm. Help is on its way. Please stay on the line and—"

"Damned straight, I'll stay on the line. Get someone the hell out here!" She was nearly hysterical, desperate to keep Grayson alive.

"Detective."

"Yeah, I know!" She heard the frantic tone of her voice, and while holding fast to her makeshift bandage of lining, watching the fabric turn from tan to deep, dark red, she managed to talk herself down, told herself she had to stay in her head to help him.

Grayson sucked in a rattling breath.

Blood colored his lips.

Oh, Lord. She blinked against hot tears.

No way would she break down. Not now. Not while she could still help him.

"Hang in there!" Shivering, she willed him to live. "Come on, Dan, you stay with me. Hear me? You stay the hell with me." But her voice cracked a little as she felt his lifeblood flowing through her fingers. Where the hell was the ambulance? She strained to hear a siren, or an engine, or any sign of help coming her way, but she heard only the rush of a brutal wind blowing through this desolate canyon.

God, it was cold. And terrifying.

Teeth chattering, she wouldn't give up, couldn't.

Could he see her? "Dan!" she yelled again. "Sheriff! Stay with me. Come on. Hang in there. Help is on its way."

The dispatcher said, "I've got a trauma doctor on the line, you can speak directly to him."

"Good," she said, though her hope was fading fast. Grayson stared up at her, his face devoid of emotion. No pain. No recognition. Nothing. Deep in her heart, she feared it was already too late.

* * *

"I've got some bad news . . . the sheriff . . . looks like a sniper wait-ing for him . . . just lucky I was here . . . bullet wound to the chest . . . still alive but . . . I can't freaking believe it . . ."

Disjointed pieces of the conversation with her partner kept sur-facing in her brain as Alvarez drove to Grayson's cabin, now a crime scene. Her throat was tight, her fingers gripping the wheel with enough force that her knuckles showed white over the wheel of her Subaru. Who would do this? Who would attack the man who'd led the department with intelligence and determination, yes, but also with kindness, empathy, and understanding?

"I'll get you," she vowed as she urged her Outback up the hill. She stopped at Grayson's private lane, two snow-covered ruts that veered off the county road. Other vehicles were parked haphazardly near the entrance: department-issued vehicles, an unmarked rig, and a van from the forensic unit. Already at his post, Deputy Kayan Rule was monitoring the nearly nonexistent traffic and keeping a log of anyone who arrived. A tall black man in full uniform, his face was a mask of quiet, seething rage. Kayan was usually affable, a rock-steady influence with a sharp wit and dry sense of humor that wasn't in evi-dence today.

Alvarez knew exactly how he felt.

Pulling her vehicle off the road as far as possible, she parked, then zipped up her boots and yanked on one glove. As she approached Rule, he said, "I hoped I'd never see this day."

"I know. Me neither." After signing in, she stretched her remaining glove over her right hand.

"Who the hell does something like this? And on Christmas?" His deep voice was angry, his lips hard against his teeth, one fist balled.

She was shaking her head, feeling as if the whole situation were surreal. "Whoever the bastard is, I'll find him."

"We," he said, his words clipped. "We'll find him."

"That's right. We will." Heart filled with dread, she started up the lane, avoiding the area roped off by the crime scene team who had managed to arrive before she had. Through the falling snow, she fol-lowed the lane that cut into the woods and followed the winding path of a stream that was nearly frozen over. Only a trickle of water was visible beneath a thin layer of ice and she noticed a snowshoe hare hiding in the brush. Any other day the area would have appeared tranquil. Serene. But not this morning.

As she trudged around a final bend, the trees opened into a clearing where Grayson's cabin, rustic and picturesque with its snow-covered steep roof and icicles dangling from the gutters, had changed into another roped-off area where officers were working and a wide stain of red had spread over the ground and seeped into the snow. Her throat tightened when she realized that the shape was irregular, showing where a human head, neck, and torso had been buried and the blood had stopped, freezing near the body. There was disturbance in the stain as well, footsteps and mashed snow. In her mind's eye, Alvarez saw Pescoli coming across the victim, kneeling at Grayson's side, trying to save him.

Her insides curdled at the image.

She spied Pescoli standing away from the scene. She was pale, her teeth chattering, leaning for support against the fender of her dirty Jeep.

Again the mind-numbing phone conversation they'd had earlier sliced through Alvarez's brain in short, painful bursts, sound bites that would be indelibly etched in her memory.

"Who the fuck would do this?" Pescoli had nearly screamed. "Who!"

"I don't—"

"Oh, hell, what a stupid question! He has so many enemies," she answered for herself. "So damned many enemies, so many sons of bitches who deserved to be sent to prison or worse!" She was railing now, talking fast, out of control. "How many hundreds of cons has he arrested or testified against, and then there are the families and loved ones of those jerks, or maybe a victim who didn't think justice was served or . . . who the hell knows?"

As Selena approached, Deputy Lazlo was saying to Pescoli, "We'll find out."

"You got that right!"

"Regan, I think you should go to the hospital. You've suffered a shock and you've been out in the elements for a while. It wouldn't hurt to have a doctor look you over."

"I'm fine," Pescoli snarled, pushing away from her Jeep, standing eyeball-to-eyeball with the shorter deputy. "How many damn times do I have to tell you?"

Lazlo held up his arms as if in surrender. "I'm just trying to help."

"I've answered your questions, so if you've got all the information you need from me, I'd like to get on with the investigation and find the sheriff's damned assailant!"

Lazlo glanced at Alvarez.

"I'll take it from here," she said to the deputy, then to Pescoli, "I know you've been over this, but humor me. Fill me in. What the hell happened, and why were you up here?"

Pescoli shot the shorter officer one last scathing look, as if she were funneling all of her hate and blame on Lazlo for just doing his job.

"I was up here to talk to Grayson," she said through her teeth, walking with Alvarez to a spot where they were out of earshot of the rest of the officers and emergency crew. "He knew I was coming over. I asked to see him."

"Why?"

"I was thinking about handing him my resignation," she admitted, then said, "Oh, great, look who just showed up. The undersheriff. Of course. Brewster."

"You want to quit?" Alvarez demanded, throwing a glance at Cort Brewster. That was crazy. Pescoli *lived* for her job. "What are you talking about?"

"Santana asked me to marry him."

"What?" Alvarez asked.

"Who did this?" Pescoli asked, swallowing hard.

Before Alvarez could respond, the undersheriff bellowed, "Whoever this bastard is, I want him!" Brewster's face was flushed from the cold and it was obvious he was dressed for church. Beneath a scarf tucked around his neck was a stiff white shirt, a necktie, and suit. His Christmas, churchgoing Sunday best.

"Stand in line." Pescoli couldn't wait to find the killer and run him in. Or kill him. It didn't much matter which.

A muscle worked in Brewster's jaw. "Tell me what happened."

"I was up here to discuss some things about the department,"

Pescoli said, omitting the part about considering leaving the sheriff's department. That idea had fled the second a bullet tore through Grayson's chest.

"What things?" he demanded suspiciously.

"Doesn't matter," she said, then gave a quick, abbreviated version of what had transpired at the cabin. "I told Lazlo all about this, twice. And I'll give another statement at the department later. Is there any word on Grayson?"

"In surgery," Brewster said grimly. "Don't know anything else. The doctor promised to call, and I sent a unit to the hospital to guard him."

"You think the assailant will try again?" Pescoli asked.

"Can't be too cautious." Brewster glanced around the area. "Don't know what we're dealing with."

"A psycho, that's what we're dealing with. A sick-fuck psycho with a high-powered assault rifle."

She felt the pressure of Alvarez's hand on her arm.

"You know the caliber?" Brewster asked.

"No, not yet, but I think because of the way he fell, the killer had to be up there on that knoll." Pescoli pointed up the hill a bit. "Crime scene team is searching, hoping to find a casing. And there should be one nearby because there were entry and exit wounds."

"Shouldn't it have been under the body?" Alvarez asked.

"You'd think," Pescoli said, "but there was just so much snow and blood. God, the blood . . ." Her voice trailed off.

Brewster turned his head to yell, "Get a damned metal detector if you have to!"

"Got it!" One of the techs who was searching the perimeter of the house suddenly plucked a bullet out of snow by the front steps and held it up.

"Now, if someone can find the shell casings up on the ridge," Pescoli muttered.

"Good luck." Scowling at the heavens, Brewster seemed to take measure of the amount of snow that was still steadily falling, destroying the scene. Even the bloody patch on the ground was being covered. "Keep looking. Hopefully we'll get tire impressions or footprints or something."

Alvarez shook her head as she eyed the knoll with its frozen brush and brambles, a thicket of pine, and a large snow-crusted stump. Two investigators were searching the area. "No car could get up there."

"Probably snowshoed, or better yet, skied. For a quick getaway." Pescoli's eyes narrowed. "Isn't there an old mining road or logging road nearby?" She was frowning, trying to picture the area in her mind. "Some kind of access road, I think."

Brewster said, "We'll check it out."

Alvarez's phone beeped and she drew it from her pocket, looked at the screen, but didn't answer. "No caller ID, but I recognized the number," she explained. "Manny Douglas's cell."

"Damned vultures," Pescoli muttered. She'd never pandered to the press and made no bones about the fact. Manny Douglas was a particularly persistent reporter for the *Mountain Reporter*, the local paper. Smart as a whip, dressed forever in outfits straight from an outdoor catalog store, Manny considered himself the local authority on serial killers and was forever sticking his weasel-like nose into police business.

"The press could be useful," Brewster reminded her, ever the diplomat. Well, except when it came to his daughters. "We might be able to use them if we need to send information out to the public." Brewster was always the authority and forever putting Pescoli in her place, but now because of Grayson's incapacitation, he truly was in charge. Pescoli's already twisted stomach tightened a bit.

The new commander eyed the sky again. Though it was now after eight, no sunshine poked through the cloud cover. "Wish the snow would give it a rest."

Pescoli said, "You'd better talk to God about that one."

Brewster cut her an unforgiving look. "It's Christmas," he ground out.

"Tell that to the freak who tried to deep-six Grayson."

Alvarez placed her hand on Pescoli's arm once again, but she shook it off. She didn't much like Brewster and he knew it. The whole damned department understood the tension between them. She and he were like oil and water, and the fact that their kids had found teenage love and trouble with the law hadn't endeared the parents to each other. The only thing that stopped Brewster and

Pescoli from an out-and-out attack was that they were professionals, grudgingly giving each other credit where credit was due. Bottom line? They were both dedicated cops.

Though it was incredibly difficult, Pescoli bit her tongue.

She didn't have time for petty squabbles or grudges.

They had to work together and nail the bastard who'd done this, put all the bad blood aside and let bygones be bygones.

After all, as Brewster kept reminding, it was Christmas.

And some sick son of a bitch was going down if it was the last thing Pescoli ever did.

CHAPTER 5

Alvarez hung up her cell phone and gritted her teeth as she stared at the computer monitor in her office. There on the screen, big as life, were pictures of a wounded Dan Grayson at the crime scene, his attack becoming her newest case. That, in and of itself, was odd as she was a homicide detective and, as of the last report, Grayson was still clinging to life, if only by a thread.

Dear God.

Her phone call had been pointless. Despite identifying herself to the person manning the information desk at the hospital in Missoula, she'd gotten nowhere. Under the acting sheriff Cort Brewster's orders, the staff of Northern General was giving out no information about Dan Grayson except to family members, which Alvarez found frustrating as hell.

She heard the sound of clipped footsteps in the hallway indicating that Joelle Fisher, ever dressed in three-inch heels, was tip-tapping along the hallway. She wasn't alone; the sound of muted voices, computer keys, and other footsteps filled the office where just the night before there had been near silence. As acting sheriff, Brewster had notified everyone who was an employee of the Pinewood County Sheriff's Department of the attack on Grayson. Nearly all of the officers, clerical workers, and even the janitorial staff who were still in town had given up their holiday to show up for a quick staff meeting and briefing.

They'd stood somber and grim-faced, most disbelieving, some

obviously struggling to rein in their emotions. Shoulder to shoulder, they'd listened in silent despair as Brewster outlined what had happened to the man who had been the sheriff for the better part of a decade and how he planned to bring the perpetrator to justice.

"I want you to look through all of the case files where Grayson brought a violent offender to justice. Not only at the offender, but members of his or her family. We also want to scrutinize Grayson's family and his financial situation, find out who would benefit from his death; who would want him dead. If you've heard anything or know of anyone who holds a grudge against the sheriff, let me know. Of course, every family member is suspect." Brewster, who'd still been wearing a suit and tie, had concluded the short meeting with, "Let's all say a prayer for Dan Grayson tonight, that God will keep him safe and that our efforts at bringing the perpetrator to justice will prevail."

Alvarez had fought her own struggling emotions during the gathering, catching Pescoli's eye. Her partner, too, had blinked hard, her jaw set in determination, her hands fisted, her lips compressed.

"Let's do this," she'd whispered to Alvarez before leaving to explain to her family why their Christmas would have to be postponed.

As unfamiliar as it was, Alvarez even prayed a little as she walked down the hallway to her office and automatically, in a throwback to her childhood, had sketched the sign of the cross quickly over her breasts. Her feelings about God and Christmas had been ambivalent for years, but now, as afternoon slid toward evening, she decided that if there truly was a supreme deity, today she'd ask for help. Any kind of help.

"I thought this was your big deal," Jeremy said from her couch as Pescoli finally stepped into the kitchen of her house, her keys dangling from her fingers, her mind still at the crime scene as she relived those horrid moments of the attack over and over again. She really didn't remember driving home from the station, was numb as she walked through the doorway to her house. "You know, a family Christmas, us all being together? I thought you were pissed that we spent last night with Lucky and Michelle, and then you're not even here when we get up at the crack of dawn and bust our asses to get here. And when we show up, you're not even here. No note, no nothin'!"

Her son was sprawled across the ever-shifting cushions of the fifteen-year-old couch and had only glanced in her direction as he played some ultra-violent video game on the living-room television. Bodies were flying, blood was spraying. In her mind's eye, all she could see was Grayson being hit in slow motion, his body spinning, the split kindling erupting from his arms. "Isn't that what you wanted? Christmas together?" Jeremy persisted, as Cisco, their mottled terrier, hopped down from his spot near Jeremy's stockinged feet. "You were all about it and . . . Damn! I can't believe I can't get past this level!" Disgusted and angry, he threw his game controller onto the carpet, then actually twisted his head to glare across the room toward the kitchen while the little dog danced at her feet, barking and twirling frantically to get her attention.

Pescoli didn't respond to either of them.

Her son's face, strong and handsome, so much like Joe's, drained of color. "Holy crap, Mom! Are you okay? What the hell happened?" He was on his feet in an instant, jogging out of the living room where the Christmas tree was listing badly near the old television. His face was a mask of concern. In a heartbeat he seemed to transform from a churlish boy to a man. "Mom?"

She must look a sight, she realized. She'd left her jacket with the crime team, in case the techs wanted to verify that the blood staining her clothes was, indeed, Grayson's, though no one thought differently. Undoubtedly, she probably still looked as shell-shocked as she felt.

"It's the sheriff. Dan. Dan Grayson." She lifted a hand and closed her eyes for a second, only to visualize the horrid attack all over again. Grayson being hit, his hat flying, his body jerking. "I went to see him at his house and . . ." Drawing in a deep breath, she gathered herself. If only she could replay the events of the morning; if only she'd gone a little earlier, spent less time in bed or arguing with Santana, maybe she could have saved Grayson. Or maybe she, too, would be in a hospital ER, surgeons and staff desperately trying to keep her alive.

From the short hallway that ran toward the stairs at the back of the house, the door to Bianca's room opened. She appeared, wearing a pink tank top and stretchy gray pants. Her hair, currently her natural black with a few streaks of blond, was twisted into an unkempt knot on her head and her ever-present cell phone was in her hand. Barefoot, she hadn't bothered looking up as she was texting rapidly, fingers flying as if the fate of the world rested in her reply.

"Hey!" Jeremy shouted.

Bianca glanced up sharply only to stop dead in her tracks. Even her frantic fingers paused over the keypad of her phone. "Mom?"

Pescoli held up a hand to cut off any further questions. "This isn't my blood. I'm okay. A sniper tried to kill Dan Grayson this morning and I got there just in time to witness it. He's at the hospital in Missoula now and . . ." She was shaking her head, wanting to reassure her children, but knowing she had to tell them the truth. Her heart squeezed and she had trouble finding the right words. "It's gonna be touch and go for a while. He was hit twice, once in the chest and then in the head, both . . . both highly vulnerable places and I don't really know much more."

"Oh, my God." Bianca's large eyes rounded, then filled with tears. "But he's going to be okay?"

Pescoli wasn't going to lie. "I hope so."

"Jesus! Who?" Jeremy asked angrily. "Why?"

If only I knew.

Bianca ran forward and threw her arms around her mother.

"Hey, there . . . It's going to be okay," Pescoli lied, holding her. "Whatever happens, it'll be okay."

"No, it won't." Jeremy stood two feet away, glaring at her. She met his gaze over Bianca's shoulder as he declared, "It wasn't 'okay' when Dad was shot, and it's not okay now."

Don't do this. Don't engage with him. He's hurting. Reliving his own loss. "I meant to say we'll get through it, no matter what happens."

"You really believe that? If Grayson dies, everything will be the same?"

"Oh, no, it won't be the same." She shook her head, felt Bianca's tears on her shoulder. "It'll never be the same."

* * *

Pescoli called Santana less than an hour after explaining to her kids that the festivities she'd planned for Christmas would have to wait. She wasn't about to rush through opening presents and a quick meal only to race back to the office. When things calmed down, then her small family would find some way to celebrate.

"So, are you calling me to tell me you've got an answer and we're flying to Vegas for New Year's?" he asked, sounding surprised and optimistic.

"Oh, God . . . no . . . I mean that's not my answer, but, no, I don't have one yet." She took in a deep breath to calm herself. "Look, Santana, there's been an attack . . ." Her throat closed for a second.

"An attack?" His voice was suddenly filled with concern. "What are you talking about?"

"Someone tried to kill the sheriff."

"What? *Grayson?*"

"Shot him at his cabin this morning. Oh, hell, Nate, I saw it all . . ." She launched into the story, her voice wavering a bit, tears tracking down her cheeks. She hoped she sounded stronger than she felt as she related what had transpired, finishing with ". . . so after I got the okay, I left to come home, talk to the kids, and change."

"I'm coming over."

"No, not now. Everything's crazy right now. I can't even spend Christmas with the kids. I've got to go back to the office."

She thought he might argue, but he understood; knew she wouldn't back away from this kind of fight. "Are you all right?" he asked, his voice softening.

"Fine."

"You just witnessed—"

"I said I'm fine." She let out a long breath. "I'm not going to rest, you know. Until the son of a bitch who did this is either dead or behind bars, I'm after his ass."

"I know."

God, she wished she could lean on him for just a second, feel his strong arms around her until she could pull herself together. Instead, she said, "I have to get back to work."

He hesitated and she imagined the shadows chasing across his eyes. "I know. You've got to do what you've got to do. Can I do anything?"

"Don't think so."

He waited a heartbeat, then said, "Look, Regan. I'm sorry. I'd like to help."

"You do," she admitted, her throat hot. "Let's just leave it at that. Okay? I'll call you later." Before he could argue, she hung up, only taking the time to change her clothes before she left her kids with bowls of canned soup, crackers, and their cell phones in front of the television.

Cisco ran around her feet, sensing something was up. She patted him on the head, then called, "See you all later," as she opened the door to the garage.

Jeremy looked her way. "Okay." His face clouded, reminding her again of Joe and how much she'd loved him at nineteen.

Bianca didn't lift her head, but she did mutter thickly, "Bye," as she concentrated on her phone.

I'm sorry, Pescoli thought, knowing she'd disappointed them but aware they were getting old enough to understand that this year, Christmas would have to wait.

Hattie Grayson's knees threatened to give way. She dropped onto her unmade bed and, with her free hand, held on to one post of the frame. "No," she whispered, her voice a strangled cry as denial swept over her. Phone pressed to her ear, she said to the officer on the other end of the line, "You must be mistaken. You *have* to be."

"I know this is a shock, but it's true, Ms. Grayson. The sheriff was seriously wounded in the attack against him," Detective Selena Alvarez was saying, her voice sounding as if it were coming from the end of a long, echoing tunnel. Hattie heard her heart pumping in her eardrums and, for a moment, blackness started edging into her peripheral vision. *Not Dan. Oh, please, please not Dan.*

"But he'll be okay?" she heard herself asking. *Of course he will. It's Dan. . . .*

"I can't comment on his condition, only to say that it's serious. He's at Northern General in Missoula."

"How serious?"

"You can call the hospital. They have more information," Alvarez said. "I really am not at liberty to say any more."

"But who?" Hattie asked, stunned. "Why?"

"We don't know yet, Ms. Grayson, but we're working on it," the detective assured her.

Hattie slowly hung up, distantly aware of her twins, their voices rising from somewhere in the living room, on the verge of yet another argument. At eight, her daughters were starting to become more independent of each other for the first time in their short lives. No longer did they want to dress alike. No longer did they protest at being put in separate classrooms. While Mallory had begun to show an interest in dance and the arts, McKenzie remained a tomboy, with a love of sports and horses.

Like her father, Hattie thought, and felt an unlikely tug on her heart. Bart hadn't been her first choice of the Grayson brothers, but he'd been the one she'd married. The only one who'd asked to marry her. And, of course, it hadn't worked. Not even the birth of the twins had been able to stop that ever-steady unraveling of their union.

And now, Dan, the rock of the family, was fighting for his life.

"Mom! She's doing it again!" Mallory screeched. Gathering her strength, Hattie walked into the hallway and nearly collided with Mallory, who was barrelling down the short corridor to tattle on her sister. She put on the brakes, skidding to a stop, then looked earnestly up at her mother. "McKenzie's cheating."

"At what?" Hattie asked automatically, then caught herself. It didn't matter. "Never mind. Look, girls," she said as McKenzie rounded the corner, "we need to talk. Come on."

Herding her kids back toward the living area, she was struck at how much they looked like their father. With their curly dark hair and big eyes, they were little carbon copies of Bart, already showing signs of high cheekbones yet to completely form, a nod to some Native American ancestor in the Grayson family tree. While Mallory always wore dresses with matching headbands and shoes that usually sparkled, McKenzie wouldn't be caught in anything but jeans, T-shirts, and cowboy boots.

"Cheater!" Mallory spat, the short skirt of her dress flouncing with each of her outraged steps as they returned to the living room and the mounds of discarded paper and ribbons from hastily opened gifts. Cards and dice from a new game were strewn haphazardly on the carpet, opened boxes with tissue paper visible were stacked haphazardly at the end of the couch, and a few more brightly wrapped boxes were still waiting under the tree, gifts for Dan. Hattie's heart ached as she thought of him lying in the hospital.

Plopping onto the worn sofa, her arms crossed indignantly over her chest, Mallory was still irked at her sister. "See!" she said, pointing an accusing finger at the upturned board game.

McKenzie wasn't about to take the accusation lying down. "I didn't cheat. Mom, she's lying!"

Mallory was shaking her head, dark curls bouncing as she pronounced, "The rules say that—"

"Girls, please," Hattie broke in. "Let's not do this, okay?" How to tell them about their beloved uncle? She usually opted for the truth, but today she just couldn't utter the words that their favorite uncle had been the target of some malicious attack. "It's Christmas," she reminded them as they shot each other looks that could kill.

Mallory pouted, "But we were playing and—"

"Mal! It doesn't matter right now, okay?" For the first time her words, or maybe her sharp tone, caused both of her children to stop their petty arguing to stare at her. "We, uh, we're going to have to change our plans a bit. Uncle Dan can't make it to dinner this afternoon."

"Oh, maaaan." McKenzie was clearly disappointed. She and her uncle had always been close.

"Why?" Mallory wanted to know. Her eyes narrowed suspiciously.

"He's been hurt."

"How?" Mallory again.

"I don't know a lot of details, but he's in the hospital and I'm going to see him as soon as Nana arrives."

McKenzie said, "I want to go."

"Me too!" Mallory wasn't to be left out.

"Not today. He's not up for a lot of visitors. But soon."

"What happened?" Mallory asked.

"As I said—"

McKenzie cut in, "Is he sick? Like when Nana got new ammonia?"

"It's pneumonia, idiot!" Mallory said, her lips twisting superciliously. Her sister had never gotten "pneumonia" right and Hattie, finding it charming, had never fully corrected her.

McKenzie glared at her sister. "That's what I said—"

Hattie stepped in. "Stop it! Right now!" Then more calmly, "And, no, McKenzie, I don't think it's pneumonia."

"But he's going to be all right?" she asked, nodding rapidly as if to ensure the answer.

Hattie could only hedge so much. She'd always been as straight as she could with her girls, but today, she was more careful. She didn't really know the extent of Dan's injuries, or his prognosis, so she thought it best to stall. "I'll know more when I get there," she said, checking her watch. "Come on, let's clean this up." She knelt on one knee and started picking up the cards. Looking up, she added, "Both of you. Not just me. Hop to."

"But it's Christmas," McKenzie complained.

"That's why I'm helping and not making you two do it alone. Come on."

Reluctantly, both girls pitched in and not ten minutes later, Zena, Hattie's mother, her arms laden with gifts, stepped through the front door. "Merry Christmas," she called in her high-pitched voice. "Come on, girls, give Nana a big hug!"

The twins forgot their squabbling at the sight of their grandmother and not only hugged Hattie's mom, but helped put her gifts under the small tree, lugged in two pies, a Jell-O mold of shimmering red and green, and a platter of cookies and candy wrapped in plastic wrap and tied with a gold bow. "For Dan," Zena said with a wink. "Bachelors! They never get enough home-baked goodies!"

"I guess." The mention of Dan Grayson was always a little tense with Zena as he had been married to her older daughter, Hattie's half sister, Cara, though the divorce was long in the past. Never mind that not only Hattie, but Zena, too, rarely heard from Cara, the old tension never seemed to quite abate.

"What about us?" Mallory asked, eyeing the platter.

"Would I forget you?" Zena bent over and tweaked her grand-daughter's nose.

"No way!" McKenzie enthused.

"Right you are, but probably your mom wants you to wait until after dinner." She looked at Hattie through the soft blond bangs of her latest wig. Zena had been battling cancer for better than half the year and though she was recovering well, her hair was still coming back. In the meantime, she wore wigs of various cuts and colors. "Why not have a little fun with this damned thing?" she'd said to Hattie once. "Chemo's hell, don't let me kid you, but I may as well see what I'd look like as a redhead or platinum blonde. I was getting sick of mouse brown shot with gray anyway! Booooring!"

Now Hattie felt the unlikely urge to fall into a million pieces. She wasn't usually so wimpy, but her mother's effervescence in almost any situation was such a relief she nearly started to cry.

"Listen, Mom, I have a big favor," she said, and pulling Zena into the kitchen, told her mother about the call from Alvarez. She kept her voice low, and the girls, eager to see the presents their grandmother had brought them, held a temporary truce as they placed the wrapped packages under the tree.

Zena's face drained of all color and she quickly made the sign of the cross over her chest even though she hadn't been a practicing Catholic for over thirty years. "Oh, my God, you have to go. Of course you do! Who in their right mind would shoot Dan?"

Hattie was already at the back door of her condo, finding her boots. "That's the thing, Mom. Obviously whoever's done this is *not* in his right mind." After stepping into her boots, she snagged her favorite down jacket from the rack over her shoes and scooped her purse from the kitchen table. Keys in hand, she took the time to tell the girls she'd be back soon, then kissed them each before heading toward the garage. "Thanks, Mom," she said, her throat catching a bit. "You're a life saver."

"Over and over again," Zena agreed, then made a quick little shooing motion with her hand. "You go. And don't worry about a thing. The girls and I will get dinner started and make that gingerbread house. Now, Hattie, you've got your cell phone, right? So you can call and give me an update."

"In my purse."

Zena's practiced smile fell slightly. "Give Dan my best. He was the one, you know. The one *you* should have married."

CHAPTER 6

"Jesus H. Christ! Just what the hell happened?" In the waiting area outside the operating rooms of Northern General Hospital, Cade Grayson glared at Pescoli as if she were the devil incarnate. Long and lean, a cowboy type, Cade sported a three-day growth of beard, a faded pair of Levi's, and an attitude that wouldn't quit. Sunglasses hung from the frayed collar of his work shirt and, Pescoli guessed, they had been left there out of convenience rather than as a fashion statement. His battered Stetson and worn jacket were tossed over one of the low-slung couches in the waiting room.

Another woman sat by the window, staring out absently, obviously waiting for news on a loved one as she knitted, her needles softly clicking, her expression a mask of despair. Next to her was a man who looked to be a generation older. He was leafing through a well-read magazine, his expression taut, probably not taking in a word of text from the article he was perusing through rimless reading glasses perched on the end of his nose.

The bell for the elevator dinged quietly and two hospital workers in scrubs, a man and woman, fell into step, their conversation never lagging as they punched in a code and the wide door to the surgical unit opened.

Pescoli had hoped for word on her boss, but so far, there had been nothing. Jabbing a finger in her direction, Cade said, "Let me get this straight. On Christmas morning, you go up to see Dan and just as you get there, he gets *shot?*"

Cade was hot. As in angry. As in furious. As in needing to punch someone's lights out. Pescoli understood his rage, even if it was misdirected at her. "We're trying to sort it all out."

"Do you think it might have something to do with you? I mean, that's one helluva coincidence, don't you think?"

The thought had crossed her mind more than once, and she couldn't help a stab of guilt. "We're still looking at all possibilities."

"Don't give me any of that police BS. It's the company line and we all know it," he declared, motioning toward his older brother, Zed, who stood near the window, one burly shoulder propped against a support post. Zed didn't say much but was working a toothpick in the corner of his mouth as he squinted through the glass to the storm outside. The guy reading the old magazine looked up sharply over the tops of his readers.

"Who the hell took a potshot at my brother? Give me a name," Cade demanded.

"I don't know. But I intend to find out. Got any ideas?"

"Isn't that your job? You're the cop!"

"As I said, we're working on it."

He shook his head, his jaw taut. "Do your job. Find the son of a bitch."

"Give her a break," Zed suggested, then, leveling his deep-set eyes on Pescoli, added, "Cade's not a big fan of law enforcement."

"I got that," Pescoli said, then to Cade, "Trust me, everyone in the sheriff's office is making this attack priority one. We all are pretty attached to the sheriff."

Cade looked about to say something else but somehow managed to keep it in.

"Anything we can do?" Zed offered.

"We could start with his enemies," Pescoli suggested.

"Don't you have that covered?" Cade demanded. "Dan's the goddamn sheriff, and before that he worked as a detective and road deputy and he ran in more scumbags than you can count."

Pescoli held up a hand. "It's the family stuff I'm talking about. You know, friends who might not be what they seemed. Anyone Dan crossed on a personal level."

Cade's gaze shifted to a spot over her shoulder and his lips tightened a fraction. He said something under his breath that sounded like "speak of the devil," and Pescoli turned to see what had caught his attention. She watched as Hattie Grayson hurried inside. She was breathless and her hair, usually so perfectly in place, was now tangled and mussed, brown strands wet from the snow. "How—how is he doing?" she asked, her question directed at Pescoli.

Pescoli threw a glance at Cade.

"Not great," Cade said, lips barely moving as he slid another accusing glare Pescoli's way. "Shot in the chest and head."

"But he's going to pull through." She looked from one brother to the next for confirmation.

"Nothing's for certain," Pescoli said, though she hated how grim she sounded. "We're waiting for the doctor."

"Oh, God." Hattie was pale, her cheeks, which had been ruddy from the cold, blanching. Slowly, she drew in a deep breath. "I just can't believe it. Who would . . . ?" Swallowing hard, she blinked back tears and shook her head, as if she were trying to dislodge a bad, lingering dream.

"How about your sister?" Cade suggested in a dangerous voice.

"What?"

"Hey!" Big Zed pushed up from the pillar on which he'd been leaning and shook his head. "Not the place," he warned his brother, but Cade was advancing on Hattie. With one hand, he swiped the air in Zed's direction, silently telling the bigger man to back off as he came within an arm's length of his ex-sister-in-law. "Cara played Dan like a damned puppet."

"But she's married to—"

"Nolan Banks, yeah, I know. Has been for years. Doesn't mean she still didn't dick around with Dan. Even when he started dating Akina, Cara still messed with him."

"He *married* Akina," Hattie reminded.

Cade glared at her and Pescoli sensed something pass between them. "And how long did that last?" Cade asked. "Ten months? A year?"

Hattie just shook her head.

"Not very damned long," Cade said, as if Grayson's failed second marriage were somehow Hattie's fault.

"It wasn't because of Cara," Hattie said, suddenly bristling. She was nose to nose with Cade and refused to back down, but it was clear, being close to him was uncomfortable for her. "If I remember correctly, Akina ran off with her high-school boyfriend."

"Because Cara kept showing up and Dan was too nice, or too emotionally attached to Cara, to tell Cara to 'get lost'!"

Pescoli was processing the information. Grayson was a private man and had kept his personal life as out of the limelight as an elected official could. She'd known he'd been married to both women, but she'd never realized Hattie was a sister to Grayson's first wife. She'd thought Hattie's relationship with Dan stemmed from Hattie's marriage to Bart, Dan's dead brother. "Wait a second," she said, holding up a hand. "Your *sister* was—"

"Half sister," Hattie corrected swiftly. "Dan's first wife. Yes." She dragged her glance from Cade to address Pescoli. "It's . . . complicated."

"Screwed up," Cade clarified, gray eyes flashing. "Depends on who you ask."

"That makes it easy," Pescoli said to Cade as she reached into her pocket and retrieved her mini-recorder. "I'll start with you. Let's cover all the family relationships, then get to the last time you saw or talked with your brother." She motioned Cade to the couch where his jacket and hat had been tossed.

Reluctantly, Cade perched on the edge of the couch, his gaze stormy, his back stiff. "I talked to him last night, late, around eleven, on my cell. But I wasn't the last person to see him before the attack."

"Who would that be, then?" Pescoli asked.

"You, Detective. You were the last person he saw."

Once more, like a piece of film replayed over and over again, Pescoli witnessed Dan's body jerking as the would-be assassin's bullets ripped through his body. Cade had a point, though, much as she disliked the man. Other than the would-be killer, Pescoli was the only witness to the crime.

She was still interviewing the brothers when she saw Santana striding toward her. Before he reached ICU, however, a deputy who had been assigned to guard Grayson and who was stationed near the door to the unit blocked Santana's path.

"Excuse me a second," she said to Cade and Zed, as Santana

looked in her direction. "I'll be right back." She hurried across the hallway. "It's all right," she told the guard as she reached the two men, then walked with Santana to a more private alcove near the stairwell. "What're you doing here?" she finally asked.

"I had to see for myself that you were okay."

She lifted both her palms toward the ceiling. "I told you . . ."

"Sometimes you tend to stretch the truth."

"Bullshit, Santana. I'm fine."

"Okay. I believe you," he said as if he really didn't. "Just don't blame me for caring, okay?"

"I don't."

He glanced down at her ringless left hand. "I'm sorry about Grayson. He's a good guy." He didn't add *"And so am I,"* but it was there, hanging in the air, unspoken.

"Just give me some time."

"And space. Yeah, I know."

He turned and headed toward the elevators, and she gave herself a swift mental kick. Why the hell did she keep pushing him away when she ached to be with him?

Because, damn it, you have a fear of commitment and a fear that if you get too close to someone you love, he will leave you.

Drawing a deep breath, she pulled herself together, then turned toward ICU, the Grayson brothers, and Hattie once more. Right now, she had to concentrate on the case. Someone was out to kill Dan Grayson. Just because they hadn't put him into his grave the first time, didn't mean they wouldn't try again.

The dog was still missing. According to Pescoli, Sturgis, Dan Grayson's black Lab, had taken off after the attack on the sheriff. Alvarez had worked most of the day and couldn't face the hospital, so she'd returned to the crime scene to trudge up the ridge, which, it seemed, was the most likely place for the killer to have set up his attack.

Using metal detectors, the tech team found two shell casings buried in the snow near an old stump. Now there were footprints all around the area; the snow had been scraped away, a fresh layer in its place as the damned stuff kept falling.

Already the detectives had searched the area and concluded that the assassin had probably skied down the ridge to a waiting vehicle on an old logging road, though no fresh tracks had been found, new-falling snow having obliterated any significant tread marks. The team was still searching, but so far, they hadn't come up with anything of use. And there had been no dog sightings.

"Where are you, Sturgis?" she wondered and let out a whistle before calling to the dog and hearing her voice echo back through the icy canyon. Listening, hoping to hear an excited bark, she stood still for a second, the frigid forest silent and, she thought dourly, unforgiving. She knew the pain of losing an animal, her own recently adopted puppy had gone missing once and she'd been frantic. So, along with nailing Grayson's would-be killer, she intended on finding his dog.

"Sturgis!" she yelled again. "Come, boy!"

In answer, a clump of snow fell from the laden branches of a hemlock tree and she turned quickly, half expecting the Lab to appear.

No such luck.

She was alone.

And getting nowhere fast.

Her cell phone jangled and she dug it out of her pocket. Caller ID flashed with O'Keefe's name and number. "Hey," she answered, smiling as she turned toward Grayson's cabin and returned along the path she'd broken in the snow.

"Merry Christmas. I've been trying to reach you all day."

"Been a little busy," she admitted as the wind brushed against her cheek.

"I know. It's all over the news. Where are you?"

"The crime scene again. Looking for more evidence and his dog." She glanced around the hills again. Dusk was approaching and the temperature would fall further. Where the hell was Sturgis?

"Any luck?"

"Nada." Uneasy, she watched the shadows ooze through the forest allowing darkness to close in. She could feel the iciness of the wind as it whispered, moaning audibly through the gorge.

"Tell me what I can do."

As a private detective, O'Keefe had his own way of investigating and could possibly break the rules she wasn't able to touch, much less bend.

"I can't allow you to do anything," she said, refusing to compromise the case, though what he did on his own time, without her okay, was something else again and he knew it. "Where are you?"

"At your place. Making dinner."

"Then I lied, you can do something. Feed the dog and cat for me, would ya?"

"Anything your heart desires," he said with a laugh that was devoid of any real sense of humor. Today, with Grayson battling for his life, no one was in a jovial mood, least of all her.

"Thanks," she said.

"Oh, and, Selena?"

"Yeah?"

"I meant it: Merry Christmas."

Her throat tightened and for the first time she felt tears burn the back of her eyelids. That's the way it was for her; she could be all tough and in-your-face, a cop who had tight rein on her emotions, but a little kindness—that did her in every time.

"Merry Christmas, O'Keefe," she said, before clicking off. She peered through the house one last time, noting that it was a mess, fingerprint dust everywhere, drawers left open, cushions on the old couch overturned, and there on the kitchen table, the contents strewn over the scarred wooden top, were two red foil bags that had been tied with ribbon, name tags reading: *McKenzie* and *Mallory*. Girlie gifts in tissue paper for his nieces. Each with a check and a notation: *"College fund."* Her heart twisted a little when she thought of the big, kind man actually trying to buy and wrap gifts for the girls.

She remembered him walking the halls of the department, a tall, rangy man wearing cowboy boots and a sheepskin jacket, his mustache a little bushy, his dog forever at his heels. Her heart twisted and she reminded herself that she wasn't in love with Dan Grayson, that she never had been, that her infatuation had been nothing more than admiration for the man.

Of course she was lying to herself and she knew it, which only made the pain worse. She loved O'Keefe. Her feelings for him were real, based on a shared history and a new commitment.

Right?

Then why was she so conflicted?

Maybe it was just the holidays, that time of year she hated and feared, the festivities only a reminder of how her life had taken such an ugly turn.

"You're over that now," she reminded herself and, again, studied the cabin that Dan Grayson called home, an isolated retreat for a man who lived alone.

Who would do this?

She looked around his house and tried to keep her emotions in check, seeing the cabin through the eyes of an investigator, not an employee and not a woman who had once fancied herself in love with him. Even so, as she walked from room to room, noting the rag rug the dog had claimed as his own, the pegs where his fishing gear still hung, or the oversized bed with a tan comforter that showed evidence of black dog hair, she struggled to remain detached. The only pictures were of Mallory and McKenzie with their uncle at a lake, and another in which a much younger Grayson was proudly displaying a large brook trout, its scales glinting in the sun, the ground on which it was laid lush with spring vegetation.

Someone from the department had already taken all of his private papers including his bills and a copy of a will.

In a cupboard in the living room, she found a stash of toys, dolls, Legos, and puzzles, probably for his nieces. There were also playing cards, a carousel of poker chips, a chess set, cribbage board, and a case that held backgammon pieces. Leaning back on her heels, she wondered how often he played cards or rolled dice with friends.

And what friends were they?

His brothers?

As far as she knew, Dan Grayson was a solitary man, on the verge of being called a loner.

But then, she hadn't known him all his life, and from the dust that had collected, and the looks of the playing boards, the games had seen most of their action years ago, when he was in college, possibly, or later when he was with one of his wives.

She found nothing more of interest and walked through the living room to the kitchen where the smell of coffee still faintly lingered in the air.

Alvarez left the house again, called for the dog and waited once more, but no bounding retriever appeared from the surrounding wilderness. She left the door to the woodshed ajar, so, if the dog did return, he could find some shelter, then whispered to herself, "I'll be back," and jammed her hands into her pockets as she headed outside to her ten-year-old SUV.

CHAPTER 7

"So get this," Sage Zoller said an hour later as she strolled into Alvarez's office. Though it was after five on Christmas Day, Alvarez was still on the clock. Then again, Zoller and Alvarez weren't alone. The sheriff's department still buzzed with voices, the ring tones of cell phones, hum of computers and televisions over the ever-present rumble of the overworked furnace.

Sage dropped a thin legal document onto Alvarez's desk. "It looks like the person who inherited the bulk of Dan Grayson's estate is his ex-wife," she said. "And not his most recent ex-wife, but the first Mrs. Grayson, aka Cara Grayson Banks."

"Seriously?" Alvarez, who had already skimmed Grayson's phone records and credit card statements, was now looking for notice of releases of any con Dan Grayson had been instrumental in convicting.

"Uh-huh." Zoller was a junior detective, smarter than smart, and worked long hours. Only two inches over five feet, Zoller ran marathons, her muscles tight, her face, surrounded by springy dark curls, definitely elfin. "I checked everywhere, including with Grayson's attorney, who didn't mind being pulled away from his Christmas dinner to talk to me. It looks like the will was last changed five years ago, *before* he married wife number two." She held up two fingers, nearly a peace sign. "So Akina was never cut into the family fortune. According to the lawyer, that, too, had been in the works, but the marriage was so short, it hadn't happened."

"What about his nieces? He's crazy about them."

"Oh, yeah, they're mentioned. They each get ten thousand, in a college fund, nothing to sneeze at. But the bulk of his estate looks like it's in real estate. His cabin is owned outright and his portion of the Grayson ranch, that would be one-quarter, which is run by his brothers Zedediah and Cade, goes to Mrs. Number *Uno*."

Alvarez leaned back in her chair. "Seems odd."

"Odder yet? His retirement beneficiary and life insurance?" She nodded at Alvarez.

"Cara again?"

"Bingo. His lawyer said Grayson wanted to meet with him after the first of the year to change things, but so far that hadn't happened."

"Anyone else know about that meeting?"

"I asked, but the lawyer, Cromwell Buckner the Fourth—really, would you name a baby that four times?" She shook her head. "This one, in the long line of Cromwells, at least goes by Buck, and he said he has no idea who the sheriff told about the meeting."

"Grayson's pretty private," Alvarez thought aloud. "Maybe no one."

"Yeah, I know, I thought there was a chance Joelle might have known about the appointment as she pretty much runs the sheriff's schedule, but, no, according to Buck, Grayson set up the meeting himself."

"So, all we know is that the people in the law offices and Dan Grayson knew about it."

"If it's even significant," Zoller said.

"Hmmm."

"I already checked on the first missus. Alibi locked up tighter than a miser's safe."

"Who?"

"The current husband, of course."

"Nolan Banks." Alvarez had heard his name before but knew little about the man. He and Cara had children, though, she was pretty sure.

"One and the same."

Zoller's phone jangled and she plucked it from a pocket, saw the display, and, smiling for the first time that day, mouthed, "Bruno," whom she often referred to as So, her shortened form of Significant Other. "Gotta take this. He's pissssssed about me missing the meal

with his folks. Guess it was a command performance with the PILs—
Potential In-Laws—but, hey, too damned bad. Someone starts taking
shots at my boss and I don't like it, so all bets and command perfor-
mances are off!" She swung the phone to her ear and said sweetly,
"Hey, Bruno . . . what's up? Yeah, yeah . . . I know . . . me, too, but
this is a really big deal . . . um-hmm . . . Give them my love and I
know they'll understand. . . ." She sauntered into the hallway still cajoling Bruno while Alvarez checked her watch. She'd avoided the
hospital all day, instead working the case, putting her efforts into
finding the bastard who had tried to kill her boss. Yet she knew she
would have to spend some time in the hospital, would *want* to be
close to him. But the idea of sitting around with Grayson's small family, doing nothing but waiting and silently praying, feeling impotent
while Grayson battled for his life, wasn't something she wanted to
face.

So she turned her attention to Grayson's will.

Feeling a little like a Peeping Tom, Alvarez started reading the Last
Will and Testament of Dan Grayson even though the man was still
struggling for his life. If he pulled through, and she prayed fervently
that he would, she'd feel even more guilty of voyeurism, but in the
name of bringing his assailant to justice, she really didn't give a
damn.

"I'll be home soon, I hope," Hattie whispered into her cell. She
was standing outside the wing of the operating rooms at the hospital, in a hallway of Northern General where cell use was permitted.
She'd taken a much-needed trip to the restroom, then stopped to
call her mother and check on her daughters. "Just feed the girls and,
if I don't get home before bedtime, please let them each pick out a
story to read, and tuck them in."

"They're asking about you," Zena said, and Hattie detected a hint
of recrimination in her mother's voice. "Mallory's complaining about
not seeing her mama on Christmas."

"I was there this morning, and we had breakfast and opened the
gifts from Santa and . . ." Why was she arguing the point? Zena
wouldn't understand, nor would she listen. She bought into her grand-
daughters' acts hook, line, and sinker, and Mallory, a bit of a conniver

who'd already announced she planned to be an actress when she grew up, knew exactly how to play her grandmother and get what she wanted. Zena never understood that she was being manipulated. Today was no exception.

"Well, honey, they're worried about their uncle, of course."

They should be. Hattie backed up to let a man with a walker and his wife ease past. His wife was tending to him, guiding him, her hand patiently placed upon the middle of his back, leaning forward to whisper to him, as he tried to steer the walker toward the elevator bank.

"I don't suppose Cara has shown up?" Zena said, drawing her back to the conversation.

"Not yet, but I called and left her a message." That had been a little weird. "I'm not even certain I have her correct cell number, my call went right to voice mail."

"I don't have her cell, just the house."

"I'll try that later if she doesn't call back."

"When's the last time you talked to Cara?"

Hattie remembered distinctly. "A year ago. I called Christmas night to wish them all Merry Christmas."

Zena gave off a little huff of disgust. "She sent me a card last year. One of those preprinted things with a picture of the family. No note. Nothing."

Hattie imagined her mother's face as she talked about her eldest daughter. Her face would be tight, her lips pursed in disapproval, her eyes sharp with pride, her chin inched up a bit. Zena always felt as if she were the persecuted one, the victim.

But today, it wasn't about her. "Look, I've got to go." She glanced down the short hallway and saw a grim-faced man in scrubs appear and draw Dan's two brothers and the detective aside. "I think the doctor's got some news about Dan." Before Zena could say another word, she clicked off and hurried to the waiting area where she heard the tail end of what the doctor was saying.

". . . with this kind of trauma to the brain, we just can't be certain. He'll be in intensive care, where he can be closely monitored around the clock, but that's no guarantee." The doctor, a neurosurgeon named Kapule, took their questions and explained some more about decompressive craniectomy, in which part of Dan's skull was removed to take pressure off his brain where swelling had occurred. The more the doctor talked about blood loss and brain trauma and infection, the more worried Hattie became. She wasn't alone. Detective Pescoli was somber, Big Zed's eyebrows slammed together, and even Cade had lost some of his bluster and anger, his rage replaced by dread.

The long and the short of it was that even though a neurosurgeon who had worked with brain injuries on soldiers from the battlefields of Iran and Afghanistan had operated on the sheriff, Dan was still in critical condition. Since the wound had been through and through, the bullet entering and exiting his brain, back to front, with no major blood vessels hit, he surprisingly had a chance of full recovery; though, of course, the odds were against him. "He'll be in ICU within the hour. It's on the third floor and he'll be monitored closely."

"There will be a guard posted," Pescoli said and the doctor nodded, understanding that the cops were going to take care of their own. Already there had been a parade of deputies and detectives through the doors of Northern General, and Hattie had seen several police cruisers and SUVs in the parking lot. Obviously, someone bold enough to strike Grayson at his own home on Christmas morning might not be deterred by the hospital's security.

"He's a fighter," Zed said when Kapule, his cell phone ringing, had left them alone in the waiting area. Others, including the woman who'd been knitting and the older man thumbing through magazines, had left, replaced by a Hispanic family of four and a nervous middle-aged woman with her daughter, but they, too, had just departed from the hospital. Because Grayson's surgery had been so involved and lengthy, their group had remained, and though Detective Pescoli had sometimes left the area, she'd always returned within the hour, sometimes moving away from them to talk quietly on her cell phone.

"I need some air," Cade said, stalking away.

Zed's bushy eyebrows shot up and Hattie had a short, sharp memory of Cade and her in an argument that had ended with him throwing up his hands and telling her he needed some air. It was inside his pickup one night after a high-school football game. She remembered the way he'd slammed the door and the breadth of his shoulders and leanness of his hips as he'd strode away from the stadium lights, leaving her to either wait for him or slam out of the vehicle as well. She'd chosen the latter, done with his anger over her relationship with Dan, which had been more a benign high-school romance than the hot affair Cade had accused her of. Still, it hadn't been his place to question her, but now, her throat felt hot at the memory; so many things had come and gone between them since.

"Mebbe you need something like this," Zed said as Cade retrieved his jacket and hat. He reached into the back pocket of his jeans, as Cade turned around, dug out a can of Copenhagen, and tossed it at his brother, who caught it in his free hand.

"No, thanks." Cade tossed the tin back. "I could use a drink." He sent one blistering look Hattie's direction, then headed toward the elevators. To Zed, he said, "I'll check with J.D., make sure the herd is okay, and I'll be back. Meet you at ICU."

Detective Pescoli let out her breath in the wake of Cade's departure. "Why don't we all go down to the cafeteria for a while, until they get the sheriff moved and you can tell me about Dan, who you think might want to harm him." She held up a hand as if she expected an argument. "I know we've been over this up here, but by now you've had some time to think about it. Maybe something's bubbled to the surface of your memory."

"Okay," Hattie said, and at the mention of the cafeteria her stomach rumbled a bit, though she couldn't really imagine eating anything. "Dan's always been private. Holds things close to the vest."

Zed was already walking toward the elevators. He was the one Grayson brother Hattie hadn't dated, and he'd never much liked her, probably because she'd made a fool of herself first over Dan, then Cade, and lastly Bart, whom she'd eventually married. She'd been accused of "settling" and of being so enamored of the Grayson rumored wealth that she would have married any of the brothers, or worse yet, that she'd married Bart because her pride had been wounded when Dan had ended up with her half sister.

It was all pure fabrication and gossip, she tried to convince herself as she rode the elevator car to the basement level where Northern General's cafeteria was located. True, she'd been fascinated with the

Grayson brothers when she was in high school, but she wasn't the only girl who had dreams of dating any one of the good-looking hellions. All four boys had grown up without a mother, wild sons of Brett Grayson, a rodeo star in the sixties and seventies, who had not only inherited his ranch, but, with his success on the circuit and smart investments, had expanded his ranch land and his fortune.

The Grayson clan wasn't Kennedy-rich by any means, but for a town the size of Grizzly Falls, they were royalty, if a bit tarnished. Hattie knew that her interest in them had nothing to do with money, but sure, she'd probably been looking for stability like a lot of young women of that age. Still, to be involved with three out of four of the brothers could be viewed as obsessive. She probably would have been interested in Zed, too; he was handsome enough. But there was a darker side to him, one that ran much deeper than Cade's wild streak.

She walked through the cafeteria line, ordered a salad and bowl of tomato bisque, and feeling uncomfortable, carried her tray to a table where Zed was already chowing his way through the first of two pastrami sandwiches and the cop, Pescoli, had begun to pick at chicken strips and fries. She was an interesting woman, tall and rangy, athletic-looking with wild reddish hair and intense eyes that shifted from green to gold. She came off kind of folksy, and Hattie couldn't determine if Pescoli really was all country-girl or if it was an act. One thing Hattie was sure of, Detective Pescoli hadn't asked them to the cafeteria because she was lonely and wanted someone to join her for a meal. No, Hattie thought, the other woman was forever on the job, listening, asking questions, hoping to find some little nugget of information that would help the case.

Well, bring it on, Hattie thought. She had nothing to hide. The trouble was, she didn't know if she could help. She really had no idea who would want to harm Dan Grayson.

As she took her seat, she said, "I know this is far-fetched, but"—she slid a glance toward Zed, who was studying her while chewing thoughtfully—"but, as you know, I don't believe for a second that my husband took his life."

"Ex-husband," Zed clarified and grabbed his Coke for a long swallow.

Hattie ignored Zed. She'd always found him irritating. To Pescoli, she went on, "The point is that Bart's dead from an apparent suicide, if you believe that nonsense, which I don't and never have, and now someone's tried to kill his older brother." She looked from Pescoli to Zed. "What're the chances of that?"

"As he's the sheriff, putting scum away for years, pretty high, I'd say," Zed muttered.

"I don't think it's some felon bent on revenge," Hattie declared. "It's something else, and maybe it even circles back to Bart's murder."

"Suicide," Zed corrected.

"Whatever."

Cade drove his pickup to the nearest bar, which was about two miles from the hospital; but then he just pulled into the parking lot, parked the vehicle, and sat with his hands on the steering wheel. He thought about his brother, hooked up to God knew how many monitors and IVs and shit, lying in distant twilight, part of his skull removed, his brain swelling, unconscious to the fact that he might never wake up.

"Son of a bitch," Cade swore, his breath fogging the windshield. He'd already lost his youngest brother to a self-inflicted noose around his neck.

Cade was the one who'd discovered Bart and, now, the scene unfolded in his head yet again: walking into the barn on a wintry morning, the sun not yet up, snapping on the lights and noting that the cattle and horses seemed spooked by something, then spying the body of his brother hanging near the huge sliding door at the back of the barn.

"Noooo!" he'd yelled, his boots ringing on hundred-year-old floorboards, denial ripping through his body. In an instant he'd found the ladder that had been kicked to one side and righted it. He'd frantically climbed the metal steps as he reached for his pocket knife in the front pocket of his jeans. "Bart! Bart! You son of a bitch," he'd screamed, hoping to startle his brother into waking, which he'd known even then was impossible. "No, no! Oh, God damn . . . !!!"

The horses had kicked at their stalls whinnying nervously, the cattle had snorted and lowed as Cade sawed through that thick rope and his brother's body fell, collapsing onto the floor with a mind-numbing thud.

"Help!" Cade had screamed at the top of his lungs as he'd jumped to the floor, feeling for a pulse in his brother's neck. Nothing, no sign of life beneath the beard stubble. He'd listened for even the faintest of breath, but knew there was none. Bart's skin was cold and losing color, his eyes fixed. He'd been dead for hours. Still, Cade had pounded on his brother's chest, and with tears streaming down his face, he'd kept at it, his hard fist useless in reviving a brother who had already left this earth.

He'd finally given up, just as Zed, swearing, had thrown open the barn door and then bawled out his own grief at the sight of his dead brother.

Now, with Dan fighting for his life, what he couldn't come to terms with, what he couldn't deny, was the guilt that was eating him up inside. It invaded his heart, making it ache as if he were having a goddamn heart attack. He'd cried out, *"Why?"* when he'd found Bart swinging in the barn, but he knew the answer then, and he knew now why Bartholomew Carlson Grayson hadn't been able to stand another day on this earth.

And Hattie, Bart's ex-wife, knew why as well, no matter how hard she tried to convince those around her that Bart had been murdered.

She knew.

CHAPTER 8

Leaving a deputy to stand guard near the intensive care unit and Hattie Grayson still seated in a waiting area, Pescoli drove away from the hospital a little after eight. "There's nothing more you can do," Pescoli had said to Hattie, but the woman hadn't budged, just nodded tightly and stared out the wide glass windows to the night. Grayson's brothers, after a discussion about returning in the morning, had taken off as well.

Her Jeep's headlights danced upon the glistening snow as she drove the country road that wound through the foothills toward Grizzly Falls and overhead, in a field of winking stars, a nearly full moon illuminated the night.

She thought about Grayson, about her job, about her kids, and of course, about Santana. The ring he'd given her—Lord, was it just last night?—was still in its box, tucked deep inside her underwear drawer, a reminder of the life she could have. If she wanted it badly enough.

As she drove over a small bridge, she saw the lights of Grizzly Falls glowing in the distance. She wouldn't quit her job now, of course, not until Grayson was out of the hospital and recovering. Then she'd tackle that problem; Santana would understand.

"Ultimatum, shultimatum," she muttered under her breath and resisted the urge to open her glove box to search for her emergency pack of cigarettes. A hit of nicotine was a crutch, nothing more. Instead, she listened to the police band crackle until her phone rang. With a glance at the screen, she recognized Alvarez's number.

"What's up?" she asked, squinting against the bright headlights of a pickup tearing by in the opposite direction.

"I've been reading Grayson's will. If he doesn't make it, his ex-wife inherits the bulk of his estate. That's Cara, the first wife. She's got an alibi, of course, her current hubby, and it's unlikely she would actually try to kill Grayson herself, but I haven't ruled out a murder-for-hire thing."

"Wow. Seems far-fetched, but okay."

"She benefits the most financially. That's all I'm saying."

Again, Pescoli looked at the glove box, and again resisted the temptation within. "What else?"

"Well, there's the political angle. The sheriff's up for reelection soon and he's got a couple of people who've made noise about running."

"Please don't tell me Brewster's already making moves," she groaned as she passed a snowplow scraping snow from the oncoming lane as it moved slowly in the opposite direction.

"Not that I know of, no. I'm talking about Cal Moran and Shirley Braddock."

"Both good cops." Pescoli, too, had heard that Cal and Shirley might run, each having political ambitions. Cal was a fiftyish father of five, grandfather of two, and Shirley was a single woman, a dedicated cop who was probably being urged by her lawyer boyfriend, Hans Tobias, who just happened to be an assistant district attorney. Hans was pushy, his mind as sharp as the crease in the pants of his Armani suits. However, even when you threw ambitious Hans into the mix, a political angle didn't quite wash. "Far-fetched," she said.

"I agree. Next up are the ex-cons."

"Now you're talkin'. Who's around?"

"Of all the dirtbags Grayson sent up the river, I've got several possibles. I'm checking with their parole officers, but the most likely suspects are, first, Floyd Cranston. He's been out two months after doing time for domestic violence; tried to kill his wife and her lover with an ax."

"Nice guy."

"Then there's Maurice Verdago. In and out of jail for domestic abuse before he finally ended up in Judge Samuels-Piquard's courtroom. Once he was sentenced, he gave her the finger, pointed at her, and yelled, 'You'll get yours, bitch.' "

"Another charmer." Pescoli had always thought Verdago was a blasting cap with a very short fuse. She loathed the guy, and he seemed to feel the same way. She'd been with Grayson when Verdago had been nabbed and the hatred in his eyes had zeroed in on her. He'd gone so far as to call her a "cunt cop" and then spat on the ground when she'd handcuffed him. She figured him for a woman hater: the kind of guy who can't live with them, can't help roughing them up. "Really, he's out?"

"For the last six months. Attempted murder of his brother-in-law."

"Ah . . . yes. Sucks for the sister."

Alvarez nodded. "He had a whole arsenal of weapons. Military stuff, all kinds of weaponry, even Russian guns. Everything from grenades and an AK-47 to some kind of fancy sword. What got him arrested, though, was that he tried hacking up his victim with a butcher knife. Business partners. The brother-in-law, Ronnie Watkins, was skimming funds from their recently started trucking company. Supposedly, Verdago's been staying out of trouble, working as a janitor in a Helena apartment building."

Pescoli snorted. "Once a crook, always a crook. And he'd been in the army, right? A sharpshooter?"

"Uh-huh. His file mentions that he was the prime suspect in the disappearance of Joey Lundeen, someone he knew, but the case went cold."

"Quite a résumé."

"Not only that, but he hated Grayson's guts, or so he told his cell mate. I found mention of it when that guy, what's his name, oh, here it is, Gerald Resler, was released."

"He's out too?"

"Resler? Yeah, walking the straight and narrow for three years now. Married. With a kid."

Pescoli said, "Resler took a can opener to his girlfriend."

"When he was nineteen."

"Still . . ."

"I'll double-check on him, but Resler wasn't Grayson's collar."

"He was mine," Pescoli said, remembering the scruffy kid with a bad case of acne, shaved head, and hate-filled eyes. "A real piece of work. Now he's married with a kid?" She let out a huff of disbelief and finally opened the damned glove box for her cigs.

"He found God."

"Good for him." Discovering the pack, she yanked both it and a lighter from the compartment.

"I think he's a better bet than Verdago and Cranston."

About to light her cigarette, Pescoli had second thoughts and tossed both her filter tip and lighter onto the passenger seat. No reason to take up the habit tonight. Maybe tomorrow. "Any others?" Turning the wheel and edging her Jeep off the county road, she eased onto the long lane leading through the trees to her house. The lane hadn't been plowed, and a fresh layer of snow covered the packed tire tracks.

"Oh, yeah, we've got more. These are just the most obvious. So, let's see . . . here we go. How about Edie Gardener?"

"Geez, I'd forgotten about her."

"Well, she's back. Got out last spring, married a man who corresponded with her while she was in the pen."

"For killing her boyfriend, if memory serves." And it did. Edie was the daughter of antigovernment extremists who lived in a compound near Cougar Ridge. Deceptively small, Edie had sat in court expressionless, dark hair pinned away from her face, her hands folded in her lap. Pretty, petite, and self-possessed, she'd won the hearts of the jury without uttering so much as one word in her own defense. She'd let her lawyer and other witnesses do her talking.

"Self-defense," Alvarez reminded her.

"Yeah, with a bullet to his back."

"I'm reading the report. She claimed he was abusing her, and her sister-in-law backed her up."

"I know." Edie had always claimed her innocence and blamed Grayson for putting her away. She'd said as much in court. "She got an alibi?"

"I'm still looking into it. Currently, she's MIA, but I've got a call in to her parole officer and her brother. No one's answering. It is Christmas, you know."

"Yeah, but she's a dead-eye when it comes to rifles and with her family armed to the teeth, she would have access."

"Maybe. So far she hasn't surfaced."

"Let's find her." Pescoli drove over the small bridge that spanned the creek on her property and saw her house, lit with Christmas lights, one strand dark while the rest of the colored bulbs outlined the gutters. "Who else?" She hit the garage door opener and the light came on as the door started its slow, noisy ascent into the tracks mounted on the ceiling.

"Carlos Mendoza." She hesitated. "He was released just ten days ago and has disappeared. The thought was that he headed south, back to Guadalajara, but that's not been confirmed."

"Remind me."

"Armed robbery with an assault rifle. No one other than one of his gang was hurt. He was arrested and his brother-in-law died in a shootout eleven years ago. A cop was injured but survived."

"Lonnie Milton." Pescoli remembered now that her memory was jogged. "He retired a few months later." Braking, she rolled into the garage and hit the garage door switch.

"That's the short list. I'm going to visit Grayson before heading home. You get anywhere with Dan's brothers?"

"Nothing significant, but it's weird, you know, about Hattie, Bart's widow. If I didn't know better, I'd swear she'd had something going with Cade once upon a time."

"You mean Dan," Alvarez said as the garage door cranked slowly downward. "The sheriff."

"Nope, I'm talking about his younger brother, the hothead. Man, he was pissed, not only at whoever had done this to his brother, but at Hattie too. And she wasn't much better. You could cut the tension between them with a knife."

For a second Alvarez didn't say a word and the garage door settled onto the concrete floor with a thud. "You think she was involved with Cade as well as Bart, and . . . maybe even Dan?"

"Maybe." Pescoli cut the engine, then tossed her cigarette and lighter back into the glove box before grabbing her computer case. "Just a vibe I got."

"Worth looking into."

"Everything is. I'll see ya tomorrow." She hung up and walked from the garage to the house where, with a sharp excited yip, Cisco hopped off the living room couch. Jeremy was sprawled on the cushions, playing one of his video games. "Hey. Merry Christmas."

He actually paused the game and rolled over to look at her, his controller still in his hands. "How's the sheriff?"

"Hanging in there, I guess. It's probably going to be touch and go for a while."

"Grayson's tough, he'll make it," Jeremy predicted with the faith and invincibility of youth. "You catch the fuck—um, the bastard who shot him?"

"Not yet."

"But you will." His eyebrows raised, pushing up the edge of a stocking cap that, these days, seemed forever on his head.

"Oh, yeah," Pescoli said, dropping her computer onto a chair at the table and unzipping her jacket. Cisco was still spinning crazily at her feet, so she took the time to bend down and scratch him behind his ears. "Hey, there," she said to the dog and was rewarded with a wildly wagging tail and a few more quick circles. "Yeah, I missed you too."

"Mom?" Bianca appeared in bare feet, pajama bottoms, and a sweatshirt that looked two sizes too big for her small frame.

"Hi." Pescoli threw her daughter a wan smile. "Sorry about all this."

"It's okay," Bianca said as Pescoli tossed her coat over the back of a chair.

"But I was going to cook a ham with scalloped potatoes, you know, try to have a real Christmas dinner."

"Who cares?" Jeremy was sitting up though his fingers were still attached to his game controller. "I had Cap'n Crunch."

"Swell. Cereal for dinner."

"And Gatorade."

"Mmmm." She noticed a half-full plastic bottle set on the floor next to a mixing bowl—the remains of his dinner. "Terrific." Lifting an eyebrow, she glanced at her daughter. "You?"

"A protein bar."

"And? Gatorade?"

"Yuk, no. Diet Pepsi."

"Even better. Zero calories and zero nutrition." Pescoli made a face, then cringed inside when she thought of her own childhood and all the traditional meals eaten around the dining table on polished silver. Even after her father had abandoned them when she was eleven, her mother had, each and every year, held Christmas dinner at the big table where she and her three older sisters had sat with various aunts, uncles, and cousins. If too many family members showed up, the long table was extended with a series of folding tables that pushed into the living room. The tantalizing aromas of roasting prime rib and hot baked pies filled the old house where laughter rang, the piano was played, and, after a flurry of opening of presents, dice were tossed when board games were played . . . a far cry from what her children were experiencing. "I'll make it up to you," she promised, her throat suddenly thick. "I swear."

"We had a big dinner last night at Dad's," Bianca said, uncaring.

"Michelle cooked?" Pescoli imagined the Barbie doll–like woman in her pink, strappy high heels and a tiny embroidered apron that barely covered her tight dress as she glazed the Christmas ham.

Jeremy barked out a laugh, as if he'd seen the same image in his own mind's eye. "Michelle's mother cooked a goose. I think it's their family tradition or something."

"It was gross!" Bianca pulled a face and stuck out her tongue. "I tried to eat some, really . . . but . . ." She shuddered violently. "Ick!"

"A protein bar was better?"

"Tons!" Bianca said, nodding. "Oh! But Michelle got me a string bikini for Christmas."

"A bikini? In Montana in the winter?" Pescoli inwardly sighed. What was wrong with Lucky's wife?

"She had to order it online, and she also bought me a round-trip ticket to Phoenix for a girls' spa weekend!" Bianca's blue eyes were bright with anticipation.

"She's going, too, I take it?"

"Uh-huh, and we're going to get all-day massages, manis, and pedis, and then lay around the pool, oh, make that pools. She and Dad have a time-share and there are six pools on the property!"

"And when is this trip planned . . . ?"

"Spring break!"

"And you?" she turned to Jeremy.

"Luke got me a new rifle."

"Seriously?"

"Yeah," Jeremy said, and he, too, grinned widely. "It's really cool. And airline tickets too. Spring training. Luke's already lined up a couple of games!"

"Good, I guess." *Weaponry, trips to the sun country, tiny bathing suits. For Christmas.* "Nothing says Peace on Earth like guns and string bikinis."

Bianca rolled her eyes and groaned, and Pescoli thought about the gifts she'd bought for the kids, gifts not yet wrapped and hidden in a back corner of her closet: a pair of jeans and iPhone cover for Bianca; two new sweatshirts and a video game for Jeremy.

"Tomorrow," she said, "I'll make spaghetti. The day after Christmas, that'll be our new holiday tradition from here on in. And we'll have presents. Tonight, though, we'll just let it slide."

"If that's okay with you," Jeremy said. "You're the one who was so dead set about us all having Christmas together. And I thought Nate was coming over."

"No, we discussed it last night and he thought it would be best if it was just the three of us today."

"Why?"

"Who cares?" Bianca said, but then she wasn't looking for a father; she had always accepted Lucky for what he was. But then, biologically they were linked. Not so for her brother. Jeremy was still searching for a father figure and maybe always would be.

"Well, even if we'd planned something, it wouldn't have worked because of what happened this morning."

"You asking Nate over for tomorrow?" Jeremy asked, his expression taut. He vacillated between concern for his mother and contempt for anyone she dated, just as he kept stepping into adulthood, then cowering back to being a self-involved teenager.

"Maybe. Depends." She thought of Santana stopping by the hospital, only to leave as quickly as he came. "We'll see what tomorrow brings."

* * *

The man lying in the hospital bed could not have been Dan Grayson. Pale, eyes closed, unresponsive, hooked up to all kinds of monitors, tubes, and bags as he lay beneath crisp white sheets and thin blankets he was far from the vibrant man Alvarez knew. Now, he appeared weak, his face unshaven, his mustache still thick, but grayer somehow. His head was bandaged, seeming nearly twice its normal size, and she saw the edges of surgical tape at the neckline of his hospital gown, indicating further surgical dressing taped to his chest.

Don't die, Grayson. Fight. You can win this battle, but please, please, do NOT give up. She blinked against a surprise attack of tears and beat them back. Crying wouldn't help, and she wasn't going to let herself think that this man she admired so much would let go of life.

He was in good hands here, she told herself, the best health care this part of Montana had to offer. In this isolated unit, there were several beds, each separated by a curtain as they fanned out from a central hub, which was the nurses' station. Two women in hospital scrubs manned the large, semicircular desk that looked as if it were designed by NASA, while another tended to the only other patient in the ward, a woman whose curtained room was on the opposite side of the desk as Grayson, separated from the sheriff by five empty beds.

The ICU was quiet aside from the hushed tones of the workers and the soft beeps of computer monitors as patients' vital signs were recorded. The only access was by a door with a punch-in code for those authorized, or a buzzer that would alert the staff to a visitor. The guard, currently Kayan Rule, a deputy from the department who Alvarez liked and trusted, was posted outside.

This area of the hospital was safe.

Secure.

The best place for Grayson to start his long recovery.

As she gazed down on his face, Alvarez felt a tug on her heart. She loved this man. Trusted him. He'd been a mentor, yes, but her feelings ran much deeper than that of a student to a teacher; she'd often thought if circumstances had been different, she and he could have become lovers.

Silly, really, but as she stared down at his serene face, she couldn't help but wonder, *What if?*

She wasn't the only one who had fantasies about the man now struggling to survive; Hattie Grayson was definitely romantically interested in him as well. While driving into the parking lot designated for visitors, Alvarez had seen Hattie hurrying to her car. One arm had been firmly around her middle, as if holding her coat closed as she'd gripped her purse, while with her free hand she'd swiped at tears. She'd looked so much younger than she had when Alvarez had run into her when she'd made the mistake of crashing Dan Grayson's family's Thanksgiving dinner one year. Alvarez had been greeted by Hattie, the mother of his nieces, who'd looked like a combo of Martha Stewart and June Cleaver in her frilly apron and pearls. Tonight, in a quickly donned coat over jeans, her hair flying from her face as she ran to her car, Hattie had appeared fresh-faced, but tortured. She'd climbed into her Toyota, gripped the wheel, and, probably thinking she was finally all alone, had completely broken down, her shoulders shaking with her sobs.

Alvarez understood the feeling of utter frustration and hopelessness now, as she witnessed how close Grayson had come to death.

And he wasn't out of the woods yet.

She touched the rail of his bed, then backed away, her eyes hot, her throat tight, her chin set. She wasn't one to break down in public, nor, for that matter, in private, and she didn't intend to start now.

"Thank you," she said to a nurse who pushed a button behind the sleek desk. As a buzzer sounded and the door unlocked, releasing Alvarez, the RN nodded and offered a small, encouraging smile.

Her chest so tight she could barely breathe, Alvarez walked into the hallway where Rule sat, unread sports magazine on his lap.

"How is he?" Rule asked, his trademark grin absent, his dark eyes filled with concern. A tall African American, Kayan Rule looked as if he'd spent years in the NBA as a power forward and was a head taller than Alvarez.

"Hanging in there."

"Any prognosis?"

She shook her head, then felt the muscles in the back of her neck tighten as she noticed Manny Douglas stepping off the elevator.

There was just something about the reporter that bothered her. Maybe it was his always-smug expression, as if he knew more than you, or the tinted glasses that often shaded his eyes, or maybe he was just one of those reporters who rubbed her the wrong way. Whatever the reason, he was here. "Son of a bitch," she whispered under her breath. She'd never liked him, never would, and it wasn't just that he was a member of the press, it was his damned attitude.

"What?" Rule glanced down the hallway, then muttered, "Great." Rule, it seemed, shared her feelings.

Heading their way in his usual flannel shirt, khakis, and down vest, the reporter for the local newspaper forced a smile as if he'd just come across long-lost friends.

"I'll handle him," Rule said, straightening and seeming to grow another two inches.

"Detective!" Manny said. "Any word on the sheriff?"

"Nothing I can talk about," Alvarez answered. "I'm sure there will be a press conference tomorrow."

"But I've got a deadline tonight and my readers would love to know how the sheriff is doing!" A thin, persistent man with a mouthful of crooked teeth, Manny was a pain in the backside. "Any leads on who attacked him?" Manny had already pulled a mini-recorder from the pocket of his vest.

"You know I can't talk about that."

Rule stepped between them. "The hospital's off-limits, Douglas."

"I know, but we've worked together before."

Selena wasn't going to be sweet-talked or bullied. "Not this time, Manny."

Manny tried again, "But Grayson's an elected official. His public, the people who put him into office, have the right to know what happened to him and how he's doing."

"You heard the detective," Rule said a little more sternly. "We're not talking about the sheriff."

"I can't tell you any more than what you can get through the hospital patient information desk," Alvarez added.

Manny hesitated a bit, then shifted gears. "All right," he said finally. "What can you tell me about Judge Samuels-Piquard?"

Alvarez stopped short. "What about her?"

"She's missing."

"Missing?" Alvarez repeated, thinking of the tall, athletic woman whose opinions were usually fair, but her sentences harsh. With short red hair and a demeanor that brooked no arguments, she was a big, blowsy woman whose tongue was as sharp as her wit. "You mean, officially? Someone's filed a report with Missing Persons?" Alvarez clarified, just to make certain the reporter wasn't on a fishing expedition.

"That's the word on the street."

"What street is that?" she said skeptically. For years she'd suspected that Manny had someone on the inside who was giving him information, a leak in the department. "Who said—"

"Uh-uh, don't even go there." He held up a hand as if to fend off an attack. "You know I'll never reveal my sources."

Rule snorted his disdain and folded his arms over his chest, stretching the shoulders of his uniform, appearing more intimidating than ever.

Selena said to Manny, "Cut it out. This isn't an episode of *Law and Order.*"

"Yeah, yeah, I know. But I've got rights, as does my source."

"Your source?"

"I'm just relaying what I heard. I thought you could confirm. Obviously not." He was already backing up, easing toward the bank of elevators. A cynical smile slashed across the stubble on his jaw. "Looks like Grayson isn't the only one having a bad Christmas."

CHAPTER 9

Hattie tossed her keys into her purse, dropped her bag onto the kitchen table, then started down the hallway past the girls' room where she cracked open the door and saw they both were sleeping soundly, both in mussed twin beds, both with stuffed animals spread over the quilts and onto the floor. Blowing them each a kiss, she closed the door softly and walked to her bedroom on the other side of the hallway.

Her mother had already left, though Zena had come up with dozens of questions Hattie couldn't answer as she'd reluctantly grabbed her coat from the small front closet.

"I could spend the night," she'd offered, genuinely concerned. "This is horrid for you, and you could sleep in. Get some rest. I'll watch the girls in the morning."

"Thanks, Mom, but I can't. I've got paperwork to catch up on, and I've got to plan for a dinner party I'm catering this weekend. The twins are already scheduled to spend the day with Rachel and her boys." Rachel McCallister was a single mother who babysat for extra money and lived only six doors down, in the same complex, so it was handy, and over the years they'd become fast friends.

"It would save you some money," Zena sniffed, putting up the pretension of an argument as she slid her arms through the sleeves of her coat, then yanked on a pair of red leather gloves.

The cost with you just can't be counted in dollars, Hattie had thought, because Zena always found a way to extract her fee. "Thanks, we'll do fine." Hattie had closed the door behind her mother, then watched as Zena walked to her Cadillac and slid behind the wheel. Her mother had paused to light a cigarette, a practice she thought she hid from everyone, including Hattie and her doctors. Then she had driven off, her taillights winking Christmas red as the big car lumbered out of the lot to the road. Once the Caddie disappeared from view, Hattie had bolted the door and turned off the outside lights.

Now, she went through her nightly ritual, checking on her daughters, turning off the hall light, then walking into her bedroom where she kicked off her shoes a little too hard and one of her heels slammed against the footboard. She thought about Dan and about her life as she flopped onto the bed. Tears surfaced. Again. She'd been fighting a losing battle with them all day, it seemed.

Heart heavy, she felt the weight of guilt settle over her and press down on her lungs until she felt as if she couldn't breathe. When Bart died, she'd insisted he didn't kill himself, but only Dan had listened, and even he couldn't do anything about the ME's verdict of suicide, even though no note or message of any kind had been found. If Bart had truly taken his own life, she reasoned—and she didn't want to go there . . . couldn't most of the time because deep down, she knew she was to blame. She was the one who'd wanted the divorce and had pushed for it, and though she'd promised Bart that he would have joint custody of the twins, sharing the girls had been difficult for everyone. Bart's depression had grown deeper and deeper and . . . maybe there was something she should have seen or guessed, some warning sign. But if there was, she sure hadn't picked up on it, other than to know he was angry at her.

She just hadn't been able to believe that he'd taken his life.

She still couldn't. Not really.

And now Dan was near death's door. A tear trickled down her cheek and she swiped it angrily away. She'd always been close to Dan, had dated him in high school. When he'd gone to college, they'd agreed to see other people, though Hattie had been broken-hearted, or at least thought she had. Then she'd caught Cade's eye, and with Dan gone, she'd turned her attention to the bad boy of the clan. Whereas Dan had been a stand-up kind of guy, the responsible brother, Cade was the rebel who spat at authority. She and Cade circled each other for a bit, then dove into a hot affair soon after she graduated. The romance, if you could call it that, fizzled out pretty fast because he had a roving eye and Hattie, in those days, if nothing else, demanded fidelity. She wanted Cade's heart and a ring, but he couldn't give either and one day, he just climbed onto his motorcycle and drove off, heading west, she'd heard later, though he didn't contact her for years. And when he finally did, that had spelled disaster with a capital D.

Now, she bit her lip thinking about him and their always mercurial relationship. They were bad for each other, had always been, never mixing. She'd forced herself to get over him, to turn to the one man who had always loved her, his younger brother Bart, baby of the clan and always a bit of a dreamer.

When Bart asked her to marry him, so soon after Cade had left for the last time, she'd not only said yes, but insisted they elope. He, more traditional, had talked her into a quickie marriage at the ranch, and she'd reluctantly agreed. As long as it was soon.

She remembered her wedding day, of course, but those memories weren't the kind that a bride should carry with her for the rest of her life. Nine years earlier, she'd stood beneath an arbor that the florists had constructed in the wide yard on the west side of the Grayson farmhouse. The day had been Montana sunny and bright, the sky June blue and cloudless, a summer breeze bending the hollyhock and columbine as it whispered through the pines.

Friends and family, around forty in all, were gathered on the yard where the rented white chairs had been festooned with bouquets of roses, carnations, and baby's breath, the bouquets trailing long blue and coral ribbons. Each guest had already been given a glass of champagne or sparkling cider to toast the bride and groom as soon as the ceremony ended.

The officiant was someone her mother knew, a short man with rimless glasses and a bald head glistening with sweat. His smile was beatific, his face weathered, as if he'd spent his youth in the sun, a man of the outdoors as well as God.

Facing her, Bart had been clean-shaven, tall and handsome in his black, western-cut suit, his gray eyes focused on her, the hint of a smile teasing his lips. He loved her. She knew that, had known it long before any words had been spoken. And that should be enough. Right.

She was making the smart choice, she'd told herself, over and over again. They were friends. Lovers. And if the lovemaking wasn't as fiery as she'd hoped, that could change. She would make it change.

Dan was Bart's best man, and Hattie made certain her own gaze didn't wander in his direction, not once. There wasn't a chance of her heart betraying her, not on this, her wedding day, and her sister, standing so closely by her, watching her, made Hattie's convictions all the stronger.

She was marrying Bart now. He was her world, so she'd stood with her hands linked to his, uttering vows she hoped she would keep. Not looking at Dan, not thinking about Cade, not letting the doubts that had chased her up to this moment catch up to her.

Life would be good.

She vowed to be Bart's "wedded wife," for better or worse, in front of God and country, her mother and her sister, Cara, who was Hattie's matron of honor.

Despite her valiant efforts to believe in the future, the wedding, even at that point, seemed cosmically off-kilter, the ceremony and all the players staged, like pawns on a giant chess board. *This is your choice, Hattie,* she'd told herself. *Don't think that way. Don't lose faith. It will work out. Bart's a good man. An honest man. He'll be true and faithful and everything you could possibly want, and he is a Grayson.*

Oh, God . . .

Her hands were clammy, her heart beating a wild negative tattoo, a warning. *This isn't right. You're marrying with your head and not your heart. Yes, he loves you, but you know you don't love him. Not the way he deserves.*

In that moment she could feel her face drain of color, but she wouldn't listen to the arguments in her mind. She couldn't. Swallowing back any lingering doubts, she told herself that this would be her life. She would be a Grayson, and the love she felt for Bart, if not as deep as she'd felt with Dan or as passionate as it had been with Cade, was strong and vital. She would make this marriage work. She had to.

Because she was pregnant. *Just* pregnant. She'd found out only two days before and she'd told no one. Not her best friend, not her mother, and certainly not Bart. There would be no shotgun wedding. This was a planned event. So what if the planning had been less than six weeks.

Her cheeks burned at the thought of the life growing inside her and hoped everyone in the small circle of family and friends who had been invited thought that she was just a "blushing bride," though that was far from the truth and she wasn't the type.

". . . it's my pleasure to introduce to you Mr. and Mrs. Bartholomew Grayson," the officiant had said proudly, and their guests clapped and held their glasses high, pale liquid catching in the light from a lowering sun. Then to Bart, he said, "You may kiss your bride."

It's over.

You're married!

Hattie had closed her eyes and kissed Bart just as the sound of a motorcycle's engine reached her ears. Her heart beat a little faster, but she told herself she was imagining things, that it didn't matter, that she was a married woman, that . . . But then Bart's muscles tightened for a second, and he released her too quickly as the sound of the engine grew louder.

Then she saw it, as they walked down a short makeshift aisle between the chairs, a harsh glint of sunlight bounced off shiny metal. With a roar, the big bike tore up the driveway, spun near the front porch, spraying gravel.

Hattie's heart did an unexpected and unwanted kick at the sight of Cade finally slowing the Harley and cutting the engine.

"What the hell's he doing here?" Bart demanded, a muscle working furiously in his jaw.

"He *is* your brother."

"Who's supposed to be in goddamned California!"

Cade yanked off his helmet, left it on the bike, and strolled leisurely toward the crowd, all of whom were staring at the disruption. His hair was longer than Hattie remembered, bleached from the sun, his face tanned, a new scar showing on one cheek. Tall and athletic, like the rest of the Graysons, he swung up the path as if he owned the place, which, she knew, he did, at least partially.

"I'll take care of this," Dan said, and Cara's weak protest of "Dan, just leave it alone," went unheeded as he started toward his younger brother.

Too late.

Cade, in battered denim and a worn leather jacket, was already through the side gate and striding up the path that ringed the house. At the final row of chairs, where a waiter stood with a tray of champagne glasses, he said, "Ah, don't tell me I missed the nuptials." His grin lopsided, his gaze was dark with emotion as it landed squarely on Hattie.

"What're you doing here?" Dan asked.

"Same as you." Cade was forced to stop as Dan was blocking his path. "Just here to give the happy couple my best."

"Bull," Bart said under his breath. He was still holding Hattie's hand, his fingers nearly crushing her bones as they tightened.

"Maybe you should leave," Dan suggested. "Come back later."

"*You're* here, brother," Cade said with meaning.

Dan held up a hand, hoping to cut off any further remarks from his headstrong brother. "Not now, Cade. It's not the time."

"For what?" Cade feigned innocence, but fooled no one, least of all any of his brothers.

Even Zed, never a fan of Hattie's, stepped up, shoulder to shoulder with Dan. "You don't want to do this," he whispered loud enough for Hattie to hear.

"Do what?" Cade was having none of it.

"It's over, okay?" Zed said a little more loudly. "They're married now. Give it up."

"Nothin' to give." Quickly, he stepped around his brothers, but Zed grabbed his arm.

"Cade," Hattie whispered desperately, all too aware of the curious eyes turned in her direction.

"What?"

Shaking her head, feeling her veil start to fall, she said, "Thank you for coming."

His jaw slid to the side and for a tense moment there was silence, just the sough of the wind and chatter of birds breaking the quietude. With his gaze still locked to hers, he grabbed a full glass from the tray held by a stunned waiter and lifted it into the air. "Here's to the bride and groom," he said. "May they have a long and happy union." Still eyeing Hattie, he drank the glass down in one long swallow, then tossed his glass to the ground. "Good luck, Hattie," he added.

At that second, Bart released Hattie's hand, burst past Zed and Dan, who were blocking his path, and swung wildly, his fist connecting with Cade's jaw with a crack. Cade's head snapped back and he reeled away. "You bastard!" Bart spat. "Why can't you just leave us the fuck alone!"

Cade landed on his butt, his fists curling, but instead of throwing himself to his feet to tear into Bart, he sat for a second on the drying grass, and again he looked at his new sister-in-law. "See what I mean about luck," he said, standing and dusting his hands as Zed and Dan restrained a furious Bart. "You, darlin', are going to need it. A lot of it."

Now, as she lay on her bed, Hattie scowled up at the ceiling. Cade had been right, unfortunately. Bart's mood swings had been wide, his anger ignited by a trigger switch, his deep soul-searching depression sometimes taking him near despair, his happiness, when he found it, euphoric. There was just no leveling him out, and therein lay the problem, one she hadn't seen before she was married. Had she suspected? Of course. But she'd turned a blind eye to her suspicions and had satisfied herself with being married.

"Fool," she whispered to the dark room.

She thought again of her husband's death; how with his depression, suicide was definitely possible, but still she refused to believe Bart would take his own life. In anger, he'd flash to fury, but he'd rarely been violent, except to his brothers, never to her. And when he was feeling down, he became morose, but not, she believed, to the point of actually carrying out a suicide plan, not taking his life, and without saying good-bye or leaving an explanation for his girls. No way could she believe that!

Even though Bart had died nearly six years earlier, wasn't it possible that someone, the same someone who tried to kill Dan, had murdered her husband? Somehow forced him up the ladder before kicking it from his legs? She knew others were sure she was grasping at straws, but she wouldn't give up, especially now that Dan had been attacked. He'd been decent to her after the divorce, and while Zed and Cade seemed to think that she'd spent the last six years trying to squeeze the last blood from a corpse by insisting Bart's death wasn't suicide, Dan had looked into his brother's death. Not only had he comforted Hattie and made some inquiries, he'd also pulled the medical examiner aside for a private chat. In the end, however, he couldn't come up with any proof that Bart hadn't hung himself, and there just hadn't been enough evidence in the ensuing years to reopen the case. Bart had been buried in the family plot, labeled forever as a victim of his own hand.

Despite what others might think, her battle wasn't just for the insurance benefit that had never been paid because of the medical examiner's ruling, nor was it to preserve his name. Certainly she didn't want her children believing their father had taken his own life, but the real reason behind her determination was justice. She hated to think that someone had tricked or coerced Bart onto that ladder and then taken his life, just as her blood boiled to think that some sicko had attempted to kill Dan.

No. It just wasn't right, and damn it, she wasn't going to back down, not until she was satisfied that the truth had come out and Dan's attacker brought to justice.

Or dead. That would be okay too. In fact, the bastard's death would be a whole lot better.

He couldn't believe he'd missed. Grayson was alive!

He drove through the streets of Grizzly Falls undetected, furious enough to consider going to the hospital in Missoula and finishing the son of a bitch off once and for all.

All day he'd waited to hear that Grayson had gone to meet his maker, but through the miracle of modern medicine and the damned luck of that stupid detective, the bastard had survived.

Be patient. What're the chances that he'll pull through? You know you hit him in the chest and the head. It will just take a little more time.

His gloved fingers tightened over the wheel as he slowed for a stoplight on the road that cut through the lower part of the town.

CHAPTER 10

"You're a dead woman, Pescoli," the voice threatened, echoing as if it were carried down a long, snaking tunnel.

Her heart slammed in her chest. Where was she? In the forest? There were trees everywhere, branches shivering and chattering in the wind, and the voice . . . it seemed disembodied.

Where are you, you bastard?

Freezing cold, Pescoli turned slowly, her eyes wide as she searched the wooded terrain where trees rose to impossible heights, their skeletal branches covered in ice, their rough-barked trunks thick enough to hide a man. Or an army.

"Who are you?" she demanded, crouching, keeping low as she reached for her sidearm. Her fingers came up empty.

Damn!

Nothing in her shoulder harness!

"Count the seconds," the voice ordered.

She whipped around. Where the hell was the bastard? Her gaze scraped every square inch of the white landscape, blinding to the point that she had to squint. Still, she saw nothing. Her heart was trip-hammering, every muscle tense. *Think, Pescoli, think. You've been in tighter spots than this. Keep him talking. Zero in on him. You don't have your weapon, but you can get the upper hand. You're a trained officer, for God's sake.*

Adrenaline pumping through her bloodstream, she yelled. "What do you want?"

"Five!" he called, his voice firm and harsh, seeming to come from

Running parallel to the river, this street was as old as the town itself. Shops and restaurants, even the old brick courthouse with its imposing forty-foot Christmas tree, flanked the street.

Waiting at the light, he tapped his fingers on the wheel, fighting the urge to try to attack Grayson again, knowing it was too big a risk. The chances were too small that he could pull it off. Still, his eyes narrowed through the windshield as he watched a large group of pedestrians, all bundled in ski jackets and fleece, strolling across the street in front of him. He wondered vaguely why they were out, decided it wasn't his business, concentrated instead on how he could get past the security guarding Grayson.

Tick. Tick. Tick.

Time was running out!

Grayson needed to die so that he could continue with the next step.

Honk!!!

A horn blared and he glanced at the light, now glowing a bright green. He stepped on the gas quickly. His concentration was shot. That was the problem, he needed rest. Then, once he'd refueled, he would tackle the Grayson problem. The sheriff wasn't getting out of this alive.

all directions at once. Was he in front of her, hiding behind the heavy bole of the hemlock? Or was he coming up from behind?

Whirling quickly, she hoped to surprise him, but saw only more dense forest.

"Who are you?" she demanded. *Come on, you coward, show yourself!*

She was breathing rapidly, her breath fogging the air as she ducked low, moving quickly under the low-hanging branch of a pine tree.

"Four!"

"Just leave me alone!" She had to get the drop on him. Somehow. Without her weapon. Using only her wits and bare hands.

"Three!"

From the corner of her eye, she saw movement. Spinning quickly toward the noise, she felt a pine needle scrape across her eye, temporarily blinding her. Where the hell was he?

"Two." The voice was almost familiar. The sheriff's . . . ?

"Grayson?" she called before remembering that he was hurt, lying in the hospital . . .

She blinked, her vision blurry, her ears straining. Over the hollow rush of the wind, there was another sound, the familiar tinkle of laughter.

Out here? In the middle of no-damned-where?

And children's voices. Giggles. Shouts.

No! There couldn't be kids out here in the middle of nowhere with a maniac on the loose!

As her vision cleared, she saw him, a tall figure backlit by a street lamp in the middle of the forest. His face was obscured from the enormous tree under which he stood, but she could tell he was athletic. And dressed in white—almost like a space suit.

Worse yet, just creeping into her line of vision, not ten yards from the freak, was a small child, a girl with dark curls and a pink jacket. Holding a stuffed rabbit upside down with one hand, she allowed the bunny's fuzzy ears to drag on the ground and leave a trail in the snow.

"No!" Pescoli screamed. The girl couldn't be more than three!

Where was the kid's mother?

Pescoli's voice seemed to alert him and he turned, revealing the rifle strapped to his back. As she watched in horror, he deftly clicked the weapon from its case and lifted it to his shoulder, sighting on the child.

"Noooo!" Pescoli screamed.

From the surrounding trees, a dog began to growl and bark.

The child's stuffed rabbit suddenly came alive, squealing and baring its teeth, a red stain appearing in the trench in the snow, blood flowing like a river from its ears. Twisting, it bit the girl on her wrist.

Heart thundering in her ears, Pescoli yelled at the kid. "Run!"

He swung the barrel around, sighting directly at Pescoli. Who was he and why was he doing this?

"One!" He pulled the trigger.

Bang! Bang! Bang!

Her eyes flew open.

She sat bolt upright in the darkness. Took in long, deep breaths.

"What the hell?" she whispered, shaking, her teeth chattering, starting to realize that it had all been a dream. Another horrid nightmare.

The door to her room opened.

A man's silhouette filled her doorway.

Tall. Backlit. Like the monster in her dream.

Scooting back on the bedclothes, she automatically swung her arm toward the nightstand for her service weapon just as she woke up fully.

"Mom?"

"For the love of God, Jeremy, you scared the living crap out of me!"

"You were screaming."

Holding up a hand, she waved him off. Her mind was starting to clear. It always took a second or so. Even reaching for her gun was a mistake; she'd kept her weapons locked away ever since Jeremy had arrived home from the hospital twenty years earlier. Letting out a long, slow breath, she tried to clear her mind. "Bad dream."

"Mom, this is, like, the fifth one in a month."

"Yeah, yeah, I know." Nodding, feeling foolish, she wondered what the hell was wrong with her. Lately, she'd been having nightmares—bizarre, horrid dreams where she awoke with her heart thundering.

In some cases, segments of the dreams were from old cases she'd worked. Other times, she was a young woman, with little kids. In some cases, Joe was dying in her arms, blood pouring from a wound she couldn't locate, blood she couldn't staunch.

She wondered if she should see a shrink but quickly decided against it. With Santana's ultimatum looming, and after witnessing the attack on Grayson, she was just stressed.

Lord knew she'd seen enough horror in her job to create the sick images that crawled through her brain at night. Coupled with what she'd seen, she'd physically and mentally experienced her own terror at the hands of a madman.

If she had bad dreams, she'd earned every last one of them. Drawing her legs up around her, she wrapped her arms around her knees. She was still cold, shivering inside; she realized she'd kicked her covers off sometime during the restless night.

"You're okay?" Jeremy asked from the doorway.

"Yeah." Pushing her hair from her eyes, she glanced at the clock: 3:37. Inwardly, she groaned when she thought of how soon she'd have to get up. Clicking on the bedside light, as her eyes grew accustomed to the illumination, she saw that her son's hair was mussed, his clothes disheveled. "I, um, I don't suppose I want to know where you've been."

"Don't think so. No."

She wanted to argue, but it was too late, and it would only be one more heated, angry discussion that went nowhere.

No doubt he'd been with Heidi until all hours of the morning. He knew where she stood about sex, condoms, his future, Heidi's . . . bringing it up now would only exacerbate an already prickly situation.

"Nothing good happens after midnight," she reminded him.

"You're wrong, Mom, and you know it."

"Okay, okay." Who was she to argue the point when she and Santana had made love into the wee hours of the morning so recently? "Not a discussion for the middle of the night."

"You're right." Hand on the doorknob, he started to turn away.

"Jer?" she said.

"Yeah?"

"Thanks."

"You're welcome, Mom. Good night." He closed the door softly and she knew he was lying. As she slapped off the light and the darkness crept in, she knew it wasn't a good night, not a good night at all.

As Christmas celebrations went, this had been the worst ever, Pescoli thought, hanging up her coat on the hook near the door of her office. It didn't even seem like the holiday. The last twenty-four hours since the attack on Grayson had been a disaster that wouldn't end. Last night, she'd hung out with her kids for a while, talked to Santana on the phone for nearly an hour, then flopped onto her bed long after midnight, though she hadn't slept much, the nightmare destroying whatever chance of getting the shut-eye she needed. She'd barely caught two hours of sleep, and this morning her eyes felt gritty and red, as if she were hungover. So far, there didn't seem to be enough Visine on the planet to help.

She made her way into the near-empty lunch area where she poured herself a cup of coffee, emptying the glass carafe in the process as she watched the dregs slide into her mug. Sometimes, when she grabbed the last cup in the pot, she'd take the time to brew more. Not today. Not when Dan Grayson was lying near death in a Missoula hospital.

Sipping from her mug, hoping the coffee had enough caffeine in it to give her system the jump start it needed, she walked down the short hallway, nodding at a couple of deputies sauntering in the opposite direction, their conversation hushed.

The entire building seemed to have turned down the volume a bit—no loud jokes, cackling laughter, or rattle of chains as a suspect, handcuffed and shackled, was herded through the department. Cell phones still rang, but they seemed quieter, and the conversation, if there was any, was muted.

Had it been just a little over a day since she'd driven around the bend in Grayson's lane and seen him hit? God, it seemed like a lifetime as she passed Grayson's darkened office and noticed Sturgis's empty dog bed in the corner. Her heart twisted and her jaw tightened as she remembered the old dog taking off like a black bullet, streaking after the assassin. "Shit," she said and wished to hell she had a cigarette.

"Hey!" Alvarez called from inside her office and Pescoli paused at the doorway. "Brewster's on the warpath."

"When isn't he?" Whether he was the acting sheriff or not, Cort Brewster was a prick, at least in Pescoli's biased opinion. "And by the way, that's not PC."

"Nothing is anymore."

"You got that right. So what's up?"

"Have you heard that Kathryn Samuels-Piquard is missing?"

"The judge?" She stepped inside the office where she noticed for the first time that the image on Alvarez's monitor was of Judge Piquard.

"I heard it last night at the hospital. Manny Douglas was more than pleased to drop that particular bomb, and I double-checked this morning, with Taj in Missing Persons. Turns out it's true. Piquard's son called it in and claimed the judge was last seen a few days ago, before she took her usual holiday up at her cabin. She goes there every year, the week before Christmas, stays through Christmas Eve, and then always returns Christmas afternoon."

"But this time she didn't show up?"

"That's right. And the family can't get her to answer her cell, which they swear is always on. Brewster's already sent deputies to the cabin, which is just this side of the county line, way up in the hills."

"It hasn't been twenty-four hours."

"Doesn't matter, after the attack on Grayson, the family got worried and called Brewster, as he's a family friend."

"They think the two incidents are related?" Pescoli asked, surprised.

"I don't know what they think, but they're nervous as hell and Brewster is concerned."

"Let's just hope she just forgot and let her cell phone battery run down."

"Yeah," Alvarez said, though she sounded as unconvinced as Pes-

coli felt. "Just a sec"—she glanced down at her phone, which was trying to vibrate across her desk. "O'Keefe's texting again." A bit of a
smile brushed her lips. "What a way to spend the holidays—elec-
tronically."

"When are you going to see him?"

"Tomorrow night. Gabe too." She smiled at the mention of her
son. "Better late than never, right?"

"Right."

"Detective?" Cort Brewster stuck his head into Alvarez's office,
but his gaze was fastened on Pescoli. "I'd like to talk to you. In my office."

Pescoli couldn't help but bristle. She'd never liked Brewster and
the feeling was mutual. While she considered him an egocentric,
hypocritical prick, he thought she was a loose cannon who was a fail-
ure as a mother. She thought he hid behind all his churchgoing,
long-lasting marriage bullshit, and he thought she was a woman who
couldn't hold on to a man or keep a marriage together.

Now, as she walked down the hallway to his office, she decided
maybe they were both a little right about each other. Of course, they
were at odds because their children had gotten into serious trouble
together in the past, and he was scared to death Jeremy would get
his precious little daughter Heidi pregnant. Pescoli could have issued
him a news bulletin: She was even more frightened of Cort's princess
getting knocked up than Brewster was.

She snorted. They each blamed the other one's child. Brewster
made no bones about the fact that he considered Jeremy a do-nothing,
dope-smoking loser, and Pescoli considered Heidi as conniving and
wily as a con woman twice her age. The one thing she and Brewster
agreed upon was that the kids weren't good for each other and
should break up, which they did, on a regular basis, only to come
back to each other over and over again.

"Have a seat," Brewster suggested, pointing to one of the visitor's
chairs, then rounding his desk and settling into the executive chair
on the other side. He was flanked by bookcases where he displayed
awards for service and pictures of his family, including his wife, Bess,
to whom he had been married for over a quarter of a century, and

their four blond, stepping-stone daughters, the youngest of which was Heidi, who, Pescoli had to admit grudgingly, was drop-dead gorgeous with her wide smile, dynamite figure, and air of innocence. Only her eyes, even in Brewster's photograph, gave away the essence of her true personality. There was a smoldering naughtiness in them, as if she held some great feminine secret she would just love to share.

Turning her attention away from Brewster's photo display, Pescoli sat in one of the chairs. Though she wasn't comfortable seated at Brewster's desk, at least he hadn't already claimed Grayson's office; that would have been too much for Pescoli and a lot of the other officers.

"What's up?" she asked.

Brewster got right to the point. "You said yesterday you went up to Grayson's place to talk to him."

"That's right."

"But you didn't say why."

"I know."

Placing his elbows on his desk, he tented his hands. "So what was it about, Pescoli, and don't tell me again that it doesn't matter, because everything does in this case. We're trying to track down the person who put Grayson in the hospital."

"Yeah, I know . . ." She was reticent to confide in Brewster. Not only had she never really trusted him, even though he'd been an exemplary cop for a solid twenty years or more, but now that Grayson was injured, she didn't want to stop investigating his attack, didn't want to give Brewster even the slightest whiff of a notion that she might want to quit the department. But she couldn't lie; this was an investigation. So she hedged.

"A couple of reasons," she said, feeling Heidi's eyes staring down at her from her school picture. "First, I wanted to make sure that I was solidly back with Alvarez again. Gage and I, it was all right, but with Alvarez back from her injury, I needed to know that we were reassigned. Permanently."

He frowned a little, as if he smelled BS. "You said a couple."

"I was just going to ask him if he wanted to join my family for dinner. He's single now, again, and I thought he might like to come over."

"You didn't want to call?"

"No."

Brewster stared at her a second. "So on Christmas morning, early Christmas morning, you go busting up there just in time to see him being hit by a sniper's bullet?"

She met Brewster's disbelieving stare. "What're you saying here?" She climbed to her feet and leaned over the broad expanse of his desk. "That I *knew* something was going down? That I was . . . what? A part of it?" she asked, horrified and angry as hell.

"I'm just asking questions, Regan, the same questions you would be asking if the situation were reversed." He arched an eyebrow, encouraging her to deny what they both knew to be true.

"Okay, you're right . . . I'm sorry," she said, half choking on the apology. Brewster was a decent enough cop and now, whether she liked it or not, he was her boss. At least temporarily.

"You have a problem working with Gage?"

"No." She waved off the idea. "It's just that he's the chief criminal detective and it makes it a little stiff. He's good, don't get me wrong, but he and I don't click quite the same way I do with Alvarez. Besides, he has more important things to do."

"Like pushing paper?"

"Like organizing the cases and overseeing what's happening, making sure everyone is doing his or her job. He doesn't have time to be running around investigating with me."

"We're down people right now. No money in the budget to hire more."

"Alvarez is back."

"Yeah, fine." He leaned back in his chair again and took a second to look out the window to the gray day beyond. "I'm not going to argue with you. We've got too much to do." His face hardened as he turned his attention back to the situation at hand. "Any headway on suspects?"

"Just the usuals; the cons who are back on the street. So far they've all alibied up."

"Family?"

"Haven't really sorted all that out yet."

"Incestuous, isn't it? Brothers marrying sisters and whatnot."

"No one with a clear motive aside from the first ex-wife, Cara. She stands to gain, big time. But I don't see her as a murderer with an assault rifle."

"Hired assassin?"

Regan shook her head; she'd already considered the money angle and discarded it.

"Double-check. Not just the ex-wife who's inheriting, but the second one who might just hold a grudge."

"We're on it."

"And don't forget Grayson's sister-in-law and his brothers and any other shirttail cousin, uncle, or aunt who might hold a grudge."

Did he think she was a moron? "Of course, as well as any political enemies he may have picked up along the way."

Brewster made a sound in his throat that could have meant anything. "This is Grizzly Falls, Montana, not Las Vegas or Chicago or New York, but, yeah, look into that angle as well." He stood, signifying the meeting was over. "Let me know what the ex-wife has to say, that could be interesting."

For once, Pescoli agreed. "Alvarez and I are going to see her in an hour."

"Good."

He appeared about to dismiss her, so she asked, "What about Judge Samuels-Piquard? I heard she's gone missing."

"Yeah." He drummed his fingers on the top of his desk and frowned. "Maybe. Maybe not. I've got people checking, working with the sheriff's department in the next county as her cabin's so close to the county line, just in case. Let's hope it's all a mistake and she turns up. Soon."

"Right. Anything else?"

"No, that's it." He was already turning away, his cell phone ringing, the familiar notes of the James Bond theme song. He snorted and said, "My oldest daughter did it behind my back."

As she left, Pescoli had the uneasy suspicion that Brewster might just be human after all, a theory she hadn't subscribed to in the past. However, most of her jaded opinions of the undersheriff were because of Heidi and her relationship with Jeremy. Maybe Brewster was just particularly touchy when it came to his youngest daughter, maybe she was his blind spot or Achilles heel or whatever. There was a chance, she thought, skirting Joelle who, carrying several platters covered in plastic wrap, was quickly marching down the hallway toward the lunchroom, that Brewster wasn't the demon she'd always thought he was. But it was a small chance. A very small chance.

CHAPTER 11

Alvarez got nothing off Grayson's phone but a bad case of regret. Though none of the received or outgoing calls provided her with information she found helpful, the list of photographs she viewed on the phone's small screen gave her a deeper insight to the man. He was in a few of the shots, of course, but there were dozens of pictures of his nieces, Hattie's twins, and a few of Hattie herself, a couple of photos of his brothers on their ranch, and too many shots to count of his dog: Sturgis sniffing at a woodpile, or splashing across a creek, or curled up by the fire, or riding in the passenger seat of Grayson's old pickup. Picture after picture of the black Lab.

As she scrolled through his photo list, Alvarez felt like a voyeur again, as if she were treading on his personal property. Nonetheless, she kept at it, searching for clues she was certain were hidden somewhere behind the screen.

"You ready?" Pescoli asked, startling her as she studied a picture of Hattie in summer, dressed in a sundress, her two girls with her, arm in arm as they sat on a large rock somewhere in the foothills and squinted at the camera.

"To visit the wives?" She clicked off Grayson's phone and slipped it into her pocket. She wasn't done with it quite yet and didn't want to leave it unattended.

"Ex-wives."

"One of which is still in his will," she said, rolling her chair away from the desk.

"Grayson's probably just a busy man who never took the time to update things."

Alvarez found her service weapon, strapped it on, then snagged her jacket from a peg near her office door. "Maybe marriage number two was rocky from the get-go. And then after the divorce, he just didn't bother."

"Usually when you go through the trouble of getting a divorce, you make damn sure your ex doesn't get a dime. Especially when no kids are involved."

"It's a moot point anyway," Alvarez reminded her. "The sheriff's still alive."

"Thank God."

They walked to Pescoli's Jeep together, braving a blast of arctic air sweeping down from Canada.

Pescoli had just started the engine when a phone rang. "Must be yours," Pescoli said, "not my ring tone."

"Not mine either. Belongs to Grayson." She was extracting the cell from her pocket and noticed the number on the screen was one of the county numbers.

She clicked on and said, "Sheriff Grayson's phone," she answered. "Detective Alvarez."

"I was hopin' someone would answer," a gravelly male voice said. "This is Louie at Animal Control. I've got the sheriff's dog."

"You do?" Alvarez shot Pescoli a brilliant smile.

"Yeah, the black Lab. Found him off of Kordell Road, just past the Cougar Creek bridge. A woman who lives down that way called in about a stray and I picked him up myself this morning. The sheriff's name's on the tags and I knew he was in the hospital, but I took a chance that someone would answer his phone. How's he doin', by the way?"

"I think stable," she said, mouthing to Pescoli, "Sturgis." Pescoli gave her a relieved thumbs-up.

"Jesus, you'd think a man would be safe in his own house on Christmas morning," the man said.

"You'd think," she agreed.

"All of us here at Animal Control, we're pulling for him."

"Thanks. Everyone is," she said. "Look, I'm in the car with my partner now. We'll swing by and pick up the dog. We're just ten minutes away." She glanced at Pescoli, who was already searching for a spot to turn around.

"Good . . . that would be good."

"Just have him ready."

Louie cleared his throat. "I'll . . . um . . . I'll waive the fees?"

That was Louie's train of thought? Fines and fees? "Good idea, Louie." Not the brightest lightbulb on the county payroll.

"But you'll have to sign for him. Be responsible."

"Not a problem." She hung up as Pescoli finished her quick U-ey and melded her Jeep into the slow-moving traffic, wending through the campuses of the county offices. Though the courthouse was located in the old part of town, on the banks of the river, the business offices, jail, juvenile complex, and sheriff's department were newer buildings, constructed higher at the top of Boxer Bluff, which overlooked the older part of town far below. "The dog catcher nabbed Sturgis out by the Cougar Creek bridge."

Pescoli said firmly, "Let's go get him."

Dan Grayson's first ex-wife, now Mrs. Nolan Banks, wasn't happy to see two detectives on her broad front porch when they arrived nearly half an hour later than planned. They'd called, explained why they'd been held up: taking time to pick up the sheriff's dog before dropping him off at the local vet to make certain he was as fit as he appeared.

The Bankses' house was massive, three stories of cedar and stone perched on the side of a cliff and overlooking a creek sliding through the canyon far below. She held open one of the oversized double doors, each of which was festooned with an oversized wreath of silvery twigs, clear glass balls, and big silver bows. "I don't know how I can help you," she insisted, holding on to the door as if she intended to slam it shut at any second. She was a petite woman in a slim gray dress and a pink, tightly knit sweater. A cap of short curls lay close to her head, and her large eyes were dark with suspicion.

"We just need to ask you a few questions. Do you mind if we come in?" Alvarez asked.

Her lips pursed; then she opened the door wider. "Sure. Why not?

I'm so, so sorry about Dan, but"—she bit her lip and lifted her shoulders—"I don't think this is any news flash. Dan and I rarely speak. We've been divorced a long time."

She stepped aside as they entered a three-storied foyer where a staircase wound upward around a twenty-foot Christmas tree decorated in lights, ribbons, and all manner of sparkling ornaments. Large rooms fanned from the main hallway, each with at least a peekaboo view of the tree. "This way." Leading them toward the back of the house, she walked stiffly ahead, ballet slippers padding noiselessly, then motioned to a group of chairs situated near a fireplace that rose to a soaring ceiling where the paddles of a huge fan turned slowly.

"What can I tell you? I already explained that Nolan and I and the kids were here on Christmas morning." When Pescoli pulled out her pocket recorder, she said reproachfully, "Really? You need to record our conversation?" Letting out a long breath, she added, "Okay. Fine. Who cares?" Taking a seat on a modern couch set near a wide bank of windows, she folded her arms over her chest and said, "What is it you want to know?"

"Let's start with the finances." Pescoli was never one to beat around the bush. "Do you know you're the primary beneficiary of your ex-husband's estate?"

She blinked. "But he was married to Akina!" Her hand flattened over her chest and she seemed sincerely surprised. "No, um, I knew at one time, of course. He told me. But that was long before we were divorced. I was pretty sure he changed that a few years back. He wasn't happy with the divorce settlement . . . but . . . Geez. Wow." She sat back against the cushions and Pescoli wondered if she was mentally calculating the value of her ex's fortune. "You're sure about this?"

"Looks like," Pescoli said. "Of course, the sheriff is still alive."

"Of course and . . . and thank God," she added quickly, but her cheeks had taken on a rosy glow and obviously the news that she would inherit from her ex someday was good. Never mind that he was still alive or that he would have to predecease her.

Alvarez said, "So how do you feel about your ex-husband? Have you and he ever reconciled?"

"Of course not. I'm married to Nolan. Have been for years."

"Then maybe you just flirted with him?" Alvarez said, and Pescoli saw Cara's cheeks flush brighter.

"What are you insinuating?"

"You know how it is," Alvarez said. "Some sparks never completely die, no matter how hard you try. Sometimes first love is the best love."

"Really? That's the way you're going?" Cara asked, then turned her gaze on Pescoli. "What about you, Detective? You've been married a couple of times, right? You think 'first love is the best love'?"

Pescoli was saved from answering by the rumble of a garage door winding upward. *Oh, good. Company*.

Alvarez said, "We just heard that you and Dan Grayson always had a thing for each other, even after the divorce."

"Who told you that? *Dan?*" Outraged, she shot to her feet just as the rumbling stopped with a hard clunk. Cara's head snapped around, as if she'd just realized that someone was home. "I think we're done here." She sent a hard glance toward the recorder. "And you can turn that thing off."

Alvarez said, "We just have a few more questions."

"I've told you everything I know. I was married to Dan for about three years, dated him for eighteen months before that. End of story. I had no idea I was an heir in his estate, and that's probably a mistake anyway, so please, it's time for you to go." Cara didn't wait for a response, just walked quickly toward the front hallway.

"What about your sister?" Alvarez pursued.

"Hattie? We barely speak." She was standing by the enormous Christmas tree, dwarfed by its height.

"She seems to have had an interest in the sheriff."

"Of course she did, his last name is Grayson, isn't it?"

A back door creaked open.

"What's that supposed to mean?"

"Honey?" a voice called from the back of the house before a tall man in long overcoat appeared. "Oh, I wondered who was here."

"Detectives Alvarez and Pescoli," she said, somehow able to grab hold of her composure again, maybe because her husband was home. Her rock. Or maybe someone she could hide behind. "They're from the sheriff's department and they came by because of the attempt"— she cleared her throat—"the attempt on Dan's life."

Banks looked appropriately somber. "Helluva thing, that," he said, taking off his coat. With it still draped over his arm, he extended a hand, first to Alvarez, then to Pescoli. "Nolan Banks."

They introduced themselves and Alvarez even flipped open her badge as Pescoli sized the man up. She'd seen him around town before, a businessman in a dark suit, crisp white shirt, and striped tie. His hair was neatly trimmed, his face clean-shaven, his blond hair thinning near the temples. An aquiline nose separated close-set, intelligent eyes. In Pescoli's opinion, Nolan Banks looked as out of place in this part of Montana as a thoroughbred at a workhorse show.

"So what's going on here? Why are you questioning my wife?"

"Covering our bases," Pescoli said, deciding she'd let Cara, herself, explain.

"How's the sheriff doing?"

"He's a fighter," she said, wondering at the anxiety in Banks's face.

"We'll pray for him."

Of course you will.

Quick footsteps pounded wildly on the stairs only to stop suddenly. Pescoli glanced up to see a girl in her early teens on the landing. She'd been gathering steam on her way downward, but at the sight of the gathering in the hallway she'd stopped short to peer over the rail.

"Oh, this is our daughter, Allison." He smiled up at his teenager. "Alli, come on down, meet the detectives."

"Why are they here?" she asked suspiciously, not budging an inch.

"Some questions for your mom. You heard about the shooting on the sheriff?" he asked.

"Yeah, it's like everywhere." With more than a little impudence, she flipped her dark hair over one shoulder. "So why are you here, questioning my mom?" A pretty girl in jeans and a tight T-shirt, her inquisitive eyes fell on the detectives.

"All part of the investigation," Pescoli answered. "We're talking to anyone who knows the sheriff."

"And Mom was married to him," Alli said flatly.

Cara glanced from her husband to her daughter. "A *long* time ago, Alli."

"Yeah, I know. Like ancient history." She almost smirked as she finally deigned to clomp down the remaining steps in her boots.

"Exactly." Cara was nodding, obviously happy that particular fact had been mentioned.

Pescoli wondered. Cara was almost too quick and too emphatic in her negations of any link to her ex.

"I thought you were Eric," the girl said a little petulantly, and Pescoli noticed her jeans were ripped. By design. Allison's boots, too, Pescoli knew, were expensive. Bianca wanted a pair just like them, and even the knockoffs were more than Pescoli wanted to pay.

"Eric's coming over?" Cara asked with a disapproving tone.

"Yeah." Allison shrugged. "I decided it would be okay."

"*You* decided?" Nolan joined his wife's concern. "That boy should get a job or go to school."

"*That boy* has a job," Allison threw back at them. "And he's taking night classes. He got his GED, you know."

"I mean a real job," Nolan said. "Working as a busboy at Dino's Pizza Parlor isn't exactly a career path, and his night class is in tae kwon do."

"So? What was your first job?" his daughter charged, eyes flaring. "Haven't you bragged about, uh, what is it? Working your way up? And starting by shoveling shit for some rich guy's horses? Herbert Long, or something."

"Alli!" Cara admonished.

"Hubert," Banks corrected. "Brady's father. Herbert is his cousin . . . but that's enough. The detectives don't want to hear our argument." He turned to Pescoli and Alvarez. "I'm sorry. Is there anything else I can do for you?"

"No, for now, we've got all we need," Pescoli said. She and Alvarez walked outside where the day was remarkably still and clouds were hugging the ground, sending wisping tendrils of fog through the thickets of snow-flocked mountain hemlock and spruce.

A damned winter wonderland, a perfect setting for Nolan Banks's large, perfectly decorated home. Pescoli could just imagine what the imposing structure looked like at nightfall, when the thousands of tiny lights were illuminated, showing off the angles and pitches of the roofline in the forest. But appearances were often deceiving, smoke screens for what really occurred, and she wondered if the cracks within the foundation of the Banks family ran jagged and deep.

Once she and Alvarez were inside the Jeep and she was driving back down the curving lane on the Banks property, Pescoli asked, "What was your hit?"

"Did Cara Banks seem nervous to you?"

"Yep," Pescoli agreed as she fiddled with the defroster so that air would warm the windshield where condensation had formed. "Maybe she's hiding something. Or someone. Hey, hand me some tissues from the glove box, will you?" Alvarez complied, and while driving with one hand, Pescoli swiped the inside of the glass above the dashboard, giving her a modicum of visibility. "Better."

"What's the problem with the defroster?" Alvarez asked.

"Good question. Had it into the mechanics, but they can't find anything. It's an intermittent problem. Don't get me started." Stuffing the used tissues into an empty cup holder, she turned back to business. "The whole conversation with Cara seemed off. Stilted. Not right."

"Think it had to do with Grayson?"

"Hard to say. Some people just react to the law showing up on their doorstep."

"That wasn't what this was," Alvarez disagreed.

"Yeah . . ." They reached the end of the lane where Pescoli rolled to a near stop, then hit the accelerator to turn onto the county road. "What did you think of the daughter? I hate to say it, but she reminds me of Bianca with her attitude. They're about the same age."

"They're in school together?"

"Oh, I don't think so. Pretty sure the Banks kids all attended the private school in Missoula."

"And you know this how?"

She shook her head. "Nolan has some older kids, boys, one was in Jeremy's class in elementary school but transferred after fifth grade. Isaiah, I think. Has an older brother, Ezekiel."

"Books of the Bible?"

"Maybe the first Mrs. Nolan was into the Old Testament."

"Or just likes old-time, solid names," Alvarez said. "She live around here?"

"Don't know. Something we should look into."

She was already fiddling with her cell phone, probably making some kind of note to herself as Pescoli continued driving. The surrounding landscape changed, forested hills giving way to snow-crusted fields stretched to the hills.

Alvarez took a few calls and the conversation was one-sided, and when she hung up the last one, she let out a disgusted puff of air.

"What?"

"Looks like Verdago skipped. Didn't show up for work today, didn't call in, according to his supervisor at the Chambers Apartments in Helena."

"What about yesterday?"

"His day off."

"Crap," Pescoli said. "What time did he get off the day before, on Christmas Eve?"

"Don't know."

"It's a three-and-a-half- to four-hour drive from Helena in decent weather, with no traffic, so let's stay he would have had to get off work four-and-a-half to five hours before Grayson was hit because he'd have to have time to ditch the car, ski into position, and set up. If he worked until two-thirty or three in the morning, it's an impossible feat."

"But if he didn't . . . ?" Alvarez posed, then said, "I'll check."

For the first time since seeing her boss cut down, Pescoli felt a ray of hope. Maybe, just maybe, they'd get this bastard. Verdago had sliced up his brother-in-law, but he was a marksman. And he hated Grayson. But what would have caused him to go after the sheriff now? He'd been out of prison for six months. Had something triggered his attack or was he just patient, this being his first real opportunity?

"Let's find him."

"Brewster's already got two detectives on it."

"Good." Pescoli visualized the man, who, now around thirty-six, was short and muscular. The last time she'd seen Verdago, his head was shaved, a skull tattooed where once there'd been hair, and he sported a thick horseshoe mustache along his upper lip and cheeks. "Maybe we'll get lucky."

"Maybe." Alvarez was thoughtful, brows pulled together.

"In the meantime, onto Grayson's second wife, Akina." Pescoli threw her partner a look. "Might as well see what's behind door number two, wife-wise."

CHAPTER 12

"I just don't like it, none of it," Cade said as he turned off the faucet to the main trough in the stable. "Dan's condition is still critical and the doctors aren't really telling us what's what."

"Maybe they don't know. It is his goddamned brain." Zed tossed some oats into the manger as the horses, on the other side of a half wall, crowded around, burying their noses into the food.

The stable was usually a calming place for Cade. With its dimmed lights, smells of dust, dung and leather, and sounds of hooves rustling in straw, this area of the ranch was where he felt most at home. Bridles hung from the rafters, saddles sat on sawhorses, hay filled the loft overhead, and all manner of tools and gear was displayed upon the wood walls. He couldn't remember a time in his life where being near the horses didn't have a calming effect on him.

Until yesterday. Then, while feeding the stock and even whistling some old western tune under his breath, his cell phone had jangled. Not paying any attention to caller ID, he'd answered the call from a seemingly disembodied voice from the sheriff's department who told him that there had been an assassination attempt on his brother.

Now, the place wasn't quite as comforting.

"I'm going to the hospital." He climbed up the ladder to the hay-loft, his boots ringing on the metal rungs.

"Not that way, yer not."

"Funny." Hoisting himself onto the hundred-year-old floorboards, he waited for his eyes to adjust to the dim light, then grabbed a nearby bale and yelled, "Incoming!" then kicked it to the floor below.

Lifting another bale from the stacks, he pushed it through the opening and it slammed to the floor below with a satisfying thump.

"That's enough!" Zed hollered.

Cade started for the ladder again, but hesitated as he caught sight of the round window mounted high beneath the eaves. Glazed in ice, it was a shadowy portal to the dark day beyond. Dusk was riding low over the mountains, shadows chasing across the hills.

A memory cut behind his eyes in a brilliant flash, a quicksilver picture of a naked woman, laying facedown on a blanket, the slope of her back and rounded buttocks pale in the moonlight streaming through the window. The hayloft was warm, with a summer heat that, inside, wasn't cooled by the wafting breeze.

The back of his throat caught as he remembered the smell of fresh hay and the buzz of insects, the sound of a coyote crying in the night, and her lying on the old blanket he kept in the back of his pickup. His senses were alive that night, sharpened by the sexual need running through his veins, the anticipation of passionate lovemaking, that special kind that had an edge to it because to some, it was forbidden.

That night, his brain had been disconnected from his soul, and any sense of integrity that could have stopped him had been left behind with the taste of her first, frightened kiss. Trembling lips, still red from a little too much wine, had transformed, turning warm, pliant, and oh so tempting.

She hadn't resisted when he'd reached beneath her shirt, his fingers scaling her rib cage; then the two of them had ended up here, naked, stripped of their clothes by eager fingers and mutual assent.

Somewhere off in the distance, a rattling train rolled noisily on century-old tracks. The hay mow was hot, August heat sweltering, sweat breaking out on his skin. He leaned closer, smelling a whiff of perfume as he reached around her, touching her breasts, feeling her nipples harden under his fingertips.

His groin tightened and his cock, already hard, strained. Thunder rolled through his brain.

"We shouldn't," she whispered, the sound disturbing the horses below. One sent up a soft whinny.

"Too late." He slid his naked body atop hers and she moaned and writhed slowly on the blanket, her hands curling into fists.

"Cade—"

"Shhh . . . no regrets." Running his hardness along her spine, he felt her need, saw the raise of her hips. She wanted him, as desperately as he wanted her, with the same pounding need. "It's all right."

When she didn't say anything, he squeezed his eyes shut and tried like hell to cool off, but his blood was running hot, his cock straining, the feel of her soft skin so damned intoxicating.

"You want me to stop?" he forced out. Hell, was that possible? His heart sounded as if it were pounding in his ears, his flesh on fire.

Hesitation. Then finally, "No."

"I feel a 'but' coming."

"This is wrong. You know it. I know it."

Well, shitfire.

"I assure you, darlin', there's nothing wrong about this, about you and me, about feelin' good."

"It's not about feeling good and you know it!" Oh, God, was she going to cry?

He wanted to argue with her, *needed* to argue with her, though he knew exactly what she meant. He just wasn't going to think about the ramifications of what they were doing. Hell, tomorrow was another day. But tonight, she was here. Ready and warm and willing . . . well, almost willing.

"I could stop," he admitted and twisted the end of her nipple just a bit, eliciting pleasure with just a hint of pain.

Her back arched and she was his again, he knew it, felt her resistance ebb.

"Tell me you don't want me," he said.

In response, she moaned softly and her buttocks rose a little higher, inviting him to the dance.

He slid closer. Pressed his weight into her. Reached around with his other arm so that he now had both her breasts in his palms, her nipples hard as he rubbed.

"Oooh," she whispered as he touched her. "Cade . . ."

"What?" he asked into the shell of her ear.

She shuddered.

"What is it you want?"

"Everything." It came out in a rush as she began to move. "I . . . want . . . everything."

And he did too. Closing his eyes, he crossed the frail barrier that was loyalty, thrust himself inside her, and changed the course of his damned life forever.

Now, years later, standing in the cold hay mow, looking through a window covered in ice, he felt as empty as he had the next day when he'd left her.

Even so, his cock twitched at the memory, and he knew in a heartbeat that if he were given the chance to replay his life, he'd do it all again.

Shitfire, he was a bastard. Raking stiff, frustrated fingers through his hair, he tried to dispel the vibrant memory. It was over. Done. Lives changed. Lives lost. "Sweet Christ," he muttered almost inaudibly.

"Hey, you leavin' or what?" Zed called from below.

How long had he been up here, caught in the web of memories that always left him a little breathless and a lot mad at the world?

"On my way!" He jumped onto the ladder and holding on to the metal rails on either side of the steps, let his hands glide down the metal handles like he'd done as a kid and slid to the floor without touching the rungs. As his boots landed on the floor below, he saw that Zed was just finishing strewing the hay in the mangers.

"What the hell were you doin' up there?" Zed demanded.

"Nothin'."

"Sure, jack-off."

Cade felt a corner of his mouth lift. *Close enough, brother. Close enough.*

"You got this handled?" Cade asked, motioning to the mangers where all the horses had plunged their noses.

"What do you think?" Zed snorted a laugh and the roan gelding, His Majesty, lifted his head to stare at Cade. God, he loved that gelding. At twenty, a lot of His Majesty's good years were behind him, but the quarter horse still had a spark in his eye and was ready, when asked, to gallop wildly across the open fields with Cade riding bareback.

Cade grabbed his hat and squared it on his head. "In that case, I'm out."

"Give the doctors hell and call me if there's any news." Zed settled the pitchfork onto the nail where it had hung as long as Cade could remember.

"Will do." Slipping through the door into the frigid dusk, Cade watched his breath fog. Hands in his pockets, he jogged along the path of broken snow, through a rusted gate to the ranch house, where he snagged his keys from a hook near the back door and made his way to the garage.

He wondered if he'd see Hattie at the hospital again, then decided it didn't matter. In fact, it would probably be better if he didn't.

Akina Grayson Bellows didn't know anything, Pescoli guessed. From the moment the detectives knocked on her front door, to the minute they left, Grayson's petite, second ex-wife kept looking at her watch while holding her one-year-old daughter.

At least ten years younger than Grayson, with straight black hair knotted at her nape and almond-shaped eyes that seemed to miss nothing, Akina was as open about her relationship with Grayson as Cara had been closed.

Akina admitted to remarrying soon after she and Grayson had divorced, and now she had a child. She seemed genuinely sorry that the sheriff had been attacked. "Oh, I read about it, I can't imagine. Poor Dan. Come in, come in," she said, waving them into a small duplex filled with baby toys, a playpen, a fake Christmas tree that was listing a little, and general chaos. Dishes littered the kitchen table visible through an archway, and the door to a back room was open, exposing two baskets overflowing with laundry and pet dishes on the floor.

While balancing her daughter on a hip, she'd shooed a white cat from the couch, cleared a spot for the detectives to sit, and said, "If there's anything I can tell you, anything I can do, just let me know. This is horrible!"

Her phone chimed on the table, she glanced at it, smiled, and said, "Just a sec. My husband. I've been waiting for this text." With flying fingers, she responded to him while her chubby baby cooed happily.

"There. Now, what can I tell you?" Smiling, she sat on the edge of a recliner.

"Let's start with yesterday morning," Alvarez suggested.

"Christmas. We were all here. My husband, me, and his son, Monty. Rick was married before, too, so Monty, he's six, was over here too." She seemed genuinely happy and the missing boy explained the Nerf gun boxes and toy trucks tucked into a floor-to-ceiling bookcase. "Anyway, this was our daughter's first Christmas, so it was very special." Akina's eyes were bright with the pride that comes with a first child. Pescoli felt a little pang as she flashed to a memory twenty years old, when Jeremy was so tiny she and Joe stuck a big red bow on his bald head, laid him beneath the tree, and snapped dozens of pictures as he stared up at the lighted branches. And now . . . Joe was dead and she couldn't even make the time to celebrate with her kids on Christmas morning. *Extenuating circumstances,* she reminded herself, but she still felt guilty.

Meanwhile, Akina, who had been an accountant before her maternity leave, was bubbling over about Sachi's first Noel. She did stop herself once to say, "It's just such a bummer about Dan," but otherwise, Grayson's attack almost seemed something in the abstract to her.

They spoke to her for nearly half an hour, but in the end she'd been able to tell them nothing that appeared to help. Her marriage to Grayson had been short-lived, the relationship a whirlwind that had occurred soon after her father had died. Akina flat out admitted that she'd been looking for a father figure, but Dan's job and their age difference had come between them, and living in a cabin in the woods while her husband spent upward of sixteen hours of his days working as a cop just wasn't her idea of a life.

"I spent a lot of time on the computer and reconnected with my husband. We'd dated in high school but lost touch. I'm not proud of it," she admitted, her dark eyes flashing as her baby stuffed all the fingers of one hand into her mouth, "but that's what happened. Rick and I began communicating. E-mailing, texting, and talking on the phone. Dan found out, but it didn't matter, by that time I'd already

READY TO DIE 115

talked to a lawyer. Rick and I got married and now we have Sachi."
She smiled at the baby and her daughter, around her wet fingers,
smiled back. "I couldn't be happier," Akina insisted, and Pescoli believed her.

"What about Dan's first marriage?"

"Oh, Cara." Akina rolled her eyes and when Sachi started putting
up a fuss, found a pacifier to place between her lips. Immediately her
daughter was appeased. "It was all kind of weird, if you ask me. Oh.
You just did, didn't you?" She smiled, then let out a long sigh. "She
was remarried to Nolan, but she kept calling Dan. Like, to come and
fix things, you know. I remember an overflowing faucet once, and it
was after hours, and Nolan was out of town, but Cara couldn't get a
plumber, so good old Dan to the rescue, and then once . . . Geez,
what was it? Oh, a lightbulb broke off in a fixture. Dan went trit-
trotting right over there again, like a damned trained pony. Oops,
sorry, we do *not* swear in this house. Little ears, you know?"

She slid her eyes to her daughter, who had spit out her pacifier.
"Cara's excuse was that her husband was useless when it came to
home repairs." She gave Pescoli a woman-to-woman-you-know-what-
I-mean look before continuing. "So, she'd call and off he'd go. After
working overtime. Leaving his *wife* at home alone. Again. And that
was just the way it went." Akina lifted her free hand as if she couldn't
understand it. "I didn't like it. At all. At first I was jealous, but it didn't
make any difference. He'd been a rancher before a cop and he can fix
anything, so she took advantage of him."

"What did you do?"

"Like I said, I started connecting with old friends on the Internet.
Rick and I got together while we were planning a high-school re-
union. He was divorced, I was . . . unhappy, and we just clicked again."

"Do you blame Cara for your divorce?" Alvarez asked.

"Oh, no. I was insecure anyway." She shook her head. "I don't
think I even blame Dan. I blame myself and Rick, and trust me, it was
the best decision ever."

Alvarez prodded, "Was Dan upset when he found out?"

"About Rick? Relieved is more like it. He might have been a little
upset, but, no, not really. I don't think he was even surprised. Seri-

ously, the marriage was a mistake. We both knew it." For a second she seemed a little sad. "But he's a good guy, and I'm sorry about what happened. Do you have any idea who would do this?"

"We're working on it," Pescoli said, giving Grayson's ex the company line. "Can you think of someone who might want him dead?"

"Any of those freaks he sent to prison, for sure." Akina lowered her voice, as if afraid of being overheard. "Some of those guys are real psychos."

"Any of them in particular?" Alvarez asked casually.

"Uh, he mostly kept his work out of the house and, as I said, he wasn't home much. Oh, wait," she said suddenly, as if an unlikely thought had struck. "There *was* one guy who really bothered him. Someone . . . Geez, I can't remember his name, though." She bit her lip and slowly shook her head as she thought. "Was it Renfro? Nah, or . . . Red Neck!" she giggled at that and her eyebrows drew together. "Oh, shoot! Rennick?" Akina looked to Pescoli for the answer. "I know it, I really do. It's on the tip of my tongue!"

"Resler?" Alvarez asked.

"Resler! Yes! That's it." She nearly jumped off her chair, as if she'd just solved the final puzzle on *Wheel of Fortune.* "Gary Resler!"

"Gerry," Alvarez supplied.

"Oh. Yeah, that sounds right. Gary. Gerry. One of those."

Her phone made a noise again and she glanced down at the table where it sat. A new text was being sent her way. "Gerry Resler," Akina repeated, as if to embed it into her brain forever. "Now I remember, a real whack job." But her attention had been diverted to her phone.

Pescoli asked, "What about Nolan Banks?"

She picked up her phone, but her head snapped sharply up as she texted a response. "That weenie? A killer? Don't make me laugh."

"He could have been upset with Dan's attention to his wife," Pescoli said.

Grayson's ex glanced up from her screen. "There's 'upset' and then there's '*upset,*' y'know, with rage and all that. I don't think Nolan has it in him."

Alvarez put in, "What about Grayson's money?"

"What money? A retirement and an interest in the family ranch?"

She set her phone back down on the table. "Dan Grayson is not a rich man. And anyway, what would Nolan Banks care?" Then the light dawned. "You mean *she's* the one who would inherit? Cara? Son of a bitch!" As if she suddenly heard herself, she winced and glanced at her daughter. "Well, if that's the case, Dan's an idiot. I can't believe it."

Alvarez asked as a final question, "Did you think you would get his estate?"

"Are you kidding?" Akina shook her head, and her daughter started reaching for the band holding her hair away from her face. "I didn't think about it much, but if I had, I would have thought he would leave everything to his brothers or his nieces. He's nuts about them!"

CHAPTER 13

"I'm sorry, Mr. Grayson, I just don't have any other answers for you." Karen Skinner, the critical care nurse at the desk, glanced at the chart on her computer monitor. "Your brother's vitals are surprisingly strong considering the trauma he's experienced, but he's still in critical condition."

Cade turned his head to view Dan on the bed, then spying all the tubes and monitors and electronic equipment, turned back to the nurse. "When's the doctor coming back to see him?"

"Dr. Bennett will be here later this afternoon. She was already here this morning. Dr. Kapule is scheduled to return this evening." She saw his hesitation. "I could have them call you."

"Do that," Cade said, snaking another look at his brother. Poor son of a bitch. Who could survive what he'd been through? Dan was strong, but this was too much. Hazarding one last glance at the bed, he felt his jaw tighten. The unconscious man on that hospital bed in no way resembled the brother Cade had known all his life.

After waiting two hours, he figured it was time to go. Nothing had changed. Nothing would change for a while. His brother just had to heal.

At least in the hospital he was safe.

From what?

From whom?

He'd already considered all the enemies Dan had made in his life, from football rivals, to political challenges, to people he worked with, and he'd come up blank. Aside from some crook Dan had sent up the river, or maybe that particular loser's family, Cade couldn't think of anyone who would resort to violence.

And whoever had tried to take him out was a good shot with a rifle, a hunter or military man, or maybe even another cop. But he couldn't come up with anyone Dan had pissed off to the point of attempted murder.

The same damned questions that had been rattling around in his brain for the past two days still nagged at him, wouldn't let him go. If a man couldn't be safe in his own home on Christmas morning, things were bad.

Buzzed out of the ICU, he walked into the waiting room and past the female guard, giving the woman a nod. The guards, like the nursing staff, rotated, which he understood. He just hoped that the security offered by the county was enough.

As he made his way outside the building, he thought again about Hattie's claims that someone had killed Bart, but Cade had never put much stock in that theory. He remembered Bart's despair, his depression. Once, soon after Bart's divorce from Hattie, Cade had heard the television in the den of the ranch house after he'd come in from his trip into town. As he'd walked down the hallway, shedding his coat and hat, then dropping his keys and wallet on a small table near the stairs, he'd recognized the sounds of a football game in progress. The room was dark, illuminated only by flickering images on the forty-two-inch screen.

Bart was seated in the battered leather recliner. A half-empty bottle of whiskey was on the coffee table, an empty glass on the side table, their daddy's Colt .45 in Bart's hands. The gun hung between his legs and he kept spinning the cylinder as he watched the Forty-Niners being handed their heads by the Seahawks. On the table was a thick manila envelope addressed to Bartholomew Grayson. The return address was for the law firm Bart had employed during his divorce.

"Bart?" Cade had asked cautiously.

"Hey." But his eyes had stared blankly at the television.

"What's up?"

"Nothin'. Just watching the game."

"With a gun."

Bart had blinked, looked down at his hands, and frowned. "Yeah, guess so."

"Why?"

A shrug.

"Is it loaded?"

"Guess so."

"Maybe you should put it away." Cade held out his hand and his brother finally looked up. What he saw in that moment caused his heart to freeze. There was a deadness in his brother's gaze, and the only other spark, other than the reflection from the images on the television, was a quick, silent accusation.

"Maybe you should go to hell."

Cade's hand was still stretched forward, palm up, fingers splayed, waiting to accept the weapon.

His brother held his gaze.

Cade felt the seconds tick by as a drip of sweat ran down his spine as Bart considered his next move.

"Come on, brother. Give it up. You know whiskey and firearms don't mix."

The beams of headlights flashed across the windows and Bart blinked for the first time since Cade had entered the room. "Someone comin' over?"

"Dan."

"Why?"

"Thought the four of us could watch the end of the game and play a little poker."

"Zed's gone. Went to Missoula. Meetin' Sally."

Sally Eberhart was the widow of a good friend. Zed had been seeing her off and on for a couple of years.

"Then it'll just be the three of us. Come on. Maybe this time we can beat Dan, get a little of our money back." He heard the back door creak open only to slam shut. "Ready to lose some serious cash?" Dan bellowed from the kitchen. Boot steps pounded on the floorboards, growing louder.

Bart squinted up at Cade, his nostrils flaring a bit. "You're an asshole."

"So I've been told."

Slowly, Bart handed his brother the .45. "I wasn't plannin' on poker tonight."

"Plans change," Cade had said, emptying the cylinder of the Colt and finding a single bullet. "Y'know, just so we're clear: Russian roulette isn't such a good idea."

"You don't know what you're talking about," Bart had said with more than a little venom as he'd capped the whiskey bottle and climbed to his feet. "But you always have been full of shit."

Cade saw no reason to argue.

The Seahawks scored again and the crowd went wild.

Bart shuffled out of the room, only listing slightly.

Cade kept the .45.

To this day it was locked in the bottom drawer of the night table next to his bed. Hidden beneath the family Bible.

A rush of warm air tinged with the scents of oregano and tomato sauce hit Pescoli full force as she walked into Dino's Pizza Parlor. It had been a long day of spinning her wheels. She and Alvarez were following up on some of the information they'd gathered today, but still, the investigation seemed caught in a quagmire. Grayson's condition hadn't changed. The alibis of the ex-cons in the area hadn't been broken, at least not yet, and though it was a separate matter, the missing judge still hadn't been located.

She'd called ahead and ordered two pizzas, a meat lover's for Jeremy and a vegetarian for Bianca. That's how her kids were, opposite as night to day. For herself, she figured she'd sample a little of each, while the family gathered around the tree to exchange gifts in the spirit of the rapidly passing season.

Was it late? Yes, but not *too* late, she figured.

Was it untraditional? You bet, but maybe she preferred to think of it as "unique," as theirs wasn't a particularly religious family. Nonetheless, she liked to inject a little bit of Christ into Christmas. Really, that was the point. Right?

She wended her way through tables that were half filled. A few families gathered at the smaller tables near the fireplace, while groups of teenagers who had apparently devoured more than their fill of Grandma's home cooking had come down to the pizza parlor to hang out. Clusters of the kids filled one section of booths, spilling over to nearby tables, laughing, talking, eating, and, of course, texting. Busboys couldn't keep up with the half-drunk sodas and plates covered with unwanted crusts that littered some abandoned tables. She paid for her order and a surly-faced twentysomething found her two boxes under the warming lights. His name tag read "Eric," and Pescoli pegged him as the much-disliked boyfriend of Allison Banks.

Huh.

"You're Allison Banks's boyfriend?" she asked as he carried the flat boxes to the cash register. Something flickered in his dark eyes.

"Yeah, I know her," he answered, suspicion heavy in his voice.

"I think she thought you might be stopping by."

"Who are you?" he asked, then glanced at her ticket. "Regan?"

"Actually, I'm a detective with the Pinewood County Sheriff's Department."

A little bit of panic rose in his eyes. "What are the cops doing talking to Alli?" he asked as she reached for the boxes. "She do something wrong?"

"No, we were just asking questions. Mrs. Banks was married to Sheriff Grayson at one time."

"So?" he asked.

"He was shot yesterday morning."

"Oh, yeah." He nodded. "It's, like, *all* everyone is talking about, how some sniper dude tried to take him out, but that don't have anything to do with Alli."

"It was just a few questions."

His boss, a man in his seventies with a thick gray mustache, was staring at Eric with the sharp eye of an owner anticipating someone skimming money from the till.

Lowering his voice, Eric said, "Alli don't know nothing."

"Do you?"

"Are you crazy?" He glanced over Pescoli's shoulder to the couple who were impatiently standing behind her. "Can I help you?" he asked as Pescoli scooped up the boxes and headed outside. She didn't really consider Eric a suspect in an attempted murder plot, but it didn't take a rocket scientist to figure out that he had a problem with the police. She made a mental note to check into his record and see what it was that made Allison Banks's boyfriend so nervous around the cops.

After finding her car in the parking lot, she placed the boxes on the front seat, then dashed across the street to the veterinary clinic and dog shelter.

Jordan Eagle had spied Pescoli approaching and brought Sturgis into the reception area, his black coat gleaming, a jaunty red kerchief knotted around his neck. At the sight of a familiar face, Sturgis let out a sharp yip and began straining on the leash. All the while, his tail wagged furiously.

Pescoli felt a rush of relief at the sight of the dog as Jordan said, "Guess he's glad to see you."

"The feeling's mutual."

A petite woman whose coppery skin and straight black hair hinted at her Native American heritage, Jordan was barely over five feet and probably not much more than a hundred pounds soaking wet, yet she had a quiet way about her that was calming to the animals she treated, even if they outweighed her.

"Is he okay?" Pescoli asked.

"Fine," she said, patting the old dog, whose muzzle was graying. "A little concerned as he's out of his routine, I think, but physically strong. All his vitals are normal, he's not dehydrated, and no obvious signs of any trauma. He needed his nails clipped and his teeth should be cleaned soon, but that requires anesthesia, so I thought I'd wait to find out what Sheriff Grayson wants." Her eyes clouded a bit. "How is he?"

"I only know what the doctors tell the department," Pescoli said. "He's alive, holding steady, but has a long way to go. You might get more information from the hospital."

"I doubt it." Jordan's smooth brow was etched in concern.

"I'm sure the undersheriff will hold a press conference," Pescoli said. "Hopefully there will be more information then. So, what do I owe you?"

She smiled down at the dog. "This one's on the house. Grayson's a good guy and I hate that this happened to him. Besides, this guy here," she said as she stroked the dog's head, "is a favorite of mine. I'm just glad he's okay after a night out in the elements."

"The department would—"

"I know, but no." Shaking her head, the vet was having none of Pescoli's attempts to pay, so she gave up. Once outside, Sturgis jumped willingly into the backseat of her Jeep to sit up and peer out the window as she drove.

"Wish I knew what you saw," Pescoli said to the dog as she nosed her vehicle out of Dino's lot and turned in the direction of her home. Through town, she passed storefronts decorated with painted snowmen and Santas and elves, as well as the First Presbyterian Church with its lighted creche. Now that Christmas was over, all the decorations seemed tired, as if they couldn't stand to be adorning buildings and trees for one more day, let alone another week. "Perspective," she told herself, knowing it was from her own viewpoint, that she was one of those people pulling at the bit to bury the current calendar and start the New Year. While others turned nostalgic as January approached, she was glad to shed the previous 365 days.

"You know, you're wishing your life away," Santana had once told her when she admitted, not for the first time, how good she'd feel once a particularly hard week was over. They'd been driving in his truck, heading to a rare dinner out, he at the wheel, she in the passenger seat. It had been autumn with the weather beginning to turn.

"Yeah, well, don't give me any of that 'live for the moment' stuff. I get it, okay?" She'd finished her flat Diet Coke and tossed her empty cup into the trash, a grocery bag he'd tucked just behind the driver's seat. "I just think some of those supposedly special moments aren't that great."

"Could that come with being a cop?"

She'd stared out the windshield as fat drops of rain had drizzled down the glass. "Trust me, it's not all the 'dark underbelly of society' that gets to me. It's just the way I've always been, ready for the next challenge." She'd swiped at the condensation collecting on the passenger window. "The way I was born."

He'd lifted a dark eyebrow in disbelief but had let any further argument slide. Thankfully. She hadn't been in the mood for an ideological discussion and figured those kinds of talks were better left to the great philosophers, of one she definitely was not.

Santana had learned when to press an issue and when to back off.

Well, most of the time. The arguments that did flare between them were always white hot, furious, and, it seemed, rarely resolved.

She thought about the ring he'd given her and the realities of marrying him. If nothing else, it would be interesting. "And challenging," she said aloud and caught her worried expression in the rearview mirror. "Commitment-phobe," she told herself and knew that she had to come to some decision soon.

Santana wasn't the kind of man who would wait around forever; he'd said as much and she believed him. And though it was true that the attempt on Grayson's life had thrown her and the department into a tailspin, Santana would still want an answer.

She drove into the garage, killed the engine, then, carrying both pizza boxes and her laptop case, shoved open the back door with her hip. Sturgis bounded out and eagerly followed her into the house. Cisco, spying an intruder, barked loudly, the hackles on his neck rising and his teeth flashing. "Enough!" Pescoli said to her dog as Sturgis, intimidated by the smaller terrier, immediately sat beside her. "We're all friends here."

Cisco wasn't about to be appeased and rather than rush up to greet her, climbed onto his favorite pillow on the couch and growled his dissatisfaction, all the while staring at the offending Lab. "Yeah, fine. Whatever," Pescoli said as she slid the pizza boxes onto the counter, the laptop on the table, and unwrapped her scarf. She yelled loudly, "I'm home. With pizza!"

When no one appeared, she walked down the short hallway and heard music pounding from her daughter's room. Knocking softly on the door before pushing it open, she found Bianca, clad only in her bra and a scrap of underwear, standing in front of her full-length mirror. Scowling at her image and cocking her head, she pulled some skin from her tiny waist.

"What're you doing?" Pescoli said and Bianca visibly jumped.

"Mom!" She grabbed a hoodie that was tangled in the sheets of her unmade bed and threw it over her head. "Don't you believe in knocking?"

"I did knock."

"I didn't hear you."

"I wonder why."

Pushing her head through the sweatshirt's neck, Bianca said angrily, "You should wait 'til I answer."

"Too late." Pescoli walked over to Bianca's desk, where between the bottles of fingernail polish and makeup, Pescoli found her daughter's iPod docking station. She yanked out Bianca's phone and the pounding music suddenly ceased.

"I was listening to that!"

The device vibrated in Pescoli's hand. "So what were you doing, there at the mirror?"

"Just looking, okay? I'm going to be taking that trip with Michelle and I want to make sure I look okay in a bikini. Give me my phone."

"You look fabulous."

"You think so?"

"I *know* so."

"You don't think I'm fat?"

"Good God." She couldn't believe what she was hearing. Bianca had always been slim and athletic, not an ounce of excess fat on her body. "Of course not."

"You're just saying that cuz you're my mom. You have to. Can I have my phone back?" She held out her hand and wiggled her fingers in a "come-on-gimme" gesture just as the damned thing vibrated again.

Pescoli tossed the cell to her daughter. "Trust me, runway models would kill for your figure."

Bianca glanced at the cell, then sent a sidelong look toward the mirror again, her expression clouding. "You sure? You're not just saying that cuz you're my mom?"

"I speaketh the truth." Pescoli sat on the edge of the bed where she spied a shimmering turquoise bikini lying in an open box. God, it was tiny.

"I just think I could look better," Bianca confessed.

"You look great. Trust me. And enjoy it. While you're young. Okay?"

Bianca shrugged.

"Come on, let's have some dinner. I told you we're starting a new tradition tonight."

"Oh, right. No Christmas or something."

"Most *Un*-Christmas. We're still going to celebrate the real deal on Christmas Day if we can, but when we can't, let's do something different. We'll have our pizza and open gifts and I have a surprise guest tonight."

Bianca rolled her eyes. "*Un*-Christmas, Mom. Really? And don't tell me, the surprise guest is your boyfriend." Her expression turned to disgust and Pescoli clamped her teeth together in frustration. In her daughter's mind, it was fine for Luke to have carried on while they were married *and* to marry a much younger woman. Bianca accepted Michelle, for the most part, with open arms as her stepmother. However, that's where the understanding stopped. When it came to Santana, or any other man Pescoli had dated since her divorce, Bianca didn't hold back. She was vociferous in her dislike of all of them, *especially* Nate Santana.

Pescoli figured it's because Santana was her first serious relationship and thereby a threat of some kind.

"Sorry to disappoint you, but the other guest is Sturgis," she said and whistled to the dog.

"Who?" Bianca was confused for a second. Then the Lab cautiously stuck his nose into her room. "Oh!" Her face lit up. "We're keeping him?"

"More like he's on loan. Just until the sheriff is well enough for the both of them to go home."

"Awesome!" She turned to the dog and patted her bed, indicating for him to jump up. "Come on, boy!"

Unsure, Sturgis hung back, glanced at Pescoli.

Pescoli plucked at the pink quilt on her daughter's canopy bed. "Maybe he's intimidated by all the girlie stuff."

"Come, Sturgis!" Bianca threw her mother a don't-even-go-there look and patted the bed again. This time the black Lab, head down, tail swinging slowly behind him, sauntered into the room. At another round of urging, he bounded on the bed and got lost in the myriad of blankets.

"I don't know if this is such a good idea," Pescoli said. As if to back her up, Cisco appeared in the doorway and yipped for attention.

"You never think *anything* is a good idea."

About to argue, Pescoli changed her mind and said instead, "Let's just remember he belongs to the sheriff and we already own a dog whose nose is more than a little out of joint." Cisco began doing quick twirls in the hallway. "He been out lately?"

"Don't know."

"I'll take care of it. But in the future, pay attention, okay."

No response.

Don't pick a fight, it is the first ever, hopefully not *annual, Most Un-Christmas.*

After letting both dogs out and then wiping their paws, she fed them both on opposite ends of the kitchen and was gratified that Cisco had quit growling long enough to snarf down his dinner.

Pescoli left her daughter's room and started down the narrow staircase at the back of the house, to the basement and Jeremy's room. Rapping on his door with her knuckles, she felt it give way, opening to a dark room where a lava lamp was slowly burping, its weird-shaped, gelatinous lumps giving off an eerie glow. "Jer—?"

"He's not here!" Bianca called from the floor above. Pescoli looked up to find her daughter leaning over the rail. She'd found a pair of jeans and her hair, as she leaned, fell forward around her face. "I just texted him."

"Where is he?"

Bianca gave her mother a knowing look. "Where do you think?"

"With Heidi."

"You got it."

"I thought it was over between them."

"That was last week."

Great. Pescoli had hoped that after the last breakup Jeremy wouldn't get back with Heidi, but, it seemed, they were forever doomed to their on-again/off-again romance. Her only hope was that one of them would grow up enough to move on, get out of Grizzly Falls, start making a real life for him- or herself. So far, it wasn't happening. Heidi was still in high school, and Jeremy was struggling with classes at the local community college. He seemed lost, sometimes not enrolled in college at all and working at the local gas station, only to "go back to school," only to change his mind and make a stab at something else again.

All the while, he'd never been able to break it off with Heidi. The undersheriff's daughter seemed to be his grounding point, which scared Pescoli to death.

"I texted him, he's on his way," Bianca said as Pescoli started climbing the stairs.

"Well, let's eat. The pizza's getting cold."

"I thought you were making spaghetti."

"Ran out of time. Maybe tomorrow."

Bianca was following her into the kitchen. "I'm not really that hungry."

"Why not?"

"I already ate."

"When?" Pescoli asked.

"I don't know. A few hours ago." She leaned over again, scooped her wild curls together, and snapped a colored band around her fistful of hair.

"What did you eat?"

Bianca straightened. "A power bar and a Diet Coke."

"Again?" Pescoli groaned. "Listen, I'm not going to get into it about the merits of eating well. We'll skip that lecture tonight, but between you and me, the protein bar and soda? Doesn't count as a meal. Maybe not even a snack."

"You just said you weren't going to give me a lecture."

"I might have lied."

"Geez." Bianca stalked to the refrigerator and pulled out a bottle of water. She took a long swallow before recapping the bottle as Pescoli warmed slices of the pizza in the microwave and both dogs waited impatiently, eyes on the platter.

"You wouldn't like it," she told them as the first plate was the Vegetarian's Delight. Looking at the thin, limp strips of peppers and onions, Pescoli silently agreed with the dogs. "Here ya go."

"Yummy," Bianca said without enthusiasm as she kicked out a chair and sat down.

"You usually love Dino's," she said as she shoved plate number two into the microwave and hit the Start button.

"Only pizza parlor in town."

"It was kind of quiet there tonight. The guy who helped me was Eric Ingles. I think he went to school with Jeremy."

"Dropped out sophomore year." She picked at a piece of artichoke on the pizza.

"You know this how?"

"He was a friend of Chris's older brother, I think."

Chris was her ex-boyfriend.

"What do you know about him now?"

"Nothing. Why?"

"He just seemed nervous that I was a cop."

Bianca snorted her disdain. "Y'think?"

The microwave timer dinged and Pescoli retrieved the second plate of pizza just as she heard a truck's engine rumbling ever closer. "So it looks like the prodigal has returned."

Less than a minute later, the beams of headlights splashed through the windows and Jeremy's truck came into view. It slid to a stop near the front of the house and he flew out of it, then pounded snow from his boots as he reached the front door, and Cisco, giving up on any scraps dropping his way, ran to the living room to do his happy dance.

"Hey, Bud," Jeremy said, scooping up the terrier and getting his face washed. "Pizza?" he asked, his face flushed, his eyes bright. "Great!" He let the dog hop from his arms, tossed his cap onto a side table, and began unzipping his jacket. "I'm starved!" He took the plate from his mother's outstretched hands and stopped at the refrigerator for a soda.

"That's the reaction I was hoping for," she said to her daughter.

"The rest of this"—he made a circular motion with a finger not wrapped around the neck of his Coke to include the remaining pizza—"it's mine. Right? All of it."

"You're such a Neanderthal," Bianca muttered with a long-suffering sigh.

"Oh, shut up," he said, half joking, his good mood making him almost euphoric. Dear God, she hoped he wasn't high on something. He'd been known to smoke a joint or two, but so had she in her youth. Leaning across the table, his nose inches from his sister's, he said, "I was only asking."

"Huh. Sounded more like marking your territory. You know, kinda like pissing in the corners of the kitchen."

"Okay, no squabbling," Pescoli intervened. "This is a holiday."

"Yesterday was a holiday," Jeremy said.

"Mom's got one of her lame ideas going. If you haven't got it yet, you're celebrating some anti-Christmas Day."

"It's *not* anti-Christmas. It's in addition to the holiday." When Jeremy looked at her she waved away the questions in his eyes. "I'll explain later, and to answer your question, *most* of the meat pizza is yours. I want a slice or two."

"Afterward we'll open presents," Bianca said.

"Good." Jeremy twisted off the cap of his Coke and washed down his bite. "Because I want to celebrate."

Pescoli looked up sharply. Her insides froze. He'd just been with Heidi. It was still the holidays . . . she thought about the ring Santana had given her and waves of denial swept through her. "Celebrate?" she whispered.

"I hate to ask," Bianca said, shoving the barely touched slices to one side.

"Then don't. You're looking at the newest deputy for the Pinewood Sheriff's Department," he declared with pride.

"What?" Pescoli whispered, thinking this was some kind of joke. Surely he was kidding, right? Pulling her leg? But she barely heard the hum of the microwave over the pounding of her heart.

"It's just one of those temporary things, until I finish school, but I went in and talked to Heidi's dad and he made me a deputy. Can you believe it?" Jeremy positively beamed, his grin stretching ear to ear. "See? I told you I wanted to be a cop."

"A deputy? But—"

"Okay, *kind of* a deputy." He cut off Pescoli's desperate-sounding words before he could get an all-out "no" from her. "He called it something else."

"A volunteer?"

"Yeah."

The rush in her ears was almost deafening. "I'm . . . I'm surprised you didn't talk to me first." She leaned against the counter for support, the way she had when she'd learned that her husband had been killed in the line of duty so long ago. He'd been older than Jeremy, of course, but the pain of that loss, whenever she thought about it, was still visceral. It didn't matter that their marriage had been in trouble. It was just . . . hellish on all of them.

And to think that her son wanted to walk in his shoes!

"I've been telling you about this, Mom." He took another large bite, stuffing the crust into his mouth, washing the whole wad down with another swallow of Coke. "For a long time. But you haven't been listening. You're always too busy."

"No, she isn't," Bianca said from her chair at the table where Cisco had taken up guard duty, his nose twitching upward. "Don't you get it, dumbass?" she asked, gesturing toward Pescoli. "She's in denial."

"It's not denial, and don't call your brother names." Pescoli held up both hands and kept her gaze on her boy. "I just didn't think you were serious."

"Maybe I wasn't. Before." He swiped another two sections of the pizza and didn't bother to heat them. "But then someone tried to kill Sheriff Grayson." Jeremy was suddenly dead serious. "Just like some jackass killed my dad. It's time for me to step up. Help find the dick who did this." Before she could argue, he continued, "You're the one who's always trying to get me to do something, aren't you? You, know, always wanting me to set goals. So I am."

"But, law enforcement?"

"It's what I want, Mom. Like you. Like Dad. The only thing I want to do. So I just went for it." He took another bite and kind of grunted in satisfaction. To Bianca, he said, "And from now on, you can call me Deputy or Officer."

"Like sure. Get real." Bianca's phone vibrated and she started texting as Jeremy looked in his mother's direction again. "Don't worry, Mom. I won't fu—mess this up. You'll see." He grabbed another slice. "Didn't you say there were presents or something? What're we waiting for?"

CHAPTER 14

The last person Hattie wanted to run into was Cade Grayson, but it seemed as if her luck had run out and sure enough, as she was walking into the hospital, he was striding through the first set of wide doors at the entrance to Northern General.

If she'd thought he would pass her by without making a comment, she was sadly mistaken. Keeping his thoughts to himself, especially where she was concerned, was just not his style.

"If it isn't Mrs. Grayson," he said, pausing as she slipped from the outside to the inner vestibule and the exterior set of doors whispered shut behind her.

"How is he?" she asked, ignoring his attempt at getting under her skin.

His eyes darkened a shade. "The same."

"You talked to the doctor?"

"Not yet." His cockiness had evaporated. "I tried, but . . . you know. The nurses in ICU said they'd pass along the information that I wanted a call."

"Maybe there's just nothing new."

"Probably." His gaze shifted from her face, to the doors and night beyond. Jaw tightening, he added, "I guess I don't have to be an ass."

"You don't have to be. You choose to be."

"Ouch." He actually winced.

"Let's not do this," she said. "I came here because I care about your brother, who just happens to be my brother-in-law. If you think that's a crime, sorry, guilty as charged." Cade's expression darkened, and Hattie went on, "I don't know what it is I do that pisses you off so much, but it's your problem, not mine. And if I really looked at the issue long and hard, I think your attitude might have a lot to do with what happened between us."

"That was a long time ago," he said cautiously.

"Yes, it was. A long time ago. Long enough that we should get past it all." She regarded him coolly, intent on not letting him get to her anymore. His eyes were dark, his pupils large in the dim light, his chin covered in a beard shadow that was somewhere between scruffy and sexy, and he stared at her as if he couldn't believe that she'd thrown off her polite little shell to tear into him.

"I guess I might deserve that," he allowed.

"You've been a real ass, Cade. It's *not* my fault that Bart is dead, and it's certainly not my fault that Dan is here. So quit blaming me."

"I don't."

"Really," she said between clenched teeth.

The doors from the hospital opened and an older man pushing a walker stepped through. He was accompanied by a woman who looked to be his daughter, as she, thirty years or so younger, was helping him guide the walker through the second set of doors. Hattie stepped out of their way, and in so doing put more distance between her body and Cade's, so she could actually start breathing again.

Once the doors behind the couple had closed, she said, "I didn't mean to get into it with you, but no matter what you think, I do care about Dan and this, what's happened to him. It's horrible."

"Yes, it is."

"And I have this need to come and see him, to somehow convince myself that he'll be okay." When Cade didn't respond, she said, "I don't even know why I'm trying to explain myself. It's not as if you'd believe me." She started for the interior doors, when she felt his fingers clamp over her elbow.

"Hattie," he said, his voice so soft she barely heard it.

Jerking her arm from his, she whipped around to stare him squarely in the face. When he didn't immediately speak, she said wanly, "This is just so . . . exhausting." Then she stepped through the doors and into the hospital lobby, hazarding one last glance over her shoulder, watching the exterior doors part. In the hazy blue glow of the security lamps, Cade walked quickly outside, kicking his pace into a jog as he crossed the parking lot to his truck.

Hattie attempted not to notice but found it impossible. She didn't know whether she hated Cade or if her feelings ran in another direction entirely. But she didn't have time to examine them now. After most of the day spent at the office, she'd gone home for dinner; then she'd felt compelled to drive to Missoula and see for herself that Dan was, if nothing else, stable.

Her mother had eagerly come to watch the girls again, and Hattie had already missed their bedtime, again, but she planned to make it up to the twins tomorrow. So thinking, she hurried through the second set of doors and stepped into the main vestibule of the quiet hospital and made her way to ICU where yet another deputy was guarding the outer area. A chill passed through her as she thought about anyone trying to kill the sheriff. Would the assassin try again? She hated to think so, but it was the question she'd read in the newspaper and seen on the news; she'd even heard speculation about it while grabbing a quick lunch at the local sandwich spot where two women who looked to be in their seventies were gossiping while a young waitress attempted to take their drink orders.

". . . can't believe they haven't found whoever did it yet," one of the women said to the waitress. Dressed in jeans and a Christmas sweater, she'd added, "It's just awful! There's just no respect these days, y'know. Oh . . . and I'll have an iced tea. With extra lemons. Three slices."

Her friend, a woman in a blond wig set in a 1950s "flip" style, nodded vehemently. "I know! It's awful. To think, on Christmas morning! What's the world coming to?"

"It's probably an ex-con. Lord knows there are lots of those. And being the sheriff and all, he's a major target."

Blonde agreed. "You'd think the police would be all over it."

"Would you like anything to drink?" the waitress interjected. Barely out of her teens, her hair pulled into a ponytail, she was standing on one foot, then the other, waiting for the women to order.

"Do you have Diet Coke?" the woman in the wig asked.

"Pepsi."

"That's fine, thanks. Oh, and a glass of water."

Her friend agreed. "Yes, for me too. And don't forget the extra lemons."

"I'll be right back to take your order," the girl promised as she'd hurried to the drink station.

The woman in the wig had reached into her purse for a small vial of pills and shaken one tablet into her palm. "I'm just shocked that someone would take a potshot at the sheriff. I mean, hasn't that family had enough to deal with? His younger brother, you know, hung himself a few years back. Left two little kids."

Hattie had felt the muscles in her back tighten. She'd wanted to step in and say something in Bart's defense, but she'd held her tongue rather than make a scene as she'd stood in line to order, deciding at that moment she'd take her Caesar salad to go.

Now, as she identified herself to the security guard, she wished she'd told those old hens exactly what she'd thought, but what was the point, really? Shoving her annoyance aside, she waited to be buzzed into the ICU, feeling compelled to be here, to even hold a vigil at Dan's bedside, though she knew it would do no good.

But he deserved someone to care about him.

And she did.

She always had.

At first as a teenager in the throes of what her mother had called puppy love, or so she'd thought, and then over the years into something that ran much deeper. She touched the fingers of his left hand, to reassure him, but there was no response.

"Hi, Dan," she whispered, blinking rapidly. "It's me. Hattie." She rubbed the tips of his fingers and felt her throat clog. "The girls and I, we can't wait for you to come over again." Her words caught in her throat and she wondered if that day would ever come.

Of course it will. It will just take time. He's strong. In the prime of his life. A fighter!

She hoped for some sign that he was improving, that he'd heard her, but there was no rapid movement of his eyes beneath his lids, no twitch of his lips, no faint shift of his finger caught between hers.

"Just wanted you to know that we all love you," she said. Then, realizing that there was nothing she could do for him, she reluctantly left the building and drove home through the cold, dark night.

He'll be fine, she told herself over and over as her tires hummed against the frozen pavement and her headlights cast twin beams into the darkness. And yet, despite all of her encouragement to herself, she wondered if that were really true. Who had tried to kill him? she asked herself again. And, more chillingly, was the assassin planning to try again?

"I can't believe you deputized my son!" Pescoli was livid as she stood over Cort Brewster's desk, hands planted on its smooth edge, her gaze pinning the tall man to his chair. His office, just down the hall from Grayson's, was slightly smaller and filled with bookcases that were stuffed with books on law enforcement, business, psychology, accounting, and a Bible. Between the volumes were pictures of Brewster and his family, the stepping stone blond girls at various ages, his diplomas and awards, even a few trophies used as bookends. One wall was covered with a map of the county, and the other, high above his desk and opposite the door, boasted a small, high window, above a credenza littered with more family photos.

His desk was neat, a picture of his wife front and center.

Pescoli got it: Brewster was a family man and proud of it.

"Hey, hold on. He wanted to volunteer and I agreed. He's not a deputy, you and I both know that, but his title or duties are beside the point. He wants to work here and I said yes. You know, Pescoli, I'd think you'd want to thank me," he said when she'd finished lambasting him. "That kid of yours has been searching for something to make of himself for a long time, and now he's shown some interest in law enforcement and you're ticked off."

"You bet I am!"

"For the love of God, Pescoli, what's with you? Quit enabling him and let him be his own man."

"It's not for you to say!" Pescoli sputtered.

"He's twenty years old and you keep trying to run his life."

" 'That kid' you mentioned is still trying to find himself," Pescoli declared, fighting back the urge to rant and rave. "And he has some whacked-out notion that he wants to follow in his father's footsteps."

"Or his mother's."

"What if your daughter came to me and wanted to be deputized?" she threw back at him. "How would you feel about that?"

Brewster rose from his chair and his face turned red. "Leave Heidi or any of my kids out of this. You're deflecting, Pescoli. It's your boy and he came to me. I didn't go looking for him. He wants to do his part, and I said, 'okay.' Actually, more like 'Hallelujah. Finally.' "

"As if you care."

"Let him grow a pair."

"I can't believe this. And why would you want to help him anyway? You've always been on his case, letting me know what a loser he is. No. Uh-uh. This makes no sense."

"I've never said he was a loser."

"Oh, yeah, I think so. Or at the very least implied it."

"I just think that you haven't let him be the man he could be. It's not him I have a problem with. It's really you."

"Then don't take it out on my kid!"

"I'm not. I'm helping him, and if you weren't so damned bull-headed, Pescoli, you'd see it."

"Not that it's any of your business."

"It is when he's dating my daughter and when he comes into my office and wants to help." Brewster's eyes narrowed, his jaw tightened, and he looked about to explode with that same hatred that always seemed to appear whenever they were talking about their kids. Then, as if he suddenly realized where they were and how out of hand the conversation had become, he looked away to gather himself. After letting out a long breath, he was calmer again. "We're getting off course here. Let's take you and me and our kids out of this equation."

"We're talking about my son."

"Yes, but hear me out," Brewster said, holding up a hand as if to physically stop her from spouting any further arguments. "We're not talking about an exclusive club here. Jeremy's not the only person who was deputized yesterday, or at least asked to help out. Informally, we 'deputized' half a dozen citizens. If you've forgotten, not only are we looking for someone who tried to kill the sheriff, but we're short-handed on top of that since Van Droz is still on a leave of absence. Who knows if she'll return?"

Though she wanted to, Pescoli couldn't argue that point. Trilby Van Droz was one of the best cops on the force, and she'd threatened to quit after her last near-death experience. Grayson had refused her resignation, talking Van Droz into taking some time over the holidays to rethink her position and consider her options.

Brewster continued, "We're down two officers, counting the sheriff, and a few others are on vacation. It's the end of the year, and there are people on holiday leave, not to mention that with the bad weather and uptick in domestic issues that always occur this time of year, we're stretched thin. Real thin. I figured we'll deputize a few who asked to be, and even though they're not on the payroll or officially part of the staff, they can help. Your kid volunteered. You should be proud, instead of going off half-cocked. That's your problem: never keeping a level head. You're a rogue, Regan, and it doesn't work for me. Just calm the hell down."

Damn it all to hell, Brewster was right, on too many levels.

Sensing capitulation in her silence, he added, "As I said, you should thank me."

She wasn't going to go that far.

"Okay. Now, we both have a helluva lot of work to do. If you want to talk about this when we're not in the middle of a crisis, fine, but for now—"

"Sheriff?" a woman's voice said from somewhere behind Pescoli. Straightening, she turned to find Sage Zoller holding on to the edge of the doorframe and sticking her head into the room. "Sorry to bother you, but it looks like they've found Judge Samuels-Piquard," she said solemnly. Obviously the news wasn't good.

"Is she all right?" he asked, but Zoller was already shaking her head, dark curls shivering around her face.

"She's dead, sir. Found less than two miles from the cabin where she was staying. Looks like a gunshot wound."

"She was murdered?" Pescoli said in disbelief, the fears that had been fractured in the back of her brain suddenly gelling.

"I was afraid of this," Brewster said soberly. "I sent Watershed up there, but he didn't see anything. Nothing was disturbed . . . I should have known. Pressed it."

Pescoli met the undersheriff's gaze and for the first time since striding into his office, she wasn't angry. "God, Cort, I'm sorry. The judge was a friend of yours."

"Of my wife's." He was nodding. "I was close with her husband, George, while he was alive. We served together. Damn. This is going to kill Bess." He reached for his jacket, hanging on a peg near the door. "Does the press know?"

"I doubt it, but I'm not sure," Zoller said, stepping out of the doorway so that he could pass. "I just got the call."

"I need to stop by the house and talk to Bess. Then I'll be up there."

"I'm on my way," Pescoli said. "What's the address of the cabin?"

"It's in the mountains. Somewhere north of Elk Basin, right?" Brewster said to Zoller. "On Spangler Road?"

"Monarch," Zoller corrected, mentioning the spur. "2700 Monarch. According to the deputies that are out there, it's not much of a road. Dead end. Only a couple of cabins anywhere near it."

Pescoli was already out of Brewster's office and on the hunt for Alvarez, who, as usual, was seated at her desk, phone to her ear, computer monitor showing the most recent report on an older model SUV, which, Pescoli saw, was registered to Wanda Verdago, Maurice's wife.

"Let's go," she said, catching Alvarez's attention. Her partner looked up, her phone still pressed to her ear. "Kathryn Samuels-Piquard's body has been found in the foothills."

"Oh, no," Alvarez said, then switched her attention back to her phone call. "Sorry. Gotta run. Just e-mail me the report. Thanks!" Hanging up, she twirled in her chair and was on her feet, reaching for her jacket, sidearm, and hat. "What the hell happened?" she asked as together they headed toward the back of the hallway, both skirting around Joelle hurrying the other way. The receptionist, like everyone else in the department, had been grim since the attack on Grayson, her spirits flagging; though, Pescoli noticed, Joelle was wearing the stupid little holly earrings that Pescoli had bought her, part of her ridiculous "Secret Santa" campaign she organized every holiday season. Today, with Grayson in the hospital and Samuels-Piquard found dead, and Christmas a day past, the tradition seemed even more foolish than ever.

CHAPTER 15

"You'd think they could have told us this to begin with," Alvarez complained as she clicked off her phone in the passenger seat of Pescoli's Jeep.

She was antsy, and it didn't help her mood that they'd almost reached Judge Samuels-Piquard's cabin only to be rerouted to backtrack along an old mining road that wound closer to the crime scene. Alvarez had taken the directions while Pescoli put her rig into four-wheel drive and the Jeep had scaled the steep, overgrown road that already showed a single set of tracks from another vehicle.

For most of the drive to the judge's retreat, Alvarez had been on the phone, still tracking down the whereabouts of Maurice Verdago. The fact that he'd disappeared so quickly after the attack on Grayson was more than suspicious, a very unlikely coincidence in Alvarez's mind.

To make things more difficult, cell phone service was sketchy in these hills, and of course, Verdago's friends and family were being of no help whatsoever.

It was frustrating as hell.

While Pescoli seemed to be zeroing in on Grayson's first ex-wife, Alvarez was checking and double-checking on the violent offenders that Grayson had put away. Those who had served their time and were back on the streets could very well hold a grudge against the sheriff, as well as the judge, as many of the cases overlapped. Dan Grayson had brought the offender to justice and, if guilty, Judge Samuels-Piquard had come up with the appropriate sentence.

Alvarez felt they would find their killer among the criminals Grayson had put away. After serving time, some parolees might walk the straight and narrow, happy to stay as far away from the law as possible, while others jumped right back into their practiced life of crime. But there were also a few who had spent every day of their time behind bars contemplating their sorry lots in life and blaming those who had put them away: witnesses, family members who ratted them out, victims who got away, or law enforcement officers who had sent them up the river. Those cons, the ones who harbored grudges and plotted revenge, were a nasty, hard-assed group. They were the suspects she was trying to weed out of the crowded pack.

Maurice Verdago was at the top of Alvarez's list of suspects, though he'd climbed to that particular rung mostly due to the fact that he'd been out a while and now, after the shooting, had vanished.

Poof.

Just like that.

Definitely suspicious.

And Pescoli had always thought he was a prime suspect; she was pissed that, so far, he was nowhere to be found.

Pescoli had mentioned talking to Eric Ingles, Allison Banks's delinquent of a boyfriend, but he'd given up no info on the Banks family, and anyway, Cara Grayson Banks didn't really seem the type to set up the killing of her ex. No, Alvarez thought, as Pescoli parked in a roped-off area near the beginning of a snowy hiking trail, the Banks family wasn't likely to be involved, especially now with the discovery of Samuels-Piquard's body. She believed that the two attacks were linked and couldn't imagine why anyone in the Banks family would want the judge dead.

Still, Pescoli was keeping the Banks family in the mix, so Alvarez wasn't going to rule them out yet either.

At the end of the road, they found another county SUV, parked at an angle, the tracks in the snow ending at its rear tires. Pescoli cut the engine and they climbed outside.

The wind had died and the surrounding forest was silent, eerily serene, towering hemlock and fir trees flocked in white, the sky above blue, sunlight sparkling on the blanket of snow.

As if she could read her partner's mind, Pescoli said, "Doesn't really feel like a crime scene, does it?"

"What does?"

Pescoli shrugged.

They both strapped on snowshoes, then hiked the remaining quarter mile to where the judge's body had been found, the sound of their boots crunching through the snow the only noise disturbing the tranquility. As they emerged from a thicket, they crested the ridge and, looking downward, saw the spot where the judge had fallen. A deputy, Beau Darville, dressed in uniform and relatively new to the department, stood over the half-frozen body. Sunglasses shaded his eyes and his jaw was set, his mouth a grimace. A second officer, Deputy Patrice Ferrier, was twenty yards away and talking to a couple, both of whom were in their twenties. Alvarez guessed they were the unlucky duo who had found the body.

"Clear shot from up here," Pescoli said before they made their way the final fifty yards to the killing ground.

"Yeah," Alvarez agreed. From the top of the rise, it would have been far too easy for anyone who was capable with a rifle to hit the judge, who, it appeared from the skis strapped to her feet, had been out for some exercise.

As they made their way down the short hill, Darville motioned them over to the body. The judge's body was lying faceup; though, from the disturbances on the snow-covered ground, it was evident that her frozen corpse had been moved.

"Sweet Jesus," Pescoli breathed. For the first time that Alvarez could remember, Pescoli looked away from the corpse before pulling herself together.

"Looks like a single bullet to the brain. Clean shot," Darville explained, pointing to a hole above the judge's right eye. "Probably lodged inside. Not through and through." Bloodstains on the ground confirmed what he'd already concluded.

"Those are the hikers who found her?" Alvarez asked, with a look to the couple who were standing just outside the clearing with Deputy Ferrier.

"Yeah, showshoeing. Liam Maxwell, twenty-one, and his girlfriend, Raney Gorski. She's twenty. Both home from Seattle, where they go to school at the University of Washington, for the holiday break. They're both pretty shaken up. Ferrier and I caught the 911." Darville sent the couple a sympathetic look. "They stayed up here with the corpse until we arrived."

Blood had caked, then frozen around the area of the wound. Alvarez knelt down to get a better look, noting that the judge's hat was still partially on her head, red curls iced into position, eyes open as if she were staring upward.

"They'd thought there might be some chance to revive her, but . . ." Darville shook his head. "No use. She's been dead awhile."

Pescoli was eyeing the tracks from the judge's skis, partially covered in snow. "She was coming from the direction of the cabin," she said aloud, then scanned the surrounding woods. "He could have been anywhere up on the ridge. We saw several spots on the trail as we came over the hill."

"Haven't looked yet," he admitted. "Waiting for backup."

"We're it." Sheltering her eyes with a hand, she stared upward, along the crest, back to the trail on which they had just walked, searching for the exact spot where the assailant could have hidden. "Crime lab and coroner on their way?"

Darville said, "Should be here anytime now."

"No other tracks?" Alvarez asked. "We only saw yours."

"None that we've seen, not a vehicle or a footprint or a ski track."

"They've got to be here somewhere unless someone helicoptered him in and out," Pescoli said, her breath fogging in the icy air. "We got dogs? A K-9 unit on its way?"

"Not yet."

"We might need them." Still studying the area, her gaze scraping the frigid terrain, she squinted toward the forested crest.

"You think dogs would help?" he asked.

"Sure as hell won't hurt." Staring up the hillside again, her eyes scanning the ground, Pescoli said, "I'm going up to take a look." Then to her partner, "Don't worry, I won't mess up the crime scene."

Alvarez was more interested in the witnesses. Gesturing to them, she asked, "They were the ones who moved her, right?"

"Yeah, they admitted it." Darville lifted a shoulder. "Just trying to help."

"I'd better talk to them," Alvarez said, and started trudging through the calf-deep snow toward the small group. One of Liam Maxwell's arms was wrapped protectively around his girlfriend's slim shoulders. Even so, she appeared to be shaking, either from the cold or the horror of what they'd discovered, or, more probably, a little of each.

". . . it's just awful," the girl, Raney, was saying as Alvarez approached, her eyes round, her nose red and running. Strands of brown hair poked from beneath a heavy, Nordic-looking stocking cap with long, braidlike ties hanging by her ears.

"It'll be okay," her boyfriend said, giving her a hug, but no smile reached his eyes. He appeared as upset as Raney but was trying to hide it. A reddish, scraggly beard covered the lower half of his face while shaded ski goggles obscured his eyes.

"I know this is rough," Alvarez said, "but can you tell me what happened? How you got here? What you saw?"

"Again?" Raney swiped at her nose with the back of her gloved hand.

"Please. Everything."

"That's just it," the girl said. "There's not much to say. We were just trying out our new gear and . . ." Her gaze slid to the frozen body of the judge and she visibly shivered.

Maxwell finished her thoughts. "And we saw something that didn't look right, y'know, a flash of red on the ground. So we checked it out and saw that it was the judge. The red was her jacket."

"How did you know who she was?" Alvarez asked.

"Her picture's been all over the news," he answered. "We saw a report about her on TV just last night." He glanced at Raney, whose head was already bobbing up and down in agreement, the long braidlike ties of her stocking cap dancing weirdly around her chin.

"I . . . uh, I just never thought we would, you know, find her," the girl said, her chin wobbling a little. "Can we go now?"

"Just a few more questions and then, sure," Alvarez said, learning that they'd been staying in her grandparent's cabin since winter break began, about three miles north. They'd started today's hike from that cabin, had seen no other tracks, and their car had been parked in the lean-to garage ever since they'd first arrived.

Which meant all the tracks in the snow now belonged to the police or, maybe, the killer's vehicle, assuming he had one. First, of course, they had to locate those tracks and hope no one else had traveled the surrounding, little-used roads over the past couple of days.

"Did you hear or see anything or anyone up here during your visit?" Alvarez asked.

"Nuh-uh," the girl said, shaking her head vigorously.

Maxwell added, "Not even a mailman or neighbor or paper delivery guy."

"That's why we came here, to be alone," his girlfriend said. "It's way different at U-Dub. People are out all day and night. We . . . we just wanted to do something together. By ourselves." She linked her gloved hand with her boyfriend's and bit her lip.

"No one out in the woods, skiing or sledding or anything? Maybe you heard the sound of a snowmobile or truck's engine?" Alvarez suggested.

"Uh-uh. Nothing. Until today. When we found"—Raney glanced at the corpse again and her face crumpled in on itself. "Could it have been a hunter?"

"Maybe," Alvarez said, knowing that it was legal to hunt some species at this time of year. Mountain lions and wolves came to mind. "But it's unlikely. He'd have to have been blind not to recognize a human, and I think a hunter would have reported this kind of accident."

"Unless he didn't want to get in trouble," Maxwell pointed out. "People are such cowards." His arm tightened over his girlfriend's shoulders.

"No reason to speculate." This was getting her nowhere and Alvarez felt time slipping away. "Just tell me what you do know," she suggested. "Go over your last few days."

"Well . . ." Raney began, then went on to say that she and Liam had left Seattle on Christmas Day. Only stopping for gas and food, they'd driven directly to the cabin where they'd built a fire, hung out, cooked over the hearth, and played cards and checkers on the board her grandfather had painted half a century earlier.

They'd seen no one and nothing, aside from three deer peering through the leafless trees the day before.

They claimed they couldn't tell the police anything else, and though they dutifully answered any and all questions Alvarez could think to throw at them, they didn't offer anything further. Nothing new came to light. They simply didn't have any more information that would help the investigation.

Alvarez let them go and returned to the body just as Pescoli returned from her reconnoiter. She said she'd found several spots where the assassin could have lain in wait for his victim, but the landscape hadn't been disturbed, and enough snow had fallen that it would have obliterated the evidence if the judge had been dead for several days, which seemed highly likely by the state of the body.

By the time the coroner showed up and the witnesses had snowshoed away, back toward their cabin, Alvarez and Pescoli decided they'd seen what they could. They trekked back to Pescoli's Jeep, where the windows were fogged and the interior was ice cold. "Maybe we'll find something at the judge's cabin," Alvarez said, clicking her seat belt into place.

"I'd kill for a cup of coffee." Pescoli fired the engine and backed around the coroner's wagon, then slid her partner a glance. "What're the odds of finding a java kiosk up here?"

"About as likely as Santa Claus and the reindeer showing up."

"It's too late for them anyway."

Alvarez smiled for the first time that day, though she didn't feel any joy whatsoever. "You know, I heard once that if you throw a quarter up in the air in any major city in the U.S., chances are it'll land a hundred feet from a Starbucks coffee shop."

"I don't think whoever came up with that theory has ever been to the Bitterroots."

"I said, 'major city.' "

"Yeah, I know. Still, a cup of anything hot sounds good." She fiddled with the Jeep's heater, which only allowed cool air to blow onto the inside of the windshield. It lent no heat to the interior but did start defogging the glass. "Should warm up soon," she said, turning the rig around, jockeying between the other county vehicles that had parked haphazardly at the end of the trail.

"Good."

Ramming into first gear, she eased the Jeep down the hill. "You think this is the same shooter who tried to kill Grayson?" Alvarez asked.

"No doubt in my mind," Pescoli responded. "What are the chances that we'd have two similar attacks on the heels of each other? Slim and none . . . No, just make that 'none.' Whoever dropped the judge is an ace, a sharpshooter, so that should narrow the field."

"What happened with Grayson, then?"

"I showed up just as the attack was going down. Probably rattled the guy, destroyed his concentration."

"So now you're the hero?" Alvarez asked, but the joke fell flat.

"Hardly." Pescoli squinted as she guided the Jeep onto the little-used road. Sunlight was streaming through the woods now, dappling the forested terrain in beams that fractured and dazzled against the snow. "My bet is that when they dig that bullet out of Judge Samuels-Piquard's brain, it matches the ones used on the sheriff."

"Looks like we've got a crack shot with a grudge against not only Grayson, but the judge as well." Alvarez slid a glance at her partner. "Probably not Cara Grayson or any of the family."

Pescoli's jaw tightened as she reached for a pair of sunglasses she kept on the dash. "I guess." Slipping the shades over the bridge of her nose, she added, "At least it narrows the field."

"Potentially. If we cross-check violent cons Grayson sent up the river with those sentenced by the judge and find out which ones are out, we might find our killer."

" 'Might' being the operative word." The heater was starting to kick in, a little warm air filling the interior.

"Here's the turnoff," Alvarez said, spying a barely visible sign marking Monarch Lane.

Pescoli hit the brakes a little too hard and the Jeep slid a bit as she made the turn.

"Fresh tracks," Alvarez observed. "Probably from the deputies Brewster sent up here."

"They make a report?"

"Just that she didn't answer and her car was there."

"Did they go in?"

"Yeah, her kid; Winston, told them where the spare key was hidden. And don't ask; yeah, it was under the welcome mat."

"You talked to them?" Pescoli asked as the cabin appeared, a log structure with a sharp peaked roof nestled between thick stands of snow-flocked evergreens. The windows were dark, a holiday wreath hung near the clear glass door.

She parked fifteen yards from the house. Several sets of footprints had broken through the snow and, true to the son's word, a key was wedged beneath a doormat decorated with a reindeer's head, colored lights twisted through its antlers.

They let themselves in.

"Nice place," Pescoli observed, an understatement as usual. The living room stretched from the front porch to a back wall of floor-to-ceiling windows offering a peekaboo view of the lake far below. Water as blue as a summer sky shimmered between the snow-laden bows of fir and hemlock and spruce.

Apart from Rudolph on the front porch, there were few decorations to remind the owner of the season, though candles were tucked between dozens of books that filled a bookcase, which, in turn, flanked a stone fireplace that rose to the peak of a wood-plank ceiling. A small display on the table, a glass bowl filled with red and green ornaments, was the only other bit of decor that gave a nod to the holidays.

Neat and dust-free, the cabin was sparse, a chess set on the coffee table, a backgammon board, pegs ready, on the bookcase near a well-worn leather recliner.

The kitchen was also uncluttered, no dishes left in the sink, nothing but a single place mat on the eating bar that separated the kitchen from another cozy space with an oversized chair and ottoman; three books and an e-reader sat on the small glass table nearby.

Upstairs, the bedroom, a loft that held a king bed and a daybed under its sloping roof, was tidy—the bed made, the clothes in a walk-in closet hung with care. The judge's medications and vitamins were arranged in a neat plastic case marked with days of the week. Judging from the contents, she'd taken her last dose on Christmas Eve.

They walked through the house, searched the grounds, and came up with nothing other than her purse, laptop, iPad, and cell phone. A quick check of the incoming calls to her phone showed the same number dialing over and over again. Probably the judge's son, Winston, who had called Missing Persons. The lab would go over each item, and technicians would check the data from the judge's e-mail and social media accounts, anything she'd done online in the past few weeks and months. Maybe something would turn up, some piece of information that would link the killer to his victim.

Outside they discovered her vehicle, a new Lexus SUV, parked in a separate garage. The keys were in the ignition, registration and insurance information in the glove box confirming that the SUV belonged to Kathryn Samuels-Piquard. Aside from the keys, a receipt for gas and an empty coffee cup in the holder, the vehicle was clean. Also, nothing seemed disturbed in the garage, though they would double-check with the judge's family, and, of course, crime scene techs would process every inch of the house, garage, and surrounding grounds.

Maybe they'd find something.

Pescoli could only hope.

"Doesn't look like robbery was a motive," Alvarez said as they walked along the broad porch that connected the two buildings, then wrapped around to the back of the house to the spectacular view. "So we're back to the scumbags who are out of prison."

"And the family."

"Always the family."

"Kind of warms the cockles of your heart, doesn't it?" They waited for the crime scene unit, though Pescoli wouldn't bet on them finding much. They'd go over the place looking for trace evidence or prints on the off chance the killer had been inside; though, it seemed, from the looks of things, it was unlikely. To her practiced eye, the house and garage looked clean.

But she'd been wrong before.

"I don't think he was here," she said, wondering about the killer, what was his motive, how he knew the judge. "I think he waited for her on the ridge."

"For how long? Unless he knew her routine, he might be sitting up there for hours, maybe days. Did she go skiing every day? Did he just get lucky?" Squinting at the surrounding forest, she nodded, as if agreeing with herself. "I'll bet the guy knows her, knows her routine, or else knows someone who told him about the fact she comes up here and goes skiing every year."

"Maybe they overheard her talking."

"Could be, but no one's going to camp out on the ridge in this cold without knowing he's got a chance to take her down."

"So he knows her."

"Or she . . . could be a woman," Alvarez corrected, still deep in thought.

"Or a hired hit man."

They heard the rumble of an engine, and within seconds another van from the crime scene pulled into view only to stop by the Jeep.

Pescoli recognized Mikhail Slatkin at the wheel and felt a little better. Slatkin was one of the best techs in the business. If there was evidence of any kind to find, Slatkin would locate it.

They spoke to the techs for a few minutes, then walked back to the Jeep.

Next up, after a quick stop at the station to catch up on e-mail, tips, and reports that had come in, she and Alvarez would check the judge's place in town and start tearing through Judge Samuels-Piquard's private and public lives, hoping they'd find some clue as to who would want her dead so badly as to actually put a bullet in her brain.

CHAPTER 16

When Pescoli returned to the station, she didn't expect to see her son, but there he was, big as life, washing out the coffeepot—a job he would never deign do at home—in the lunchroom that smelled of burned coffee and chili peppers and cilantro.

"What's this?" she asked, walking up to him. He'd shaved, combed his hair, and was wearing a pair of jeans that didn't hang so low on his buttocks they were in danger of falling off. He was even wearing one of his two dress shirts and a damned tie, the one she'd bought him for his high-school graduation.

"I told you, I'm . . . like a deputy now."

"I just don't get it."

"Only because you don't want to." He was rubbing the glass pot so hard, she thought he might break it. Soapy water splashed onto his shirtsleeves. "I told you before, I want to be a cop. Like Dad. Like you."

"Oh, Jer—"

"Don't, Mom. Okay?" he said, turning fast and glaring down at her. Then in a lower voice, he whispered, "Not here."

When the hell had he gotten so tall? In those seconds, when anger flashed in his eyes and determination set his jaw, he looked so much like Joe she was flung back in time to one of the many arguments in their marriage. Again. This déjà vu thing was beginning to become a habit. And not a good one.

His face had flushed and belatedly she realized she was embarrassing him. Oh, for the love of God, as if anyone cared. But Jeremy slid his eyes to one side where a grouping of tables was strewn with empty cups and pages of the newspaper. A few other cops were taking a break, though none was showing the least amount of interest in their discussion.

Brett Gage, glasses set on the end of his nose, was working a Sudoku in the newspaper while eating what looked like a tuna sandwich, and two road deputies were just pushing back their chairs, their break over. Rhonda Cafferty was finishing a Diet Coke, draining the can, while Shanna from Dispatch carried the remains of her lunch, a Lean Cuisine lasagne, and tossed the scraps and box into the trash.

"Come on, Mom," Jeremy said softly. "Give me a break, would ya?" He looked over her shoulder at the sharp staccato sound of high heels clipped against the old tile floor. It didn't take all of her detection skills to realize that Joelle had arrived.

"Oh, let me do that!" the receptionist insisted, and before Jeremy could refill the coffeepot with fresh water, she'd nudged him with her hips away from the sink. Her pre-Christmas holiday colors had been replaced with a blue suit and snowflake earrings. The glitter in her hair was missing and some of the sparkle had left her eyes, but she managed a small smile for Jeremy. "Look at you," she said, sizing him up and down as he stood, still holding the coffeepot. "All grown up!" With a glance in Pescoli's direction, she said, "Aren't you proud?"

Jeremy arched a dark brow, silently urging her to argue.

"Always," Pescoli lied . . . it was really just a half-truth. Of course she was proud of her children, yes, but frustrated as hell with each of them at times. The pride thing . . . it wavered with the situation. She thought about last night, how relieved she'd been that he'd checked on her, how disappointed she'd been to know that he'd been out doing God knows what with Heidi Brewster.

"You should be!" Joelle was taking control of the kitchen area. Locating a premeasured package of coffee in the drawer, she eyed it and discarded it. "Decaf? I don't think so. Not today with all that's going on. Everyone needs to be on their toes!" Slapping a caffeinated packet into the basket of another pot she found in the cupboard, she sent a sharp look at Pescoli's son. "And you. Why don't you help me out front with the phones? The undersheriff is going to hold a press conference, and no doubt Vera and I will get swamped. Also, you can take over Vera's job of pointing people in the right direction. If anyone walks into the department, you'll be who they talk to, and don't worry, we have maps up front at the desk." She motioned toward the glass pot still in his hand. "Put that carafe away and come along, I'll show you where we keep the maps and give you a crash course on reception."

"Sure . . . fine," he agreed.

"Just give me a sec." Filling the new pot with water, she added, "And we'll make it official. Find you a shirt and hat from the department. Trust me, you'll be all set!" Joelle pushed the appropriate button on one of the coffeemakers, then swiped the counter with a towel. "There we go!" Smiling in satisfaction, she snapped the towel, then hung it on a rack near the sink. "All done." Kitchen to her standards again, the coffeepot already gurgling, hissing, and dripping, she headed toward the hall.

"Don't you, like, have some work to do or something?" Jeremy whispered to Pescoli as Joelle in the archway wiggled her manicured fingers in a "come along" gesture, then clicked her way out of sight.

"More than 'or something.' And lots of it."

"Then shouldn't you be doing it?"

She almost told him to shove his attitude but decided to back off. For now. "Okay, but this isn't over," she warned. "We'll talk about it tonight," she said.

"Whatever." Gone was his earnest expression, replaced by sullen rebellion as he slammed the coffeepot back into the brewer hard enough that she was certain the glass would shatter. Gratefully, it didn't.

"Jeremy, c'mon. This is my workplace."

"Mine, too, Mom." Turning away from her, he followed after Joelle and Pescoli sent up a rare, silent prayer, just as she thought she heard a barely audible, "I just don't know what the fuck you expect from me."

Realizing that her fists had clenched and that Brett Gage had looked up from his puzzle, Pescoli tried to think of something to say—and failed.

"Teenagers," he said into the silence, his smile knowing. "Can't live with 'em, can't shoot 'em."

"But you can ground them, if they still live with you," she said, and silently added, *Even when they're in their twenties.*

"Yeah, well, the carrot or the stick, that's the age-old question." He picked up his newspaper and snapped it before turning the page. "Personally, the stick, it never helped me when I was growing up. Just made me want to beat the crap out of my old man." Looking over the top of the sports page, he smiled, his lips twisting wryly. "I was smart enough to never try as he was an all-state fullback and would have whipped my ass."

"Is that advice? Because you don't have any children that I know of."

"Just sayin'." He snapped his paper loudly.

"I'm handling this."

"Didn't seem that way much to me. But, hey, he's your kid. I was just trying to give you the teen-male perspective."

"Which is?"

"If it moves, screw it."

"That's *not* what was happening here, and this has nothing to do with a girl or—"

"Doesn't he date Brewster's daughter?"

"No . . . well, sometimes." Why was she even engaging in this conversation?

"And Brewster hired him? Your son wouldn't be the first boy trying to score Brownie points with a girl by buddying up to her old man."

The very thought was appalling. Jeremy would never stoop so low. *But he did go to Brewster behind my back, didn't he?*

As if Gage could read her mind, he smirked, then stuck his large nose into his paper again and, gratefully, out of her business. Remembering that she'd come into the lunchroom for a reason, she reached into the refrigerator for the can of Diet Coke she'd left earlier, only to find that it was missing. Someone had decided to help himself to the unmarked can.

"You'd think you could trust people not to steal in the damned sheriff's department! Aren't we supposed to uphold the law, not break it?" Slamming the refrigerator door shut, Pescoli let her breath out slowly. She was on edge, no doubt about it, and overreacting.

Hadn't she herself "borrowed" a can of soda now and again, never quite replacing it?

"Payback's a bitch," Gage muttered as he folded his paper.

Irritated by the chief criminal detective's remarks, probably because of lack of sleep and the fact that Gage's sentiments echoed Santana's, she strode out of the lunchroom in a dark mood.

Only last week, while lying naked in Santana's bed, she'd vented her frustrations with her son to him. Santana had listened, his arms tightening around her, holding her close, and then he, like every man she'd come into contact with lately, had offered his own thoughts. "Let him grow up, Regan. Quit fighting the inevitable. For Christ's sake, Jeremy's nearly a man."

"Haven't you heard? Twenty's the new twelve."

"Only from overprotective, control-freak mothers."

"Nice," she said, trying to roll away. Santana, damn him, had chuckled, pulled her close, and kissed her. With his hands caressing her body, she'd let the argument drop and concentrated on the tingles he'd elicited with his warm, wet tongue on her skin.

Now, though, she was pissed. It was just so much like a man to use sex to end an argument.

Oh, and you haven't done that too? Along with taking a can of Diet Coke or Pepsi now and again? Face it, Pescoli, you're no saint.

Self-doubts assailed her as she walked into her office. For the first time in a long while, she wondered if, as a mother, she was more a hindrance rather than a help. What she did know was that having Jeremy working and doing something, *anything* was positive. However, having him work in her space wasn't all that great. She just couldn't afford not to have full concentration on her job; her focus had to be razor sharp so that she could find Judge Samuels-Piquard's killer and Grayson's assailant.

Time was going by and being distracted by her son's presence wasn't conducive to keeping her attention razor sharp, but she couldn't see what she could do about it.

"So you're okay?" Hattie asked, her Bluetooth microphone and receiver strapped to her ear as she drove into the heart of Grizzly Falls. She'd finally caught up with her sister. With the girls in the backseat of her Toyota, she was headed to Wild Wills, a restaurant situated in the lower level of the town, the older section built on the banks of the Grizzly River.

"I'm fine. We're all fine," Cara replied from the other end of the wireless connection. "I don't know what the big deal is, why everyone is so concerned. Dan and I have been divorced, like forever. I know that sounds so cold and heartless, and that's not how I feel."

Hattie wondered but didn't say it as she drove down the steep slope of Boxer Bluff.

"Of course I'm worried sick about him," Cara said. "And I feel awful, just awful that someone took a shot at him."

Not just "took a shot." Whoever it was actually hit and wounded him. Big time. Hattie slowed for the railroad tracks at the bottom of the hill, waiting for the empty flatbed truck in front of her to roll under the open arm of the gate.

"And now someone's killed that judge, which is frightening," Cara added with a little shiver.

"First Dan and then Judge Samuels-Piquard," Hattie murmured.

"You think it's the same killer?"

"I don't know," Hattie said, but had been troubled ever since she'd heard the news on the television earlier in the day. "It's a pretty big coincidence if it's not, considering the timing." The assassination of the judge, so like the attack on Dan, was causing her to rethink her position that whoever had shot the sheriff had previously killed Bart. Was it possible that her ex-husband, depressed over their divorce and life in general, really had hanged himself? All these years she'd convinced herself someone had actually killed him and staged the scene to appear as if he'd taken his own life, and with the attempt on Dan's life, it had felt like a replay.

But now, she wasn't certain of anything.

"I don't understand why everyone is calling me," Cara was saying as McKenzie, from the advantage of her booster seat, spied a mother holding the door open for her son who was carrying a double-dip cone from the ice-cream parlor situated less than a block from the railroad tracks. She began pointing frantically, her finger tapping against the glass. "Can we get ice cream? Mommy, please?"

"Please, please, please!" Mallory chimed in.

"Today? It's freezing outside," Hattie said automatically, which wasn't a lie, and the clouds rolling over the mountains were threatening snow.

"But I want ice cream," McKenzie argued.

"After dinner, maybe," Hattie said, then added, "Shh, girls! I'm on the phone with your aunt." To Cara, she said, "I'm sorry, minor distraction here. You were saying?"

"Just that the police showed up here and started asking me and Nolan all kinds of questions. Like I would know anything about Dan's life these days. It was just so weird, and even Alli was pulled into the interview." Cara sounded distraught. "Thank God the boys weren't around."

The boys, Hattie knew, were Nolan's sons from his first marriage. "They're in town?"

"This year. Judith had them at Thanksgiving," she said, the last phrase with just a trace of a sneer in her voice. It was no secret that Cara and Nolan's ex had never gotten along, probably due to the fact that Cara was involved with Nolan long before he and Judith had divorced. "And if you ask me, it's all kind of moot anyway. Ezekiel's twenty-two and Isaiah is only a couple of years younger. They only show up to appease Nolan. They'd much rather be snowboarding or drinking or God-only-knows what." Cara's relationship with her stepsons had always been rocky; partially because of Judith's hatred of her ex's second wife and partially because Cara had always treated them as if the "step" was more important than the "son" in her relationship with her husband's boys. "So," she said, more than ready to change the topic, "how's Mom?"

"Good, I guess. Still wanting to run my life and still sneaking cigarettes."

"While she's being treated for cancer?" Cara's tone was disbelieving. "She's nuts. Does her doctor know?"

"What do you think?" She slowed for a light and waited as a woman crossing the street stopped dead center to check her cell phone. "She doesn't know that I know."

"Have you called her on it?" Cara accused.

"Oh, yeah. A couple of times. But she denies it, and since she doesn't light up in front of my face, she thinks she's pulling a fast one. As she says, repeatedly, it's her life."

"I know how hard it is to quit, but it *is* possible." She sighed loudly. "I suppose I should call her."

Hattie could envision her half sister gnawing at her lip in indecision. The light changed and the driver of a pickup heading the opposite direction honked, causing the woman in the crosswalk to visibly start and scurry for the curb.

Hattie eased through the intersection and started searching for somewhere to park. Downtown was clogged today, traffic stalling near the brick courthouse where a gigantic tree still festooned in holiday lights rose over the small patch of grass on which it had been planted over a century earlier.

Cara, earlier reticent to talk, was now on a roll. "With Mom it's just so damned complicated."

"Yeah, I know," Hattie agreed. Then feeling closer to her half sister than she had in years, suggested, "Why don't you come over to the house soon? Maybe before New Year's sometime? The girls would love to see you. Bring Alli and Nolan and the boys."

"Oh, God . . . no! I mean, maybe just me and okay, Alli, if I can pry her away from her phone, but trust me, Isaiah and Ezekiel wouldn't be interested. They're barely ever at the house as it is, only here now because of winter break. As I said earlier, they're far from being "boys." And Nolan's *always* busy, like twenty-four/seven busy."

Hattie got really lucky. Despite the throng of people who were bustling along the sidewalks where shops boasting after-Christmas sales were doing a banner business and cars were jamming up the side streets, a parking spot was actually opening up. *There is a God!* Hattie turned on her blinker and waited as an elderly woman at the wheel of an older Buick the size of Manhattan backed up slowly. "Okay, then it'll be just us girls."

"Yeah . . ." Cara didn't sound very convincing. "I, uh, have gifts I didn't get over before Christmas for Mallory and McKenzie. Just let me check with Nolan and look over the calendar, okay?"

"Anytime would be great. Let me know." Finally, the big boat of a car lumbered off and she hit the gas to zip into the oversized space.

"You know," Cara admitted, "I've thought about going and seeing Dan, but . . . he's in intensive care and I don't think he ever really forgave me for Nolan and . . . since we're divorced . . . I mean, I'm not even his most recent wife. Has Akina seen him? Wait. Stop. Sorry. What she does isn't the issue, is it?" Again a long-suffering sigh as Hattie slid her Camry into Park. "I suppose you've seen him."

"Yes."

"Is he going to pull through?"

"I hope so. You'll have to ask his doctors."

"They won't tell me anything," Cara complained. "With you it's different. You've always had the real connection to the family, to Dan or Bart or Cade or whomever," she said with enough irony to make Hattie cringe a little. "I don't know what you find so fascinating about that family, but . . . oh, well. Look, I'm not going to call the hospital. You can just update me, okay? Hey, I've got to go; Alli's calling me on the other line."

Before Hattie could say "good-bye," her sister had ended the call.

"Great," she said to the empty airspace as she yanked off her headset and cut the engine. The girls were already working their seat belts to get out of their booster seats, which as Mallory had mentioned time and time again, they were nearly too big for. "Becky Davis doesn't have to sit in one," she'd argued just this afternoon when Hattie had insisted the girls climb into the boosters.

"Becky Davis sits in the seat without a booster," Mallory had complained.

"She must be older than you."

"Nuh-uh, she's in our grade," Mallory had said as she'd reluctantly plopped into the dreaded booster seat. For once McKenzie had been nodding in complete agreement with her twin. "And Stacy Kendall and Lena, they don't have to either."

"Or Charlie or Robert," McKenzie chimed in.

"Well, they don't live with me and until you're eighty pounds *and* Dr. Lambert says it's okay, you'll use them."

"It's not fair," Mallory pouted, her lower lip protruding as she crossed her arms over her chest.

"You know, that's right: life isn't fair," Hattie declared as they'd each reluctantly strapped in. "But for now, this is the law. Mine. And the state of Montana's, so it's no use arguing."

"I hate booster seats!" Mallory declared and McKenzie echoed the sentiment.

"I know. Oh, do I know," Hattie said.

Mallory had maintained her bad mood for the entire ride while McKenzie, after pointing out which classmates had escaped their booster seat regulations, had seemed to forget the discussion and looked out the window and drawn on the condensation collecting on the glass.

Now, they were unbuckling their restraints and scrambling to get out of the car. The girls loved going to Wild Wills, not for the food, which they both assured her was far less appetizing than the menu at McDonald's, but because of the decorations.

"I'm gonna see Grizz first," McKenzie claimed, mentioning the gigantic stuffed grizzly bear that stood near the door of the restaurant and was always dressed for the season. She took off, pink cowboy boots flashing, unzipped coat billowing like a cape, dark curls bouncing as she ran down the snowy sidewalk. Like a shot, she was gone, swallowed up by the crowd.

"Hey! Wait!" Grabbing Mallory's hand, Hattie, the strap of her purse slung over her shoulder, ran to keep up with her daughter. "Slow down! We hold hands at the street! Remember? McKenzie!" Attempting not to panic, cutting through pedestrians wrapped in their winter coats, she was running, dragging Mallory, worried that McKenzie, in her need to always be "the first," would forget the rules and barrel headlong into the street where traffic was bottlenecked, but still moving, still dangerous. "McKenzie Grayson! Stop right there!"

McKenzie looked over her shoulder. Damn it, she knew better! And really, she probably wouldn't run into the street, but she could slip and fall, and the whole idea of her running off was a worry.

Hattie nearly tripped over the leash of a fortyish woman walking a greyhound who was currently straining to sniff the base of a lamppost.

"Watch out!" the woman snapped, her nose red with the cold, her eyes accusing behind fogging glasses.

Hattie ignored the warning and kept running through the throng. "McKenzie!"

She'd just about reached her, when McKenzie, realizing she was getting near the crosswalk, tried to slow down and slipped, her boots sliding over a thin patch of ice.

Down she went, legs flying, hair whipping around her face, skidding toward the street where snow and slush were piled and dirty vehicles rolled past, their tires spraying water.

Hattie leaped forward just as a big, gloved hand grabbed hold of one of McKenzie's flailing arms. A half second later, she was pulled to her feet.

"Whoa there, cowgirl," Cade said to his niece as he hauled her into his arms and Hattie, still dragging Mallory, almost slammed into him.

"Thank God," she whispered as McKenzie, surprised to be rescued by her uncle, began to sob, probably more out of embarrassment than pain.

"Hey, it's all right," he said, more tenderly than Hattie would have ever expected. His jacket had seen better days, his jeans were faded, and he hadn't shaved since she'd last seen him, and still he exuded that sexy confidence she'd always found irritatingly attractive. And yet he seemed at ease holding his niece.

"Are you okay?" Hattie asked her daughter, fighting back the urge to scream at her. Her heart was tattooing with fear.

McKenzie sniffed and nodded as she blinked against tears, but she didn't break down. "My leg hurts."

"Bad?" Cade asked.

"Kinda. No . . . it's okay."

Where Mallory would have been screaming bloody murder, McKenzie, stoic like the Graysons, seemed to have a high threshold for pain.

"Will ice cream help?" Hattie asked.

She brightened immediately. "Yes!" Then, "I'm sorry, Mom."

"Okay, we'll go up to the ice-cream parlor, but it has to be after dinner and you can't just go running off like you're three years old again, okay?" Hattie said.

"I wasn't going to go into the street," she said, wiggling to the ground.

McKenzie was fearless and more than a little bullheaded. Though she seemed to be growing out of her impulsiveness, every once in a while she reverted, as she had today.

As the stoplight changed, the woman with the greyhound walked past. Her lips were pinched as if she'd just sucked on a lemon, and the look she sent Hattie was meant to remind her that she'd lost control, bothered the woman and her dog, and quite possibly was a horrid excuse for a mother.

So what else was new?

Hattie chose to ignore her some more along with the other passersby who sent them curious looks.

"That was stupid!" Mallory announced.

"It wasn't stupid," Hattie disagreed. "It was . . . rash."

"Stupid." Mallory lifted her little chin up a notch and confided in her uncle, "She knows better."

Cade barked out a laugh. "Well, if she didn't before, I'd bet she does now." He winked at McKenzie, who, now embarrassed, turned away.

"I want to see Grizz!" she insisted.

Mallory rolled her expressive eyes. "Oh, brother."

"Maybe I want to see him, too," Cade said.

Hattie held up a hand. "You don't have to—"

"Do anything. I know. But I'm thinking I haven't seen how the big boy's been decked out this year."

Before she could protest, he took Mallory's hand and, when the light changed again, crossed the street with her in tow. McKenzie, still embarrassed and slightly petulant, held her mother's fingers and followed after.

By the time they'd wended through a few other pedestrians and had stepped on the sidewalk, McKenzie's mood had shifted back to her usual effervescence. "Come on!" she cried, pulling Hattie, obviously not wanting her twin to get to the bear first.

Too late. Cade held the door open and Mallory shot through, McKenzie three steps behind.

"Wow!" Mallory cried, clapping her hands at the sight. The massive grizzly bear, teeth exposed in a frightening snarl, stood tall on his hind legs. This year he was dressed in a long white nightshirt and cap, glasses perched upon his black nose. In one of his huge, out-stretched paws was a copy of *The Night Before Christmas,* his long claws visible beneath the opened pages. Behind the enormous bear, half hidden on fake stairs, a smaller bear was hiding.

"He's beautiful," McKenzie whispered.

"Beautiful?" Cade cast a glance in Hattie's direction and their eyes locked for a heartbeat. In that split second, she was reminded of happier times.

Before the lies.

Before her marriage.

Before the accusations.

Before Bart had died.

She swallowed hard and looked away. Those were times she'd be better off forgetting.

"I don't know if *beautiful* is the word I'd use," Cade said, eyeing the bear again. "Comical maybe, still kind of scary, but beautiful? Sorry, cowgirl, that's a stretch."

"You're being silly, Uncle Cade," McKenzie said.

"Or worse," he agreed, and again he hazarded a look Hattie's way.

The silence stretched between them, awkward and embarrassing. A bit softly, she said, "The girls and I are having an early dinner here and, as you heard, ice cream later. If you want to join us, you're certainly welcome."

"Yessss!" Mallory said enthusiastically.

"Sorry, princess." He shook his head. "I can't. Not today. I've got to see your Uncle Dan at the hospital." Then to Hattie, "The sheriff's department is holding a press conference tonight. I want to be there." He leaned down to Mallory's level and said, "So I'll have to take a rain check on dinner."

"What's a rain check?" She skewered him with her suspicious gaze.

"It just means that Uncle Cade will have dinner with us another time," Hattie explained, though she realized she was probably lying.

"No!" McKenzie protested.

As was her most recent custom, Mallory, again, crossed her arms over her chest in defiance. "When?" Mallory asked. "When is he coming over to dinner?"

Hattie shrugged. "Up to him."

"Soon," Cade promised and was already backing toward the door. "You girls"—he waggled a gloved finger at his two nieces—"don't you give your mother any trouble. Okay?"

" 'Kay," McKenzie agreed, but Mallory didn't acquiesce. She'd heard empty promises before and recognized this one for what it was.

"He's never coming over," she complained as Hattie herded her daughters past the board listing the day's specials. They walked into a cavernous dining area filled with tables and booths. Mounted high overhead, above the wagon-wheel chandeliers, were stuffed heads of animals indigenous to the region. As Mallory climbed into a booth beneath the glassy eyes of a bighorn sheep, she said, "Uncle Cade's a big liar."

If you only knew, Hattie thought, sliding onto the bench across the table from both girls. *But then no one's a bigger liar than I am. No one.*

CHAPTER 17

The judge's house had been built over a hundred years earlier. Constructed high on a hill overlooking the Grizzly River, the two-storied Victorian sat across a broad avenue from the park. Though the official street name was Hillside, the locals referred to these eight blocks across from the park as "King's Row." With a view of the falls, the judge's manor, like all of the other homes along King's Row, was decorated with strings of clear Christmas lights, some of which were already aglow as twilight had settled in.

The house was two-toned, its upper story a darker green, typical, Pescoli thought, of the era in which it was constructed. Just like the other homes facing the park. The wide porch led to a pair of double doors that were inset with oval windows and crowned by a small balcony above. A plaque mounted near the door told them this was a historic residence, built in 1916 by John Adams Thompson, one of the founding fathers of the town.

The house was locked tight, of course, but Pescoli entered using a key from the ring they'd found in the Lexus parked in the judge's cabin's garage.

Inside, the Victorian was as neat as the cabin had been, though the house in town was more cluttered, holding a lifetime of para-phernalia and memories.

Through an archway was what had once been a parlor and now was a den, the old tiled fireplace the focal point in the room, a stack of kindling and logs in a carrier on the hearth. A writing table was pushed beneath the windows, and a small television was hidden among the books lining shelves built to the ceiling. She could see everything from atlases and tomes on the law, to paperbacks with broken backs and dog-eared pages.

And yet there was a feeling that this room hadn't been used in a long while, that the lingering scent of old fires and forgotten cigars was little more than a memory.

"Her husband's den," Alvarez said as she walked to a back wall where pictures of a dark-haired man in uniform was prominently displayed among artifacts of wars throughout the ages, everything from crossed swords mounted near the ceiling to medals pinned to velvet and kept under glass at eye level. George Piquard, his name originally Georges, according to his dog tags, which, along with his medals, were on display.

Pescoli said, "Like a shrine."

Alvarez was already walking through the rest of the house, where an artificial Christmas tree, its lights connected to a timer and shining brightly, stood in the living room, unopened packages spread around its base. Antique chairs and a leather couch with an oversized ottoman were positioned around an ornate marble fireplace edged with decorative tile and currently covered with a hood as it wasn't in use.

Tiffany lamps were interspersed with more modern pieces, and holiday candles and bowls of colorful glass balls reminded them that, for the owner of this home, Christmas was far from over. Pescoli felt a jab of sadness as she looked at the packages with their big bows and surprises tucked inside. Yes, Kathryn Samuels-Piquard had been a hard-nosed judge who took it as her personal mission to mete out justice, but she was a person, too, a woman with friends and family.

"You okay?" Alvarez asked.

"Fine." She walked up the stairs to the bedrooms and cursed her newfound sensitivity. She hadn't even liked the judge and now she was getting all maudlin. The attack on Grayson had really laid her low, but she needed to be tough and strong. It didn't help that Santana had delivered her an ultimatum, or that Bianca was starving herself, or that Jeremy wanted to be a cop. No wonder she was stressed and having nightmares that set her hair on end. In some ways, it was a wonder she was functioning at all.

She looked around the first bedroom, then stepped back into the hall and called down the open stairs, "Found another computer. Desktop." Then she stepped back into the room and to the walk-in closet where the judge's clothes were pressed and hung, similar colors kept together. Neat and tidy, just like the rest of the house.

She looked through three other bedrooms, then met Alvarez downstairs in the kitchen.

"Anything interesting?"

"Just this calendar," she said. "I would have thought the judge with all her electronics would have a virtual calendar, you know, hooked up to all her devices."

"Me too."

"Then why have this?" she asked, pointing to a slick, printed calendar hanging on the wall near her phone. "See, there're even entries on it." She indicated the fifteenth of the month, where a time and the name of a local dentist had been scratched.

"The only entry."

Alvarez rifled through the pages. "Uh-huh."

"Maybe she's old school. Keeps this from habit," Pescoli said.

"Should be more dates filled in. Kathryn Samuels-Piquard was one busy lady."

"Maybe she hadn't gotten to it yet, hadn't transferred anything from her electronic one . . . or maybe she happened to call the dentist from this phone, or took the call if it was a reminder for her appointment, and her phone or electronic notepad wasn't handy, so she jotted the info down here."

"So, where's this year's calendar? The year isn't over yet and this one starts January first," Alvarez said.

"Which is almost here."

"Could be she cleaned house before she left and filed it away or pitched it. She's pretty neat."

"Anal," Pescoli agreed, carefully opening a drawer and seeing each piece of flatware nestled tightly into its mates—forks separated from salad forks, soup spoons in a different slot than teaspoons. She pulled open the door to the pantry with a gloved finger and saw all of the cans and boxes were kept together by brand in tidy rows. Next the refrigerator, where there was no food aside from half-empty bottles of salad dressing and mayonnaise. The glass shelves and white drawers were gleaming under the glare of the refrigerator's bulb.

"It's not anal, it's organized. Not everyone is a slob, you know," Alvarez pointed out. "This is how I keep my kitchen."

Pescoli made a sound in her throat and thought of her own crammed pantry, her jammed closet with clothes she hadn't worn or thrown out in years. Part of it was because of lack of time, and the other part was because she just didn't care. "Are your clothes hung according to color?"

"Type of clothing, like pants or shirts, then color, then style."

"Jesus."

"Hey. It's not that unusual. Come on, you've poked your nose in more than your share of closets. A lot of them were very organized."

"Okay, fine."

"So why throw a calendar out prematurely? An organized person wouldn't."

"Let's find the damned thing, if we can." Pescoli didn't think the missing pages of the last year were a big deal, but she also didn't like anything that seemed the least bit out of the ordinary. "If this was her routine, and the year isn't over yet, and she was planning to return before the thirty-first, it should be around."

"The garbage was probably picked up right before Christmas. If she threw it out . . ."

"Wait a sec." Pescoli walked into the den again and knelt near the hearth where black, flaky ashes were visible in the firebox.

"What?" Alvarez asked, following.

"See those dark ashes in the grate?" Pescoli said, pointing toward the charred interior. "Would the judge leave ashes in the grate? Considering how neat she was, how spotless the rest of the house is kept, almost as if it was thoroughly cleaned before she left."

"Nope." Alvarez came over to her.

"I'll bet that she rarely builds a fire here in her husband's shrine. No way would she leave this fireplace with ashes in it." Pescoli slid the screen open. "And those are not ashes from firewood, those big black flakes are paper."

"The calendar?"

"Possibly. Or her will. Or maybe just a piece of paper with ID and account numbers she didn't want to recycle, but still . . . there's a shredder in her office."

"Maybe the lab can find something."

Pescoli rocked back on her heels. "Whoever made this fire might have been in a hurry; didn't want to bother with taking the hood off the grate in the living room but wanted to make sure whatever it was got destroyed." Her eyes narrowed as she thought, imagining the scene.

"So what was it?"

"If it was the calendar, then what did the killer want permanently erased?"

"A particular date with someone?"

"A lover?" Pescoli posed. "And his name was on the calendar? But if she wanted to hide it, that's not too smart and the judge was pretty damned sharp."

"Maybe she didn't want to hide it, but he did."

"Someone who didn't want their relationship known because . . . he was married maybe? Or involved with someone else too?"

Alvarez shrugged. "Or maybe it was someone who didn't want any association with the judge for political reasons."

Pescoli eyed the medals on the wall, the military award, and collection of weapons on display. "Or maybe we're barking up the wrong tree entirely and someone just burned some trash."

"We'll have the lab check the ashes. Let's talk to the person who cleans the house, find out if the fireplace was ever used." Alvarez looked closely around the room. "I'm just guessing here, but I don't think the judge mopped her own floors or polished her own silver."

"Right. Maybe the maid knows something." They started walking toward the front door when Alvarez's phone rang. "Unknown number," she said, then answered, "Detective Selena Alvarez." There was a pause as the person on the other end of the line said something.

"I'm sorry, Mr. Douglas, but I can't discuss the case. There's going to be a press conference this evening at the sheriff's department, so you can . . . Yes, I understand, but I'm sure your editor will give you a little more time with the deadline . . . Nothing to say except 'the investigation is ongoing.'" She hung up.

"Our buddy Manny is at it again," Pescoli observed.

"You got it."

"Some reporters are okay, but not Douglas." She glanced through the oval window in one of the doors. "It's go time. The techs are here." Snow had begun drifting down lazily and night had fallen; all the street lamps were now giving off their watery illumination. Though Kathryn Samuels-Piquard's home didn't appear to be a crime scene, there was a chance the killer was someone the judge knew, someone who'd been in the house and left some evidence behind.

"And they've got company," Alvarez said.

A television news van with the letters KBTR emblazoned across its side had turned down the street and was slowing in front of the house. A thin layer of dirt from the slush on the road had dimmed the letters, but the words were still legible, the driver slowing as he located a parking spot.

As the lumbering vehicle stopped on the opposite side of the street, a reporter in a red jacket and black slacks and boots hopped onto the street. She couldn't have been an inch over five feet or a day over twenty-five.

"Honey Carlisle," Alvarez said, while Pescoli opened the door to admit the techs.

"You know her?" Pescoli couldn't place the face.

"Works out at my gym. Transferred here from a station in Salt Lake City. Was Miss Utah or something."

"You know this because it was out on the club bulletin?"

"My trainer, Jed. He's definitely got a thing for her."

"Which came first, her hair color or her name?"

"Shh." Alvarez hid a smile.

"Selena!" Honey yelled, waving a gloved hand enthusiastically, just as if she'd run into a long-lost friend.

"You're on a first-name basis?" Pescoli asked, her brows lifting.

"We're in a couple of the same kickboxing and step classes, and then sometimes after, meet up at the juice bar."

"Seriously? The juice bar?" Pescoli said as Honey began marching across the snow-covered lawn.

Alvarez ignored Pescoli's comments. "Stop!" she said sharply in the reporter's direction and held out both her hands. "Let's keep it in the street."

"Oh, okay." The reporter backtracked while Alvarez stepped off the porch to greet her.

"Is this a crime scene?" Honey's big, round eyes grew wider. "I thought the judge was killed in the mountains. Oh, my God, was there *another* murder?"

"No. we're just being careful. And respectful," Alvarez reminded.

"Okay. Sure. Um, I just need an interview for the ten o'clock news!" She flashed a radiant, Miss Utah-worthy smile Pescoli's way.

"You'll have to wait until after the press conference at the station," Alvarez told her repressively.

"Really?" She was suddenly deflated.

"That's what the undersheriff ordered."

"That would be Cort Brewster, right?"

"He's in charge temporarily," Pescoli put in as she stepped off the porch herself.

"Can you give me an update on Sheriff Grayson?" Honey asked Pescoli in her cheery voice.

"Again, you can ask all your questions of the public information officer this evening," Alvarez put in firmly before Pescoli could respond.

Honey wasn't about to be denied. "You aren't going to tell me anything? Like, how the judge was killed?"

Alvarez shook her head.

"Were the two attacks, one on the sheriff and then the judge, linked?"

Alvarez didn't budge. "You can ask the public information officer."

Honey glanced at Pescoli, who stared back. She must've seen the don't-even-think-about-it censure in her eyes because she finally gave up and said, "Okay, Ralph," to a hefty guy hauling a camera on his shoulders. "Let's take some exteriors. House and grounds. I'll give a short report and we'll edit it in with footage from the conference."

She was clearly disappointed but went about her business, standing in front of the house, talking into a microphone with snow falling all around her.

Pescoli and Alvarez talked to some of the members of the crime scene unit and then, once the news van was gone and the techs were packing it in, they headed out toward their vehicle. Just as they reached the street, a woman, dressed in a long black coat, hurried out of the house two doors down. Tall and wasp-thin, she was holding a broad-brimmed hat to her head as she walked swiftly through the swirling snow toward them.

"I'm Claudia Dubois, I live two doors down, right over there." She pointed a long finger at the Georgian house from which she'd just appeared. Built of brick, with evenly spaced windows and pillars supporting a small front porch, it was more elaborately lit than the judge's.

Pescoli and Alvarez had barely introduced themselves when she broke in, "I can't tell you how devastated Barry and I are! That's *Doctor* Baron Dubois. We *adored* Kathryn, and spent so much time with her and her family while the kids were growing up. While George was alive, we would play cards or go to movies. Oh, my. Then things changed, of course. Kathryn moved on. Dabbled at dating."

"Was she seeing anyone?"

"Now? Oh, Lord, I don't know. She was always tight-lipped about that sort of thing." She was on a roll and wasn't about to be sidetracked. "Winston, well, he always was an odd child, very withdrawn, and now he's married to that awful woman. Kathryn didn't like Cecilia much, let me tell you, but I guess it doesn't matter now." She blinked rapidly, her lashes thick with mascara, her gray eyes shadowed. "It's just such a shame!" Her hat threatened to blow off again and she clamped it down with a bony hand.

"What about her maid? She had one?" Alvarez asked.

"Donna? Oh, yes. Lovely girl."

Pescoli asked, "Does Donna live around here?"

Claudia, still holding tight to her hat, shrugged as if it didn't matter. Her lips pursed and she declared, "I hope you catch that pervert!"

"What pervert?" Alvarez asked.

"The one who's been stalking her. Or, us. I'm telling you it's unnerving."

"Who is he?" Alvarez demanded.

"Well, I don't know his name or I would tell you," she said, a little ticked. "We've seen him, in the park. He seems to be casing the houses. Ours. Kathryn's. The Millers." She indicated a tall house with a turret that stood between her house and the judge's. It was dark aside from the Christmas lights. "The Millers, they're still out of town. Skiing in Utah. Been gone since before Christmas." Her hand went to her mouth. "I bet Velma doesn't even know about Kathryn unless she saw it on the news . . . oh, my." She was clearly worried sick. "But the man who was watching our houses . . . he obviously keyed in on Kathryn's place."

"This man. The stalker. You think he's dangerous, that he could be the one who killed her?" Pescoli asked, making a note to check with the Millers as well as the other people on the block.

"I'm saying it's a strong possibility." She craned her head to look over her shoulder and across the street to the park.

Pescoli asked, "Did he ever talk to the judge, accost her?"

"No . . . not that she said to me." Claudia faced them once more.

"Did he ever approach anyone that you know of?" Alvarez asked.

"No, no . . ." She bit the corner of her lip. "It was just . . . well, he acted so strange."

Alvarez suggested, "You mean, maybe he's mentally unbalanced?"

"Well, obviously!"

"Did you ever see him with anyone?" Pescoli asked.

"He was *always* alone. Under the tree. Always under that tall fir. Always staring." She shivered visibly. "I told Kathryn he was dangerous, but she didn't pay him any mind."

Pescoli looked across the street to the park with its dozens of trees and street lamps to the very tree the woman was indicating. Her heart stilled and the dream she'd had the night before reawakened. She imagined the assailant, dressed in white, standing beneath the branches and even now, there was a little girl walking near the tree, her mother pushing a stroller nearby.

So much like the images she'd seen in her mind that a cold finger seemed to slide down her spine.

"Pescoli?" Alvarez asked and she snapped to.

To Claudia, she asked, "When was the last time you saw him?"

The thin woman thought hard. "Oh, when was it? Last week, I think, before Christmas, maybe around the twenty-first or twenty-second . . . sometimes my memory isn't . . . oh, that's right!" She snapped her gloved fingers. "It was the twentieth. I remember because he was standing there as I was backing up, taking some of my pumpkin bars to the church for the evening Bible study classes. But that *person,* whoever he is, was there again. Beneath the tree as always. It's right on the jogging trail and I believe he chose that spot because it would be easy to grab anyone who passed by!"

"But you said he was focused on the judge."

"Her house. The Millers' and ours, yes! But there's no telling what he'll do. He's dangerous, I know it and now . . . oh, dear, poor Kathryn."

"What time of day did you see him?" Pescoli asked.

"Always in the evening or late at night," Claudia said hurriedly. "I've never once seen him in the mornings or early afternoons. No, no, always in the dark." She was nodding, agreeing with herself, her hand still keeping her hat in place. "And I went to drop off the cookies after five, I think, and this time of year the night comes so early."

Alvarez cast Pescoli a look, then asked, "Can you describe him?"

"Tall, fit—maybe, hard to tell. Always wearing ski gear, heavy down jacket, y'know, bulky. Camouflage white for winter, like hunters wear."

White. Like the dream.

"The hood has a bill, so his eyes are always shaded. I'm telling you it's downright spooky, takes all the fun out of Christmas." Once more, Claudia hazarded a quick glance to the park where a solitary jogger wended his way along a snowy path.

"Did you ever see him in or near a vehicle?" Alvarez asked.

"Oh, no." She stared at them as if they'd asked if the man she'd seen was from Jupiter.

"Does he carry a weapon?" Pescoli asked, thinking of her dream and the assault weapon she'd envisioned on her assailant's back.

"Of course he does!"

Pescoli focused on her. "What kind of weapon?"

"Well, how would I know? I haven't actually *seen* a gun or a knife, but he's always facing the street, observing our houses." She laughed a little. "How could I possibly know what he's got in his pockets?"

"So, you're just assuming," Alvarez clarified.

"It's not that big of a leap. This *is* Montana, you know."

Weirder and weirder, Pescoli thought. And yet . . . "Would you mind working with a police artist?" she asked, even though she was starting to question the woman's credibility. Something about all the information she was spewing seemed off, though it was so like last night's nightmare that it was spooky and Pescoli couldn't just write it off.

Coincidence.

Nothing more.

"I'd love to!" Claudia cried. She visibly brightened at the thought of actually helping, or perhaps it was just because someone in authority was taking her seriously. "You want me to come down to the police station?"

"The sheriff's office," Pescoli clarified.

"Perfect!" She was suddenly thrilled, as if she'd just accomplished an impossible feat. Her grief and dismay at her friend's death were, apparently, forgotten, at least for the moment. "I'll bring Barry too. He's just so smart. A doctor, you know. He might be able to add something!"

"Your husband saw the stalker?" Pescoli asked.

"Oh, no. Never." Her lips pursed almost in distaste. "It's the oddest thing. Whenever I noticed the stalker in the park, I'd call the doctor over, but wouldn't you know, every time Barry got to the window, he'd be gone." Her eyes narrowed suspiciously. "It was as if that stalker knew I was watching and decided to vanish. Poof!" She threw her hands into the air and her hat, caught on a breeze, went sailing. "Drat!" With surprising speed, she took off after the hat and managed to catch it against a pile of slush near the curb.

"Something's not right," Alvarez said as they followed her. "This is all too bizarre and convenient."

"You got that right." Pescoli decided not to mention the dream. At least not yet. Alvarez was even more of a realist than she was. "Let's see what *Doctor* Dubois has to say."

"If he's home," Alvarez said.

"And *if* he really exists."

Walking rapidly, Pescoli and Alvarez caught up with Claudia and walked her back to her house, where her husband, wearing sweatpants and a Texas A&M sweatshirt, was just opening the door.

Score one for the truth.

"Claudia?" he said worriedly, as round as she was thin, the reverse of Jack Sprat and his fabled wife.

"I saw these police officers over at Kathryn's and thought I should explain about the man who's been stalking us."

"Honey," he said softly, his bushy gray eyebrows drawing downward over the tops of horn-rimmed glasses. "You know there's no one there. We've been over this." Then he turned his attention to the detectives. "I'm sorry," he said, and there was a guarded sadness in his eyes. "I'm afraid Claudia has . . . an active imagination, and all this sorry business about Kathryn has made things worse."

"But I saw him, Barry! You know I did. I told you!"

"May we come in?" Pescoli asked. The man stepped aside so that they could enter a wide foyer lit by an ornate chandelier.

As he closed the door behind them, he said to his wife, "It's freezing out there, dear. I'm sure the detectives could use something to warm them up. Maybe we could rustle up some tea or coffee for the officers?"

"My goodness!" she exclaimed, tossing her hat over the hook of a coatrack positioned near the door. "Where the devil are my manners?" She unbuttoned her coat and with it billowing behind her said, "Coming right up!" as she bustled off toward what presumably was the kitchen.

Once she was out of earshot, her husband said, "I don't know what my wife told you, but ninety percent of it is fabrication." His forehead wrinkled. "I'm afraid she hallucinates and sometimes can't distinguish what is real from what is not."

"There is no stalker in the park?"

"Oh, there could be, I suppose, but as for an athletic-looking man in some kind of white camouflage gear?" His eyebrows lifted over his glasses. "I've yet to see him."

Alvarez and Pescoli exchanged glances.

Back to square one.

CHAPTER 18

Cade didn't need to be thinking about Hattie.

Not tonight.

Not ever.

But there she was big as life, playing dangerous games in his mind as he drove through the snow to the hospital in Missoula. Lately, it seemed, everywhere he turned, she was there with her tangle of hair, mischievous eyes, and quick smile that, when her lips parted, showed off not-quite-perfect teeth.

He was a fool, he thought, taking his foot off the accelerator as he was coming up much too quickly on the tail of a Chevy Suburban whose driver had decided to creep fifteen miles under the speed limit with the snow. Easing behind it, he considered his chance meeting with Hattie in town, the way that little McKenzie had been barreling down the sidewalk and how frantic Hattie had been for her daughter's safety.

No matter what else he might think of her, Hattie was a damned good mother; he wouldn't argue that.

But that's where it ended.

The Chevy turned off at the next light, taillights fading, and he was able to pick up speed again, his wipers slapping away the dry flakes as they tumbled from the sky. Traffic was thick, the glare of headlights steady as he tried, and failed, to forget about his sister-in-law. *Ex*-sister-in-law, he reminded himself. Seeing her again had kicked all the old memories back through his brain.

The turn lane for Northern General appeared, and he flipped on his signal and eased over. Ever since she'd married Bart, he'd tried like hell not to let her get to him. Not to remember how it had been with her.

Of course, it hadn't worked, and though over the years he'd forced himself to keep his distance, these past few days it had proved impossible.

Even now his favorite radio station was playing a song from that summer when they'd had their fling.

"Shitfire," he muttered and snapped the damned thing off. He'd tried to get her out of his blood, oh, hell yeah. Not only had he made a conscious effort to avoid her over the years, he'd also been with more than his share of women since the last time they'd been together, nearly a decade ago. However, none of those one-night stands and short relationships had cut into his soul the way she had. He'd told himself it was because she was off-limits, forbidden fruit, so to speak, and that the very notion of her being taboo had ignited that rebellious in-your-face attitude that had cursed him since the day he was born.

Or maybe it's something deeper.

He yanked his keys from the ignition and cut the engine. He didn't believe in soul-deep love and all that other for-the-movies crap that Hollywood fed the American public, and he wasn't going to start now. Jamming his keys into the pocket of his jacket, he climbed out of his truck and started jogging toward the wide doors of the hospital. He was a fool, there was just no two ways about it, and he'd be damned if he'd fall for Hattie all over again.

Striding through the vestibule, he remembered he'd argued with her right between these glass doors. She seemed to think it was *her* mission to see to Dan. As she'd seen to Bart. As she'd seen to him, for Christ's sakes! That was the trouble with Hattie, she couldn't leave the Grayson men alone.

Just like you can't seem to leave her alone.

His mind taunted him as he crossed the reception area.

Just before she married Bart, remember? You knew she was engaged, but you couldn't leave it alone. And no doubt Bart figured it

out or she told him. Doesn't matter how it happened, but he knew,
Cade. Your brother knew you were sleeping with his fiancée just
weeks before she finally broke it off.

If she hadn't, you'd probably still be trying to get her into your
bed. No wonder Bart was depressed. No wonder he decided to
climb that ladder and toss a rope over the cross timbers of the barn.

It served you right to find him there.

He didn't believe for a minute that he was to blame for his brother's
death, but he knew he wasn't completely innocent. Nor was Hattie.

His jaw so tight it ached, Cade pounded on the elevator keypad
and strode inside as the doors opened.

He wasn't alone. The car was already occupied with a beleaguered-
looking couple and their children. A boy of five or six was holding a
smiley-face balloon that said, "Get well," and a girl who was a couple
of years older was balancing a tray of homemade cookies that looked
leftover from Christmas, judging from the shapes and colors.

"Can we just go home?" the little boy, tugging on his mother's
coat, asked.

"Not yet, Andy. First we have to visit Grandpa."

"But I don't like it here," the kid complained petulantly as he
leaned against the back of the car and did his best to look miserable.
"I hate the hospital!"

You and me both, Cade thought as the car stopped on his floor
and he strode off the elevator.

Winston Piquard didn't look a thing like his mother.

While she'd been big-boned and fair, with fiery red hair and sharp
blue eyes that missed nothing in her courtroom, he was dark, tall,
and thin, his eyes a deep brown, maybe accented with contact
lenses.

Her tongue had been razor sharp, her demeanor all business, and
no matter how much taller you were than she, Samuels-Piquard had
been able to somehow look down her nose at you. But this man, a junior accountant with a small firm in Missoula, Pescoli knew, was a little hunched, his demeanor defeated despite the fact that he was in
his early thirties. Then again, it hadn't been a good day for him.

Standing in the doorway of his house in his stockinged feet, he blocked Pescoli's entrance as well as any view inside. Wearing khakis, a pressed dress shirt, and down vest, he was more than a little perturbed to find the officers at his door.

"I already got the bad news," he said, after Pescoli and Alvarez had introduced themselves. He stood beneath the overhang of the porch where a Christmas tree, needles drying, one forgotten ornament winking between the branches, had already been propped outside against the house.

"We're sorry for your loss, Mr. Piquard," Alvarez said. "We don't want to intrude, but we do have some questions."

"I figured." A muscle worked at his temple. "I just don't know what I can tell you."

"You have no idea who could be behind this?"

"It could be anyone, couldn't it? She didn't make a lot of friends on the bench." He ran both his hands through his close-cropped hair. "I told her to retire. But did she listen? She never listens . . . listened to anyone. Man, I just can't believe . . ." His voice trailed off and for a second, he looked at the step, down at his feet, shaking his head as he remembered something. "She didn't have to work, you know. She was set, but . . ." He lifted his shoulders and glared down at the welcome mat. "She loved it." When he glanced up again, his eyes shone. Clearing his throat, he added, "I'm sorry. We've . . . My wife and I have been worried sick ever since she didn't come back to town or return our calls." He closed his eyes for a second, gathering himself.

"If we could come in," Alvarez suggested when he seemed to have pulled himself together. "It won't take too long."

He was shifting from one foot to the other. "I don't know. My wife is pregnant and . . ."

"We just want to find whoever did this to your mother and put him away forever," Pescoli told him.

"Yeah, I know." He glanced over his shoulder to the door that was still cracked just a bit, then nodded. "Okay. Fine. Sure, why not? My daughter's about to go down for the night so it would be a good time . . . oh, hell, Lily loves Mom. They used to . . ." Again his voice trailed off as he led them inside a cookie-cutter house that looked nearly identical to the others in the cul-de-sac. He closed the door behind them, then hesitated, and Pescoli saw him take a swipe at his eyes with the back of his hand.

Moving boxes in various sizes had been stacked in the hallway and den, and toys of every shape and color littered the living areas. The sharp aromas of garlic and tomato sauce caused Pescoli's stomach to rumble. How long had it been since she'd eaten? It seemed like forever. She stepped around a toddler's plastic ride-'em toy, an orange van with a seat that opened and created a small storage space.

"Excuse the mess," he said, "we're moving. Right after the first of the year, so everything's kind of crazy right now."

"Where are you moving?" Alvarez asked as they found their way to the kitchen where a pot of tomato sauce was cooling, pasta draining in a sieve in the sink. A toddler was seated in a high chair, busy finger-painting the tray with what was left of her spaghetti sauce. The rest, it seemed, was smeared across the lower half of her face.

"Across town, to Ranch Hills Estates." Pescoli had heard of it, a newer upscale neighborhood with large lots, views of the mountains, and golf course memberships included. "This is my daughter, Lily. Can you say 'Hi,' Lil?"

"Hi!" the little girl echoed excitedly, obviously glad for the distraction from her meal-cum-artwork. Her eyes were round and blue, her hair a tuft of light brown, and a handful of teeth were visible as her grin stretched wide.

"Cee-Cee?" Winston called toward a short hallway while Lily pounded on her tray. Seconds later a very pregnant woman carrying a laundry basket appeared. "This is Detective Pescoli and Detective Alvarez. They're here with some questions about Mom."

"Oh," she said somberly, dropping the basket onto a kitchen table already littered with empty boxes, tape dispenser, and marking pens. "Can you just give me a minute to change her and put her to bed?" she asked, then found a baby wipe and started cleaning her daughter's face and hands. "We're already running late with dinner. It's almost bedtime. For her, I mean."

"We can start with your husband," Alvarez suggested.

By the time Winston had unburied chairs in the living area and they were finally seated, the cries of "Mommy! Mommy! Oooouuut!" echoed down the hallway.

"Every night we go through this . . . it's normal." Then added, "About the only thing that is, lately."

A few minutes later, Cee-Cee reappeared.

"Sorry. Duty first," she said as she pushed a bag of toys out of the rocker and sat down wearily. "I think we'll just have to ignore her." She sent a look down the hall where the child's cries were already slowing down. "I'm sorry." She forced a smile, "I'm Cecilia. Cee-Cee. This is just so awful. I mean, I can't imagine anyone . . ." Clasping her hands together, she shuddered. "If only she hadn't gone to the cabin."

"If someone followed her up there to kill her, she wasn't safe here either," Winston said.

"I suppose." To Pescoli, she asked, "Do you have any idea who would do this to Kathy?"

"We're working on it," Pescoli told her, "And we're hoping you can help. You were all close, as a family?"

Cee-Cee was nodding. "Kathryn and I got off to a rocky start, I guess. Two strong women, you know, and I'm sure she didn't think anyone was good enough for her only boy." She threw Winston a smile.

"This is old news," he responded.

"It is," his wife agreed equably. "We were always civil and then Lily came along and Kathryn was just so good with her, so into the baby. Nothing was ever said, but from the minute Winston's mother laid eyes on the baby, all the hard feelings just evaporated."

"You agree?" Alvarez asked Winston.

He lifted a dismissive shoulder. "Yeah, I guess. I didn't see it happening so instantaneously, but Mom did seem to let go a little once Lily arrived."

Cee-Cee said, "This is just so horrid."

"What about boyfriends?" Alvarez asked.

Winston looked uncomfortable. "I think she may have dated, but we never met any of them." He thought for a second. "Since Dad died she never got involved seriously, as far as I know."

"No one recently?" Pescoli asked.

"I really couldn't tell you," Winston said stiffly. "My mother's personal life was just that: personal."

"Any other family problems?" Pescoli tried.

"No." Winston was firm.

Cee-Cee glanced across the room to her husband, who rather than sit in another side chair was standing in the archway to the foyer. "There's Vincent . . ."

Winston froze for just a second and Pescoli asked, "What do you mean?"

Cee-Cee went on when it was clear Winston wasn't going to respond, "Kathryn and her brother never got along. Vince never amounted to much. He's just one of those guys always looking for the big score. Bright enough, but never held a job for more than a year. Winston's dad loaned him some money and it pissed Kathryn off because he never paid it back."

"How much money?" Pescoli asked.

"Fifty thousand dollars."

Pescoli inwardly whistled while Winston muttered, "Damn it, Cee-Cee."

"Why would Georges loan his brother-in-law money if he was such a bad risk?" Alvarez asked.

"They were friends. Army buddies," Cee-Cee responded, awkwardly pushing herself to her feet and walking to a shelf where she pulled down a huge box.

"Wait!" Winston sprang to his feet, but Cee-Cee was already digging around inside the box. She pulled out a long package encased in bubble wrap.

"He gave this to Winston years ago, right, honey?" she asked Winston, exposing a long, military sword.

"When I graduated from high school," Winston acknowledged, his gaze shooting darts at his wife. "He and my dad both had one."

Pescoli looked at the sword, noticing the detail on the pommel, guard, and grip. There was some fine etching in the guard and the weapon seemed familiar.

Cee-Cee settled back into the rocker. "Now I have to keep it away from Lily."

"I'm going to mount it on the wall in the new house," he snapped. "Up high, above the foyer. It'll be fine."

Alvarez asked, "Where's Vincent now?"

"He has a place up on Spruce Creek, but I'm not sure he's there. We haven't heard from him in a couple years," Winston said.

"He's never even met Lily," Cee-Cee said with a sniff.

"Does he know Sheriff Grayson?" Alvarez asked.

Winston stared at his wife. "You and I both know Vincent isn't capable of killing anyone!"

"We're just trying to get a clear picture here and find out who killed your mother," Pescoli reminded him.

He opened his mouth, shut it, then on the brink of breaking down suddenly sniffed loudly and cleared his throat. "Yeah, I don't know who Vincent knows. Maybe he knew Grayson."

"Do you have Vincent's phone number?" Alvarez asked.

"A cell number that's maybe still good. We haven't heard from him since a card last Christmas . . . huh . . ." His skin paled. "He didn't send one this year." He dug into his pocket and retrieved his own cell phone, scrolled through the list, then gave Alvarez and Pescoli the number.

"It can't be Vincent."

"Why do you say that?" Alvarez asked.

He shook his head. Reaction seemed to be settling in and the sword in his hands began to wobble.

"Win!" Cee-Cee admonished and he snapped out of it, reaching for the bubble wrap to cover the blade once again.

"I was afraid of this, you know," he said.

"What?" Pescoli asked.

"That some nutcase she sentenced would take it out on her. That's what happened. It wasn't Vincent or any of her family or friends. It was somebody she put away."

"We're looking at everyone," Alvarez said.

"You think it's any nutcase in particular?" Pescoli asked him as he stuffed the sword back in its box, closed the lid, and put it back on the shelf.

"She's gotten threatening letters from a bunch of those jerk-wads and their families. One woman even came to Mom's door once, called her a bitch and all sorts of names. Mom just had her arrested and got a restraining order against her."

Pescoli asked, "Who was that?"

"Edie Gardener. She came over to Mom's house around Halloween, I think, maybe just after. Went on a real tirade. Mom shut the door, called the police, and got a restraining order, but it kinda freaked me out when she told me about it." He found a bare spot on a bench near the window, sat down, and clasped his hands between his knees. "This is just so . . . fucking unbelievable!"

"Win! Please. Language. We don't talk that way. Now that we have Lily—"

"Mom is dead, Cee-Cee," he snapped, his face suddenly flushing a deep, angry red, for the first time showing some of his mother's fire. "Today, I think I can talk any fucking way I want."

"But—" She was about to argue, then backed off, rubbing her protruding belly as she leaned back into her chair. "Fine, Winston. Fine." Still slightly ruffled, with her daughter still calling to her from a bedroom down the hallway, she turned to the detectives. "It's just such a stressful time for us right now."

Pescoli understood. "We'll try to make it as short and painless as possible. Anyone else beside Edie Gardener that you know threatened your mother?" she asked Winston.

Dan was the same.

Still in ICU.

Still in a coma.

Still under guard.

Still hooked up to machines, monitors, and tubes, his head bandaged.

Come on, brother, you can pull through this.

Cade stared down at the man he'd looked up to all of his life and willed him to get better.

He'd been here for nearly an hour, but if he'd hoped to see any small sign of improvement, he'd been disappointed. There was one more bed occupied now, a teenaged girl who, he'd heard, had been in a car accident that had taken the life of her boyfriend. She, too, was comatose, didn't even know yet that he was dead.

The place was depressing and Cade was struggling to be patient. When he'd first asked, and then demanded, answers of the nursing staff and a doctor who the nurse had called in, he'd found out little more.

The platitudes hadn't helped. No soft smiles or understanding looks could make him feel the slightest bit better.

He'd heard: "Your brother is doing as well as can be expected." "He hasn't been under care all that long." "We'll know more in the next few days."

But no one had been able to give him the assurances he needed. At an intellectual level, he understood, but at a pure, raw, gut-emotional level, he was frustrated and scared as hell.

The truth of the matter seemed to be that there was no real prognosis, that every day Dan survived was a good sign, and that, for now, his condition was on a wait-and-see mode. No more surgery was scheduled and, Cade guessed, they were in for the long haul.

"I'll see ya, Dan," he said, and walked out of the big, sterile building where his brother clung to life.

He told himself to suck it up. Deal with the situation. He'd lived on a ranch most of his thirty-eight years. He knew about accidents and life and death. But he couldn't convince himself to just let things take their course, that Dan was in the best medical facility in the area, that, by the hands of skilled surgeons and the grace of God, his brother would pull through.

Cade needed to do *something, anything* to help. As he drove away from Missoula, the lights of the town appearing in his rearview mirror, before the snow and distance extinguished them, he thought about all the times Dan had come to his rescue. From the time Dan had dived into the swift river to pull his nearly drowned brother Cade to safety when he'd been ten, to keeping his mouth shut when Cade had snuck out as a teenager, Dan had always been Cade's savior. Hell, Dan had even taken the blame for a fender bender that would have canceled Cade's insurance when he'd just started driving. Even as adults, Dan had tried to hold his younger brother's rash, impulsive streak down. Hadn't he counseled Cade against pursuing Hattie? Hadn't Dan wrestled him down, put him in a choke hold, and told him that chasing Hattie while she was dating Bart was not only a fool's mission, but a show of complete dishonor? Had it stopped him, no. Dan's advice of "leave her alone" had gone unheeded. To this damned day, Cade hadn't been able to control some of his most visceral and primal of urges—not when it came to Bart's ex-wife. But Dan had tried to save Cade from himself.

Always.

Two years older, and light-years ahead of him in maturity, Dan had always been the rock of the family, the strong one, at least to Cade. Second-born, Dan had assumed the leader role in the family, a role Zed hadn't been happy about relinquishing. While Zed seemed to have been born angry and his own trouble with the law had proved it, Dan had always been pleasant and even-keeled. Cade had earned his role of hellion with every scar on his body, and Bart, the youngest, was always a step behind the rest, never sure of himself.

Now, Bart was gone and Dan was barely alive.

Cade took a corner a little too quickly and his pickup slid a bit, but he held tight to the wheel, rode out the slide, and stared into the night. He met a few cars, the beams of their headlights diffused in the snow, but he drove by rote, the heater throwing off enough air to keep the windshield clear, the radio silent; only the sound of tires humming on the frozen pavement and the steady growl of the engine disturbed the night.

Once in Grizzly Falls he stopped at the Black Horse, a local watering hole where he downed a beer and ate a chili dog, then drove on to the sheriff's office where he watched the press conference.

Darla Vale, the public information officer, stood at a makeshift podium under the cover of the overhang at the top of the few stairs leading into the building. To one side, still protected from the snow that continued to fall, the acting sheriff stood in full uniform, his face grave, his hands at his side. Next to Brewster were the two detectives working the case. Alvarez, looking as sharp as Brewster, though she was wearing street clothes, and Pescoli, taller, a little disheveled, but as serious as her partner.

Under the glare of the security lamps, Vale made a statement that said the department was using all of its resources in trying to solve the current cases, specifically the attack on the sheriff and the assassination of Judge Kathryn Samuels-Piquard. When asked for details, she wouldn't respond with specifics. A lot of answers started with "the investigation is ongoing" and petered out with not much more information given. When asked by a blond reporter about a connection between the two cases, the standard answer was once again repeated, though this time it had a caveat: the bullet that had killed the judge would be compared to the slug retrieved from the attack on the sheriff. Then, Vale promised, the police would be able to confirm or deny a link.

All the while, Brewster didn't say a word.

Neither did Detective Alvarez or Pescoli. Obviously, they were just there for show.

In the end, Officer Vale asked for the public's help in locating the offenders and gave out a telephone number, a hotline, for any information the public might have.

Cade, half frozen, left the area just as the conference was breaking up. He hadn't learned anything more today. Not from the hospital staff and certainly not from the yahoos running around like chickens with their heads cut off as they tried to locate the killer.

Maybe his opinion was unfair, colored by his personal connection. Dan had always taken pride in his officers and staff, but right now, Cade wasn't feeling the least bit kind toward anyone involved in this mess.

Climbing into his pickup, he thought about another beer, but dismissed it. One twelve-ouncer might lead to two, which could lead to three . . . and as angry and frustrated as he was, he'd best avoid anything that might fuel his anger and erode the governor that kept his temper in rein.

Driving past the Frozen Flamingo Lounge with its pink neon sign and nearly full parking lot without a second look, he headed outside of town where the storefronts and suburban sprawl gave way to snow-covered fields separated from the road by fences and snow-drifts.

He wondered, as he stared into the darkness, who the bastard was who had cut his brother down. What sick, twisted mind had laid in wait, and then, with cold-hearted calculation and near-perfect precision, put two bullets into the sheriff of Pinewood County?

His gut clenched at the thought, and he realized his hands were holding so tight to the steering wheel that the bones in his knuckles showed white. He'd been so angry when he'd left the hospital he hadn't bothered with gloves; he'd kept his hands in his pockets at the damned press conference. Now he stretched his fingers from what felt like a permanent clench.

The future was murky, not that his had ever been clear. He'd never much worried about tomorrow, was content to live day to day. That was about to change.

Somehow he'd have to deal with Dan's recovery, no matter how slowly it evolved. If it meant Dan returning to the ranch after a period of rehab at a facility, then so be it. He'd move a nurse in. Whatever it took. If Dan needed more room, Cade would move into the bunkhouse; he preferred it to the big rambling home that had once been filled with his father, three brothers, and two dogs. For a while, his mother had been around as well, but those were times he hardly remembered.

Now, the big old house oftentimes seemed empty, lacking the life and energy that was once so much a part of it.

Again, he felt his stomach clutch. The muscles at the base of his neck tightened.

"Pull it together," he said aloud as the lane for the ranch came into view. He slowed at the mailbox, rolled down his window, and grabbed the cards, letters, bills, and junk mail that had collected over the past several days, then turned into the long lane leading to the dark house. He'd already talked to Zed and made certain that he and the ranch foreman, J.D., had taken care of the stock here, as well as looking after Dan's two horses, which they'd decided to move to the ranch as well.

Zed had said he'd taken a call from the sheriff's office and was told that Dan's dog had shown up and was now with Detective Pescoli at her place, which was a major relief. The dog and Dan had been inseparable the past few years, and Cade planned to pick him up in the morning, make sure that Sturgis was comfortable at the ranch and ready to greet Dan when he arrived.

If he makes it, Cade. There are no guarantees that he's gonna pull through.

He shut down that irritating inner voice of doubt.

He couldn't listen to it.

Tick. Tick. Tick.

Time was moving onward, whether he liked it or not.

And Grayson was still alive.

He stalked through his cabin, feeling as if he could climb out of his skin after all the years of planning, all the time he'd spent making sure that everything had been perfect.

Everything but that bitch of a detective showing up when she had, splintering his concentration, ruining his shot.

A serious piece of bad luck.

He stripped down to nothing, let the cold of the cabin caress his skin and seep into his muscles, reminding him that he was alive, clearing his mind so that he could think.

Dropping to the floor, he started with push-ups, quick and fast, with military precision, his back as straight as the boards his mother had made him lie on at night, boards without the comfort of a mattress or even a sheet, thick slabs of oak pegged together, as strong and as unbending as she had been. At least they'd been smooth, from all the bodies before him, sisters and brothers, aunts and uncles, even his mother herself had been forced to lie shivering on those old planks. As a child, he'd wondered how many of those before him had peed on the wood, or if the girls had bled upon it. There were no stains. Mother had scrubbed it clean, then lovingly oiled what had been originally constructed as a workbench, the ancient vise still attached—a warning.

He'd lain at night staring at it while he shivered, wondering if anyone had been forced to place a finger, or wrist, or foot in the dual jaws with their serrated teeth. The crank always seemed to have been moved between his visits, and he wondered what had been locked in those ugly grips, if flesh had been squeezed between those harsh, steel teeth.

If ever he were forced to sleep on the bench during a full moon, he believed the vise was alive. As the moon rose, casting silvery illumination through the tiny paned window, the shadows of the night shifting eerily, he would swear the vise grew and moved, a hungry monster climbing upward, jaws exposed, snaggletoothed and ready.

Only with the morning light had the creature receded to become, again, his father's rarely used clamp, his mother's reminder of potential, painful punishment.

Now, as he held the push-up position, his cold body beginning to sweat and shake, he gritted his own teeth and forced himself to hold his muscles tight despite how hot they burned, regardless of the pain ripping through them.

Mind over matter.

Tick. Tick. Tick.

The seconds passed and finally, when the drips of sweat running down his nose were nearly a stream, he released and let his body fall to the cold floor.

Naked.

Closing his eyes, he remembered the workbench again and held his arms wide, his legs straight, feeling hard wood against bare skin, reminding him that he had a purpose.

Reminding him there were others.

Even if Grayson lived through this night, he would eventually die. If not from these wounds, then new ones.

In the meantime, he could concentrate on the rest of them.

They needed to die. Soon.

Forcing himself from the mental comfort of the floor, he walked to the desk and retrieved the slashed head shot of the judge.

"Too bad," he whispered without an ounce of feeling. He liked his trophy, but knew just what to do with it after carefully wiping it of any prints, any hint of DNA evidence. Snapping on latex gloves, his only article of clothing, he then set about his task, making sure no hair or skin was left behind. At this point he had to be careful.

The detectives and those nerds in the lab would have a field day with this, and he couldn't risk any minute trace of himself on the picture.

All of his personal information, including his prints, were already in the system, and he knew exactly how it worked, how they would find him.

He would be just as careful of the envelope, which he planned to mail from Grizzly Falls, right under their noses.

At that thought, he smiled inwardly. Havoc would reign.

Satisfied that his envelope and contents were clean, he placed them into a plastic bag that he tucked into his duffel bag. Then he sorted through the head shots again. Unfortunately, the picture of the sheriff was still intact as the man was still clinging to life. "Soon," he promised the photograph, as if the damned sheriff could hear him.

Then he sorted through the other pictures until he came up with the still shot of Regan Pescoli. She, too, was looking at the camera, never knowing she was being photographed. That was the beauty of high-tech cell phones.

They could become a camera with the press of a finger.

Which his had been.

In this shot, Detective Regan Pescoli, the bitch, was looking straight on, her eyes wide, her expression pensive, hair falling around her face. In a way, she was beautiful, he had to admit, though he hated the idea.

"You're up," he said to the photograph and felt his blood sizzle a bit at the thought of bringing her down. One shot, right between the eyes. That would do the trick.

Glancing at the clock mounted over his old desk, he realized he had to dress quickly and leave. Hours and minutes and seconds were passing.

His actions were being monitored, he was certain of it, so he had to be more careful than ever, couldn't take the chance that someone might follow him.

Not here. Not to his private space.

Again, he glanced at the round face of the old-fashioned clock, the very timepiece that had been in his father's shop, where he'd been stripped bare and forced to sleep, the place he'd come to think of as comforting.

He had so much yet to accomplish and, as always, time was running out.

Especially for Regan Pescoli.

Tick. Tick. Tick.

CHAPTER 19

"This is going to be awkward," Alvarez said to her dog as she noticed a flash of light, the wash of headlight beams illuminate the room. Keyed up, she told herself to calm down, that everything would go smoothly, but that remained to be seen.

She was ready.

She could do this.

She could have an evening with the son she gave up for adoption a little over sixteen years ago.

Straightening the hem of her sweater, she drew in a deep breath. She'd been expecting O'Keefe and Gabriel Reeve, the boy who was her birth son, the teenager she'd just met recently and with whom she'd spent so little time. Her feelings for Gabriel were conflicted: mixed with the love that comes with birth was the guilt and anxiety of giving him away. And then there was the issue of his adoptive parents.

The last time she'd seen him, he'd been lying in a hospital bed recovering from wounds he'd received while with Alvarez, the birth mother he'd sought out while he was on the run for his part in an armed robbery.

"Oh, what a tangled web we weave," she whispered.

Fortunately, Gabe had worked a deal with the D.A., in some part due to her efforts, and was now on probation and living at home with his parents, Dave and Aggie Reeve, instead of being incarcerated in the juvenile detention center that had been looming in his future.

She tried to calm herself, remind herself to take it slow. He was her son by blood only, and though he'd sought her out and wanted to have a connection to her, they were just getting to know each other, just beginning to find some footing in a tentative relationship. To complicate matters, Aggie was related to O'Keefe and, as Gabe's mother, suspicious of Alvarez's motives with her son.

Taking in a deep breath, she heard an engine die, then shortly thereafter, car doors slam. *Here we go.* She'd talked to Gabe several times since his release from the hospital and he'd insisted he was "fine" and "okay." She'd dug a little deeper and it seemed through the miracles of modern medicine and the recuperative powers of youth, he was not only on his feet, but, according to O'Keefe, nearly a hundred percent, no longer under a doctor's care.

"Thank God," she whispered under her breath and hoped that the evening ahead wouldn't be a train wreck.

Her dog, of course, didn't care about any of the human drama that was about to unveil. The mottled, half-grown shepherd puppy wiggled his way to the front hallway, while Jane Doe, her cat, alerted by Roscoe's antics that something out of the ordinary was afoot, slunk behind the couch and hid beneath it, peering cautiously toward the door.

Before anyone could ring the bell, she threw open the door just as O'Keefe and Gabe made their way to the porch. As expected, the sight of Dylan, dressed in a leather jacket and jeans, caused her heart to skip a beat. And seeing Gabe on his feet again was an incredible relief. With coppery skin, dark hair, and a gleam in his brown eyes, he seemed to have grown since the last time she'd seen him, even appeared broader in the shoulders, but, of course, that was impossible, all her perception.

"Hi," she said, and before she could move out of the doorway to let them pass, O'Keefe unexpectedly reached into his pocket and placed a piece of greenery over her head. Then recognizing the mistletoe sprig for what it was, she said, "Hey, whoa. Wait a minute, it's too late for—"

"Don't think so."

With a swift move, he wrapped his arms around her, swung her off her feet, and, while twirling her beneath the porch lamp, kissed her hard on the lips.

For a second, all of her worries melted into the night where snow was falling and the air was crisp and cold, and the man she loved was pressed warm against her.

Gabe whispered, "Oh, wow."

"Oh, wow, is right," she said, a little breathlessly when he finally set her on her feet again. "What was that all about?"

"You tell me." His eyes were dark with the night, a smoldering gray she'd always found sexy as the devil. His jaw was square and rock hard, his beard shadow evident.

"In-ap-propriate." She sent a glance at her son who stood down a step but was grinning ear to ear. "And downright corny and definitely waaaay past the season."

O'Keefe said, "Gabe was in on it. I told him what I was going to do."

She turned accusing eyes on her son. "You didn't try to stop him?"

Shrugging, the kid grinned, his white teeth flashing. "He said you might be pissed."

"No," O'Keefe corrected. "I said I wanted to give her a thrill."

"Yeah, and that she'd be really ticked."

Alvarez glared at them both, even as a grin tugged at the corners of her mouth. "Mission accomplished. On both counts." From inside, Roscoe barked impatiently, and as she stepped out of the doorway, he barreled through, galloping off the porch in his excitement, only to come bounding back to wiggle and whine at Gabe's feet.

"Hey, boy." Gabe's attention immediately focused on the dog.

"Are you out of your mind?" she whispered to O'Keefe.

He laughed, a big, throaty laugh. "Depends on who you ask."

Gabe said, "My mom says you're 'certifiable.' "

"Aggie's always had a way of putting things," O'Keefe muttered, finally letting her go. Alvarez peered around him to find Gabe leaning over, playing with Roscoe, who was jumping up and down, then bolting across the front yard only to come back yipping excitedly.

"It's a good thing you're here," she said to the boy who was a stranger as much as her son. "Roscoe's been cooped up because I've been working so much."

"All day?" the boy asked.

"I have someone walk him, but it's not the same as this."

As if to prove her point, Roscoe bolted off across the yard again, snow flying from his big paws as he disappeared around the corner, only to spin out somewhere near the hedgerow and show up again, running in crazy circles.

"He's possessed," Gabe observed. "Maybe you should name him something like Crazy Devil or something."

"*Diablo loco?*" She laughed and Gabe looked at her as if *she* were the crazy one. "I think I'll stick with Roscoe. Come on in, it's freezing out here!" To the dog, she yelled, "Roscoe! Come!" With a yip of pure joy, the puppy bounded over the threshold, but she caught him mid-leap. "Oh, no, you don't."

"You called him," Gabe said.

"That I did, but Roscoe knows the drill, don't you, boy?" Carrying the whining, wiggling dog into the bathroom, she snagged a towel from a hook near the door, then began drying each of Roscoe's big paws. He shifted and squirmed and tried to get away, but Alvarez, used to his escape tactics, prevailed. Once his paws, legs, and belly were wiped down, she let him onto the floor. "There ya go."

Never missing a beat, he took off, toenails clicking as he raced into the front room, noticed Jane Doe lying under the couch, and, ears up, tail raised, lunged in her direction. He was rewarded with a hiss and a quick view of pink tongue surrounded by long, white, needle-sharp teeth.

"She hates him," Gabe said as Alvarez, after washing her hands, returned to the living room.

"Trust me, she loves him but doesn't want anyone to know. Sometimes if I get up early and neither of them wakes up, I'll find her curled up in his bed, next to him, back to back, happy as can be. This"—Alvarez pointed at the cat cowering in her hiding spot—"is all for show."

Gabe appeared unconvinced but continued to play with the dog, roughhousing in the living room as if he hadn't been in a hospital bed so recently. Still hyped on adrenaline, Roscoe barked and leaped. His tail nearly cleared the coffee table of magazines and he bumped into a nearby lamp, sending it teetering precariously.

"Enough!" she said to the dog.

Pulling a face, Gabe said, "Sorry."

Alvarez steadied the lamp. "It's okay. Look, if you want to take him out in the back, where it's fenced, go ahead. He really does need to get rid of some energy, but take the towel and keep it by the door for when you come in."

Gabe didn't have to be asked twice. He grabbed the same towel she'd used, whistled, and opened the sliding door to the small back-yard. Roscoe bounded through, Gabriel flipped the towel onto the back of a nearby chair, and they were off.

"What do you do when a teenaged boy isn't around?" O'Keefe watched the boy shut the door behind him.

"I used to jog with Roscoe. Every day. Until I was injured."

His face darkened as he, too, remembered the attack that nearly took her life. "About that—"

"No need to go there again. Not tonight." She hazarded a glance toward the closed slider where, just beyond the glass, she spied her son standing under the porch light. *He's not your son. Remember that.* "I'm okay. Really. Getting better every day. Roscoe will have trouble keeping up with me soon." Before he could argue, she added, "Come on, you can help in the kitchen. Make yourself useful."

"How?"

"Stir the soup."

"You actually made—?"

"I ordered and picked up clam chowder from Wild Wills, bought salad in a bag, and got the last three loaves of sourdough bread at the bakery." She switched on the oven, then reached into the refrigerator and pulled out a bag of "Holiday Blend" greens—spinach, lettuce, and chard—along with a packet of dried cranberries and hazelnuts, and proceeded to pour the contents into a glass bowl. "This isn't what I had envisioned for my first meal with Gabe," she admitted, "but work's nuts, so it'll have to do. You know, originally, when I found out about Gabe and realized I'd have this chance to get to know him, I thought about introducing him to his culture. Maybe it's weird, considering the circumstances, but I wanted to make something tra-ditionally Mexican, like my grandmother used to do for us kids, es-pecially at the holidays. I figured Gabe probably doesn't get much of his Latino heritage from Aggie and Dave."

"Zero."

"Right. So once Aggie and Dave agreed that I could be a part of Gabe's life, I thought that maybe we could connect on a level that might not be as threatening to his parents."

"Possibly." O'Keefe wasn't convinced.

"It's too bad it didn't work out, at least this year, because some of the food was my favorite part of Christmas. *Abuela*, she made flan, with coconut or caramel for *Nochebuena*, Christmas Eve. And it was The Best. I'm saying that with capital letters. The Best!"

"She was a good cook, I take it."

"Is. To this day," she said, though it had been years since she'd seen her grandmother, and a little niggle of regret wormed its way through her heart.

"What about your mother?"

Alvarez placed the loaves of bread into the warm oven. "She's good, too, but I remember my Aunt Biatriz's churros. Biatriz is a musician, always playing the piano for family get-togethers, and she makes a chocolate sauce that's just slightly hot. I think it had a little chili pepper in it to give it some kick. But she would never give up her recipe, even though every year she brought it to my grandmother Rosarita's house. All of us kids, we got to dip the churros into these big bowls." She smiled at the memory of all of her brothers and sisters, as well as her cousins . . . and then her smile faded as the recollection darkened to that same forbidden territory that always crept into her heart. Clearing her throat, she refused to go down that same, painful path and forced a smile. "Trust me, it was To Die For. Again with the capital letters. Tonight, though, it's bakery brownies."

"And we'll love them," he assured her. "A brownie's a brownie. Despite it's heritage or culture or all those things you've never once shown an interest in, at least to my knowledge."

"*Bastardo!*" she said, teasing, then opened the refrigerator door again. "How about something to drink? I've got beer and . . . a bottle of pinot gris."

"Beer's good."

After handing him a chilled bottle, she checked on the bread, then glanced out the window to see that Gabe was still playing with Roscoe. "Fast friends," she observed.

"You know what they say about a boy and his dog. Inseparable."

"Except the dog's here and he's in Helena."

"He'll probably be pestering Aggie and Dave for one of his own."

"Great." The last thing she needed was Aggie to freak out about anything she was doing. It was hard enough for Aggie, as the adoptive mother, to let him have time with Alvarez and, deep down, Alvarez understood Aggie's concern. If the roles were reversed, there was a good chance she would feel the same.

She noticed that all jocularity had faded from O'Keefe's face. "So . . . how's Grayson?" he asked and she tensed a bit. Though they'd never addressed her ambivalent feelings for her boss, O'Keefe had sensed that there was a connection between Grayson and her; something deeper that she'd never wanted to face, much less address.

"I don't know," she said to the man she professed to love, the man she *did* love. "He's holding his own, I guess. Still hanging in there, but I have the feeling it's by a thread."

"I'm sorry." He sounded as if he meant it and her heart broke. When her gaze found his again, she saw the questions hiding in his eyes and realized he would never ask. It just wasn't his style.

"I'm sorry too. On so many levels." She decided now was the time to put all of her cards on the table. "Look, I care about Grayson," she said, her throat tight. "He's my boss and a good, good man. I respect him." She noticed that O'Keefe's mouth had tightened at the corners, deep brackets appearing, but she plunged on. If there was ever a chance for her and O'Keefe, she had to be honest, even brutally so. "There was a time . . . not all that long ago that I wondered if there could be anything more between us. You know, more than just a work relationship."

He didn't say a word, didn't so much as sip from his bottle.

"But then you came back into my life." She touched his arm, felt his muscles tense. "And everything changed. Everything became clear. You haven't asked, but you've wondered about the sheriff and me. Nothing ever happened between us. That was probably his choice, not mine, but now, regardless of how he recovers, or, God forbid, doesn't, nothing ever will."

She stood on her tiptoes and brushed a chaste kiss across his lips. "Seems as if I've fallen for this *bastardo* who came back into my life."

His expression softened a bit. "You didn't have to say all that."

"Oh, yeah, I did." She was nodding. "I just didn't expect to do it tonight, in the kitchen."

"Glad you did," he said, and with a glance at the door, he set his beer on the counter, drew her into his arms, and pressed his warm, eager lips to hers. For a moment she closed her eyes, allowed herself to be swept away, pushed aside all the tensions, the headache, the terror of the past few days.

The oven timer dinged loudly and she stepped away from him, out of the safety of his arms, and back to the here and now. This was a night she was planning to spend getting to know Gabe; she couldn't be distracted, she thought, as, using a towel, she pulled the warm loaves of bread from the oven.

"Any idea who did it?" O'Keefe asked, picking up his beer and taking a swallow.

"Who shot Grayson?" she asked, carving the dome off the first loaf, then removing most of the warm, fragrant bread from inside its crust. "That's the problem. Too many ideas. We've got a lot of suspects, a lot of motives, a lot of alibis. We're just trying to sort it out."

"If I can help . . ."

"Cube the bread."

"That's not what I meant. I was talking about the investigation."

"I know." She handed him a knife, then sliced the top off the second loaf.

As a private investigator, he didn't have to jump through all the legal hoops she was forced to and could bend some of the rules that she was afraid of breaking. To her way of thinking, that could be a good thing. As long as the case wasn't compromised. "I'll let you know," she said.

"I assume the two cases are connected. Grayson and the judge."

"The autopsy on Kathryn Samuels-Piquard was today. I'll have a preliminary report on the cause of death and a ballistics report first thing in the morning. Then we'll know for sure if we've got one assailant, which has my vote, if anyone's asking. What're the chances of two assassins? We can even rule out a copycat thing because the judge was dead before the attack on Grayson."

O'Keefe took a long swallow from his bottle, then pulled out the bread board and started cubing the hot centers from the loaves. "Any chance Grayson and Samuels-Piquard have a connection other than professionally?"

"You mean, like, lovers?" she asked and conjured up the man with whom she'd worked, her mentor and guide. Then she thought about the hard-nosed opinionated judge. "I doubt it. If he was interested in anyone, it was probably Hattie Grayson, his brother's widow, though actually she was his brother's ex-wife; they were divorced before he killed himself."

"Maybe they weren't lovers," he said thoughtfully, "but had some other social connection. I know it's the logical thought that the attacks had to be because of their jobs, that maybe they'd sent a nutcase to the Big House and either he or someone close to him decided to take a little revenge, but that's just an assumption."

"I know." The truth was she'd tossed around the same idea herself but hadn't found any thread tying the two victims together. "We've talked to the families, checked records, though we're still going through all of the judge's info." Once they'd finished with the bread, she looked out the slider again and saw Gabe and Roscoe still running in the snow. "They're both going to be soaked." She found water glasses in the cupboard. "I shouldn't be discussing the case, or any case for that matter, with you, y'know."

"Just giving you a different perspective, but you're right. Not tonight." He touched her shoulder and she looked up. "Are you really okay?" His gaze held hers for an instant too long, a few seconds that caused heat to climb up the back of her neck.

"I'm fine."

One side of his mouth lifted and a dark eyebrow raised. "More than fine, I'd say."

"Keep that thought, O'Keefe." She smiled. She understood that he couldn't spend the night, not with Gabe here. They'd already had this discussion via quick texts and had decided, especially upon Aggie's insistence, her maternal instincts in high alert, that O'Keefe would drive the boy home to be with his family later this evening.

Pouring soup into each bread bowl, she said, "I don't know if having the cases linked will narrow the suspect list or broaden it, but I suspect the latter. We're already double-checking anyone who knew them both and potentially held a grudge or had something to gain."

Just as she was setting plates on the eating bar, the sliding door opened and Gabe, red-faced, stepped inside.

She said, "Don't forget the towel!"

"Oh, yeah . . ."

Roscoe was already sprinting through the door, but Gabe collared the rambunctious pup and did a half-decent job of cleaning those massive paws.

Alvarez asked, "How about you? Are you wet too?"

"Just a little," Gabe said, as snowflakes began melting in his black hair. "Dry snow."

"Okay. Come on, wash up and you can help serve," Alvarez said to the boy. "Around here, it's every man for himself."

He was more than glad to find plates and put out flatware while she tossed the prepacked salad dressing with the greens and O'Keefe scooped spoonfuls of thick New England clam chowder into each sourdough bowl. She placed a pat of butter and a pinch of dried parsley on top of the soup. "Voilà," she said. "Almost homemade."

"Maybe better," O'Keefe said.

She laughed. "Nope, *assuredly* better."

Carrying his bowl to the table, O'Keefe said, "Aren't we domestic?"

"We are tonight." But this was temporary. Despite the lit tree and red candles, tonight wasn't Christmas, and though there was a heart-warming feeling of family this evening, it would be fleeting. The truth of the matter was that Gabriel Reeve wasn't her legal son and Dylan O'Keefe certainly wasn't her husband. Tonight, though, she wasn't going to allow her overly practical, realistic self to ruin the moment. This patched-together, belated holiday meal felt right, somehow, as if she actually were part of an oddly splintered family.

Outside the window, the snow fell softly, almost peacefully, while inside the fire burned quietly and the lights on the Christmas tree still glowed.

Growing up, she'd been a part of a large, pious, and happy family. At least that's how she remembered it, until as a teenager her inno-cence had been stolen, her rose-colored vision of the future destroyed. She'd left home, never to return, and the spirit and joy of the holidays were, she'd assumed, part of her oh so distant past.

Now as they sat down, Gabe asked, "Don't you say grace?" Casting a glance at Alvarez. "My mom is, like, we have to say grace before every meal."

For years, she'd avoided the holidays and any celebration, and she'd sheltered herself from others with a thick, standoffish shell.

Now, with O'Keefe, she felt that shell cracking a bit, sensed there was a chance for a new beginning.

Despite the horrors and demands of her job.

"That's a good point," Alvarez said to Gabe, "but we're going to do it my family's way, okay? A prayer to Our Lady of Guadalupe. It's kind of a tradition." She glanced at O'Keefe, caught his eye, and for the first time in a long while, she bowed her head.

CHAPTER 20

"So what the hell's wrong with you?" Alvarez asked Pescoli the next day as they slid into one of the well-worn booths in Shorty's Diner, a twenty-four-hour restaurant and bar that was located close enough to the department offices for convenience, far enough away that they weren't tripping over other officers come lunchtime.

A long red counter, circa 1958, ran the length of one end of the building. Padded stools, raised up a step, lined the customer side of the counter with a few of the seats currently occupied. Conversation hummed and a deep fryer sizzled somewhere on the other side of a large window cut into the wall separating the counter area from the kitchen.

It had been two full days since Kathryn Samuels-Piquard's body had been found. Other than establishing that the bullet removed from her brain during the autopsy when compared to the bullet retrieved at Grayson's cabin was a match, they weren't much closer to finding the culprit.

At least, though, they knew they were looking for one weapon and, most likely, one assassin, unless, of course, he was working with a partner, which was a consideration, if not likely.

With the ticking of the clock, Pescoli was getting more and more agitated. She knew it, but couldn't control the feeling that she was missing something and that time was slipping by, the case was getting colder.

"Wrong with me?" Pescoli repeated, stalling as she reached for a plastic-coated menu held next to the napkin holder near the wall. She sent Alvarez a did-you-really-just-ask-me-that-moronic-question look. "You mean other than this case? Or the fact that my kids are giving me fits? And that my love life . . . oh, I don't want to talk about it." She snapped open the menu. There was something else nagging at her as well, the same black fear that caused the demons of the night to rob her of sleep.

"Something's going to break on the case," Alvarez said as she eyed the menu. "I can feel it."

"Right now, all I can feel is hunger. I swear I could eat a horse. Make that two."

A bubbly waitress appeared at the table. Her smile was wide, her black skirt tight, her hair pulled away from her face to bob in shiny corkscrews around a thick pink headband. Her name tag read Terri and as she placed two water glasses on the table, she asked, "Can I get you something to drink?"

Automatically, Alvarez said, "Iced tea."

Pescoli skewered her with a look. "It's freezing outside," then said to the waitress, "I'll have a Shorty's Famous."

Terri didn't bother writing the order down, just said, "That'll be a few minutes and I'll come back for your order." Then, bouncing away, she disappeared through a swinging door with a porthole cut into it.

"You gave me trouble for ordering an iced tea because it's 'freezing outside,' then you order a milkshake?"

"Not just any milkshake." The Famous was a black-and-white milkshake made with vanilla ice cream, hot fudge, chocolate syrup, and crushed Oreo cookies.

"You're right," Alvarez responded sarcastically. "It's more like a surefire diabetic seizure in the making. What happened to your usual Diet Coke?"

"Don't know," she admitted, and that was the truth. "I just feel like a milkshake. No reason to make a federal case of it."

"Maybe not. It's just not your usual thing. I've worked with you a lot of years and you've never once ordered a milkshake. It just adds to my theory that something's up with you." She folded her arms over the table and stared at her partner. "So, what is it?"

Pescoli's short fuse ignited. "Well, I guess you're right. Everything isn't just hunky-dory in my life right now. First off, I've got this case I can't solve and, oh, someone killed a person I work with and tried to murder my boss. Then one of my kids decides he wants to be a cop and is invading my workspace. The other one is trying to mold herself into a real-life Barbie, I think, by starving herself and, yeah, I'm afraid she might have a serious eating disorder, but so far I've tiptoed around that issue," she said, gaining steam as all of the problems that had been eating at her came rushing out. Having no intention of unloading, she suddenly couldn't stop herself. "Then there's the trip to Arizona both of my kids are taking with Lucky and Michelle, all part of the super-duper bonanza of a Christmas present that includes firearms and possible body waxing, I'm not really sure. The upshot is that Bianca thinks she's way too fat to wear the bikini her stepmother bought her, so she's basically starving herself. And Jeremy is all about the rifle his father bought him. He takes it with him in his truck. God help me, I only hope it's not loaded. But who knows, I don't even know my own son anymore. Well, that goes double for Bianca. What the hell was Lucky thinking?"

"You're serious about this?"

"Damned straight, I am. Then there's Santana. Did I mention that he's thrown down the gauntlet and given me the do-or-die option after asking me to marry him?" Before Alvarez could say a word, the waitress suddenly appeared with the drinks. Pescoli eyed the tall, old-fashioned glass holding the very milkshake in question. Though she wouldn't admit it out loud, she did wonder why she'd felt compelled to order a drink that could possibly top her usual daily calorie allowance.

In for a penny, in for a pound. Or two. Or three.

Alvarez ordered some kind of bisque and salad, and Pescoli decided on a Reuben sandwich with a side of potato salad.

"Got it," Terri said, her smile flashing as she turned on her heel to head back to the kitchen.

While Alvarez fiddled with squeezing lemon into her tea, Pescoli grabbed her milkshake, swirled the concoction with her plastic straw, then took a long drink. It was everything it was advertised to be and more.

"You could have told me," Alvarez said.

"I just did." Another long swallow. *Heaven!* "Look, we haven't had a lot of time to sit around and chat. Time when we weren't actually working."

"So how're things with you?" she asked, trying, and failing, to hide her sarcasm.

"Don't get mad. I just asked." Alvarez ignored her iced tea. "You haven't been yourself lately."

"Oh, for the love of . . ." She wanted to argue, to rail at the heavens for all that was wrong in her life, all the frustrations. She glanced at a booth near the window and spied a couple in their seventies. They were having coffee while holding hands across the table, as if they were in love as much today as they had been fifty years ago, or whenever it was that they first met. Never in her life had she experienced anything so obviously deep and committed. No, her loves had always been white-hot in the beginning, filled with passion that spilled from unleashed ardor in the bedroom to fiery anger when things weren't going right. She suspected the fights and frustration had more to do with her than the men she chose.

Stirring her shake, she looked up and found Alvarez staring at her, near-black eyes assessing. "I didn't mean to unload," she admitted, "but you did ask."

"I did." Alvarez finally tasted her tea.

"Okay. Sorry. I have been a little edgy lately. I didn't mean to snap. So, seriously, how *are* things with you?"

"I'm fine. O'Keefe and I are good . . . we just don't get to see each other much. He and Gabe came over for dinner."

"Everything cool?"

"Yeah, I think so. It's a little strained with the parents. They're not so sure him connecting with me is such a great idea, but we're working on it."

Terri returned with their orders. Pescoli's stomach rumbled at the sight of the thick sandwich, Swiss cheese melting over the corned beef and sauerkraut.

"Anything else?" Terri asked, then when Alvarez said, "I think we're fine," she danced away to the next table where a family of three was being seated. From the looks of it, their teenaged son wasn't all that excited to be having lunch with his folks. As Mom and Dad took off their jackets and tried to engage him, he sulked, keeping his own coat zipped, his watch cap pulled low over his forehead, his arms crossed belligerently over his chest. As Mom removed her hat, her blond hair falling around a face just starting to age, she smiled and chattered, trying to jolly the boy. Dad, more stern, cast him a don't-embarrass-your-mother glare as he plucked a menu from its holder. The kid responded with grunted monosyllables guaranteed to send his parents orbiting into the stratosphere.

Pescoli had been there.

Way too often.

She picked up half her Reuben and took a bite. The succulent blend of cheese, Thousand Island dressing, corned beef, and kraut exploded in her mouth.

God, it tasted good.

"So, are you going to marry Santana?" Alvarez asked.

"Don't know," she answered honestly as she dabbed dressing off the corner of her mouth with her napkin. "I'm torn."

"Why?"

"Not my first rodeo." She took another bite and thought as she chewed. "And it's not that easy. I've got kids."

"Almost grown."

"'Almost' being the operative word. And then there's the job. Not exactly conducive to wedded bliss."

"He's a big boy. Knows what he's getting into."

Pescoli nodded, ate a little more and felt better, her blood sugar stabilizing, her temper no longer at flash point. "This didn't come at a good time."

"There's never a perfect time."

"Look who's suddenly the marriage counselor."

"I know you're not looking for advice, but from my perspective, it seems you're overthinking it. Looking at the downside rather than the up."

"This? From you?" Alvarez had always been reined in, her emotions well under check, her private life just that: private. She wasn't one to talk about feelings and emotions, and that suited Pescoli just fine. While Pescoli was apt to fly by the seat of her pants, Alvarez was always more cautious and thoughtful.

"I'll ignore that. And as for Jeremy, I wouldn't worry too much about him. I know it's weird, but under Joelle's tutelage, Jeremy's doing great. I've run into him a couple of times in the department and he seems to be able to handle the phones or some of the people who come in asking for information. He shows up on time, dresses according to department code, and does what he's supposed to. What more do you want from him?"

"I know." Pescoli set her sandwich onto her plate again. "I was probably wrong about that. I've always said he needed a purpose, something to do with his life, I just never figured it would be as a cop."

"He's not a cop yet."

"He needs to go to school."

"He will if he really wants to join the force. He'll have to." She blew across a spoonful of bisque. "So, go ahead and marry Santana."

"Easy for you to say."

She barreled on, "And you let Jeremy work at the department and find out what he really wants. Hurts nothing. As for Bianca," she said, a little more serious, "if she's really got an eating disorder, that's a real problem. You have to do something. Fast."

"I know," Pescoli said, taking another bite from her sandwich and wondering how a child of hers would deny herself food. "And I will." She polished off the first half, then tackled her potato salad. "Thanks, Dear Abby."

"Anytime." She stirred her soup. "Remember, I do have a master's in psychology."

"Well, then, that does make you an expert, now, doesn't it?"

Alvarez attempted to swallow a small grin. "Pretty much."

"Fine. So, now that you've solved every damned one of my personal problems, let's get back to business."

Alvarez nodded, her smile fading, her eyebrows drawing together, tiny lines appearing over her nose. "Because both victims work in law enforcement, we've been digging into past cases, thinking that's the connection." She glanced around the room, her gaze skating over the other customers. "But what if that's what the killer wants us to think? What if there's a connection we don't know about?"

"Between the judge and the sheriff?"

"Yeah." Alvarez was thinking hard.

"What kind of relationship?"

"That's what we have to figure out."

"Lovers?"

Alvarez hesitated. "It doesn't feel right," she said, shaking her head, but Pescoli could almost see the cogs turning in her partner's mind. This wasn't new territory for Alvarez to travel. "I still think Hattie Grayson's the only woman he'd be interested in."

"Or you."

Her head snapped up. "I think we'd better be clear about this," she said, "because I'm only saying it once, and I'm only saying it to you. Nothing ever happened between me and the sheriff. Not that I didn't fantasize. But it wasn't happening. He never would have let it, so it was just a passing thing, all on me. One-sided."

"Okay. Then why not the judge?"

"There's no evidence pointing that way. At least not yet. And if you're thinking that Grayson's name is going to magically appear out of the ashes from the fireplace in the judge's den, I think you're jumping off the deep end."

Pescoli dug into her milkshake with the long-handled spoon she'd been given, breaking up a clog of ice cream. "We need to look at them all."

"That we do," her partner agreed, clearly disturbed. The topic of Grayson's love life was hitting too close to home, it seemed.

And that, to Pescoli's way of thinking, was one more problem in a case that already had far too many.

Hattie screwed up her courage as she drove to the Grayson ranch. The road was familiar, the memories vivid, as she guided her Toyota onto the long lane that wound its way to the ranch house. Surrounded by acres of snow-covered pastures and backdropped by rugged mountains, the house sat on a small rise, outbuildings scattered around the place the Grayson boys had called home for most of their lives.

She caught a glimpse of the barn and her heart twisted when she imagined, for what had to be the millionth time, how Bart's body had swung from the cross timber where Cade had found him. In her mind's eye, she saw his ashen face, bulging eyes, dark bruises on his neck. *Why?* She wondered again but knew deep in her heart that if he did, in fact, hang himself, she was the reason he'd taken his own life. "He didn't," she said again, forcing conviction into her words, praying that she was not the cause.

As her Camry churned its way to the crest of the hill, she recognized several vehicles, including Cade's truck, parked just outside of the garage. For a split second she second-guessed herself, but she'd come too far to turn back now, and her reasons for arranging a play date for the twins so that she could track down Cade hadn't changed. It was time they cleared the air, once and for all.

For the past couple of days, ever since they'd run into him in town, McKenzie and Mallory had been focused on seeing him again. It wasn't a surprise that they were feeling uncle deprived, she supposed, as Dan had played such a large role in their lives.

Parking beside Cade's Dodge, she took a deep breath, stuffed her keys into her pocket, and bracing herself against a gust of wintry wind, grabbed her purse and trudged through the snow to the front door. Her handbag felt as if it weighed a ton, the fat envelope inside heavy with the truth.

Cade's dog, Shad, a three-legged speckled hound, sent up a ruckus as she approached, only to melt into a puddle of wagging tail and excited whines as she spoke to him.

"Hey, Shad," she chastised softly. "What's with all the barking? You know me." She took the time to scratch the old dog behind his floppy ears and was still petting him when the front door opened and Zed, standing in his stockinged feet, new-looking jeans, and a sweatshirt from Montana State, filled the doorway.

"Hattie," he said, and seemed more than a little irritated to find her outside his door.

"Hi, Zed."

"Somethin' I can do for you?"

"Yes, but first, is there any news about Dan?" she asked, wondering if the doctors had given more information to the sheriff's brothers than had been released to the general public.

"Still the same."

"I'm sorry." She hadn't expected to hear differently, but she'd hoped Dan had taken a turn for the better. "I guess it just takes time."

"That's what they say." He eyed her up and down. "But you didn't come all the way out here to ask me about Dan's condition."

"No, uh, I'm looking for Cade."

"Are ya, now?" As ever, he didn't bother to hide his disapproval, had never warmed to her.

"Is he here?" When he didn't immediately respond, she added, "His truck is here," and hitched a thumb toward the battered pickup.

"He's working."

"Here?" she asked.

Beneath his unshaven jaw, a muscle worked in aggravation. "In the machine shed."

She started to turn away, then thought better of it. She'd driven out here to clear the air, so why not start with Zed? He, too, was the girls' uncle, and she was sick of the silent treatment. As another gust of raw wind chased along the fence line, fluttering a few dry leaves along the crusted snow, she faced him once again.

"Did I do something, Zed?" she asked and saw a flicker of something dark in his eyes. When he didn't answer, she pushed it, taking one step nearer to the doorway. "You're always short with me, kind of condescending."

"Am I?"

"Don't be obtuse."

"Sure. That's what I am. Obtuse."

Sensing the tension between them, the dog let out a whimper and looked from Hattie to Zed, his tail nervously sweeping the old floorboards.

"It's not one thing you did, Hattie," Zed finally said, looking down his broken nose at her. "It's everything you did. Everything you still do."

"Such as?"

"You really want to do this?" he asked. When she didn't respond, just held her ground, he said, "Okay. Let's start with you she-cattin' around here. Searchin' out Cade. Hanging out at the hospital check-in' on Dan. Just bein' available." The disgust in his voice was palpable. "You know, woman, it's like you have no pride when it comes to my brothers. And you just don't give up, do you? Driving Bart to his grave was bad enough, but you just can't leave it alone." He took a step forward, towering over her, imposing and seething.

"I didn't drive Bart to do anything! You know I believe with all my heart that someone killed him. And whether you like it or not, I'm still a part of this family."

"You might wear the Grayson name, but you and Bart were divorced, and that was your making, your insistence. You didn't want to be married to him. Your girls are a different matter. They're blood, always will be. But you? You're just their damned guardian. Until they're eighteen. Then it's over." His face flushed beneath his beard. "You aren't even Bart's legal widow, y'know. Oh, you've been making a big stink, boohooing about him to Dan and the sheriff's department, insisting that he didn't kill himself, that someone staged his suicide, but that's just plain BS, all to ease your guilty conscience, and we both know it!"

"My guilt?" Of course there was more than a modicum of truth in his charges, yet she was horrified that he believed her to be such a phoney. "I don't feel guilty about—"

"Like hell you don't!" he thundered, his eyes narrowing to slits. "Don't make excuses, Hattie. It belittles us both. You and me and Cade, and probably even Dan, know what finally pushed Bart over the edge. It was you and Cade. He knew about the two of you. Even questioned the paternity of his own daughters. Can you imagine?"

She felt as if a knife had been thrust into her heart and then twisted oh, so slowly.

"Oh, Zed, I didn't—"

"Didn't what? Didn't sleep with Cade right before your wedding? Didn't conjure up some romantic fantasies about Dan, once Bart was out of the way and Cade unavailable? Or is it you just didn't mean to be such a slut when it comes to all my brothers?"

He glared at her with such intensity that for the smallest second she wondered if he were jealous that she'd never had any interest in him.

"Well . . . I asked you what I did, but I really didn't expect to have my character annihilated right here on the porch this morning." Her own temper had sparked and she couldn't help but add, "And who're you to judge? You've had your share of women, some of them married, always one on the side."

"I never banged one sister while engaged to another."

She drew a breath. She wanted to haul off and slap him, but instead, backed up a step, her gloved hands tightening into hard, furious fists.

"We're not talkin' about me, Hattie."

"I came here to . . . bury the hatchet. To try and make some peace with you and Cade and now, at least with you, I see it was a mistake."

"You got that right." Zed pointed a finger right at her chest. He whistled to the dog and Shad slunk past his legs to the warm interior of the house. "You asked what it was you did that pissed me off. Let's just make something clear, okay? It wasn't what you did, Hattie, it's who you are."

CHAPTER 21

Leaving the door of her office ajar, Pescoli hung her jacket on the hook near her file cabinet. She'd been fighting a headache all day, but the pain at the base of her skull had eased up a bit after lunch, which was a good thing. A damned good thing. She didn't have time to deal with a migraine, not now anyway.

Kicking out her desk chair, she sat down, her eyes already on the computer screen. She heard shouts in the hallway as one of the deputies led a suspect toward an interrogation room. The guy was handcuffed and shackled, his chains rattling. Pescoli cast a glance in his direction. Shaved head, curled upper lip, fury flaring in eyes set deep in his head; he was twitching a bit, too, probably higher than a kite, the smell of smoke clinging to him filtered into her room as he passed.

"I didn't do nothin'!" he was arguing, angry at the world, and especially Deputy Kayan Rule, who was guiding him past Pescoli's door toward a back hallway. "You can't do this to me, man! I want a fuckin' attorney. You hear that? I got rights!"

Rule said something back, but Pescoli didn't hear it. Whatever he'd muttered was effective as the scumbag immediately clammed up.

"Good," she said aloud as she refocused on her computer screen.

As for all of Alvarez's personal questions and quick-fix solutions to her personal problems, they were probably spot-on, irritating as that was. Though, of course, she hadn't been completely honest with Alvarez, hadn't copped to the fact that her nights were filled with weird, dark dreams that kept sleep at bay. Nor did she admit that sometimes she felt as if unseen eyes were watching her. She'd never been paranoid, had always been fearless, too much so, she'd been told. But lately she'd thought someone was watching her.

Just the other night, as she'd walked to her Jeep and unlocked the door, here, at the station, under the security lamps, she'd felt as if her every move were being observed, and her skin had literally crawled. She'd been alone in the lot, the wind cold and biting when she'd experienced the sensation that someone was watching, possibly targeting her. Adrenaline pumping, she'd looked over her shoulder, surveyed the lot that had been scraped free of snow. Several vehicles shone under the bluish glare of the tall lamps. It had been eerily quiet, no traffic on the side street, no cops heading to their vehicles or pausing for a smoke on the way home. She'd been totally alone, and she'd seen no dark figure hiding in the shadows, no suspicious person scuttling out of sight, no assassin sighting a rifle at her. She'd thought for a fleeting second about Claudia Dubois's assertions that someone had been watching the judge's home from the park, a man in winter camouflage. Her throat had turned to dust, her nerves stretched thin as she'd unlocked the Jeep and double-checked the backseat and cargo space, all the while feeling like a moron—a scared-spitless moron.

She'd told herself to get a grip and noticed her hands were shaking a little, her craving for a cigarette intense, though she hadn't given in, probably because she refused to buy a new pack.

The job was getting to her. As was the stress of the holidays.

No way would she admit the fact that she was suddenly a little nervous, that she'd actually reached for her sidearm . . . just in case.

No doubt Alvarez, if she had an inkling about Pescoli's night terrors, would either psychoanalyze her partner herself or send her straight to a psychiatrist's couch.

There was no reason for that, Pescoli decided, as she scanned her e-mail, hoping for something, a tip or piece of evidence that would help break open the case. As she sorted through her virtual in-box, she had to admit, at least to herself, that Alvarez had been right on several counts. She, as a mother, had to let Jeremy go, to make his own way and deal with his mistakes. Conversely, she needed to keep a closer eye on her daughter and try to find out what was going on in Bianca's brain that skewed her perception of herself. Unfortunately, some of the bad self-esteem came directly from Michelle encouraging her to "get fit" or "trim down" or however she phrased it as she handed Bianca a bikini meant for a twelve-year-old.

Muttering under her breath, she decided she'd have a chat with her ex and his petite little wife. It was irritating as hell to know that Michelle really wasn't all that stupid, despite her on-and-off-again ditzy blond act. In Pescoli's opinion, her ex's wife was far more cunning and sly than she acted. And she seemed to have a twisted idea of what a woman should be. That was all well and good, except when that ridiculous notion started messing with Bianca's self-esteem.

Lastly, there was Santana.

She loved him.

There wasn't a second's hesitation on her part to admit it, and she did want to live with him. It was just the marriage part that worried her and that, she understood, was her problem. The plain truth was she wanted to marry him, so she'd just have to pack her fear of the rite away and bury it.

To hell with the consequences.

Life was an adventure.

There were no guarantees.

She gritted her teeth. She had some major steps to take once she was home. For now, though, she needed to concentrate on finding the son of a bitch who put two bullets into Grayson and killed Judge Samuels-Piquard. Unfortunately, nothing in today's batch of e-mails helped.

So much for burying the hatchet, Hattie thought as she left the ranch house. Hands buried deep in her pockets, purse slung over her shoulder, she followed large boot prints toward the outbuildings. Zed had made it pretty damned clear how he felt about her, and there was no arguing the matter, not that she cared to. For as much as Zed despised her, the feeling was mutual. She'd always thought he was the weakest of the clan, a self-absorbed, silent man who, she suspected, had more than a few dark secrets of his own.

Not that it mattered.

What Zed thought was neither here nor there.

Not so with Cade.

Another gust of wind kicked through the buildings, shrieking long and low before dying to silence again. A few flakes of snow drifted from the leaden sky that stretched over the surrounding peaks. She'd always loved it out here, had once considered it her home.

Obviously Zed disagreed with that particular fantasy.

It, no doubt, really chapped his hide that she, as the girls' guardian, owned a quarter of the ranch. They'd worked out an arrangement when Bart had died, and any net income from the ranch was placed into an account for Molly and McKenzie at the first of every year. She never touched the money, only thought of it when the bank sent her electronic statements every quarter.

As she cut between the pump house and grain silo, she spied a light burning in the window of the machine shed. Her insides tightened a bit and she wondered if she should have called first, warned Cade that she wanted to clear the air. But then she might have lost her nerve and she really needed to talk to him. Face-to-face.

Nearing the long building, she heard a steady clanging emanating from within. "Courage, Hattie," she whispered to herself as she ducked beneath long, toothlike icicles that hung from the eaves and pushed open a wide door that slid on creaking rollers.

As soon as there was enough space for her to squeeze through, she stepped inside the cavernous shed where a tractor, combine, and disc harrow resided along with hitches, trailers, and other machines she didn't immediately recognize. As she made her way along a narrow aisle behind the machinery, the smells of dust and oil filled her nostrils. Beneath it all, she detected the scent of diesel. "Hello?" she called, shivering a bit as the shed, if it was heated, was still cold enough that her breath fogged. "Cade?"

"Hey!" His voice echoed from the length of the shed and she followed the sound to find him standing on a step stool, leaning under the open hood of a large tractor. His hair fell over his forehead, and his sleeves were pushed up over his elbows. Grease blackened his hands and forearms, and streaked jeans that were nearly threadbare and spattered with paint.

"Trouble?" she asked as he straightened and tossed his hair from his eyes.

"Nah." Grabbing a rag from the back pocket of his jeans, he climbed down the steps, wiping his fingers. "Maintenance." His smile was a crooked slash and a streak of black was visible on his jaw. "Don't let anyone kid you, it's not 'yearly' maintenance." He hopped off the ladder, still cleaning the grease from his hands. "It's 'all-year' mainte-nance."

"Ah . . ." As he closed the gap between them, she felt a second's hesitation.

"What's up?"

Here we go. "I came looking for you and Zed said you were out here. He, uh, wasn't very glad to see me and let me know just how he feels."

"Zed can be blunt."

"That's one way to say it," she said, then waved off any further dis-cussion about his oldest brother. "Anyway, it doesn't matter what he thinks, not really; I came out here to clear the air and hoped that we could find a way to get along."

"Aren't we?"

"Come on, Cade. We've never really gotten along."

He hesitated. "So, why now, Hattie?"

"I thought we needed to talk," she started, wondering why her well-rehearsed lines had left her. "It's the girls. When they saw you on the street the other day, when we were going to Wild Wills, they were really disappointed that you didn't join us." He started to ex-plain, but she held out a hand to stop him. "That's just part of it. Ever since Bart died, they've been searching for a father figure, I guess, and Dan's tried his best to fill those shoes, at least as well as he could."

"And now you expect me to . . . what? Take up where Dan left off?"

"No." Wincing inside, she shook her head, as if denying what she was about to admit. "Listen, I'm sorry. This is coming out all wrong. I probably should wait to tell you, but I've waited so long, so, so long already, and now Zed has accused me and . . . Oh, God."

She was withering inside, her confidence leaking away.

"Hattie?" He grabbed her arm, as if to steady her, and she closed her eyes. What a mess she'd made of things, of her life, of Bart's. "What?" he asked. When she opened her eyes, she found his face close to hers, his breath warm, his pupils dark, his expression clouded with concern. "Zed accused you of what?"

Mother of God, she was such a coward, such a foolish, deep-seated coward. "It's complicated," she said, aware of the tense fingers clamped over her upper arm.

"Then you'd better uncomplicate it."

The world seemed to shift at that moment as dozens of memories cut through her brain, memories of hot sex, warm winds, and cool water against her skin as she swam naked in the pond. With Cade. Beneath the wide Montana skies, smelling new grass and . . .

"Hattie?"

She blinked. Told herself to quit being a wimp. Felt sweat drip down her spine though it was cold as hell in the machine shed. Cade came back into too sharp of focus again. "Okay," she said in a voice she didn't recognize as her own. "There's just no way to say this any easier or more succinctly." She drew in a long breath and finally admitted, "The truth of the matter is that Bart wasn't the girls' biological father, Cade." His eyes, so close, darkened, and his jaw slid to one side. Slowly, the fingers grasping her uncoiled. Mixed emotions crossed his face. Disgust. Anger. And guilt. *He knew! Damn it, he's known all along. Or at the very least suspected the truth.*

The seconds stretched between them as he stared at her. "Say it, Hattie," he insisted, his voice low, nearly menacing. "I want you to actually say the words."

"Don't you blame me, Cade. You're in this with me, but, yes, you're the twins' father. That last time we were together."

"I don't believe it."

"Don't you? I see it in your eyes. You've probably suspected all along, so don't start pointing fingers. We were both adults, both knew what we were doing."

"You were engaged," he charged.

"That's right. To your brother."

He took a step backward, distancing himself. "Shitfire, Hattie, how could you—"

"*We,* Cade. You and me. We made those babies. How could *we*?"

"But you passed them off as Bart's." His face contorted in disbelief, his scar showing white, the dark smudge of grease more visible against his suddenly very pale skin.

"Bart knew."

"*What?* He knew? Jesus H. Christ, Hattie. You both knew and you kept it a secret."

"No, no, no!" She was shaking her head, furious with herself for not being clear in the beginning. "He found out when I did, and that was long after the twins were born. In the beginning, neither of us guessed that the girls weren't his, not really, though I knew it was a possibility. But it wasn't until we tried to have another baby, not too long after the girls were born. I wasn't for it; Lord, we already had two. Twins. I had my hands full. But Bart insisted. He wanted a son too. The girls weren't enough for him, and then we started trying just before the girls turned one, I think. One month went by, then two, finally six or seven, and it seemed odd as the twins had been so easy to conceive."

He was listening, not saying a word, just staring at her. The only sound was the wind outside as it rattled around the corners of the building.

"So," she said, her voice still barely audible. "Sometime just before the girls' second birthday, we went through a series of fertility tests and found out that he couldn't . . . father children."

"He was sterile?" Cade said. "Is that what you're expecting me to believe?"

"Yes."

"You could be just making this up now."

"Why would I do that?"

"I don't know, convenience. To try and rope me in."

"Trust me, this isn't the way I would go at it if I was trying to 'rope you in.' "

"You waltz in here and make this kind of announcement, that I'm a father and I'm supposed to just accept it?" he demanded, color returning to his face. "Would you?"

"You're rejecting the girls?"

"No, damn it, I'm rejecting what you're saying. For the love of God, Hattie, this is a pretty damned good jolt."

"You've suspected all along, but I knew you'd fight me," she said. "Even though it's obvious the girls are Graysons. So, I brought some of our old medical records."

"You're unbelievable."

"I suppose so." Reaching into her purse, she withdrew an envelope and set it on the fender of a flatbed trailer.

"What is this?" he asked, ignoring the thick white packet. "What do you want from me?"

"Nothing," she said succinctly, trying to keep her anger in check. *You started this, Hattie! Remember? You knew it wasn't going to turn out all sweetness and light.* "I just thought it was time you knew the truth. We've had a big jolt this week, were reminded how short life really is. I thought you'd want to know."

"About nine years too late," he growled. "For the love of Christ, Hattie, even if this is true—"

"It is. Do you honestly think I would leave my kids with Zena and drive out here as part of some kind of scam?" She sighed and looked away from the shock on his face. "I honestly thought you knew me better than that."

"Seems I don't know you at all." She looked back at him to find him scrutinizing her. "So you're trying to tell me that now, finally, you've had a change of heart, that you're . . . I don't know, doing something altruistic by letting me know that I'm the father of eight-year-old twins I thought were my brother's."

"That's the way it is."

Throwing his hands up, he asked, "So now that I know your version of the truth, did you think that . . . I don't know, you and I and the girls, we could be some happy little family, that Mallory and McKenzie would start calling me 'Daddy'?"

"Of course not." She flushed. "I haven't told the girls and I don't intend to now, unless you want to make a case of it."

His eyes slitted suspiciously.

"Don't worry, Cade, as I said, I'm not looking for anything from you."

"I don't believe you."

Her heart squeezed a bit because deep down, the truth was that she did want something for the girls. She wanted them to know their father, to feel the strength of a good man's arms to comfort them when they were hurt, the stern love and guidance from a father that they'd missed. She, as a mother, would like the solid support of the man who'd sired her children, but then she couldn't expect it.

"I messed up," she admitted. "Big time. I didn't tell Bart about us until after the problems with conceiving, and then he was . . . well, beyond pissed. At me. And rightfully so. I was engaged to him when it happened. However, the girls *always* had a father who was there for them. Bart loved them as if they were his biological kids. His feelings for them never wavered. Not a bit."

"What about his feelings for you?" Cade demanded, his anger palpable. "How fucked up were they?"

"He made it crystal clear how he felt about me, about what I'd done. How I'd betrayed him and couldn't be trusted and never loved him and on and on. I deserved it, I guess, didn't have much of a defense. He even accused me of never loving him, which wasn't true, but no amount of denial was good enough. He thought he was my third choice after you and Dan, and he made it all crystal clear, even accused me of wanting to sleep with Zed too." She shuddered at the memory, at the storm in her husband's face, the outright disgust and repulsion at her. She'd thought he might strike her, or spit on her, the way his hands had balled and his teeth had shown, but he'd turned and smashed his hand through the wall of their bedroom, blasting a hole in the wallboard and knocking the family portrait off the wall. "He moved out of the bedroom that night and we never slept together again."

"Wow." He shook his head.

"Yeah." She remembered those months, the tension in their house, the angry looks, sullen moods, monosyllabic answers to her questions. Bart had completely iced her out and had never let her forget for a second that she'd betrayed him. She'd suggested counseling, then when that hadn't flown, a temporary separation or cooling-off period, anything to repair the rift between them. Bart, ever more despondent, had refused, his fury and humiliation seething just under the surface. Day-to-day life had become impossible, to the point that

Hattie avoided being in the same room with him. While he seemed to revel in his newfound role of victim and martyr, she'd come to resent her part as an evil twenty-first-century Jezebel.

"Doesn't seem to be any other way to see things." Ignoring the envelope, Cade added, "So, after spilling your guts because you were forced to, and him turning his back on you, a few months later you walked out."

"Essentially," she admitted, unable to explain how difficult her marriage had become. "Things were never perfect between Bart and me, but the truth of the girls' paternity put a bigger strain on the marriage. I just wanted to work things out, but it wasn't going to happen."

"*You* wanted to work things out?"

"Yes, but it was too late. The wall between us was insurmountable. He wouldn't go to a marriage counselor or a psychologist or a psychiatrist, even though he was obviously suffering from depression and the marriage was unraveling."

"So you just up and left him."

"You can twist this any way you want, but Bart wasn't willing to work on the marriage. Even though they were young, the girls were picking up that something was wrong, and I couldn't lie to them any longer, or pretend that everything was fine, so, yes, I gave him an ultimatum: Get help or get out."

Cade's jaw tightened and she thought he was going to lambast her again. Well, fine. She'd said what she had to say and could leave with a clear conscience. She turned for the door, but his voice stopped her.

"I'm not blaming you," Cade said nearly inaudibly.

"Coulda fooled me."

"No." Scowling, he looked up to the rafters, then shook his head, as if he'd been searching for answers in the cold crossbeams and had come up with nothing. "I guess I want to, but I can't. You're right," he said, his voice low, a muscle working at his temple, near the thin scar still visible on his cheek. "It wasn't just you. I was there too. I should have stopped it, but . . ." He let out a disgusted puff of air. "I just wanted you so damned bad that I didn't care about Bart. That's a fact.

I didn't care that you were engaged, that what we were doing was right out of some bad movie." Regret tugged at the corners of his mouth, reflected darkly in his eyes. "You could have told me before."

"And what would have changed?" she asked.

His look was long and penetrating. "For one thing," he said, "Bart might still be alive."

CHAPTER 22

Pescoli glanced at the clock on her cluttered desk and told herself she could take five minutes to call Santana. They hadn't really spoken since he'd offered her the ring, only a quick text or message to check in. He, too, was disturbed about what was happening, and their only communication these days was about Grayson. Nothing further had been said about his proposal, but time was passing and sooner or later, she would have to face him.

Picking up her cell, she dialed and waited, but he didn't pick up, so she was forced to leave a message. "Hey, it's me. Thought we should get together. It's, uh, been a while." That wasn't quite true. He'd given her the ring on Christmas Eve, and she'd seen him briefly at the hospital, but it still felt like forever since they'd been together. "Give me a call." She hung up and stared at the phone, wondering why this was so hard. Why had she become such a commitment-phobe? Two rocky marriages didn't necessarily mean that she would have another. Right?

No reason to lose sleep over it; she had too much to do. She decided to stretch her legs, so she got up and walked a short distance down the hall. "Still no word on Verdago?" she asked as she stepped into Alvarez's much too neat office. How did anyone work that way, with everything stacked, filed, and color-coded? Even the top of her desk held only one open file and a bottle of water, its cap screwed on tightly, resting on a coaster near a cup holding several pens and pencils.

"Nothing."

It was near four in the afternoon and outside, night had fallen. Pescoli had spent the last few hours on the phone, running down tips and reevaluating the reports from the crime lab that included any trace evidence that had been collected and processed. Fingerprints, footprints, and tire treads had been analyzed and compared, the preliminary autopsy, without drug information on the judge performed, bullet striations compared, and all of the judge's personal life, from her telephone records to her bank statements, were already being pored over.

Every facet of the judge's life, like that of Dan Grayson's, was being dissected—professionally, personally, and privately—and laid bare.

The obvious link between the two victims was their work, the people they came in contact with and the scumbags they'd put away, but that was almost too easy, and nothing yet was fitting. As they'd discussed earlier, Alvarez and Pescoli were searching for any other connection between Dan Grayson and Kathryn Samuels-Piquard.

Socially, they would run into each other at occasional charity events, but they didn't really travel in the same circles, primarily because Grayson didn't seem to have much of a social life.

There was phone contact between the two, but usually during work hours, and the six times that Grayson had called the judge late at night in the last two years turned out to be on the nights he'd requested search warrants and needed a judge's signature. Samuels-Piquard had obliged. So far, they'd found no incidences when the judge had called Grayson, except at work, and those had been spotty and few.

Aside from searching for a connection between the victims, Pescoli was still looking into their personal lives, but so far, Grayson's ex-wives and Samuels-Piquard's family seemed clean. However, there was still Vincent Piquard, the judge's ne'er-do-well, and lately invisible, brother. The cell phone number Winston had given her for him had been a bust; the elderly woman on the other end of the phone said she'd gotten the number only six months earlier and, sure enough, phone records had concurred.

Vincent was off the radar.

Even though his sister's death had been splashed all over the news.

Odd.

Very odd.

Even if the siblings had been estranged, it seemed Vincent would have appeared, have talked to his nephew, or have contacted a lawyer about his part, if any, of the estate. Death of a relative usually brought out the rest of the family—the good eggs, the black sheep, and the bad seeds.

And then there was the missing Maurice Verdago. The more time that went by, the more Pescoli was thinking he might be the guy. His violent streak was a matter of record and though he'd never actually been convicted of a homicide, there was the Joey Lundeen cold case. Lundeen had disappeared nearly fifteen years earlier and had known Verdago. Maurice had been a suspect in his disappearance. Pescoli had already requested the records.

As if reading her mind, Alvarez rolled her chair away from her desk and said, "Verdago's still missing, and no one in his family or close friends seem to know where he is. I checked."

"What about his wife?"

"Nothing nice to say about him. Seems she wasn't aware that Maurice had a woman on the side. Carnie Tibalt. Actually, her full name is Carnival, and Wanda, who didn't know about his girlfriend until we started nosing around, went ballistic when she found out."

"Oops," Pescoli said. "Have you talked to either woman?"

"Only Wanda. I was the lucky person who asked her about Carnie after she told me she had no idea where her husband was. But she must've suspected he had something going on with Carnie because she didn't argue the point or scream that it was impossible. What she said was, 'That fuckin' bitch!' and hung up. Hasn't answered her phone since."

Pescoli actually grinned. "What about Carnie—geez, Carnival, really, who would do that to a kid?"

"I've heard lots worse."

"Okay, me too," Pescoli allowed. "Any luck with her?"

"Not much. She won't even pick up the phone, and no one answers at her last known address."

"Work?"

"Like Verdago, she's gone. Worked as a barmaid over at the Long Branch. Picked up her last paycheck and disappeared."

"What about vehicles? They've got to be driving something."

"Maybe her car. The wife has Verdago's old Chevy Blazer, so it's out of play. Carnie has no car registered to her, but she drives an old Dodge van according to her coworkers at the bar. No one remembers much about it, so it must have Montana plates, nothing that stood out. All I know is it's white or light gray or silver, depending on who you ask, and has a dent in the driver's side door. About twenty years old."

"Big enough to sleep in."

"You still have to park it somewhere."

Pescoli agreed, "But Montana's a big state with too many damned hidey-holes." Leaning back in her chair, she added, "Verdago could have it stashed in an old barn or shed, or just at the end of an old mining road that's closed for the winter. Camp out."

"They'd still need supplies."

"Not too many so far," she said, and that was the truth. Though it seemed like forever since she'd witnessed Grayson being shot, actually only a few days had passed. Less than a week. She knew that fact very well, as the minutes were ticking down on her ultimatum with Santana. New Year's was approaching fast. "We have a BOLO alert out on the van?"

"Yes, ma'am, the Be On the Look Out for is in place. No hits so far. And we're also checking on stolen vehicles in the area."

"All this is assuming Carnie is actually with Verdago," Pescoli said on a sigh.

"Since she's missing about the same time, a distinct possibility, I'd say." Alvarez uncapped her water bottle and took a swallow, then twisted the cap back on again before setting the bottle back onto its coaster.

Of the five recently released prisoners who might have had it out for Grayson, four had been sentenced by Judge Samuels-Piquard:

Maurice Verdago, who had tried to kill his profit-skimming brother-in-law, joined Floyd Cranston, would-be ax murderer, and Gerald Resler, who'd attempted to cut his girlfriend with a can opener way back when but had been Pescoli's collar. Edie Gardener might have won over the jury, which found her guilty of a lesser crime, but when it came to sentencing, Judge Samuels-Piquard had meted out as harsh a penalty as the law would allow.

"What about the others?" Pescoli asked.

"Mendoza never actually faced Judge Samuels-Piquard, and he's in a Mexican jail, Juarez, fighting extradition. He was definitely out of the country at the time of the attack on Grayson, so I'm scratching him for now. As for your good buddy Gerald Resler, he was at a church retreat, working on his marriage."

Pescoli had trouble believing that the acne-faced kid with the violent temper and a Texas-sized chip on his shoulder had changed. "The can-opener king found God?" She snorted. "Prison must've turned him around."

"That or having a kid. Several people at the retreat vouched for him, so, unless he's taken up with a sect of Methodist liars or he hired someone to do his dirty work, he's clean."

"Narrows the field, I guess," Pescoli said as over a soft thrum of conversation, someone's cell phone chirped from a nearby office. The department was still out of sync, it seemed, without Dan Grayson at its helm. The connecting hallways and offices, bustling with activity as usual, the sounds and smells the same, but the feeling was off, devoid of that quiet calmness Grayson emanated. Pescoli glanced down the corridor to his darkened office where once Sturgis would have curled lazily on his dog bed tucked into one corner, or Grayson's Stetson would sit atop his desk where he'd so often left it.

She missed him, from his bushy, graying mustache to the glint of humor in his intelligent eyes. With Grayson in the department, it had seemed balanced somehow.

Now, she felt the change. Now there was a void, an emptiness that reminded Pescoli that Dan Grayson might never return, that someday his office could be occupied by someone else. The thought soured her stomach.

It seemed light-years since she'd driven to his home intent on handing in her resignation, a lifetime since she'd planned to let him know that her living arrangements were changing, that she was looking forward to a life with Santana, eons since she'd watched his body, almost in slow motion, jerk with the bullets' impact, the kindling in his arms flying in all directions.

No wonder she was tired and cranky, the world seeming off-kilter.

"What about Edie Gardener?" Pescoli asked. "I don't suppose she's surfaced."

"She's definitely in avoidance mode and we haven't zeroed in on her yet, but according to her sister-in-law, she's talked to Edie, who, it seems, has been hiding out at her new husband's home."

"We know where that is?"

"Twenty miles toward the Idaho border," Alvarez said, "I just got the address out of Edie's sister-in-law. She was pretty reticent about giving out information; I think worried that the family will see her as a rat, but she felt compelled to come clean, I guess. And, even more interesting, I think, is that the sister said Edie's newfound love is an ex-con who's a major hunter. Has bragged about taking down a bull elk with a clean shot to the head from a quarter of a mile or so."

"Could be just talk."

"Maybe, but worth checking out." She was already reaching for her jacket and sidearm. "Let's see what Edie and her new hubby have to say for themselves."

"I'll meet you at my Jeep," Pescoli said, reaching into her pocket and withdrawing her keys. "One quick stop to make first." She tossed the keys to Alvarez and made a detour to the ladies' room where she downed two ibuprofen to help fend off that lingering headache and used the toilet.

Ever since lunch she'd felt a little queasy and at first had blamed her upset stomach on the corned beef and sauerkraut that she'd wolfed down, but now, she wondered if she was coming down with the flu that Bianca had suffered from just last week.

"Great," she whispered, washing her hands and heading out to meet up with Alvarez. With everything else on her plate, the last thing she needed right now, the very last thing, was to get sick.

She walked out of the restroom and nearly plowed into her son. Carrying a teetering stack of boxes, Jeremy muttered a quick, "Excuse me," before realizing who she was. "Oh. Mom."

"Got a sec?"

"I've really got to get these boxes down to—"

"This'll only take a minute," she said, "Alvarez is waiting for me. But I wanted to say . . . I was wrong." The words nearly stuck in her throat, but as she stared at her son, standing straight, hair combed, clean-shaven, wearing a pressed T-shirt with the department's logo embroidered into it, she felt pride swell her chest.

"About what?"

"You, kiddo. If this is what you want to do, then, hey, go for it."

"Don't call me 'kiddo,' " he whispered.

"Hey, I apologized, okay? Admitted I was wrong, but I'm sorry, I'm probably going to call you what comes to mind. 'Kiddo' could be the least of your worries, Jer-Bear."

He cringed at the childhood name. Years before, while still in grade school, he'd begged her to drop it and she had. Until now, when a stricken look washed over his features. "Don't, Mom. Please, just don't."

"Okay, pumpkin."

"That's *worse!*" He looked around to see if anyone had overheard their conversation. "Give it a rest."

She laughed and gave him a wink. "Just know I've got your back." And with that she was out the door.

"I guess you all didn't see the sign?" Edie Gardener said when she opened the door to find Alvarez and Pescoli on her sagging porch. She'd appeared in pajama bottoms and a faded sweatshirt while smoking a cigarette. They introduced themselves and flashed their badges, and she seemed positively bored. A small thing, probably not a hundred pounds, she oozed "I'm a badass" attitude despite her stature. Her brown hair was pulled onto her crown in a bun that was nearly the size of her head, and as she sized them up and down, she nodded to a big beware of dog sign that hung on a dilapidated fence between the carport and the mobile home. An old Buick sat on blocks under the carport, its roof sagging and covered with snow. More snow was falling, carried by a wind that was raw and gusting. "You're just lucky Buster's locked up."

A low-pitched, but frantic howl emitted from within the house, as if Buster had heard his name and was ready to charge out the door with his teeth bared, fangs dripping, his whole being intent on ripping them limb from limb. "See?" She cracked a smile that faded as quickly as it had appeared.

"We'd like to ask you a few questions," Alvarez said.

She looked down on the detectives as if collectively they were the scum of the earth. "I'm not an idiot. I know why you're here, and I'm tellin' you right out before you start askin' all your stupid questions, I had nothin' to do with what happened to the sheriff or that judge. That's why you're here, right? Because I was pissed at Grayson for lockin' me up. Well, here's a news flash"—she leaned forward a bit—"I didn't kill Johnny way back when, and I sure as hell didn't shoot the sheriff." She turned her head to one side and yelled over her shoulder, "Hey, Art, will you tell these cops that I was with you when that dumbass sheriff got himself shot?"

"Just a sec," a deep voice ordered.

"*Now,* Art! These ladies need answers." Shivering a little, she wrapped one arm around her middle, but despite the cold, she smirked as she drew on her long, black cigarette. The sound of heavy tread approached and somewhere, farther within, the wild barks and growls increased in volume.

"Buster, hush!" the male voice ordered and the dog immediately did as he was bid just as Art, all six-feet-seven of him, appeared behind her. With a shock of dirty blond hair, he towered a foot and a half over Edie and looked like an ex-NBA center gone to seed.

"She's right," he said, his eyes puffy from sleep. A flannel shirt flapped open over a once-white T-shirt. "I read when the sheriff was shot. Christmas mornin', right? We was together. Playin' Santie Claus." He smiled, showing slightly crooked teeth, pleased with himself for providing the alibi.

"Anyone else see you?" Alvarez asked.

"Yeah, we was at the pancake house—oh, what's the name of it."

Edie looked up at him. "Hot Stacks."

"Yeah, that's it," he agreed, nodding. "Hot Stacks. There in Missoula. The one that's open all day and night, every day."

"The waitress who waited on us was Rose," Edie said with a smirk. "Tall blonde with a tattoo climbing up her arm." She indicated the inside of her left arm with the hand that held her cigarette. "A rose. Appropriate, don't you think?"

"Your memory is pretty clear." Pescoli wasn't sure she was buying their story. It all seemed too pat. "What time were you there?"

"Nine," Art said, looking at Edie. Double-checking. "Maybe ten."

"The sheriff was shot earlier," Alvarez said.

"We were together. Here. It took us a while to get there, but you check with Rose and some of the other people havin' their Christmas breakfast there," Edie said. "Because Art here finally gave me my wedding ring. About damned time too." She stuck out her left hand to display a sparkling ring covered in diamond chips. "I squealed, loud enough that Saint Peter, up in heaven, heard it. You just ask Rose!"

"And anyone else in the place." Art was beaming from one ear to the other, so damned proud of himself. So that's what he meant by playing "Santie Claus."

Pescoli cut in, "I hear you're a pretty good shot."

His smile slid away. "Not 'pretty good,' I'm damned good. Ask anyone around."

Pescoli assured him, "I will."

"Oh, I get it," Edie said. "You think I had him shoot the sheriff for me? Now, ain't that somethin'?" She actually cackled. "How sweet. As if I needed someone to do my dirty work. That's a good one. But listen, if Art here was the one aiming the rifle that put a bullet in Grayson, the sheriff would be six feet under right now instead of lingering at a damned hospital. You're barking up the wrong tree, I tell you. No matter how much I hated Grayson, and I still do, I wouldn't do nothin' that would put me back in that prison. I'm thinkin' everyone else he put away feels the same."

She shivered again as a blast of wind slipped through the canyon. "I haven't done nothin' wrong. As far as I'm concerned, Grayson got what he deserved. I hope he dies. I just didn't do it." She took a final drag on her smoke, then tossed the cigarette into a snowbank to sizzle and die. "We're done here."

The sound of frantic claws scrambling toward the door caught her attention and a tiny dog that was obviously part Chihuahua shot through her legs. It barked and yapped, showing its nasty little teeth. "This is Buster?" Pescoli said as Edie picked up the tiny pooch.

"Oh, no, this here's Fifi." She held Pescoli's gaze for a second. "Trust me, you really don't want to meet Buster."

At the sound of his name, the dog in the back started growling and barking wildly again, sounding as if he were big enough to eat Fifi in one bite.

"Really, it would be a very bad idea," Edie said and slammed the door in their faces.

A father?

Cade could barely get his mind around the truth, if that's what it was, and from the medical reports that Hattie had left with him, it seemed that her story was accurate. He'd watched her leave, hadn't stopped her when she'd said, "Okay, that's why I came here, to let you know that the girls are, at least biologically, yours. You have rights and . . . and I should have told you before, but I just couldn't. So there's not a whole lot more to say." She'd looked at him with those damnably intelligent eyes and waited for him to say something, but he hadn't. Didn't even know where to start.

Her face had still been flushed from his comment about Bart. She'd nodded to his continued silence and turned away, and he'd watched her shove open the heavy shed door and disappear into the coming night. Only when he'd heard her engine turn over did he shake himself back to action. "Son of a bitch," he'd whispered as he'd turned out the lights and, head swimming with thoughts of those two little imps who he'd let himself believe to be Bart's, made his way up to the house. He hadn't noticed that Zed's Ford was missing, but the house was empty when he'd walked inside.

He was alone.

Which, all things considered, was a good thing.

Though he was covered in grime and grease, he hadn't bothered even cleaning up, just poured himself a healthy dose of whiskey and opened the envelope to spread its damning contents over the old plank table that had been in the house as long as he could remember.

Originally, when their mother was still alive, all four boys had always occupied their assigned seats. Ma and Pa had been situated at either end of the table, Zed and Dan in chairs on one side, Bart and Cade occupying the bench near the wall.

To this day, he took the seat on his end of the bench and now, he glanced down its scarred length to a spot where Bart had, after Ma had died, carved his initials into the wood.

God, that was a lifetime ago.

He looked across the table to the spot Dan had occupied, catty-corner from him, and imagined his older brother looking back at him, silently offering him advice. Cade's insides twisted when he realized he might lose the brother who had been his mentor all his life. "Damn it all to hell," he said under his breath, then swirled his drink, looking into the amber depths, unable to imagine what the world would be without Dan Grayson. Certainly not a better place. If he could get his hands around the throat of the bastard who'd done this, he would gladly strangle him. He blinked, imagining Dan in his chair. It had been decades since he'd sat on the smooth wood seat on a daily basis.

Long before all their lives had been forever tangled in Hattie Dorsey's seductive web.

Don't blame her, Cade. She's right. She didn't do this on her own.

He reread the reports and saw that Bart's sperm count was practically nonexistent, the likelihood of him fathering any children nil.

He didn't believe Hattie had been involved with anyone else; hell, the guilt she'd experienced by being with him about killed her, so he had to assume Mallory and McKenzie were his.

And really, what did it matter? Bart was dead, Dan still in a coma in the hospital, and Zed despised Hattie; always had, always would. So that left him to be the father figure to the girls he considered his nieces.

Was anything so different?

Hell, yeah! He was a father. A damned father. A role he'd never really considered playing, not that he didn't love Hattie's imps, he did, but a *father*?

Of course it had crossed his mind, but he'd put it aside, always telling himself that if there were a modicum of truth to his suspicions, someone would have told him.

Well, that someone did.

Today.

And ridiculously he was furious. Stung that it had taken her this long to come up with the truth.

"Shitfire," he whispered to no one but the dog who, lying on the couch in the living area, didn't seem to notice. "Apparently you're as blind as I am," he yelled across the room to Shad, who didn't so much as lift his spotted head.

Daughters! Two daughters! A whole vista of dance lessons, cheerleading squads, softball games, and boys with hot cars, boys who couldn't keep their dicks in their pants, randy teenagers just like he'd been, came to mind.

He shoved the faded reports aside and, carrying his drink, walked to the window to stare outside. Snow was falling, covering the woodpile, drifting against the stables and catching on the windowsills. Peaceful. Serene. In direct opposition to the storm of emotions roiling through his mind. He remembered all too clearly the night Hattie had come to him, breaking it off, sobbing that she was a horrible person for what she, what they'd, done to Bart.

Attempting to console her, he'd pulled her close and told her that it would be all right. He'd taken one whiff of the perfume lingering in her hair and kissed her cheek, tasting the salt of her tears, and she'd pushed him away, with such force he'd been surprised. "Never," she said, blinking hard, her lips trembling, outrage and guilt burning in her wide, anguished eyes. "Never touch me again."

And he hadn't. Two hours later, he was on his bike and heading west, tearing down the road twenty miles over the speed limit, putting the dust of Grizzly Falls and the heartache and confusion that was Hattie Dorsey in his rearview. He'd intended to stay away forever but couldn't resist the draw of the wedding when he'd shown up and made an ass of himself. He still cringed inside when he remembered that foolish show.

He'd been as randy and horny as the boys he foresaw trying to date his daughters.

A helluva thing.

Now, taking a swallow of whiskey he barely tasted, he noticed his reflection, pale and watery in the glass. "So now what're you gonna do, you son of a bitch?" he asked the man with the streak of grease on his face. "Just what the hell are you gonna do?"

CHAPTER 23

"You think maybe Edie, in her twisted way, is right?" Pescoli asked Alvarez as she drove into town, crossing the railroad tracks at the base of Boxer Bluff. Darkness had fallen and the snow was beginning to get serious, coming down steadily enough that Pescoli cranked up her wipers to the max.

Alvarez threw her a look. "I don't think Edie Gardener's right about anything."

"She said we were barking up the wrong tree, and there's a chance she's got a point. It could be that whoever's behind this is closer to home."

"You mean like a love triangle, or someone wanting to inherit, or something?" Alvarez said. "We've looked into that, but the trouble is we now have one assassin. Why would he want both victims dead?"

"Unless Grayson is somehow connected to the judge on a personal level."

"No proof of that," Alvarez said. "At all."

"I know, I know." Pescoli let out a frustrated breath and felt as if she were missing something obvious as she followed the road that cut along the hillside and wound its way up the bluff to the newer part of Grizzly Falls. She'd called Sage Zoller and asked the junior detective to follow up on some leads, including trying to track down Rose at Hot Stacks, the pancake house in Montana, just to double-check on Edie and her goon of a new husband.

"We've already figured that Grayson's ex-wives are out. They have no connection to Judge Samuels-Piquard," Alvarez said.

"Yeah, I know. It must be someone they both put away," Pescoli agreed and felt the heartburn that had been with her since she'd awoken kick up again. "Would you check the glove box? I think there's a bottle of antacids in there. I could use some." As Alvarez rummaged inside the box, Pescoli once more attempted to come up with some personal connection between Grayson and Samuels-Piquard. She'd tried to find some way Cara Grayson Banks or Akina Grayson Bellows wanted to harm Dan Grayson, but it was apparent neither of Dan's exes had opportunity. For Cara Banks, there was plenty of motive, but her alibi was rock solid and she appeared not to want anything to do with the Grayson family or money. Nolan Banks, from all outward appearances, was on the wealthy side of the economic seesaw. And Akina was into her own thing. The same could be said of Winston Piquard, though the judge's brother, Vincent Samuels, hadn't yet surfaced.

"So we're back to the beginning," Alvarez said as Pescoli slowed for a light and a semi, making the turn in front of them, nearly rolled up on the sidewalk before chugging down the hill. As the light changed, Pescoli stepped on it. Traffic was relatively light. Alvarez found the near-empty bottle of chewable antacids and, after they pulled into the lot, handed it to Pescoli, who downed four tablets.

"We still don't know who cleaned the judge's house, right?" Pescoli asked.

"Still working on it," Alvarez said. "There's a chance she could shed some light on the judge's personal life or any threats she may have gotten."

"And what happened to the threatening letters that her son swears she got?"

Alvarez glanced out the window to the day beyond. "Her house and office have been searched and so far, nothing."

"You think the maid would know anything about that?"

"Possibly."

"Then let's find her." As she cut the engine and stepped outside, Pescoli's cell phone went off and she glanced down at the screen. Unknown number. God, she hated that. She answered, "Regan Pescoli."

"Detective!" She recognized the voice even before he said, "Manny Douglas, here. *Mountain Reporter.*"

Damn! She shouldn't have answered. "I *know* where you work, Manny."

"I thought you'd like to see what I got in the mail today."

"What?" she asked, as the connection was a little dicey, the traffic noise and wind making it hard to hear.

"Better I show you in person. I'm just down the street getting coffee. I can be at the station in less than ten."

"I'm busy," she said automatically, assuming he was just bluffing while intending on weaseling his way into the station so he could go on another information fishing expedition.

"Trust me, you won't be too busy for this," he said, and there was an oily smugness in his voice that bugged the hell out of her. "I'll be right there." He hung up and she gave herself a swift mental kick for not meeting with him outside of the station. Once inside the doors of the department, there was a chance it would take a gigantic backhoe and light-years to get him out again.

"Problems?" Alvarez asked as they walked into the station.

Sighing, she shouldered open the door, then repeated the conversation. "I'm going to need fortification for this." She made her way to the lunchroom and eyed the coffeepot, then thought better of it. No reason to get the heartburn going again.

Making her way to her desk, she stripped off her jacket and sidearm, and looked up Claudia Dubois's, the judge's neighbor's, number. Whether she was a little dingy or not, she was there on the street. She placed the call and as the phone rang, Pescoli remembered Claudia's insistence that someone evil had been watching the Samuels-Piquard residence from the park.

Real?

Imagined?

Who knew?

Claudia answered on the fourth ring. "*Doctor* Dubois's residence," she announced curtly while Pescoli identified herself.

"Oh, yes, Detective! I'm so glad you called." She sounded absolutely delighted.

"I was wondering," Pescoli said, double-checking as she knew Claudia's memory faded in and out, "if you remember Donna's last name, the maid for Judge Samuels-Piquard."

"Donna Goodwin," she said clearly. "I told you that when you asked the other day. She lives outside of Missoula and cleans for Kathryn, well . . . did and for Velma next door."

"Velma Miller?"

"Yes." There was a perturbed tone to her voice, as if Pescoli were a cretin.

"Are the Millers home?"

"Of course they are. Their skiing trip only lasts a few days, just over Christmas. They're always back before New Year's."

"Good to know." If it turned out to be true. Claudia's sense of reality seemed to shift with the days. Another question plagued her. "Have you seen the stalker again?"

"What stalker?"

Oh, dear God.

"The man in white, maybe white camouflage that you noticed under the tree in the park."

"The park across the street from us?" she said, and there was a note of concern in her voice. "I told you about him?"

"Yes."

"Oh. My. Well, I was probably mistaken about that. My husband, Barry, *Doctor* Baron Dubois, he told me I was mistaken."

"Were you?" Pescoli asked, wondering about the little round man who had seemed so concerned about his wife when they'd spoken in the foyer of their large, brick home. Was he trying to protect his wife, not wanting anyone to know of her hallucinations, if that's what they were, or did he have another motive?

"Was I what? Oh, mistaken." She lowered her voice to a soft whisper. "Of course not. That man was there, I tell you, and if you ask me, he's the one who killed Kathy!"

"Thank you, Mrs. Dubois," she said as she spied Sage Zoller stick her head into the office. She held up a finger to indicate she was about done with the conversation and to hold on.

"You're welcome, Detective, and please, stop by anytime." As she hung up, Pescoli was left with more questions than she had when she'd first dialed. "What's up?" she asked Sage.

"A couple of things." The junior detective slid into the room, leaving the door slightly ajar. Leaning against the edge of Pescoli's desk, she said, "First off, the lab can't find anything from the ashes found in the judge's house."

"Not good news."

"I know, but there it is. No way to analyze them any further. All they can say for certain is that it was paper."

"Great."

"But we got lucky on another lead. I was able to run down Rose Hellman, the waitress at Hot Stacks, and she did confirm that Edie Gardener, now Mrs. Art Danielson, was there on Christmas morning, sometime around ten or ten-thirty, and that there was quite a stir when she was given her ring. She let out a whoop that caught everyone in the restaurant's attention; then her husband placed the ring on her finger, kissed her, and twirled her off her feet, knocking over several glass pots of warm blackberry syrup in the process. Everyone in the restaurant clapped."

"They still could have shot Grayson and made it to Missoula."

"First they'd have to ski off the hill, find their vehicle, presumably change, as I asked, and Rose said Edie was in a short skirt and tights, but yeah, it could happen."

Pescoli tapped her pencil on the desk. "I wonder what they drive?" She remembered the Buick, sans tires, gathering dust in the carport, but hadn't remembered seeing another vehicle.

"I checked. He did have a truck, big-ass Dodge, but he totaled it six weeks ago. Probably where he got the money for the ring. And she has a twenty-year-old Honda Civic."

"Which could have a ski rack." But she knew she was pushing it. "Check on that and also the Millers, the neighbors of the judge. They're supposed to be back in town, so maybe they can tell us if she was seeing anyone or if anyone suspicious was around and, oh, the phone number of Donna Goodwin. I think she may be their housekeeper as well as the judge's. And do we have any leads on a boyfriend, whom she might have been seeing?"

Sage shook her head, dark curls bouncing around her face. "Not yet, but we're still running down some cell phone numbers. There's one that she called quite a few times and it's untraceable, one of those disposable ones. Someone called her from it as well. It was bought from a store in Spokane and we're trying to run down the owner."

"Let me know when you find out who it is."

"*If* I do," she said. "But you'll be the first to know."

"Mom, er, Detective," Jeremy said, knocking on the partially open door. He stuck his head inside. "There's a Mr. Douglas here to see you. Says he's with the paper."

"He is." She shot Sage a knowing glance, then said, "Don't send him back. I'll meet him up front." Having made the mistake of being cooped up in her office with Manny once before, she wasn't going to put herself through it again. His gaze had been everywhere, on her computer monitor, checking her cell phone, which she'd left on the desk, eyeing files spread on the top of her short cabinet. Nope, not again.

"I'll get back to you," Sage promised and scooted by Jeremy, who was still standing awkwardly in the doorway.

"Okay, let's go," Pescoli said and followed her son to the front of the building where Joelle was seated at the front desk, talking on the phone, and Manny Douglas waited on the outside of the reception counter, on one foot and then the other, in front of the department's Christmas tree that had definitely lost all its luster. The star on the top was listing dangerously, and some of the decorations had fallen onto a fake, glittery carpet of snow and equally fake unopened presents. Considering the current state of the Pinewood County Sheriff's Department, the decorations seemed almost gauche, brushing on obscene. Even the silver sign in block letters strung from the exposed beams of the ceiling felt tacky and irreverent when Dan Grayson's current condition was considered.

The letters spelled out: merry christmas and happy new year!

Not a prayer, Pescoli thought as she caught Manny's eye. Today he was wearing rain gear straight out of an outdoors men's catalogue: solid blue Gore-Tex pants and jacket, unless she missed her guess.

Snow was melting on the shoulders of his hooded jacket and his eyeglasses had fogged. As she approached, he took off the glasses and cleaned them with a cloth he'd withdrawn from one of his many pockets.

Mission accomplished, Jeremy peeled off to sit on a stool near Joelle's desk. She, apparently, was his mentor, and even thinking of her in the capacity of teacher just seemed wrong. Other than Seymore, the part-time maintenance guy, Joelle was the least likely person to be a cop in the building, maybe in the whole damned department, but there she was, pointing painted nails at maps and information packets, flashing her brilliant smile at Pescoli's I-wanna-be-a-cop-like-my-dad son.

She couldn't worry about it now. "Hi," she said to the reporter and forced a smile. "What can I do for you, Manny?"

He snorted. "I think it's more like what *I* can do for *you*."

"Fair enough."

The front door opened and in with a gust of wind came a middle-aged couple who quickly approached the desk. As the woman shivered visibly, her face red, her lips a little blue, the man with her zeroed in on Jeremy and said, "We need help, or someone to call AAA. The car is broken down about three streets over and we're from out of town."

Manny watched the exchange as Jeremy stepped up to help them. "Look, we need to go somewhere where we can talk." As if to accentuate his point, the door opened again and a woman bundled head to foot in a long down coat, hat, and scarf called, "Do you have public restrooms here?"

There was no reason to argue. "Fine." She led him down the hallway but veered away from her office and found a free interrogation room. Indicating a straight-backed chair on one side of the table, she slid into the spot across from him. "What have you got?"

His eyes fairly gleamed. "I've got something important to the case, but for it, I want an exclusive."

"Exclusive?"

"On the case surrounding Judge Samuels-Piquard's killer."

"You know I can't do that. We're asking for the public's help, using all the media resources. An exclusive is out." What kind of BS was this?

"Then give me something extra, okay? First crack at a new angle on the story or a new piece of evidence."

"Why would I do that?"

"Because I'm going to help you. A lot."

"How?" she asked, folding her arms across her chest. "And I don't have time for any bull."

"Oh, I know it." He was nodding as he unzipped his jacket and reached into a deceptively large pocket to withdraw a wide ziplock bag. Through the clear plastic were two items: a manila envelope addressed in block letters to Manny Douglas, c/o the *Mountain Reporter* with the newspaper's post office address included, and a picture.

Pescoli's stomach dropped when she realized the 5x7 was a photo of Judge Samuels-Piquard, a head shot that she'd used in her latest campaign to be reelected to the bench. When she flipped the picture over, she saw, scrawled across in the back in black ink, a simple message:

WHO'S NEXT?

"This is evidence," Pescoli told him flatly. "You have to leave it here."

"I know."

"It came today, in the envelope?"

"That's right."

"Who touched it?"

"In our office, just the mail clerk and me, I think. You've got my prints on file and I told Gary, he's the clerk, that if he wasn't in the system, he needed to come down here and be printed so you can compare and eliminate him."

"It's a long shot anyway," she thought, but figured there might be a partial print and possibly DNA in the seal of the envelope from the killer's saliva.

This was their first big break.

"Kinda obvious the killer isn't finished yet. He has more victims planned."

She felt sick inside. He was right. Why else the note on the back of the photo? "So why do you think the killer decided to send this to you?" she asked.

Palms out, his hands spread wide, he said, "I'm the best."

"Oh, right. I guess I forgot for a second."

"So what do you say?" Manny asked, eyebrows raising in anticipation, arching over the rims of his glasses.

"Okay, fine. You're up to bat first, but no exclusive."

"And you should know, we're running with the story that the picture came in to us and we're working closely with the department. You have anything else I can add?"

"Nothing you can't get from the public information officer."

He sighed theatrically. "Darla Vale isn't all that forthcoming."

"You mean she denied you an exclusive too."

"Something like that."

"I guess you'd better get used to it."

"Come on, Pescoli. A little tit for tat here, okay. At least give me first call?"

She glanced down at the photograph and felt a shiver slide down her spine. Who the hell were they dealing with? What kind of psycho had decided to taunt them, and the question he asked, *Who's next?* was a warning that he wasn't yet done. She felt, in negotiating with Manny Douglas as if she were bargaining with the devil. Well, so be it. He was just ambitious to a fault. "Just don't get in the way of the investigation," she warned.

He held up both palms in surrender.

"Good."

"But I'm going to hold you to this deal, that you call me first if there's a break in the case."

"I'm sure you will, Manny," she said, scooping up the newfound evidence. "On that, I don't have a single doubt."

Stomping snow from her boots, Hattie opened the door to her house and was met with a wall of heat, and the aroma of something tangy, robust, and spicy hit her full in the face. Her stomach rumbled as she threw her car keys into her purse, then shrugged off her coat.

"Something smells just short of wonderful," she said, and from deep in the kitchen her mother laughed hard enough that the laughter gave way to a coughing fit.

"It should. Been working on it for hours," Zena called from the kitchen. She stepped into the hallway, wearing an apron and holding a wooden spoon. "My version of minestrone soup. Got the recipe from a friend of mine; you remember Tottie. Well, she never could quite get the spices right, so I tweaked it a bit. Uh-oh, here comes trouble!"

"Mommy!" Mallory yelled, and both girls came running from the back bedroom. Mallory, in a turtleneck, tutu, and ballet slippers, danced and twirled her way into the living area. McKenzie, wearing shorts, a T-shirt, and cowboy boots, clomped fast behind her sister.

"Beware the thundering herd!" Zena declared.

"How're my girls?" Hattie asked, kneeling down. All of her weariness suddenly disappeared as she hugged first one twin, then the other. "Have you had fun with Grandma?"

"They had a blast," Zena said. "And don't let them tell you differently." She waggled her spoon, pointing first at McKenzie, then Mallory. "Did we make cookies or what?"

"Yeah!" McKenzie said. "Gingerbread men!"

"Seriously?" Hattie looked over her shoulder at her mother. "You know it's almost the new year."

"I had some leftover dough." She lifted a shoulder. "Couldn't let it go to waste."

"We made gingerbread women too!" Mallory added and gave her sister a get-it-right glare. "Not just men." They bounced into the kitchen and Hattie followed to see that, indeed, lying faceup on cooling racks, two dozen or so gingerbread people were decorated, or overdecorated to the max. Neon-colored frosting, cinnamon hearts, sprinkles, and tiny chocolate chips had been pushed into the cookies in every imaginable combination.

"Aren't they beautiful?" McKenzie whispered.

"That they are. Every last one of them." Hattie glanced at her mother. "Thanks."

"No sweat," Zena said and stirred some fresh pasta into a huge pot of soup, then opened the oven door, and the smell of baking bread escaped on a warm cloud. "Dinner's about on. Go on, girls, wash up!"

With a little less enthusiasm, they raced down the short hallway to the bathroom. Zena glanced at her daughter once they were alone. "How'd it go?"

"What do you mean?"

"You told me you were going to go talk to Cade about Dan."

"Yes."

"I know there was more to that conversation."

"I don't know what you mean."

"Oh, sure you do, honey. It's the damned elephant in the room that neither of us ever talks about. But I've battled cancer and still am. God knows if I'm going to win that fight, so I don't have time for any more skating around the issue."

Hattie, standing near the kitchen table, stared in disbelief at her mother. Zena *knew*? That had to be what she was leading up to. Heart beating a little faster, she said, "What issue?"

"Hattie, for the love of God. I know you've had a fascination, no, make that an obsession with those Grayson boys since you were in high school, maybe younger. And I don't blame you. They've got it all, and I've always been one to appreciate a sexy man, otherwise I wouldn't have been married five damned times!" She gave the pot another stir. "When I was your age, I think I was married to Cara's father, Richard, at the time, or maybe I was on to Hank by that time, I really can't remember, but I never dreamed I would have said 'I do' and meant it five times. Lordy. Anyway, doesn't matter, I always told you that Dan Grayson was the brother you should have married."

"I know."

"But Cade, he was the one who was in your blood, honey. I knew about Bart's problem, y'know, about fathering kids. Wasn't hard to figure out when you tried so long and nothing happened. Yet you were pregnant in a blink with the twins."

"Mom, this is really none of your business."

"Well, I'm making it my business right now," she said and finding a tasting spoon, took a dip from the kettle. Steam rose from the small spoon and she blew across the rich broth before tasting it. "Mmmm. Perfect," she said. "Better than Tottie Juniper's, let me tell you." She slipped the spoon into the sink where several other pans and cookie sheets were soaking. "So, I'm asking again, how'd it go with Cade?"

Hattie was about to argue, but Zena sent her a look that could cut through steel. "Don't," she warned.

Hattie sighed and looked up at the ceiling. "It went about how you'd expect."

"That bad, eh?"

"Worse," Hattie admitted, remembering the fury in Cade's eyes, the anger at her, the guilt at his own participation. Hearing the pipes groan as the girls turned off the water, she said, "I'll fill you in later."

"And I'll give you all the motherly advice I can muster!"

"Perfect," Hattie said as McKenzie and Mallory reappeared, their faces red from scrubbing, their hands still moist from splashing water. "Come on, let's set the table. Grandma made us soup."

The girls helped serve and Hattie wondered how they'd react once they knew the truth; it was bound to come out now, and she hated to think how that would play out. They were eight now, though sometimes they each acted as if they were three, and kids in school could be rough. If parents talked and their children found out, there could be round after merciless round of teasing. She imagined she'd be the subject of small-town gossip and the butt of many nasty jokes, but she could handle it; she doubted her business would suffer, only her personal reputation, but she could handle it.

Not so much her girls. They were at a tender age, too young to really understand, too old not to get some of it. Would she tell them? Of course. Eventually. She just wasn't sure when. A lot of her timing would probably depend on what Cade might want, what he would do.

So far, judging by his reaction this afternoon, it wasn't looking all that good.

CHAPTER 24

Brewster went ballistic when he saw the picture of the judge. Completely and utterly ballistic! He demanded more information than Pescoli could give him, then phoned Manny Douglas at the *Mountain Reporter* as well and had a few words with Douglas's editor.

Of course he'd learned nothing more, but he'd called a meeting, and so, after five o'clock, aside from a skeleton crew left to man the desks, the detectives and some of the road deputies had been called into a meeting in the room usually assigned for a task force, which, it seemed, might be happening.

Alvarez caught up with Pescoli as they walked into the wide room and took a spot at the table. "Brewster wants us to bring everyone else up to speed."

"Perfect."

Pescoli had spent the last two hours going over the suspect lists again, separating out those who had rock-solid alibis, or those with flimsy motives. This guy, whoever the hell he was, was a whack job, demanding attention, sending a picture of the judge to the newspaper to keep attention to his crime and also taunt and bait the police.

The killer obviously had his own list as he'd indicated he wasn't finished with his business.

No matter which angle Pescoli took, she always came back to Maurice Verdago, the one ex-con who wasn't anywhere to be found. He'd never returned to his job as a janitor in a Helena apartment complex, nor returned to his home, which, according to Sage Zoller and a detective from the Helena Police Department, held nothing of interest.

So why was he in the wind?

She double-checked his résumé. Not only had he been in the army, it seemed, but he was in the special ops, a sharpshooter. He had to be the guy. Right? He had a temper. It was all there in the report and extremely suspicious that he'd gone to ground.

There was something wrong there. Very wrong.

If she could just figure it out.

"Okay, everyone listen up," Brewster ordered as chairs were scooted into the table and conversation died. The room was cold, and Rebecca O'Day, a corporal deputy, took the initiative and fiddled with a radiating space heater.

Brewster sat in the middle of the long cafeteria-type table, directly across from Pescoli, who was wedged between Alvarez and Kayan Rule in the room built of concrete blocks painted a dull industrial gray. The floor was linoleum circa 1970 and shone bright under the overhead fluorescents. A copy of the picture, note, and envelope they'd received were posted on a large white board in one corner of the room. Brewster cleared his throat and got everyone's attention.

"We've got a situation here. Well, I guess we've had it since Christmas morning or even before as it seems the judge was actually killed before the unknown took a shot at Sheriff Grayson. Now, he's sending notes and pictures to the media, taunting us, indicating that he has more victims in his sight, so we have to double up security on Grayson, just in case the killer thinks he can finish what he started, and then we need to find this guy. Before he targets and hits someone else.

"Detectives Alvarez and Pescoli have been leading the investigation and they'll tell us all where we are." He spied Jeremy, who was entering the room with a coffeepot and tray of empty cups. Brewster flicked his fingers rapidly in a come-in-quickly gesture and Jeremy, with a sideways look at his mother, set the cups and packets of creamer and sugar onto the table. He positioned the pot in front of Brewster, who pointed to one of the empty cups. As if he'd done it a hundred times, Jeremy poured the coffee for the undersheriff.

Pescoli felt a little hot under the collar and told herself that she was being ridiculous, that Jeremy asked for and wanted this, that Brewster was *not* being condescending to her son.

Still, it bothered her. Jeremy had signed on with the department to help, yes, but to learn about the responsibilities of being a cop, and today he'd been reduced to waiting tables. Maybe that was a good thing; he certainly didn't have any training to do much more. But still, it seemed demeaning somehow and she couldn't help but wonder if this was all part of Brewster's plan to humiliate her son.

"Thanks," Brewster said as he picked up his cup and other cops poured their own brew.

Get over it. Jeremy needs this lesson. He has to start at the bottom, learn what it really takes to be a cop. For now, he's little more than a "go for" volunteer.

"You go ahead," she said to Alvarez as they stood to fill everyone in.

Jeremy started to leave, but Brewster stopped him before he reached the door. "You might want to stay; see how this works," he said, and waved him into a folding chair situated near an oversized map of the county. Jeremy sidled over to the chair and seemingly self-conscious sat down.

Pescoli turned her head into the case again. She and Alvarez stood, together, at the table, and Alvarez walked everyone through the investigation, from the moment that Grayson had been shot until this afternoon when Manny Douglas had brought in the plastic bag with its contents.

The officers around the table listened and sipped coffee, and one or two scribbled notes. Watershed chewed gum thoughtfully, and Zoller used her small tablet computer. For the most part, the officers' eyes never left Alvarez as she spoke.

She was wrapping it up. ". . . so we'll wait for any evidence that can be found on the envelope and keep on running down tips as they come in. We're looking for a couple of suspects, specifically Maurice Verdago and Vincent Samuels, the brother of the judge."

"He's not actually a suspect," Pescoli clarified, "but he's missing and we want to know where he is." There were a few questions, some discussion among the officers, but in the end, they left the room not knowing any more than they had when they entered.

Jeremy lingered, cleaning up the coffee cups and gum wrappers, and Pescoli stopped to say, "I'll see you at home, but it'll probably be late."

"How late?"

"I wish I knew."

She started walking toward her office when Brewster waved her into his. She took one step inside and nearly stumbled. The walls of his office were bare, his desk cleared, boxes stacked in one corner.

"What's going on?"

"I'm moving into Grayson's office," he said matter-of-factly and her stomach nearly hit the floor.

"Why? Did something happen?" Surely if Grayson had taken a turn for the worse, she would have heard about it.

"I'll move back once he can come back to work. But the truth of the matter is, even if he makes a full recovery, it's going to be weeks, or more likely months, before he's ready to take over his responsibilities again. Things are pretty tight here already and we'll need to find a temporary undersheriff, who'll occupy this office." He gestured to the interior of the small room he'd claimed for over a decade. "But that's not why I called you in," he said, balancing one hip on the corner of his desk. "While Alvarez was explaining the case and talking about Maurice Verdago, I had a little epiphany."

"I thought they were always pretty large."

He nodded, one side of his mouth curving up. "I suppose. Anyway, did you know that Verdago was a local boy? He grew up around here. Always had a temper, always got into fights, and they kept escalating until he attacked his brother-in-law."

"Maybe before. We're looking into an old cold case. Missing person, presumed dead. Maurice's name came up."

"Oh, right. I remember that. Joey . . . Langly?"

"Lundeen."

"That's right." He snapped his fingers.

"I've looked through the files. Nothing solid there. At least at first glance."

Brewster frowned. "I wouldn't put it past him. Verdago always was a hothead and my guess is his temperament didn't improve much in prison."

"So, you knew him personally?" This was news to her. Unsettling news.

"No, no . . . he's younger than I am, but my brother knew him, and you know what, Maurice, at one time, was close friends with Vincent Samuels."

Pescoli blinked. "The judge's missing brother."

"I think they may have served together in Iraq."

In her mind's eye she saw the sword Cee-Cee Piquard had unwrapped in her home, a sword identical to the one mounted on the wall in Georges Piquard's den. "I thought Vincent Samuels served with Georges Piquard."

"Yes, that's right."

"Then . . . ?"

Brewster was nodding and, as if anticipating her next question, said, "I served with Georges too. We're old friends. But he stayed in longer than I did and that's when he buddied up with the man who would become his brother-in-law."

"And Verdago."

"I don't think they were ever close. Verdago always had a mean streak in him." He shook his head. "You know, now that I think about it, I'm pretty sure Vincent introduced Kathryn to Georges." His eyebrows drew together. "I'll have to ask Bess about that."

"I thought Kathryn didn't get along with her brother."

"That was later, I believe."

"After he borrowed money from her husband."

"Did he?" His eyebrows cocked. "I didn't know about that."

"It caused a rift between Kathryn and Vincent."

"I think there were lots of reasons for that," Brewster said. "Bess has alluded to some of them, but I never paid much attention. It was all just gossip. Until now."

"Speaking of your wife," Pescoli said, "I'd like to talk to her. She was close to the judge and she might know something about her personal life that could help."

"Well, okay, of course," he said, though he frowned and rubbed the back of his neck thoughtfully, "But, I want to warn you, she's taking this very hard."

"I'm sure she's devastated."

"We all are," he agreed. "The members of the church and Bess especially, but I'll ask her to come in tomorrow morning. I think she's free."

"Good." Hoping the judge's friend could shed some light, Pescoli still had other avenues to follow. The wheels were turning in her mind, faster and faster. Now there was another connection between the judge and Verdago through her brother. It seemed a little flimsy, but still, Verdago had the means, opportunity, and skill. "I think he's our guy," she said aloud.

"Verdago? Good. Then prove it," Brewster said.

"I will," she vowed, knowing in her gut that she was finally on the right track.

"You know this is a long shot," Alvarez said once they were nearly to Helena. The trip from Grizzly Falls had taken over two hours, closer to two and a half, and might just turn out to be a wild goose chase. Though snowfall had been light and traffic not all that bad, surprising Wanda Verdago might not be worth all the trouble, but Pescoli, as usual, had the bit in her teeth and man, oh, man was she going to run with it.

"Long shots sometimes solve cases." Pescoli squinted through her windshield, searching for the turnoff from US 12, a mile west of Helena. The night was clear enough on this stretch of road to see the lights of the city washing up to the night-black sky.

"I'm just saying don't get your hopes up." Alvarez's cell phone chirped and she answered.

"It's Sage," Zoller said on the other end of the connection. "I finally ran down Judge Samuels-Piquard's lawyer and got a copy of the will. He wasn't very happy about it as it was so late and all, but one of his junior associates was still working, so he had the guy take a copy and e-mail it to me."

"And?"

"It's pretty straightforward. Almost everything goes to her son, Winston, with a couple hundred grand set aside for her grandkids' college tuition."

"So now he can afford the upwardly mobile move into that tony new neighborhood," Alvarez said.

Pescoli shot her a look. "The will?"

With a quick nod to Pescoli, she said into the phone, "What else?"

"There's a list of charities, including the college where she graduated from law school. That combined together for another hundred grand," Sage said.

"Must be nice to be able to spread it around," Alvarez said. "Anything else?"

"Yep, here's the kicker: Seems as if the judge had more property than we knew. There's the lake house, where she went every Christmas, but there's also another property, not far down the road from the place she vacationed. I've got the address, and it, along with a monthly distribution of fifteen hundred dollars for life, unless her money runs out, goes to her brother, Vincent Gregory Samuels."

Alvarez felt that little tingle she always did when a case was coming together.

"I forwarded a copy of it to your e-mail account, as well as Pescoli's. That is, as they say, 'all she wrote.' "

"It's enough." Alvarez hung up.

"The judge's will?" Pescoli asked.

"That's right," Alvarez said and filled her in as they drove the final few miles to Wanda Verdago's apartment.

"So Vincent's in play. I knew it when he disappeared," she said, guiding her Jeep to an area of apartment buildings. "We need to send someone out there."

"I'll text Rule. See if he's available."

Alvarez was just finishing the text when Pescoli said, "Here we go. Now, which one is it?"

"Right here." Alvarez pointed to a two-story building that looked a lot like a motel straight out of the seventies. Barely lit, a sign announced that they'd reached the Aspen Grove Apartments. With staircases on either end of a long porch facing the parking lot, the units were delineated by doors surrounded by a large plate-glass window on one side and two smaller windows on the other. Cookie-cutter apartments. The Verdago unit was on the second floor, so they parked next to a black SUV with plates indicating it belonged to Wanda Verdago. As Alvarez stepped out of the warm interior of the

Jeep she was hit by a blast of cold, subfreezing air that seemed to cut through her thick jacket.

Thankfully the parking lot was clear of snow and ice, but the asphalt was cracked, several potholes gouged into the surface, and the paint on the trim of the building was peeling. The few shrubs that were the complex's meager attempt at landscaping were still dusted with snow and shivered in the breeze.

Pescoli led the way as they climbed the exterior staircase and rapped loudly on the screen door of Unit 212.

No response.

But it felt as if someone was home. Though the curtains of the largest window facing the porch were drawn, there was a thin gap between the panels, just enough space for the flickering blue light of a television to pass through.

Pescoli pounded again, more determinedly.

This time, she got a response.

"Coming!" a raspy voice called from inside the unit as the sound of frantic tread reached Alvarez's ears.

"I hope there's no back exit," she said.

"Probably only a second-story window," Pescoli said. "Swear to God, Joe and I had an apartment that was identical to these when we were first married." Nonetheless, Alvarez jogged back down the stairs and took a peek behind the building to find out that her partner was right, there wasn't even a small back deck for the upper units or patio for the lower ones.

Perfect.

She hurried up the stairs again and heard Pescoli pound on the door for a third time. By the time she reached the door, Pescoli had already fished her badge from her pocket and the irritated voice from within called, "Hold on to your damned horses, will ya?"

The door opened and a heavyset woman wearing too much makeup and too little clothing stood on the other side of the screen door. Her white-blond hair was a wild tangle, her mascara thick and clumping, shiny green shadow shimmering on her eyelids, the rest of her face washed out and pale. Struggling into a bathrobe that was two sizes too small in an effort to hide the fact that she'd been lounging in a nearly see-through T-shirt and underwear, she was already talking as the door swung wide. "Whatever it is you're peddling, I don't want—oh, shit!" She looked up just as she tried to cinch the gaping terrycloth together with a tie and saw their badges. "Now what?"

Quickly they introduced themselves, and Pescoli asked if she was Wanda Verdago, though they'd seen her picture enough times to make a visual ID. "Well, yeah, I'm her, but what the hell do you want with me? I already talked to the cops."

"I know, but we have a few more questions."

"About that shithead Maurice?" she asked, her features pulling together into a knot of distaste. "God damn, I regret the day I met that son of a bitch."

"Can we come in?"

"Hell, no!" she said automatically, then seemed to think better of it. "Oh, crap. Sure. Why not? Just give me a sec, would ya?" And before they could answer, she closed the door, locked it, and left them on the concrete porch that connected four units and where a scrawny fake fir tree sat in a plastic pot, decorated in lights that didn't so much as twinkle.

Wanda appeared a few minutes later, her blondish curls clipped away from her pale face, navy sweatpants and an oversized striped shirt replacing the pajamas. She was still barefoot, her toenails shining a deep holiday red. "Come on in and excuse the mess," she said, unlatching the door and leading them past a small entry hall and into the living room where a shag rug from somewhere south of 1972 had been stretched across the floor and shampooed so often the burnt orange had faded to a dull, hairy apricot tone. Judging by the rolling lumps in the carpet near the hallway, it was in serious need of another stretch at the very least. The house smelled of microwave popcorn, and a few tiny white kernels were visible on a dusty table where a solitary green candle burned but did little to cover up the buttery odor.

"I don't know where he is, if that's what you want to know," she said, dropping onto a corner of a once-sleek couch where the cushion definitely sagged, indicating she'd plopped into her favorite spot. An aluminum tree dominated one corner of the room, a flat-screen TV placed opposite the sofa.

"Well, that would help," Pescoli admitted.

She snorted through her nose, a sound of disgust. As Pescoli and Alvarez took seats in the two floral occasional chairs, Wanda cast a rueful glance at the television, then plucked a remote from the coffee table and paused some game show.

"Do you have any idea where he'd go?" Alvarez asked.

"I wish! But ten to one he's with that slut Carnie Tibalt." Her face looked as if she'd just sucked on a lemon. "I can't believe it. Gave him the best damned years of my life, wait for that cocksucker to get out of prison, and what does he start doing but bang that cunt of a waitress from the Long Branch."

"You don't have any idea where he'd go?" Alvarez tried again.

"If I did, I'd shoot them both. Oh, damn, though I'd have to get me a new gun as he took the rifle with him."

"He had a rifle?" Pescoli put in.

"Oh, yeah, just a couple of weeks, like he'd bought hisself an early Christmas present or somethin'."

"You know where he bought it?" she pressed.

"Nah, but it had to be from some guy off the street, right? A private owner and untraceable weapon, cuz I'm pretty sure it wasn't legal for him to have it."

"You know what kind it was?" Pescoli tried again.

"No." She held out her fleshy palms as if she'd been offered poison. "I don't know much about guns and I don't wanta know. Trouble. That's what they are."

Pescoli kept the questions coming. "Does Maurice have any enemies?"

Wanda looked at her as if she'd grown horns. "Only about a million." She snorted. "He had tons of people who didn't like him or who he didn't like, and I remember him talkin' about the 'Dirty Half Dozen.' Yeah, that's the name he gave for people who really screwed him over."

"Did he ever say who they were?"

"No, but you can bet that judge was on the list. He hated her. And the sheriff." She eyed Pescoli critically. "Wasn't all that fond of you, either, but don't take it personal, it was a pretty big club."

"I won't," Pescoli said. "So who are his friends, who does he hang out with?"

"Nobody. Shit, most of his 'friends,' if you'd call them that, are up at the big house. Still in prison. Oh, I guess Elders got out, not that it's a big deal."

"Elders?"

"Cameron Elders. From the first time he was in prison, you know, for trying to hack me the hell up. But he hasn't talked to Cam in years. Every time Maurice was out, Cam was in, or that's the way it seemed. Besides, he wasn't interested in any of his old buddies." Her eyes narrowed with renewed fire. "The only person, and I use the term loosely, he hung out with was that piece of ass Carnie Tibalt! Man, it really pisses me off to think how he screwed me over for that little cunt with her perky little fake titties! Twenty-nine, that's how old she's supposed to be, but I'm bettin' she's at least five years older." She sniffed loudly as if she'd encountered a bad odor. "Younger'n me, though, you can bet on that. When I think of them together . . . son of a goddamned bitch, it makes my blood boil."

And she wasn't kidding. Her normally pallid complexion had turned beet red during the conversation.

"He must've had some other friends," Pescoli said.

"No time for 'em. Too busy humpin' Carnie. God, I hope he fucks himself to death. Both of 'em!"

"What about Vincent Samuels?" Pescoli ventured.

Her head snapped up. "Vinny? He did know someone he called Vinny. But I never caught his last name."

Bingo.

"Did they get together recently?"

"Dunno. Maybe. He did mention the guy. Probably another prick who screws around on his wife."

"Vincent Samuels isn't married," Alvarez said.

"Smart guy." As if she'd just thought of something, she curled the fist of her left hand and shot it out so that they could see her knuckles. "See this," she said, pointing to the ring sparkling on her fleshy finger. "My damned engagement ring. Big-ass rock, yeah? Maurice swore it was real, that he lifted if off some old broad and then had the stone reset and I bought his story, hook, line, and sinker. Turns out it's cubic Z. I'm thinkin' he never had the ring he swiped, or he hocked it and replaced it with this, or maybe he was so damned stupid he stole a cheap knockoff. Oh, crap, what does it matter."

With all her effort she tugged on the ring in question, finally getting it over her knuckle and hurling it across the room to the area where a small table sat off the kitchen. "That's what I think of that bastard. If I ever see his face again, I swear, I'll rip off his lying lips, then gouge out his eyes! And that's before I pull a Loretta Bobber and cut off his damned dick."

"Lorena Bobbitt," Alvarez said automatically.

"Yeah, that's the one!" Wanda growled. "You know he's got a temper, Maurice does. Threatened me with a chainsaw once . . . can you imagine? A fuckin' chainsaw? Good thing he didn't have a gun then or one of us would be dead now." She let out a long, world-weary sigh. "That Bobber chick? She's a goddamned hero in my book." Wanda glanced down longingly at the remote for the TV but decided to let it lie and folded her arms under her large breasts. "Damned fucker."

She seemed to be calming a little and Alvarez decided to try and get Wanda back on track. "Do you have any idea where Vinny might live or hang out?"

" 'Course not. I don't even know the man."

"And you don't know anything about Maurice, where he might go?"

"Not a clue," Wanda replied. "But then why would I know anything about him, huh?" A tear slid from the corner of her eye and as mascara ran down her cheek, she added, "I'm just the dumb bitch who was stupid enough to believe it when her cocksucker of a husband told her he loved her."

CHAPTER 25

"Gee, I can't imagine why Maurice would cheat on a sweetheart like that," Pescoli said sarcastically as she drove out of the parking lot of the Aspen Grove Apartments and headed for the highway.

"He's not exactly a gem in my book," Alvarez said, and while she'd originally thought driving all the way to Helena might prove to be a wild goose chase, they had learned a few things about Maurice Verdago, his violent temper and his relationship with Vincent Samuels. "Rule hasn't gotten back to me," she added, texting some more.

"What are you telling him?"

"Just to check out if the cabin is occupied. I'd like us to do the Samuels interview."

"Good." Pescoli clicked on her blinker, then eased into a sluggish line of traffic on the main road. "Wonder where Maurice got the rifle."

"Wonder what its make and model is." Alvarez finished her text and sent it.

"It would have been nice if Wanda had any clue about firearms," Pescoli said. "I want to talk to both Vince Samuels and Cam Elders." Her mind was already spinning the possibility that Maurice might have connected with the missing Vincent or his ex-cell mate.

"Let's hope he's not in the wind too."

"Has to check in with his parole officer."

"Make that *supposed to* check in."

"Right." Spying her opportunity, Pescoli gunned it around a pick-up hauling a fifth wheel trailer as Alvarez's cell phone rang.

"Selena Alvarez," she said, studying the taillights in the distance.

"Oh, Detective, hi." The voice on the other end was soft, barely audible over the hum of the Jeep's tires and the rumble of the engine. "This is Cecilia. Cecilia Piquard."

"Yes, Mrs. Piquard."

Pescoli glanced her way for a split second, then slowed, cutting the road noise.

"You, uh, you told me to call you if I thought of anything else?"

"Yes?"

"Well, there was something, but I didn't want to say anything with Winston in the room. He's out now, ran to the store for diapers and milk, just to the mini-mart on the corner, and Lily finally fell asleep, so I have to make this quick. Winston won't be gone long."

"What is it?" Alvarez asked.

"Win told you Kathryn didn't have a love life, but that just isn't true. She was pretty discreet, you know, never talked about dating, but we both knew she used one of those matchmaking services a while back."

"Did she ever mention any of the men? Or did you meet any of them?"

"Oh, no, no . . . nothing like that, but a friend of mine, a guy, was on the same service and came across her profile. It was kind of a fluke cuz it's a double-blind deal, no real e-mails or phone numbers, but he recognized her picture and it said she was a lawyer, not a judge, so he showed me on my computer. Sure enough, there she was even though her picture had to be at *least* from ten years earlier, before she started coloring her hair, y'know? Anyway, it was really surreal and I shouldn't have, but I told Win about it, kinda thinking it was funny. Win, not so much. In fact, he hit the roof. First with me, accused me of being a snoop, and then with his mother. He really flipped out and told her she was a professional woman and what was she thinking and who knew what kind of creeps were lurking there, ready to prey on her and blah, blah, blah. Really hit her with both barrels. Like, oh, yeah, right, anyone would prey on Judge Samuels-

Piquard." She hesitated and then said more softly, "I guess someone did, didn't they?"

Alvarez was listening hard, trying to digest the information and put it into her mental image of the judge. It seemed off, somehow, but she didn't doubt that Cee-Cee was serious. "Do you know the name of the service she used?"

"I did. But now, I'm not sure. It was something like matchmadein heaven.com, or something similar. Anyway, like I said, she gave up her subscription or membership or whatever it is, or so we thought, but then, maybe three months later, last summer, just after the Fourth of July, I think, we were all at a party at the Jamisons', friends of the family, and she took a phone call and stepped into the den.

"I had to go to the bathroom and it was one of those connecting ones. You could access it from the hall or the den, but I didn't know that when I went into it. So there I was on the toilet, just on the other side of the door, and I heard her . . . oh, this is weird, but it sounded like she was kind of talking dirty. Like she was flirting. Sexually, you know?"

"What did you hear?" Alvarez asked, her pulse jumping a little.

"As I said, the door was closed. Kathy didn't know I could hear her, but I could and she said, 'You know what I like . . .' and then there was a pause as if she was listening to someone on the other end and then she chuckled and said, 'Well, that, too, but not on top. I like to be under the sheriff.' "

"You're sure about that?"

"That's what it sounded like, and then she giggled, you know, low and throaty, and then said, 'I'll see you later,' and it was already nearly midnight. I mean, I thought she went to bed around nine with nothing more than a good book, but it shows you how wrong you can be about someone."

"Who do you think she was talking about?" Alvarez asked, thinking about all the implications. Just now, when they were thinking that Maurice Verdago was the culprit, was this a new love triangle wrinkle?

"Obviously she was talking about the sheriff, of course. Sheriff Grayson. The guy who's in the hospital. If you ask me, someone didn't like him messing around with Kathy."

Alvarez's hands clenched around the phone. Could this be right? "Or maybe it was the other way around?"

"Like someone didn't want her messing around with Dan Grayson?" she said. "Yeah, sure. It could be, I suppose."

But who would care? One of his ex-wives? Hattie Grayson, his sister-in-law? Hattie seemed interested in him, but she didn't seem the type . . . neither did Cara nor Akina. And why try to take out the sheriff too?

"Oh! I gotta go. I hear the garage door going up. Win's back. Please, please, please don't tell him I called you. He would be so ticked off!"

Before Alvarez could say another word, Cee-Cee hung up.

She lowered the phone from her ear, trying to wrap her mind around Sheriff Grayson and the judge. Really? She felt more than a little disappointment and she didn't want to analyze that too carefully.

"What the hell was that all about?" Pescoli asked, speeding up again.

"Cee-Cee Piquard thinks she overheard the judge setting up a lover's rendezvous with Dan Grayson."

"Oh, come on. I thought we'd ruled out the whole love triangle thing."

"We had," Alvarez said, then repeated the conversation, finishing with, ". . . so Cee-Cee assumes that the judge and the sheriff were having an affair."

"If it's true, someone knows about it," Pescoli said. "There'll be phone messages or love letters or texts or more overheard conversations. One of them would have told someone something. Tomorrow, we'll start with Bess Brewster and talk to Samuels-Piquard's maid. Then, if that doesn't work, we'll try the sheriff's brothers."

"And hopefully Rule will have learned if Vincent's in that cabin, and we can go talk to him," Alvarez said.

Pescoli nodded as she stared into the night and the distant glare of oncoming headlights from the eastbound lanes.

"You think the ashes we found were old letters?" Alvarez asked.

"It's possible," she said, "but who the hell knows?"

"Why is it with this case that just when we think we're getting somewhere, like with Verdago, we learn about a possible love connection?"

"Just because Kathryn Samuels-Piquard had a private love life, even if it was with Grayson, doesn't mean it pissed someone off," Pescoli said.

"But it could be the motive."

"Maybe." Pescoli was cautious.

"I thought you were the one who was thinking the case might have a personal angle to it."

Snow was starting to fall again, so she hit the wipers. "I just have a feeling about Verdago. What was it he said to the judge when he was sentenced?"

" 'You'll get yours' accompanied by a nice finger gesture."

"Right. And his prison cell mate said he hated Grayson." She scowled as the wipers slapped snow off the windshield. "He's gotta be our guy."

"I think we need to keep our minds open."

"Always," Pescoli agreed, but Alvarez knew her partner and when she got an idea in her head, especially about a killer, it took heaven, earth, and maybe a signed confession from another suspect for her to change her mind.

He hung up his clothes with the precision of military training. The cabin was cold enough to elicit gooseflesh on his skin, yet he didn't approach the banked fire until he was completely naked.

Only then did he drop and, starting with push-ups, go through his routine of exercises, stretching, and testing each muscle, feeling the strain, watching sweat drip from the tip of his nose to the cold stone floor.

He was tired. Exhausted. And yet he forced himself to go through his routine, to push himself. Soon, he would be tested and he had to prevail. Already there had been one mistake, and it ticked him off to think that Dan Grayson wouldn't just give up the ghost. Surely he was mortally wounded. Had it not been for that damned Pescoli and the quick response of the EMTs and the skill of the surgeons—

"Stop!" he ordered, breaking the silence within this tiny cabin. He couldn't afford negative thoughts, had to persevere. He was on a path that had only one end.

Once the exercises were complete, he walked outside and through a snowbank to the woodpile. Icy crystals caressed his bare skin and stung the bottoms of his feet. A gust of wind rattled the naked branches of a sapling and cooled the beads of sweat upon his skin.

Calming himself, he drew in a long breath and reminded himself that sending the picture of the judge had been a success.

Renewed, he split the kindling, remembering Grayson with his own armload of firewood, how he'd aimed at him and missed. He closed his mind to that particular mistake. It could, and would, be rectified.

Back inside, he stoked the fire, coaxing flames to crackle and leap; then he warmed his backside as heat emanated from the hearth. Allowing himself one drink, he donned gloves and walked to the desk, his father's old workbench.

Lovingly, he ran a finger along the old wood. Arranging the four pictures on his desk, he tried to calm down, to think clearly, to think of the days ahead. His timing had to be precise. Impeccable. If any mistakes were made . . .

No. Don't let it happen. Take a deep breath. Count to ten.

When doubts entered his mind, he pushed them steadfastly aside. *The first bitch is dead, isn't she?*

Soon, the second will go, and you know what will happen with the others . . . it is only a matter of time.

CHAPTER 26

The killer *had* to be Verdago, Pescoli reasoned as she pulled into her garage. The threats, his violent nature, the perfect timing of his disappearance—all stacked up to one conclusion: guilty as sin. It boiled her blood to think that sicko had killed the judge and put Grayson in the hospital.

Cutting the engine, she grabbed her computer and purse, and once out of the Jeep, shut the garage door. She couldn't wait to find the sorry bastard and haul his ass back to jail.

Wild scratching on the other side of the door indicated the dogs had heard her arrival. They were waiting as she opened the door, and immediately vied for her attention as she dropped her computer case and purse onto a chair at the table.

"Okay, okay," she said, bending down as Sturgis's tail worked double-time while Cisco spun in happy little circles and stood on his back legs. Yep, she thought, unzipping her jacket as the warmth of the house hit her full force. The dogs, of course, were ecstatic to see her. Her kids? Not so much.

Jeremy was laying on the couch, video controllers in his hands. He barely looked her way as she walked into the living room. Gone was the enthusiastic, clean, Johnny-on-the-Spot volunteer from the station and in his place (and body) was her disinterested-in-life-around-him son.

"Hey," she said, noticing that his rifle was propped next to the couch. His cell phone buzzed. From where she stood, she saw that it was a text from Heidi.

"Hey," he mumbled back at Pescoli, then, not responding to the text, swore under his breath as some opponent annihilated him and the entire television screen turned a bloody crimson.

"Good day at work?"

"Yeah."

"Sorry about coffee duty."

He shrugged as if he didn't care.

"Do you ever think that Brewster is picking on you or making an example of you?"

"Of course. He's a prick. Likes to rub it in that he's bossing me. I think it's his way of getting back at me for dating Heidi. At the office, I can't disagree with him, have to do his bidding."

"And you're willing to?"

"To be a cop?" His lips rolled inward. "Yeah, why not?" He was still working the controller for all it was worth, never taking his eyes off the action on the screen. "But if he thinks he can humiliate me into quitting or can make me look like a jackass, he's wrong, and sooner or later he'll figure it out. Oh, damn! That guy's going to get me!"

For a second she thought he was still talking about Brewster, but then she realized he was angry about the game he was playing.

"How is Heidi?" she asked, daring to stick her toe into dangerous emotional waters.

"She's cool."

Hardly. Hot as a pistol was more like it.

"You guys still going together?"

He paused, then looked over his shoulder. "And this is your business how?"

Here they were again, arguing because Jeremy considered himself an adult, yet he lived under her roof and oftentimes was more immature that his younger sister. But she wasn't in the mood for a fight. Not right now. "Just asking," she said.

"We see each other, Mom. We go out. Are we exclusive? Yeah." He threw another challenging look at her, but she didn't say it, just hoped, as always, that he used his head around Cort Brewster's beautiful and sexy daughter.

"Okay," she said, changing the subject. "So, have you had dinner?"

"Grabbed tacos with Cody." A pause. "And, yeah, Heidi and Cody's girlfriend were there."

Of course. *Get over it. He's right. He can date whomever he wants.*

"What about your sister?" she asked, sneaking a look at the hallway leading to Bianca's bedroom. "She's here, right?"

"In her room." He actually glanced in Pescoli's direction. "I have no idea what she ate or what she did. That's on her, Mom."

"Fair enough." Tonight, she didn't want to pick a fight, but he really had to do something about the damned rifle. "You know, in my house, all firearms are locked in the gun closet."

Again he looked at her, this time as if she'd gone suddenly stark, raving mad. "Yeah, I know. Cuz we were kids, but now there's no reason."

"Sure there is. I'm not here all the time and neither are you. Bianca could have friends over and they start horsing around and before you know it, someone gets hurt. They are still kids." *And so are most of your friends,* she thought, but held her tongue.

"Give me a break."

"I'm serious. Plus, if anyone is poking around, you know, casing the house and they see a rifle, it's more incentive to break in."

"It's registered, Mom. In my name."

"Doesn't mean it couldn't be used in a crime if it were stolen."

"Who's going to come all the way out here."

"We're fairly secluded, you know that. No one could see an unfamiliar car in our drive as the neighbors are a quarter of a mile away."

"Huh?"

"Just lock up the gun."

"No!" He was suddenly angry. "Lucky's right, you know," he charged, giving her a shot. "You really do jump off the deep end."

"Me? No way!" She wasn't taking this from anyone, especially not her son. "The rules in the house are that guns are locked up, separate from the ammunition. That's all. Just do it."

"The rifle's always with me."

"Jeremy . . ."

"Jesus, Mom. Why do you have to be such a damned ruleser?"

"A what?"

"You've got too many rules!" He threw his controller on the floor in a fit of disgust, then snagged his phone. "And don't start with the 'my house, my rules' lecture. I've heard it before. About a million times!" Grabbing his rifle and texting on his cell with his other hand, he turned and stalked downstairs to his bedroom. She let him go. Their gun closet was right next door, so Pescoli allowed him the dignity of putting his weapon away without her chasing down the steps after him, like a nagging shrew.

She would check later, however. Sturgis, though, slunk down the stairs after him, clearly thinking he was in trouble too.

Pescoli sighed. Unfortunately, all of Jeremy's arguments hit home. She'd never been a person who played by the rules, but she expected it of her children, and as for jumping off the deep end, true, she had a quick temper, but she tried like hell to keep a rein on it. Lately she hadn't been doing such a hot job, as Alvarez had so deftly pointed out.

Reminding herself that motherhood wasn't always easy, she walked to Bianca's room, rapped with her knuckles on the door only to have it whisper open.

"Hey, Mom," Bianca said. She was seated at her makeup mirror, polishing her nails with a glittery hot-pink color. Cisco followed Pescoli into the room and whined to jump onto the bed, a feat he'd managed as a younger dog with no problem.

"Okay, you," Pescoli said, and picked him up to drop him unceremoniously onto the mussed pink duvet and assorted pillows. "What's up?" she asked her daughter.

"Nothin'." Bianca stroked a glossy patch onto her right index finger.

"I never could get the hang of that, you know," Pescoli admitted, sitting on the edge of Bianca's mattress while Cisco dug frantically at one pillow. The mattress sagged a little under her weight. "Polishing my right hand. The left was a breeze, but the right? No way. Ambidextrous, I am not."

"Oh, come on, when did you ever polish your nails?" Bianca laughed, meeting her mother's gaze in the mirror of her small table.

"I did, or tried to, with my sisters, when I was your age or maybe a little younger."

Gently, Bianca blew across her wet fingernails. "I thought you were all jocks with attitude or something."

"We were, or at least I was, but that doesn't mean I didn't want to be pretty, or hip or popular."

"And you thought fingernail polish would do that?" One of her eyebrows arched skeptically.

"I thought it might help."

"I can't imagine you *ever* caring about anything so girlie."

"It was a phase. Didn't last long."

"Did it help make you popular?"

"God, no." Pescoli laughed. "I didn't take the time or was too impatient to do it right, and my sisters got sick of having to do my right hand, so I gave up on it."

"You want to learn?"

Pescoli hesitated and saw the earnest look in Bianca's big eyes. "Well, sure. Not tonight, though."

"Too busy."

"I promised I'd see Santana."

"And you're late. Again," Bianca said. "Wow."

"Work."

"Like always."

"I know, I know, I'm thinking about changing that."

Again, she elevated a disbelieving brow. "Was that right after hell freezes over?"

"You know, on Christmas morning, the reason I was going to the sheriff's house was to talk about my options, possibly turn in my resignation."

"What?" Bianca spun on her stool to face her mother. "I don't believe you. You'd *never* quit, Mom. What would you do?"

"Pay more attention to you and your brother."

"You've gotta be kidding. Jer and I are never here, and we're not gonna change just because you suddenly decide to become a stay-at-home mom. Get serious. Oh, wait a minute." Her smile slid from her face. "Does this have to do with Santana? Oh, God, Mom . . . you're not thinking about doing anything . . . stupid. I mean, I know you talked about moving in with him, but I thought you changed your mind."

"Not completely."

"Because that just wouldn't work, you know," she said hurriedly. "Not for me. Or Jer for that matter. I mean, I might have to live with Dad and Michelle."

"Would you really want that?" Pescoli asked, bracing herself for the answer.

"I don't know Nate Santana and I really don't want to. It's just weird that you're dating him, y'know." Her polish forgotten, she crossed the room and plopped onto the bed next to Pescoli, her legs folding beneath her. Please, please don't do something stupid," she begged.

"Trust me, Bianca, I spend my life attempting to do just that." It burned her a little that the kids had oh so readily accepted Michelle when Luke had remarried. However, whenever Pescoli dated, her kids both cried "foul" as if they were threatened by her interest in men.

"So what did you have for dinner?" Pescoli changed the subject.

"Soup."

"Is that all?" she dared to ask.

"It was enough."

"Bianca," she said, "tell me what you ate today."

"I told you."

"Soup. That was it?"

"Oh, I guess I had a power bar and a Diet Coke."

"Anything else?"

"I wasn't all that hungry."

"There was leftover pizza and some ham and a spinach salad in the refrigerator."

Bianca's eyes darkened. "So?"

"So, it seems like you're intentionally starving yourself."

"No way." She climbed off the bed and glanced at herself in the mirror, caught herself, and turned away sharply, plopping onto the stool.

"What did you eat yesterday?"

"I don't know." When Pescoli waited she added, "Mom, really. I don't remember."

"Start with breakfast."

"I don't know . . . an energy drink."

"That all?" When she saw belligerence in her daughter's eyes she said, "Okay, lunch?"

"I made a salad."

"Any protein in it?"

"No, but I had a protein bar at Jana's and we went out for coffee at Joltz."

"You drink coffee?" This was news. Dear God, how did she miss something so basic? For all her life, Bianca had turned her nose up at anything close to coffee.

"I had a mochaccino. With whipped cream and chocolate. *Tons* of calories."

"Anything else? What about dinner?"

"What is this, the Spanish Inquisition?"

"Close enough."

"Pizza, okay?" Before she could comment, Bianca added, "At least two slices, vegetarian, with tons of cheese. At Dino's. We had ice cream afterward. So what do you want me to do now, keep track for you?"

"That would be nice, yeah." Feeling the argument escalating, she pulled back. "I'm just a little concerned."

"Oh, Mom, get a life!"

"I have one and it's busy enough for two or three more people. I really do need a clone, you know. But, honey, you're a major part of my life, you and Jer are the most important."

"Hard to tell sometimes," she muttered.

Pescoli couldn't argue that point; her job and hours away from the house were a simple fact of life. "Listen," she said, not going to be drawn into that particular discussion, "I know girls your age sometimes struggle with body image and I just want to make sure that you're okay."

Bianca rolled her large eyes. "Mom, I eat a lot. Like tons! But ever since I had mono last year I haven't had a major appetite. It's not a big deal. I think that might be a good thing."

"Because?"

"Because America's fat and I don't want to be part of that."

"You aren't even close!" The girl was thin, but with curves. "I just want to make sure you're getting enough nutrition, that's all. It's my job to worry about you."

"I thought your job was to catch the bad guys," her daughter charged.

"That too."

"Well, stop worrying about me. Really." Her cell phone clicked and she looked down, saw a text, and frowned.

"Bad news?"

"No, just . . . Chris."

"I thought you and he were over."

"We are." She looked her mother squarely in the eye. "He sometimes doesn't get it." She tossed her phone onto the counter. "He's such a dick."

"I don't think you should talk like that."

"Funny, isn't it?" she said, and for a second she sounded just like Michelle. "Because I don't think you should either."

"You got me there," Pescoli said and pushed herself off the bed. It was hell going around and around with her daughter. "Aren't you due for a checkup with Dr. Lambert?"

"For the mono?"

"Well, hopefully that's long over. I'm just talking about a physical, y'know, to check on your general health," Pescoli said, not convinced that her daughter wasn't sliding down the slippery slope of a serious eating disorder. It was one thing to eat poorly, as a lot of teenagers did, it was another to avoid food due to some freakish perception of weight.

"I'm fine," Bianca insisted. "At least I was until you got home."

"Enough said. I don't have time for this right now." She heard the words and inwardly winced. Even though she realized that an argument now would only escalate into a full-scale battle, she hated to think that she was running away from a fight that had to happen. Bianca was still glaring at her. "We'll talk about this tomorrow," she promised and was rewarded with an overly dramatic groan.

She didn't wait for a further argument. Despite her texts to Santana, she was really late, so she made a pit stop in her bedroom and changed, slapped on fresh lipstick, and added a touch of perfume. After grabbing the box with the diamond ring in it, she was out the door again, and all the while, not too far in the back of her mind, she was thinking about Maurice Verdago and wishing to heaven above that she knew where the son of a bitch was hiding.

He had to be close; she felt it. As she drove away from her home, she checked her rearview mirror more than once. "Get over yourself," she whispered, but couldn't shake the feeling that someone was making note of her every move.

She pushed those thoughts aside and turned on the radio, half-listening to the music while mentally making a list of all the projects she'd have to do when she arrived at the office the next day.

She'd check with Kayan Rule and find out what he'd learned about Vincent Samuels. She wanted to interview Cameron Elders too. She felt in her gut that Samuels or Elders, or both of them, might know where Maurice Verdago had gone to ground. Alvarez could interview the judge's maid and Brewster's wife.

Maybe something would shake out.

As rapidly as her tires sped along the snowy streets, her mind spun with the case and by the time she reached Santana's place, she'd nearly forgotten her fear that someone was watching her. "Paranoia's a bitch," she said as she followed a broken path in the snow to his front door.

Using her own key, she let herself in to the warmth and semidarkness of his cabin. One strand of Christmas lights was lit and the muted television was tuned to the news, silent reporters and anchors on the screen. A fire crackled in the hearth, embers red and glowing, flames offering a flickering light.

By the fire, Nikita yawned, the only energy expended at her arrival, his wagging tail thumping rhythmically against the floor.

Stretched out on the couch, Santana opened an eye and a slow smile spread across his beard-shadowed jaw. "Hey, darlin'," he said, raising up on an elbow, that damnably sexy grin doing what it always did to her.

As she dropped her coat over the back of a chair, he said, "I wondered if you'd actually show." He stretched, arms overhead, the hem of his long-sleeved T-shirt inching upward to show a slice of his muscular abdomen. Her blood heated a little when she remembered running her fingers along a body sculpted by hard physical labor on the ranch. She also thought about the return heat he gave off whenever she toyed with the buckle of his belt, her fingertips delving and teasing at his waistband.

As if he knew where her mind was wandering, his lips curved into a slow smile. Yes, they had passion all right. She couldn't and wouldn't deny that very obvious fact.

Pescoli dropped her coat over the back of a chair. "I didn't think it would be this late."

"You never do."

"I know."

"It's okay," he said, moving so that she could sit on a bit of cushion that was exposed due to the bend of his hips. He wrapped his arms around her waist. "I'm just glad you're here now." His voice was low from sleep and she didn't resist when he pulled her down to lay beside him, their bodies spooned together tightly.

"I can't stay."

"Sure you can."

Sighing, she closed her eyes, feeling the strength of his arms, the warmth of his body. The house smelled of wood smoke, but her nostrils were tingled by the hint of soap, as if he'd just stepped out of the shower. "Don't even think about leaving," he said into her hair, and she knew this was where she belonged, or at least a very vital part of her belonged, with this man.

"Okay, I won't think about it," she promised, "but I do have to go. Soon. I just came over because I have an answer for you."

She felt all his muscles tighten as, with an effort, she pulled the ring from her pocket and noticed how it glittered in the firelight. For a second, she wondered if she were making one of the biggest mistakes of her life. There had been so many already.

Taking his hand in hers, she wrapped his fingers over the band with its sparkling stone.

"You're saying 'no'?" He was suddenly awake, propped up on an elbow, dark eyes searching hers.

"Well, I guess that's an option, but I doubt I would have driven all the way out here in the middle of the night just to turn you down."

He grinned in delight. "You witch!" Then, "You're serious?"

"I just thought it would be nice if you asked me again, on your knee, and this time put the damned ring on my finger."

He stared at her as if he could not believe it.

"That's right, hotshot," she admitted. "You win."

Lithely, still holding her close, he rolled them both to the floor and then, on his knees, pulled her to the same position, so they were nearly eye-to-eye.

"Let's do this thing, cowboy." Feeling oddly shy, she tossed the hair from her eyes.

He took her hands in his and asked tenderly, "Regan Pescoli, will you marry me?"

"I can't wait," she whispered, her heart soaring as the weight of the decision lifted, all of her doubts scattering to the four winds. "And, let me tell you this, Santana. I'm serious about this, okay? This time it's forever. So don't even think about backing out of the marriage. Otherwise I might just have to shoot you."

"Wouldn't have it any other way," he vowed.

"I'm dead serious when it comes to the 'till death do us part.' "

"Then let's hope that death parting us is a long way off." Before she could say another word, he kissed her as if he meant every promise, his lips molding to hers, his arms surrounding her as they rolled as one onto the floor. Melting against him, hearing the steady beat of his heart, in counterpoint to her own, she told herself this was the right decision, that nothing bad would ever happen to them, that they would be together forever.

"Make love to me," he whispered against the shell of her ear.

Outside the wind began to howl, the storm suddenly intensifying, and with the instant rush of wind, the fire flashed brighter for a second.

Feeling her body respond to his touch, she told herself that they would make love until they were breathless, that they would love each other until they got old, that time was not racing through the hourglass, and that something dark and horrifying did not lay in wait.

But deep beneath the surface of all of her hopes and dreams, under the bravado and self-confidence that she forever called up and in a place she barely acknowledged, she knew that she was lying to herself, that somewhere the patient, but relentless angel of death was simply biding his time.

CHAPTER 27

"I just don't understand why I'm here," Bess Brewster said for the second time since dropping into one of the visitor's chairs in what was now Brewster's office, though there were still boxes stacked in one corner, all clearly marked in bold black marker: PROPERTY OF SHERIFF DANIEL GRAYSON.

It all seemed so wrong, almost surreal, Alvarez thought. Seated in another visitor's chair next to Bess, with Brewster now firmly in Grayson's old executive chair situated on the other side of the desk, she'd already asked a few preliminary questions and Mrs. Brewster was not happy about it.

Trim and petite, Bess was in her late forties and just beginning to show the signs of middle age. A few wrinkles fanned from intense blue eyes, a little sag was visible under her chin, and gray hairs that she hadn't yet decided to disguise were visible in her no-nonsense bob of thick blond hair. No doubt, she'd been a head-turning beauty in her youth.

Just like her daughters, Alvarez thought, scanning a few of the photographs arranged on Brewster's newly claimed credenza. Four daughters, all blond, like their mother, all blooming into beautiful women. A picture of Heidi was front and center, Cort Brewster's youngest, the one he referred to as his "princess" and clearly the prettiest. In the photo she was dressed in a long, strapless gown in a shimmery aqua fabric, and tucked into her sun-streaked hair was a glittering tiara, as if indeed she were royalty, if only prom princess.

"I'm your wife, Cort, not some common criminal or suspect," she said, obviously agitated. Her spine was stiff, two points of color showing on her high cheekbones.

"Bess, honey, it's just standard procedure. You know that. All of Kathy's friends and family are being questioned." Hooking a thumb at his chest, he said, "Even me. And I'm the sheriff."

Acting sheriff, Alvarez thought silently.

"It was bad enough two weeks ago, having to explain about your gun," she complained. "All those questions. As if I knew what had happened to it."

Brewster said to Alvarez, "A rifle was stolen from the house. Probably kids."

"Not any kids the girls associate with!" Bess jumped in. Then, looking at Alvarez, she said, "Someone broke into the basement, but that door never locks properly." She shot her husband a damning look. "It was supposed to be repaired months ago."

"Bess, stop. It's been fixed now. All that was taken was the rifle and an old laptop in the basement. They didn't even bother looking for the shells."

"If you'd ever clean out all that stuff down there . . . you're lucky they didn't get into your college things or all that military memorabilia you have stashed away. Cort, it's been years."

"Bess, enough. I'll work on it." To Alvarez, he reaffirmed, "It was probably kids from the neighborhood. I reported it."

"Has the rifle been found?" she asked him.

"No." He shook his head. "Remington .30-06."

"The same caliber as the weapon used in the attacks on Grayson and Samuels-Piquard."

"What?" Bess gasped. "Oh, no. You don't think . . ." Her eyes rounded. "Would someone have stolen your gun, Cort, and then used it to kill Kathy?"

"That's pretty far-fetched," he said, but obviously from the worried look in his eyes, it had crossed his mind, if only fleetingly.

"Stranger things have happened," Alvarez said, making a note.

"I suppose, though I hate to think that some kid—" Brewster started.

Bess broke in, "You don't know who broke in and neither do I.

Maybe it wasn't a kid, but a criminal, the kind that would go out and shoot an innocent woman!"

"You're jumping to conclusions." To Alvarez, he said, "Check it out. I filed the report with Chas Aiken in Theft, about five weeks ago."

"It was the Friday after Thanksgiving," Bess clarified.

"You're right," he agreed.

With a sigh, Bess said, "Let's just get on with this."

Brewster turned his attention to Alvarez once again. "I think we can keep this short." An order. Not a question.

"We're just trying to learn a little more about the judge's life," Alvarez said to Brewster's wife.

"From me?" With a questioning gaze to her husband, Bess said, "Kathy and I were close, but really, she was a very private person. This whole thing is awful. Just awful! I just don't see how I can help." Her fingers played with the collar of her prim jacket for the third or fourth time since being seated, and realizing she was fiddling, she quickly folded her hands in her lap, forcing a smile.

She hates this, Alvarez decided. "Do you know if the judge was seeing anyone?"

"You mean dating? You think I would know that?" She shot another disbelieving glance across the desk at her husband. "If Kathy had a boyfriend, or was dating someone, I didn't know about it."

"She'd been on a dating service."

"Really. Well, she never brought a man with her to any of the church functions. The last one I saw her with, at least romantically, was Georges."

"What can you tell me about her family?"

She thought for a moment. "I know her parents are gone, her brother and she don't speak much. Her son and granddaughter were close with her, though I'm not really sure about the daughter-in-law. Cee-Cee and Winston never attended church or Bible study despite repeated invitations by our minister and several of the elders. Cort, you talked to Win once or twice, didn't you?" she asked, her neatly plucked brows drawing together.

The acting sheriff rotated his hands, turning his palms toward the ceiling. "Probably. I don't remember specifics if I did."

"There's just nothing more I know about her." Bess touched her collar again. "I'll help with the funeral arrangements when the time comes." She glanced at her husband pointedly. "I hear the body hasn't been released."

"Today," he said.

"Oh, that's good. The ladies of the church are helping with the gathering afterward, coordinating the service with the meal. We're expecting quite a crowd." She actually seemed more interested in the ceremony than her friend's death.

As if she'd read Alvarez's thoughts, she frowned slightly and said, "A lot of people knew and respected Kathy. We have a big job on our hands."

Alvarez asked a few more questions, but Bess didn't offer up anything further on the judge's private life. "Did she ever mention the sheriff?" Alvarez finally asked.

"Cort?" She turned to her husband. "Just in casual conversation, asking me what we were doing."

"She's asking about Grayson," Brewster said tautly.

"Oh. Oh." She flushed as she realized her gaffe. "No, not that I remember. They knew each other, of course, but how well? I have no idea."

"No romance between them?" Alvarez asked.

"Kathy and Dan? I don't think so. I suppose it was possible, but he's not a member of the church."

"Meaning?" Alvarez questioned.

"Well, it's just that I don't see Kathy seriously dating anyone outside the congregation. Georges, you know, was a very devout man." She was nodding, her eyes again on her husband, her fingers toying with her collar once more. "An elder. Like Cort." She turned her gaze to Alvarez. "Is there anything else? I promised Heidi I'd take her shopping this afternoon. She has some Christmas presents she wants to exchange. Teenage girls, you know. They live and breathe on their phones and make 'shop till you drop' their mantra."

"Yeah, we're done here," Brewster said and Alvarez silently agreed. If Bess Brewster knew anything important about her deceased friend, she wasn't offering it up.

"If you think of anything that might help, or you may have forgotten—" Alvarez began.

Bess cut her off with, "Really, I've told you everything. I can't help you any more. You just need to find her murderer and put him away." Again she glanced at her husband.

"We will," he promised.

"Oh, I have faith," Bess said, sliding her arms into the sleeves of her long, black coat trimmed in a silvery fur that was most likely mink. Make that a dead mink. Into PETA, Mrs. Brewster obviously was not. She'd grabbed her purse and was heading for the door before Cort could scoot his chair out, round the desk, and assist her. "Even if you don't find him," she was saying as she paused to pull on a pair of long, black gloves, "God will punish that man. Make no mistake. Judgment Day will come."

With her final declaration of divine wrath, Bess marched out of Grayson's old office, her pumps slapping against the tile floor in rapid, staccato steps as Brewster followed, hurrying to catch up to her.

Alvarez was left with a weird feeling, as if she'd missed something important, though she wasn't sure why. It was probably due to the odd, out-of-sync vibe between Brewster and his wife, and Alvarez guessed it wasn't anything good. It didn't help that conducting an interview in Grayson's office, while he was still unresponsive in a hospital bed, felt more than a little strange as well, as if she were already walking on his grave.

"Hi, Mrs. Brewster!" Jeremy's voice rang out and Alvarez quickly walked into the hallway.

"Jeremy," Bess responded, her voice as icy as the day outside, her footsteps never once breaking stride. A cold fish was Bess Brewster, and one who obviously had no use for her daughter's boyfriend.

The acting sheriff didn't respond, but within a second or two, Jeremy looking back over his shoulder, nearly ran into Alvarez. "Oh, sorry. I was just going into this office."

"You have clean-up duties?" she guessed.

"They're putting the sheriff's stuff in storage." He walked in and picked up two boxes, then returned to the hallway, catching up with Alvarez as she headed to her own office. When she peeled off, he went on past her.

Alvarez exhaled heavily as she sat down at her desk. She'd received a text from Rule, who'd been unable to drive up to the cabin and see if Vincent Samuels resided there. Too much new snow and a ton of traffic problems that the deputy had needed to attend to first. Maybe it was just as well. She and Pescoli could drive up there later.

So far, the day had been a bust. Brewster's wife hadn't given her any more information than she'd retrieved from her interview with Donna Goodwin. This morning Donna had just been finishing cleaning the Millers' house when Alvarez had caught up with her, but everything she said was just a confirmation of what they already knew. Pushing fifty, Donna was short, compact, and wiry. Her hair had been clipped into a close-cut buzz that made her appear mannish, and though the temperature was in the teens, she was wearing cargo shorts and a tight-fitting thermal shirt.

The problem was that she only cleaned the judge's house once every two weeks and rarely spoke to the woman who'd hired her. She knew of no family problems or boyfriends, and agreed the judge had kept a calendar, though Donna had never paid much attention to it. She thought it was for doctor's appointments and the like. As for the fireplace in the den, "It was spotless when I left it, the week before Christmas. Fact is, I've never seen any ashes in there. She doesn't use it." She'd seemed genuinely sad as she'd loaded her cleaning supplies and canister vacuum into her hatchback and driven away.

Alvarez had hoped Velma Miller could fill in the blanks, but the judge's little round neighbor hadn't been much help either. The interview in the Millers' parlor off the foyer lasted all of half an hour. Velma wanted to help, but she, like so many others of the judge's friends, knew very little about her personal life.

Alvarez asked if Velma had seen anything suspicious or odd in the neighborhood, and the little round woman had shaken her head slowly. "Not really. Every once in a while I would see a car over at Kathy's that I couldn't place, but she was a judge, you know, had a lot of friends . . . I didn't think anything of it."

"What kind of car?"

"Oh, I don't know. A smaller one, sedan . . . kind of a goldish beige color. I think they call it champagne or something just as high-brow and silly, but like I said, it was probably someone from her work or the church."

"Have you ever seen anyone just hanging out? Watching the judge's house?"

She actually laughed. "You've been talking to Claudia Dubois, haven't you? Claudia's imagination is wild at times. I mean *wild*. I've heard about the stalker, but as many times as I look out upon the park, and it's often, as I knit right here in this room, by the window, I've never seen the man she described or anyone remotely suspicious."

Alvarez had walked to the window to stand near a well-worn rocker with a basket of yarn beside it. Peering through the glass, she said, "Mrs. Dubois said he stood under that tree. Maybe you couldn't see him from your angle. The tree could block it?"

"Well, maybe, but you do know that Claudia isn't always . . . clear."

"We talked to her husband."

"Oh, the *doctor*." She sobered a little. "It's sad, you know. At one time Claudia Dubois was the smartest woman I knew."

Now, as she paused in the doorway to her office, Alvarez dragged her mind from the interviews and responded to a text on her cell phone from O'Keefe, firming up plans to meet later.

Joelle came hurrying along the hallway, stopping momentarily to peek into the sheriff's office. "Oh, I don't like this at all," she said with a shake of her blond bouffant. She shook a long-nailed finger at Alvarez, as if she were to blame for the recent departmental changes. "Sheriff Grayson is coming back, you mark my words. It's just going to take time. Some people around here just jump the gun, if you know what I mean!" And then she was off, her heels clicking on the tile floor, her expression as perturbed as Alvarez had ever seen it. For the first time since joining the department, she was on the same wavelength as the receptionist.

Sage Zoller was practically beaming when she dropped into Pescoli's office two hours later. "Who said persistence never pays off?"

"What have you got?" Pescoli asked, frustrated as ever. Her stomach growled loudly and her neck ached from bending over the computer, searching reports and maps of the county for hours. A jumble of files was strewn across her desk: papers in disarray in her in-basket; various pictures of her kids; a half-full coffee cup placed an inch from a supersized cup of soda with a straw that was flattened by chew marks. She'd learned that Rule hadn't made it to the cabin where they assumed Vincent Samuels was, and she was ready to yank Alvarez out of the station and get out there.

"I struck out with the dating service, matchmadeinheaven.com. Those people take their privacy *very* seriously, let me tell you. I finally got some information on the judge, though. She used the site but hadn't logged on in over a year. If she connected with someone there, they've moved off the site. It looks like a bust to me."

Pescoli glanced at the clock on the wall. "What was that about persistence?"

"Look what I just got from Nettie in Traffic." She slapped a grainy photograph onto the desk, stacking it on an uneven pile of papers.

Pescoli stared at the image impatiently at first, then leaned closer. It was a photo from one of the traffic cameras in the city. In the shot, a white van was streaking by, two people inside the cab. "Carnie Tibalt's van?" she guessed, her pulse speeding up.

"Looks like it, though the plate is obscured."

"The driver. Son of a bitch. That's Verdago!" For the first time in days, she felt a surge of excitement. Finally, some of their hard work was paying off. "Where was this taken?" she demanded, noting the camera location.

"North of town, at the junction heading into the mountains." Sage folded her arms over her chest and leaned against the door. "On the road that leads up into the hills, the main county line where all the spurs break off."

"Toward Elk Basin," Pescoli said, already ahead of her.

"That dead-end road where the judge's cabin is."

"Monarch," Pescoli said, but her mind was scrambling ahead. If Vincent Samuels was at the cabin, maybe that's where his old buddy Maurice Verdago was heading. "Take a look at this," she told Zoller as she pushed aside her half-drunk coffee and soft drink, and flipped through several maps she'd printed off the Internet. After all of the dead ends with Grayson's ex-wives and searching for a disgruntled boyfriend of the judge, she finally could see the path. "Here we go," she said, a thrill of adrenaline tickling her blood.

Laying the map flat, she pointed to a red dot she'd inked on the map. "Monarch Drive. This is where the judge's cabin is, where she was staying." Moving her finger due north, she stopped at another red spot. "And here's where the judge's body was found."

"Got it. But over here"—she moved her finger west a little bit—"here's where Vincent Samuels's more rustic cabin is."

The three points created a perfect triangle.

"Accessed by this same road where Verdago was heading."

"With his girlfriend." Picking up the soda, she chewed thoughtfully on the protruding straw.

"So where's Vincent Samuels?"

"With them? In the back of the van? Dead?" The possibilities were endless, but Pescoli was beginning to believe the answers to the entire case were hidden in that cabin, holed up with Verdago and his girlfriend.

"Let's go find out."

"With backup, right?" Sage said.

"You come with Watershed or Rule or whoever's available. I'll get Alvarez. The important thing is to not go in guns blazing. We don't want to scare them off. They might already be spooked if they've realized they got caught by the traffic cam."

"Right."

"So we'll go in softly, check the situation out, and if it pans out and we think we've got them, we'll call for the team." Kicking her chair back, Pescoli was on her feet and reaching for her sidearm and shoulder holster.

"Aren't you going to run this by the sheriff?"

"The sheriff is unavailable right now, in the hospital."

Zoller shot her a look. "I was talking about—"

"Brewster, I know, but he's out of the office too. Another meeting." She snapped the holster into place.

"He's gone more than he's here," Zoller said.

"Politics." And Cort Brewster reveled in them, in the power. In the few days he'd been appointed the acting sheriff, he'd taken his administrative duties to heart, the part of the job Grayson detested. God, she wished Grayson would improve, show some sign of returning. "I'll get Alvarez. We were about to go see Samuels anyway."

"I'll find a partner," Sage said.

"Where are you going?" a male voice asked from outside the open door.

Damn!

Pescoli ran a litany of swear words through her mind as she recognized Manny Douglas, wearing his signature parka as well as his ever-present smirk, hovering just outside the door.

"How'd you get in here?" she demanded. She didn't need the press. Not now. Not when she felt the case could finally be breaking.

"I brought him." From the hallway, Jeremy poked his head into the room and Pescoli's day, which had so recently been looking up, took a nosedive.

"Don't you know you need to check with me first?" she asked her son, trying to hold on to her temper. This situation could have been so easily avoided had Jeremy been properly trained. But the worst part of it was that facing off with Jeremy was just the kind of scene she'd been concerned about ever since her son had started volunteering at the offices, the kind of scene she never wanted to experience.

"It was okay the other day," Jeremy pointed out, his back up as she grabbed her purse and zipped her jacket.

"And I came out to meet him, remember." For the love of God, her son could be so clueless sometimes. "Always let me know," she told him. "Always. Give me a heads-up. I could have sensitive material on my desk, or someone else in the room. You can't just let anyone walk in here."

"Hey, hey, hey!" Manny butted in. "I insisted. And it's a good thing. What happened to 'first call'? That's what you promised."

"I know what I said," she snapped as he backed up a step to allow her to pass, so now, she and Zoller were adding to the clog of people near her doorway. "That call will come when there's something to report."

"This seems like a breaking story to me."

"Nope, it's not. Not yet. We've got nothing so far. As soon as we do, you're first on my list."

"Huh," he snorted.

"Mom!" Jeremy said, a new urgency to his voice. "What's on your finger . . . are you *engaged*?"

Everyone stopped to stare at her left hand where her new ring winked under the fluorescent lights.

"Umm, yes . . . yes. I was going to talk to you and Bianca tonight."

"But—"

"Seriously, Jer. Tonight."

"You said you would talk to us first before you did anything," he said. "But it looks like you've already made your decision." He was positively stricken.

"Not keeping promises, Detective?" Manny asked.

"Tonight, Jer," she said again firmly. Before he could argue any further, she shouldered past him and Manny, and said in an undertone to Zoller who was right on her heels, "Under the radar. No sirens, no lights."

"See you there . . ." Zoller said quietly as she headed down the hall and Pescoli turned into Alvarez's office.

"What do you mean, she's getting married?" Bianca asked and Jeremy wondered how his smart little sister could be such an idiot sometimes. He'd picked her up from her current BFF Amy's house and now they were cruising through the lower section of town, near the falls, and were scouting out food, cheap food as neither of them had a job and therefore no extra cash.

"It musta happened last night. That's why she had to leave, to be with that douche bag Santana." He looked around. "There's nothing good down here. Let's check the hill."

"You think Santana's a douche?" Bianca asked as they headed toward the road that connected the upper part of Grizzly Falls, which was above this section near the river.

"I don't know."

"I think he's kind of sexy, well, in an old man kind of way."

Jeremy groaned. "Are you kidding?" As they passed the courthouse, he shot a glance her way and caught her smothering a smile. "Oh, yeah, you're so funny."

"What's really bugging you?"

"I just don't think we need some jerkwad coming into the house and telling us what to do," he said, though she was right, he was irritated at his mother, in fact, mad as hell. His mom thought she could tell him who he could date and what her opinion was about his choice, but man, he couldn't give her advice on anything, and the way she'd chewed his butt in front of the other detectives and that reporter today was a real pisser. Then again, he didn't like Santana much either. They'd come to blows before and it could happen again.

"Maybe he won't get in our way."

"Jesus, Bi, what planet are you living on?"

She looked at him as if *he* were from Jupiter; then she reached over and turned the heater up, as if that would help.

"It's broken. Remember?" he said.

"Get it fixed. It's freezing in here."

"When I get some extra money." Shifting down, he turned the nose of his truck up the hill and bounced over the railroad tracks. Man, did he need new shocks, but he couldn't afford them yet. Just like he couldn't fix the heater. Not while he was a volunteer; he needed a paying job and was almost to the point of begging for his old job back at Corky's Gas and Go, but he'd left there on bad terms, to the point he wasn't sure he even could use the service station/mini-mart as a reference for another job. Nor could he ask the mechanic on duty to give him a deal any longer. So he'd had to let the maintenance on his pickup lag.

He gave the truck some gas as the road was steep as it cut into the sheer cliffs of Boxer Bluff. As a kid he'd imagined the cliff face splitting and falling down on their car, burying his mom's old Explorer and them in it, but he'd gotten over that somewhere along the line.

"You're just being overprotective," Bianca theorized as her cell phone buzzed for like the zillionth time since he'd picked her up. "It's because she's the only mother you have."

"The only parent I have," he clarified. "You've got Lucky."

She wrinkled her nose and thought about it as she scanned the text. "Yeah, I guess, and Michelle."

"They don't count. Not for me."

If Bianca was surprised at his feelings for the couple she embraced so wholeheartedly, she didn't show it as she texted back with lightning speed.

"What's so important?"

Again she looked at him as if he were from outer space. "Like everything. My life."

They crested the top of the hill and drove past the sheriff's department. He glanced at the parking lot, saw his mom's Jeep was missing, and wondered where she was. It worried him, how gung ho she'd been to go after the judge's killer. She was a little reckless at times, and as he'd heard Heidi's father remark so often, she could be kind of a "loose cannon." Not that he really put much stock in Sheriff Brewster's opinion. That guy was a bastard with a capital B and it irked Jeremy that he had to suck up to him.

But someday it would all be different.

When he was a cop and Heidi was his wife.

They'd already talked marriage, though he knew it was in the far-off distance. Heidi was pushing him, but he wasn't ready, and as stupid and immature as his mother seemed to think he was, he knew better than to tie the knot before he'd figured out his life and she'd figured out hers.

So he put up with her dad. For now. And even Heidi was coming around about him, saying he'd "changed" ever since becoming sheriff, that he wasn't around as much or as into his family.

Just like his mom had warned. But that's what happened when you were an officer of the law. So Heidi better get used to it, because someday, she was going to marry one.

"How about Dixie's?" he asked Bianca, as he spied the neon sign of the local burger hut at the next stoplight.

She was still texting like mad, not paying much attention. "Do they still have garden burgers?"

"I think."

"Okay."

Bianca flirted with becoming a vegetarian, just as she flirted with bulimia. Their mother was wising up to the fact, and Jeremy had given Bianca a lecture because it was just plain stupid, in his mind. Yeah, he'd heard it was a serious eating disorder, but he just wanted her to stop being so dumb. Bianca seemed to be coming around, or so he thought as he pulled into the parking lot of the burger joint and, smiling, caught a glimpse of Heidi Brewster seated in one of the booths.

The night was suddenly looking better.

CHAPTER 28

Cade's patience had run thin.

He ordered a beer at the bar of the Black Horse Saloon and nursed it slowly. Country music twanged from the speakers, pool balls clicked at a table in the corner, and several televisions were turned onto a variety of sporting events, none of which held his attention.

J.D. and Zed were handling the evening chores, so a few hours earlier Cade had driven to Missoula to check on Dan.

It hadn't gone well.

With each passing day, the usually cheery nurses and aides at the hospital seemed less hopeful for his brother's recovery, or at least that was the impression that Cade had gotten. The security guard posted outside the ICU wing was ever changing and appeared to become either more grim at each of his visits or more bored. Neither boded well.

Finally, just two hours earlier, he'd cornered an ICU doc entering the unit as he was leaving and, sick and tired of what he perceived as the runaround, he'd demanded answers.

Though the doctor, a neurologist, tried to be encouraging, there was something in her eyes that warned Cade against expecting miracles.

"Some people recover, if not fully, then nearly," she'd said to Cade, "but some people don't. We're doing everything we can and I, personally, have talked to my colleagues around the country who have dealt with this kind of trauma. That's the good news, that we're linked by computer to the best hospitals in the world, so I can assure you we are giving your brother the best level of care possible." She smiled and touched Cade on the arm. "I hear the sheriff's a fighter, so try to have some faith," she suggested while her eyes had soundlessly warned him to brace himself.

He'd left Northern General and Missoula with the feeling of doom dragging him down.

It hasn't yet been a week, he reminded himself as the attack had been Christmas morning, but New Year's was fast approaching, and in a few days he wouldn't be able to offer himself that bit of false hope.

Then there was Hattie and the girls.

What a mess that was.

The bartender, a redhead with a tattoo peeking from the open collar of her blouse and who definitely didn't look old enough to serve, slid an old-fashioned glass filled with peanuts his direction. He caught it before it went past and she offered him a sexy little smile. He tipped his head, silently thanking her, but that was the end of it.

There had been a day when he'd taken any subtle flirtation as an invitation and reacted. Usually, whatever had ensued had ended up badly.

But he wasn't interested, he thought, downing his beer and leaving enough cash on the bar to cover a hefty tip.

Not tonight.

Maybe not ever again.

Alvarez didn't share Pescoli's enthusiasm that they were going to catch Verdago, haul him off, and extract a confession for the attempted murder of the sheriff and the killing of Judge Samuels-Piquard. Just because a vehicle that looked like Carnie Tibalt's was heading in the general direction of Vincent Samuels's cabin, didn't mean that Verdago was holed up there, and the picture of the van wasn't as clear as it could have been, the image of the driver and his companion blurry. She wasn't even sure that the passenger was a woman, much less Carnival Tibalt.

"You said there are dozens of places to hide in this section of Montana. Verdago might not be at Samuels's cabin."

"Maybe."

"But you think he'll be there."

"I'm hoping." She hit the wipers as the snow that had been falling off and on all day was definitely on again, dusk descending, darkness ahead as the lights of the city faded behind them. "Nothing ventured, nothing gained."

"Yeah," Alvarez said as Pescoli drove north of the city, "Maybe Verdago will be sitting around a table playing poker with the Zodiac Killer, D.B. Cooper, and Jack the Ripper."

"Fun group," Pescoli said dryly.

"Masters of evasion."

Zoller had rounded up Pete Watershed and they were following, about a mile behind, keeping in contact via the radio and cell phones. Of course, Manny Douglas was probably in the mix as well, following at a distance, but wanting to be on the scene and, probably, getting in the way. Though Pescoli had ordered him to back off, that was unlikely. The man wasn't stupid; he wouldn't blow the assignment or get in the line of fire. Hopefully.

"Did you know that Brewster had a rifle stolen recently? Remington .30-06. Same caliber we're looking for. Stolen right after Thanksgiving and, I checked, he reported it."

"Coincidence?" Pescoli asked.

"Maybe. Common gun."

"What the hell is that all about? His house is broken into and then the attacks?" Pescoli's eyes narrowed. "I don't like it."

"Neither do I. I'm going to do some more digging."

"Good." The road wound upward, through the forest, where the frozen conifers, covered in white, knifed upward, seeming to pierce the darkening sky.

They talked about the break-in at Brewster's house, trying to fit it into the mix, and all the while Alvarez's nerves were strung tight as she thought about the upcoming confrontation. Would they find Verdago, armed to the teeth? She glanced at her partner and noticed, as Pescoli turned a tight corner, the ring on her left hand. "So, you gave in to the ultimatum, huh? The one you went off about the other day in the diner."

"What?"

"You're engaged," Alvarez said.

"Oh. Yes. Thanks to my son, the whole department heard." Pescoli glanced at her partner. "Don't tell me you're going to be pissed that I didn't tell you personally."

"I was just going to offer congratulations."

"Good."

"Just thought I'd acknowledge it. You can tell me about it later, when we're not in the middle of this."

"Maybe then I'll be in the mood to talk about girlie stuff."

"Not likely."

She finally scared a smile out of Pescoli, who changed the subject with, "Okay, I think we turn off in about a quarter of a mile."

"Got it." Alvarez said, focusing again on the task at hand. She called Watershed and Zoller, explaining their position, as Pescoli cranked the wheel and the Jeep veered off the main highway and headed deeper into the mountains. The plan was to park the cars out of view from the cabin and hike in. Pescoli and Alvarez would secure the front of the building, Zoller and Watershed the back. Two other units were patrolling the area and were on standby should they need to be called in. Alvarez prayed that wasn't the case, and that the capture of Maurice Verdago would be swift and without incident.

Then there was Manny Douglas, jonesing for a story, anxious to be a part of the action and record it all, though Pescoli had been firm and succinct when she'd ordered him to stay put. When, if ever, had that happened?

"Here we go," Alvarez said, checking her GPS, which could be spotty in these desolate areas, but today, at least was working. The lane into the cabin showed tire tracks. "Someone's been here recently."

"Maybe it's just Samuels," Pescoli said.

But Alvarez could feel her excitement, the electricity in the car, and it infected her as well.

Pescoli checked the rearview. "Zoller and Watershed caught up." Her hands flexed and opened over the wheel, her gaze focused hard on the narrow, winding double set of ruts cutting through the stands of hemlock, pine, and spruce. No lights glittered through the massive trunks; no sounds reached their ears as they pulled closer to the lake and Vincent Samuels's hideaway.

"Let's hope this isn't a bust." This all felt a little rash, which, of course, was the way Pescoli ran all aspects of her life, personal to professional. Alvarez had been cautious and played by the rules ever since a collar that had gone terribly wrong while she was with the department in San Bernardino.

Maybe too much so.

Still, she was nervous going into this. As Pescoli cut the lights and drove around a final bend in the lane, she checked her service weapon and thought of Dan Grayson still fighting for his life in a hospital bed at Northern General.

"Any closer and Verdago might see the headlights." Pescoli parked below a rise in the road and Watershed's county vehicle tucked in behind her. Without a word, they climbed out of their SUVs and walked along the lane until they saw the cabin, dark except for the light in one window, a flickering golden patch that reflected on the snow. Through thickets of trees the lake stretched wide beyond them.

The rustic cabin with its crumbling rock chimney and paned windows was small and square. Set on the forested shores of the lake, the building was slightly decrepit with a tiny porch tacked on right in the middle of the structure. Its snow-flocked roof sagged a bit, yet the cottage had a quaintness and serenity good enough to grace a Christmas card. *May joy and peace be with you this holiday season . . .*

Verdago's hideout? Oh, God, please let this go without incident, Alvarez thought, switching off the safety of her sidearm.

As the scent of wood smoke wafted in the cold winter air and snow fell in fat, heavy flakes, Alvarez began to sweat.

A single-car garage had been built ten feet off the front porch of the cabin and tire tracks in the snow led to the lowered door.

Someone was home.

Alvarez's stomach tightened. She caught movement in her peripheral vision and spied Watershed.

Armed with a rifle and his sidearm, he checked the garage and shook his head, indicating the building was locked tight. He held out a gloved hand and spread his fingers wide, indicating he needed five minutes to get into position and secure the back of the house.

As he and Zoller slipped through the trees flanking the lake side, Alvarez hit the stopwatch feature on her phone. They'd go in when everyone was in position, but these last minutes of waiting would be excruciating, her muscles jumping.

Like San Bernardino.

Was it possible that this was a setup? Were they being lured into a deadly trap? Her mind jumped ahead to all the ways this capture could go wrong.

A shadow passed by the window.

Something felt off about this and she wondered if they should hold off, call in the backups, warn Brewster what was going down. . . .

Then she saw the stain.

Dark, reddish, a pool of what she could only assume was blood had spread in the snow near a pine tree approximately twenty feet from the edge of the rickety porch.

Her heart nearly stopped. Silently, she caught Pescoli's attention and pointed to the large stain and, upon closer inspection, more carmine-colored drips leading to the garage. Footprints in the snow, now buried and uneven, indicated one person, or possibly two, had walked to the blood pool. It was too dark to make out which direction they had been headed, but there was a definite drag mark, a deep trough, where something had been hauled away.

A body?

Had Verdago gotten rid of Carnie? Had she become a liability? Or was the dead person the missing Vincent Samuels, owner of the property? Or someone else? Someone on his hit list?

Her heart was pounding hard, her mouth dry. Something definitely was going down here and she no longer expected the capture to go quietly.

Noiselessly, she walked onto the porch, and while Pescoli took a spot on one side of the door, she flattened herself to the wall on the other, hard enough that she felt the shingles pressing against her back through her jacket.

When the time came, Pescoli would knock and announce that the police were here and then hopefully, the confrontation wouldn't end in gunfire.

But that was unlikely.

Her cell phone clicked softly.

The five minutes were up.

It was on.

Pescoli's gaze met hers and with a nod, ordered Alvarez to call for backup. Alvarez pressed another button on her cell phone, silently alerting the two backup units that they were needed.

STAT!

Alvarez braced herself.

Pescoli banged hard on the door, the sound echoing through the hills. Before it was answered, she quickly stepped away from the entrance and pressed her body into the siding again, just in case Verdago came out guns blazing.

Nothing happened.

Silence reigned.

No frantic footsteps ran wildly through the house.

No panicked shouts were yelled.

No movement could be felt in the old timbers.

And definitely no door was opening.

Pescoli waited, her weapon aimed squarely at the door, just as Alvarez's was.

"Maurice Verdago?" she yelled again, disturbing the stillness. "Open up! This is the Pinewood County Sheriff's Department! Come out with your hands over your head."

Silence, and then something . . . footsteps.

Alvarez set her jaw. Adrenaline poured through her blood, the hand on her weapon was steady.

A second later, the door swung inward.

Standing in the doorway, unarmed, was Vincent friggin' Samuels.

His eyes, behind his glasses, were round, and as he focused on Pescoli with her weapon pointed at him, his mouth dropped open and he looked as if he might pee himself right then and there.

"What the hell is this?" he said and his hands shot skyward. "Don't shoot! For the love of God! Don't fucking shoot!" Looking as if he might actually faint, he cried, "For the love of Christ, it's only an elk!"

"An elk?" Alvarez said and Samuels's head jerked in her direction.

"Oh, shit. I mean, I know I poached the thing, but don't kill me over it." He licked his lips nervously, his eyes darting back and forth in his head as she lowered her weapon. "I shot a damned elk. Yeah, not in season. With no tag. But . . ." As his mind cleared a bit, his expression changed slightly, fear giving way to confusion. "You . . . you thought Maurice was here?"

"Isn't he?"

"No." Samuels looked even more stunned than before. "Why would he be? I haven't seen him in ages . . . last I heard he got himself sent to the big house by hacking up his brother-in-law. Kathy, er, oh, excuse me. I mean the 'Honorable Judge Kathryn Samuels-Piquard' threw the book at Verdago. He never forgave me. Like it was my fault or something."

"You think we're here because you killed an elk?" Alvarez clarified and thought of the bloody pool, the drag marks in the snow.

"The damned thing just wandered over here and so I nailed it. It . . . it's hanging in the garage. A buck," he added quickly, as if the animal's sex mattered.

Pescoli wasn't convinced. Her weapon was still trained on Samuels. "You don't mind if we look inside?"

"Well, Jesus." He was getting a little pissy now. "Go right ahead. Knock yourself out."

"Step off the porch," she ordered. Then as Alvarez heard the back door open, Pescoli, sidearm aimed in front of her, moved cautiously into the house and out of sight just as in the distance the scream of sirens cut through the night.

"Clear!" a male voice yelled from inside the house. Watershed. Again: "Clear!"

Slowly, his gaze on her gun, Samuels lowered his hands and said to Alvarez, "I don't know what you people think you're doing, but trust me, you've got it all wrong."

"Do we?"

"I'm not blowing smoke when I say that I haven't seen Maurice.

He's a con, for the love of God. I just don't know why you came up here! Did Kathy send you?"

Alvarez had wondered at his earlier tone. Now she realized he was still unaware of his sister's death.

"That would be just like her," Samuels was going on, annoyed. "And trust me. All of you people and that dick Grayson aren't going to hear the last of it either. I know people . . . attorneys and . . . Oh, shit. What's this?" He looked over Alvarez's shoulder as blue and red lights flashed in the night, reflecting on the snow, splashing off the trees. Engines rumbled and sirens shrieked as headlights appeared over the rise. "More cops? What the fuck do you think I did?" And then more soberly, "What is this? What's Maurice got himself into?"

"You've been at this cabin awhile," Alvarez started.

"What the fuck's going on?" he demanded. "Yeah, I've been out here for weeks and there's no phone, no electricity—just the way I like it. Kathy thinks I've got a screw loose or something. Accuses me of being a damned hermit, but I don't really give a rat's ass what she thinks. I suppose she's the one who signed the damned search warrant for you guys to come bustin' into my place. And, oh, by the way, I haven't seen that warrant yet. Better show it, or get the hell off my property."

"We don't have a warrant, Mr. Samuels," Alvarez responded, all but shouting to be heard over the sirens. Something in her serious tone or expression must have gotten through, because suddenly he dropped all his bluster.

"What's wrong? Why are you here?"

"I'm sorry to inform you that your sister is dead."

"No . . . no . . ."

"She was shot, Mr. Samuels, not too far from here, probably a few days before Christmas."

"That can't be right. I don't believe it. Who would shoot her . . . oh, Jesus . . . who wouldn't?" Swallowing and blinking, he appeared to be trying to absorb what she was telling him, make some sense of it. "Verdago? You suspect him? And you think he was hiding here at *my* place?" Finally putting the pieces together, he sagged against the doorjamb. Alvarez reached out to keep him from falling and helped slide him down onto the single crooked step of the porch. "No . . . This can't be true. We had our problems, me and Kath, but oh . . . God." His attention was caught by the cop cars, the beams of their headlights illuminating the small clearing as sirens were abruptly cut and the SUVs slid to a stop. Doors flew open. Two deputies from each vehicle slid to the ground to use the doors as shields.

"Stand down!" Alvarez yelled, still keeping her gaze trained on the judge's brother.

"What?" The first deputy, Jan Spitzer, called from the other side of her open car door.

"I said, 'Stand down.' Verdago's not here!"

"About time you figured that out," Samuels said. He swiped at his nose with the back of his hand. "Oh, what the fuck?"

He looked past the cop cars and Alvarez followed his gaze to spy a man, bundled in a heavy jacket, hurrying along the snowy landscape. Ducking furtively, running from one tree to another as if expecting a barrage of gunfire at any second, he carried a small bag.

With a sinking feeling, Alvarez recognized Manny Douglas. "Get back," she yelled at him, then to Spitzer, who was starting to approach the scene, "Secure the perimeter! Nothing's going down here!" She located Spitzer's partner and shouted, "And get him"—she indicated the crouching reporter—"the hell out of here!"

At that moment, Pescoli, weapon at her side, disappointment etched on her face, walked out of the house and onto the porch. "Nothing," she said just as a bright light flashed in the darkness. Alvarez instinctively raised her weapon, rolled into a crouch, and saw the reporter, camera in hand, a smile splitting his weasel-like face.

"I said, get him out of here!" she yelled at the rest of the officers who surged forward.

Manny lifted his hands and backed away, and Alvarez knew their fiasco at the cabin was about to be splashed across the front page.

CHAPTER 29

She probably should never have admitted to Cade that the girls were his, Hattie thought as she closed the back door of the commercial kitchen from which she ran her catering business. There were two parties looming in her near future: The Robbins's New Year's Eve dinner, which she had catered for the last three years, and for the first time, the Knapps's open house the following afternoon. Her business was growing, slowly but surely, and she'd actually thought about taking on a partner so that she could spend more time with the girls.

Weeks ago, she'd worked out the menu and budget with her clients and purchased the items that weren't perishable. Today it was down to the wire and she'd spent most of her day purchasing and organizing all of the fresh food for the two events; tomorrow she'd start pre-prepping and cooking.

For the most part, she and the girls lived on the girls' share of the profits from the Grayson ranch, but it wasn't enough to meet the monthly bills. Her catering business filled that gap, though work was spotty; some times of the year she had more parties than she could service, other times not so much. During the lean months, she spent more time with the twins and in the busy months, like December through New Year's, she was run ragged.

Wiggling the exterior door's handle to double-check that the temperamental lock had actually latched, she told herself to quit worrying. Of course she hadn't known how Cade would react when she'd dropped the bomb on him that he was a father and had been for eight years, but she certainly hadn't expected silence. Cade had always been vocal and hotheaded, but lately, even dealing with Dan's condition, he'd been a little more in control of his temper. But not like this. Not to the point of noncommunication.

His initial reaction in the machine shed hadn't surprised her, but the silence since had. Though she told herself to just be patient, that he was processing, that everything would work itself out, it felt as if she were experiencing the calm before the storm.

"He had to know," she reminded herself again, her breath fogging in the air. Picking her way through the iced-over puddles in the lot to her Camry, currently parked beneath a utility pole with a high-wattage security lamp, she finally noticed the pickup a few spaces away.

Cade's truck.

And he was inside, she could see him in the driver's seat as a car drove past, the wash of headlights illuminating the interior of the pickup and his face: hard. Grim. Uncompromising.

Her heart lurched.

As much as she wanted some kind of communication from him, the thought of actually facing him again was daunting. Would he be reasonable? Would he want things to stay as they were? Would he want to be a bigger part of the twins' lives? Or would he be nursing his anger, ready to do battle again?

As he observed her approach, he climbed out of the cab, a tall, dark silhouette against the backdrop of the street lamps.

"I wondered when I'd hear from you," she said, screwing up her courage as she made her way to the space between their vehicles.

"Had a lot to think about."

She nodded. "I laid some heavy stuff on you."

He was leaning against the driver's door of his Dodge, the brim of his hat shading his eyes from the dim glow of the security lights, snow catching on it and the shoulders of his sheepskin jacket. "That you did." Nodding slightly, he looked away from her for a second, then refocused on her face. "I was wondering what we're going to do about it."

"You mean what *you're* going to do about it. I plan to live my life the same way I've been living it, raising my kids, taking care of my business"—she tossed a hand outward, toward the back of the building housing the kitchen—"and dealing with my screwball family. Mom's had some health issues, I haven't heard from Dad in years and suddenly he sends a Christmas card with two checks, one for each of the girls." She shook her head. "And then there's Cara."

"Yeah, Cara." He said her name as if it tasted bad.

"I know she's concerned about Dan. She said so."

He made a sound of disbelief. "She's your sister. I get that. But she's no saint, so don't bother making excuses for her. She is who she is. She never loved Dan. When they were divorced, it was over, at least for her, and she married some other guy. End of story." A lift of his shoulders said it all: Cara Hyer Grayson Banks was of no consequence.

"So back to you. What do you want, Cade?"

He hesitated for just a second, and his gaze touched hers for a heart-freezing instant. In that moment she saw a life with him, with the girls, all of them at the ranch together. McKenzie on horseback, Mallory demanding her father take her to her next dance recital, a Christmas tree decorated by the staircase, tinsel and lights glittering, she and Cade . . .

Her lips parted at the absurdity of her fantasy. What was she thinking? She and Cade would *never* work. Yes, they'd been good in bed; she'd never been as turned on by any man, though she would never admit it. And they could appreciate each other's sense of humor, wry and wicked, but that's where the compatibility stopped.

Sex and laughter did not a relationship make.

But children might.

"I want the girls," he said succinctly.

"What?" she asked, shocked by his bald declaration even though she'd worried he'd say something like this, do something like this.

"Not all the time, but half," he amended. "Joint custody."

"No . . . I . . . why?" She was struggling to keep her fear under control.

"Isn't that why you told me about the girls now? You expected some kind of help with—"

"I thought I explained all that, Cade." She snapped back to the moment. "I thought that we, you and I together, would *eventually* tell them the truth, when they were old enough to understand."

"They'll never be that old. Hell, I don't understand it and I participated."

"More than willingly," she reminded.

"No argument there."

"I want the girls to know their father, that they have a father, and that if something . . . something were to happen to me, then they'd have another parent. They've already lost the man who claimed them as their own, and they could be on the brink of losing their favorite uncle."

He flinched at that.

"Life is short, Cade. We don't know what's around the corner, and the girls need someone in their lives besides me, and an aunt who doesn't care a lick about them, not really, and a grandmother who's battling cancer. They need *you*, Cade, yes, just like they sure as hell need me."

"So you expect me to just stay in the shadows? Pretend that I'm still just their uncle for the next five or six years, and then when they're into puberty and boys and God knows what else, spring it on them that I'm their father? How do you think that'll go, huh? If anything, it'll cause another rift so deep it might not be bridged for years, if then. They're eight now. Better they find out the truth now, so that by the time they get to junior high, when kids can be *really* cruel, they've already dealt with it. They'll be used to the situation and so will all the other kids. The gossips in this little town will have moved on to other, juicier, fresh grist to run through the rumor mill."

"So, what? You want to go back to my house and make the announcement?"

"Yep, I'll bring dinner."

"I was joking."

"I know."

She stared at him. "I'm not ready for this."

"I am," he said. "And who knows? They might just say, 'We want to spend the night with Daddy.' Then you can pack them up and send them on their way to the ranch with me."

She almost laughed. "That's not going to happen. What do you know about taking care of eight-year-olds?"

"I'm a quick study."

"What're you going to do when Mallory wakes up with nightmares, or McKenzie gets one of her wild hares and takes off?"

"I can deal."

She snorted, worried that she'd just made the worst mistake of her life. And that was quite a feat considering all of the blunders she'd racked up over the years.

He took a step closer to her. "You can't have it both ways, Hattie. Either I'm in or I'm out. And you're the one that let me in, so, like it or not, there's no turning back. Now, I'm going to visit my kids. You coming?" He climbed into his truck, fired the engine, and waited.

At least he didn't drive off in a spray of gravel and ice, she thought as she anxiously followed him to her place. She parked in the garage while he found a spot on the street, right behind Zena's Caddy. They met at the front door.

"Okay," she said, her nerves tight. "But we're not telling them anything tonight, right? For now you're still Uncle Cade."

He hesitated.

"It will be confusing for them, so we need to take it slow. Ease them into it." She could hear their questions already.

What about my real dad?

Aren't you still my uncle?

How can you be my uncle and *my dad?*

"Fine, for tonight," he agreed. "But before this year is out, we're going to broach the subject." As he stood under the porch light, his features set, she saw the tight line of his jaw. There was no turning back. Cade was determined to step into the role of fatherhood, which was what she'd wanted, right?

They headed into the house and the girls, who had been coloring in front of the television, suddenly looked up and screamed in delight. Markers and crayons flew every which way as they flung themselves at their "uncle." He swung them each deftly off their feet, giving them each a quick hug before planting them back down. Hattie could hardly watch as, completely ignoring their mother, they giggled and laughed, vying for Cade's attention before he could even take off his coat. "More!" McKenzie cried, practically jumping into his arms again. A lump filled Hattie's throat as she watched him with them. Already they adored him, and the feeling was obviously mutual. Her eyes burned. This was so right, yet it could have far-reaching consequences for her.

Clearing her throat, she said, "Hey, girls, give your uncle a break," as she slipped out of her coat and left her boots by the front door.

"He's not our uncle," Mallory said with that superior know-it-all attitude that was just beginning to bloom and really get under Hattie's skin.

"What do you mean?" she asked carefully.

Zena appeared from the kitchen. Wearing an apron, an apricot-colored wig, and a smile that seemed painted on, she said, "I'm the culprit!"

"*You* took it upon yourself to tell them?" Hattie was aghast.

"So it's true?" Mallory asked eagerly.

"Mom! What were you thinking?" Turning to her daughters, she said, "Uh, yeah. From now on Cade is your daddy."

"Did you get married?" McKenzie asked.

"No, we're not getting married."

"But then how come he's our daddy now?" McKenzie's little face twisted into a knot of concentration.

"Mommies and daddies don't have to be married," Mallory said. "Neva's mom and dad are divorced and so are Charlie's. He's got a new dad."

"That's right. Families can be pretty mixed up. Look at Aunt Cara and me. We have different fathers," Hattie said desperately, shooting Zena a dark look.

"What about our real daddy?" McKenzie asked.

"He's dead, dummy! That's why we need a new one!" Mallory had it all figured out.

Hattie chastised her daughter, "Mallory, don't call your sister names." To Cade, she added, "Uh, you talk to the children, I need a word with my mother." Hustling Zena into the kitchen where a pot of bean soup was simmering on the stove and a pan of corn bread cooled on racks set near the window, she said in a low, furious voice, "I can't believe you did that!"

"It's time the girls know who their father is."

"But, Mom, you had no right! This was for me to decide."

Picking up a wooden spoon lying in a holder, she stirred the soup, turning the beans from the bottom of the kettle. "It's been nine years of lies, Hattie, and I, for one, don't have any more time for this."

"You're so wrong about this."

"Maybe. Call me 'selfish' or a 'meddler' if you want, I deserve it. But I need to leave this earth knowing that my family is settled."

Dread crawled up her spine. "What're you talking about?" she asked, even as a cold awareness was taking hold of her. And then she saw the quiver of Zena's jaw and the tissues that had been used and wadded before being tossed into the trash. "Mom? What is it?"

"I got the call today." She touched her cell phone lying faceup on the counter and took a deep breath to steady herself. "It's the cancer. It's grown, honey."

"No, don't say it."

But, as usual, her mother ignored her. "According to the doctor, there isn't much more they can do."

CHAPTER 30

"Are you out of your friggin' minds?" Brewster roared, the veins in his neck protruding, his face a nasty shade of red that was turning purple. "What the hell were you thinking, going out into the woods half cocked with some asinine theory about Verdago? All because of a damned picture from a traffic cam?" Standing over the desk in the office he'd claimed, he was dressed in full uniform, leaning forward, obviously expecting Pescoli and Alvarez in their visitor's chairs to cower.

Pescoli wasn't giving an inch and neither, it seemed, was Alvarez as they tried to explain themselves. The door to the office was closed and the room felt suddenly foreign, a sterile place without Grayson's easy demeanor, without his dog, and definitely without his class.

Pescoli argued, "This was good info."

"It was thin," he said, his eyes narrowing. "Very thin. You can't even tell if the driver really is Verdago. His passenger is unidentifiable, and even if it was Verdago and his girlfriend, they could be in Canada by now, or Oregon or, hell, halfway to Mexico. What the hell made you think they would end up in Samuels's cabin? This was outrageous action on faulty data."

She wanted to throw it all back at him, but no matter what she said, he had an answer.

"And you know what?" he railed. "It all backfired. Worse yet, I have no idea what the fuck you did to piss Manny Douglas off, but tomorrow, come hell or high water, the *Mountain Reporter* is printing a story about eight of my officers, *eight* deputies and detectives on the public payroll, making a huge blunder that will cost the county thousands of dollars to what? Run a poacher in? The only reason it hasn't cost us more money is that the department's bending over backward in the hope that Vincent Samuels doesn't make a stink. *Vincent Samuels*. Did you all forget that he's the judge's brother, one of the bereaved? He didn't even know that he'd lost his sister, and you two, along with *six others,* go in, weapons drawn. Son of a bitch!" He kicked the air in frustration.

Pescoli had never seen him so angry, so worked up. She'd always thought he'd had somewhat of a level head, except when it came to her son and his daughter, of course. Those times when she had witnessed his agitation, it had been intense, his temper blasting hot when it came to his kid. However, at the office, he'd been able to control his emotions.

Not today. Not now that he was in power.

He threw a look at the ceiling, as if hoping God Himself would intervene.

"Samuels is talking about getting a lawyer, you know, for all his pain and suffering. They'll drum up other charges, too, starting with there was no warrant and that there was no reason to think anyone was in danger out there, or a crime was being committed, or whatever. It won't stop there, let me tell you. Some hungry attorney wanting to make a name for himself might just take his case and either way, the department will have to deal with the consequences!" He glared down at Pescoli with pure hatred. "This is on you, Pescoli." Then his attention moved to Alvarez. "You, Detective, should know better. She's always flown off the handle, breaking or bending any rule that got in her way, but you, you're supposed to be the cool head."

"I'm with Pescoli on this one," Alvarez said tightly.

"Then you're both idiots!"

His phone rang and he dismissed them with a sharp wave of his hand.

"That was fun," Alvarez said once they were in the hallway and walking to their offices.

The shifts had changed, most of the officers who worked days having left, the night crew settled in. Still there were voices and the hum of computers, ringing phones, and the glow of interior lights that kept the station abuzz with activity long into the night.

"Maybe we were too quick to pull the trigger," Alvarez said as they reached Pescoli's office. Closing her eyes, she shook her head, as if she couldn't believe the image she was seeing in her mind's eye. "A damned elk."

"If it weren't so pathetic, it would be funny," Pescoli said heavily. She inwardly cringed as she recalled walking through the small cabin, her weapon raised as she checked all the rooms and closets, and even the crawl space and tiny attic, all the while hoping to flush out Maurice Verdago and put the case to rest. She'd checked the garage, too, and sure enough, the huge carcass of a bull elk had been hung from the rafters. Just seeing the skinned animal suspended from a hook had made her stomach lurch. Fired up on adrenaline and then the ultimate humiliation for being so damned wrong, she'd nearly upchucked right then and there.

Fortunately, Manny Douglas didn't get *that* reaction on film. How had she read the case so badly? For the love of Christ, Vincent Samuels, oddball loner that he was, hadn't even known that his sister had been shot and killed.

"You won't think it's funny when the story runs tomorrow morning," Alvarez said. "I can see the headlines now: county sheriff department searches for murderer, finds dead elk."

"Accompanied by the picture of us holding the judge's brother at gunpoint?" Pescoli considered the public reaction and the fact that every TV station within a hundred miles would want to delve deeper into the story. Already she'd ignored a call from Honey Carlisle from KBTR and another one from Nia Del Ray of KMJC, a rival station, both reporters obviously having tapped into the police band. The newspaper article in tomorrow's paper was just the tip of the iceberg.

"Yeah," she said as she peered into her darkened office where she'd left her Big Gulp with its flattened straw. "It's going to be great."

Alvarez looked tired as all get out. "Look, I need a break and I'm taking it. This really messed with me today, and O'Keefe and I are getting together tonight, alone for the first time in a while. But if you need me for anything, my cell will be on."

"You're safe. I think I've used and abused enough of the staff for the day," Pescoli said.

Alvarez snaked a glance into the direction of the sheriff's office. In a low voice, she confided, "O'Keefe said if we need some extra help, you know, the kind that isn't . . ."

"Legal?"

"I was going to say 'orthodox.' If we want that kind of assistance, he offered his services."

Pescoli was tempted; it would be so nice not to play by the rules or deal with the likes of Brewster. She'd screwed up more times than she'd like to remember in her career, but never had it been the kind of screaming dressing down that she'd just experienced with the acting sheriff. Brewster was a head case pure and simple. So he had a pristine record in law enforcement; that didn't mean he was a great guy. In his case, far from it. And she felt badly that she'd dragged Alvarez and all the other officers into her own personal hyped-up mess. She'd been so eager to nail the son of a bitch who'd shot Grayson, she'd misread the signs, and now everyone, not just she, was paying the price.

"I think we'd better play this one by the book," she said. "We want to nail Verdago before he gets another crack at the sheriff or anyone else."

"You still think it's him?" After the day's debacle, Alvarez sounded skeptical.

"Got any better ideas?"

"Nope."

"Me neither," Pescoli admitted, and that was what really ticked her off. Outwardly, she acknowledged she'd screwed up. Inwardly, she seethed, her gut telling her she was right, that Verdago was the guy.

But she couldn't figure out how, despite another couple of hours going over reports, info, and maps of the area. Brewster could deny it all he wanted, but the picture taken by the traffic cam was Verdago. Pescoli would stake her badge on it.

Still without answers and stung by her enormous mistake, she drove home nearly two hours later. As she'd reconstructed what went wrong today, writing it into the report she'd hand to Brewster in the morning, she'd also sought to come up with another avenue. But each mental path she traveled down, each new possible scenario she explored presented a major roadblock.

The suspect list had narrowed.

Grayson's brothers had no beef with him, or the judge. Cara Banks didn't seem to have any real animosity toward her ex, and Pescoli had already crossed her off as having the desire or wherewithal to hire an assassin. Besides, why would she knock off the judge in the process? The same went for Akina Bellows, wife number two. The dating angle hadn't been proved or disproved, but she couldn't find any evidence linking Grayson and the judge romantically, and even if there were an affair, who would care enough to try and take them both out? Yes, the judge had called the station over the past few months, but that wasn't all that out of line.

So she buried that old theory as well.

Which left the people they'd sent up the river and right at the top of the list, without the alibi most of the other ex-cons had come up with, was the missing Maurice Verdago.

A headache was pounding behind Pescoli's eyes and she once again had the nagging thought that she was missing something . . . something important, and right under her nose, but whatever it was, she couldn't quite grasp it, even though she concentrated so hard that she nearly hit a rabbit that hopped into the road in front of her car, hesitated, then turned quickly, missing her tire by inches as it disappeared into the icy brambles flanking the road.

Resler, Cranston, and Gardener all had rock-solid alibis.

Swearing under her breath, feeling her stomach begin to act up again, she turned into the long lane of her home. Recent tire tracks suggested Jeremy was home. She crossed the single-lane bridge to round a final bend and spy her house sitting in its clearing. The Christmas lights strung on the eaves were glowing, aside from one strand that had decided to give up the ghost, but Jeremy's truck, usually parked out front, was missing.

Huh.

For a second she thought someone was watching her, that same eerie sensation that had prickled her skin when she was alone and created the nightmares that ruined her sleep. Was it possible that whoever was following her had come here for her children?

For the love of God, check your paranoia at the door.

As she drove into the garage, she had one hand on her sidearm, her adrenaline pumping in spite of herself. Then she heard the dogs starting to make a ruckus and Bianca's voice: "Hey! Hush! Calm down. Cisco, you troublemaker!" The smaller dog continued to yap while Grayson's Lab quieted immediately.

She returned her gun to its holster and breathed a long sigh of relief.

Get a hold of yourself, Pescoli. You are doing no one, including yourself, any favors with all these mind games.

Once inside the house, she greeted both dogs and found Bianca sitting at the kitchen table, a bottle of soda and a small bag of some kind of chip at her fingertips as she read on her new e-reader and somehow still was able to text on her phone.

At least she was interested in some kind of food. "Hi," she said, actually looking up.

"Hey." Pescoli dropped her things on a nearby chair and hung her coat on the hall tree near the door. "What's up?"

"I'm *eating*. See."

"Mmm-hmm."

Her daughter sent her a dirty look, snagged a chip, and snapped it between her teeth.

"Where's your brother?"

"Take a wild guess," Bianca suggested, then before Pescoli could make a stab at it, said, "He hooked up with Heidi tonight when we went to get dinner. I think it was a setup."

"How did you get home?"

"Oh, *they* brought me. Heidi was already at Dixie's with friends and so we ate there. They brought me home and then left again. They're probably at her house. She said she had something to show him."

I'll bet, Pescoli thought but didn't say it, though her stomach tightened at the thought of her son under the same roof as her disgruntled—make that so-furious-he-was-frothing-at-the-mouth—boss.

"He's mad at you, you know," Bianca said.

Pescoli let out a humorless laugh. "He'd better take a number." Walking to the refrigerator, she decided she'd have a glass of wine, but the minute she opened the bottle of chardonnay, poured herself a glass, and took a sip, her heartburn acted up again. "What a waste," she said, then jammed the cork into the bottle and set it back into the refrigerator. "Let me guess why he's mad at me. Was it because I embarrassed him at work, or because I told him to keep his rifle locked up, or my attitude about Heidi or—"

"Because you didn't tell us you were getting married," Bianca supplied.

"Oh."

"Yeah, 'oh.' "

"I was going to tell you both tonight," she said, "but I really didn't think about Jeremy seeing me at the office." She met her daughter's curious gaze. "Things have been a little crazy, you know."

"Aren't they always?"

She nodded. Walking back to the table, she added, "I didn't mean to upset you guys."

"You didn't upset me." She said it sincerely, with a dismissive lift of her shoulders. "It's your life. I kinda like Santana, but Jeremy's not a fan."

"I know."

"And he thinks he's got to be all protective and stuff. You know, the guy thing." She rolled her eyes as her phone beeped. For once, she ignored it. "He's like a total doofus, you know. Jer, he tries to be all cool and grown up, but he's really . . . just clueless."

"Did you tell him that?" Pescoli asked.

"I'm not suicidal." She flashed her mother a smile as she wadded up the empty bag of chips. "He thinks he's so badass. So, come on, show me your ring." A little self-consciously, Pescoli thrust her hand across the table and her daughter actually squealed as she touched the stone. "So damned awesome!"

"Oh, I take it you approve?"

"Does it make a difference?"

"I *am* trying to take your feelings into consideration. But, no, I suppose not."

"Are you going to have a big wedding and can I, like, be your maid of honor and Jeremy can walk you down the aisle?"

"Oh, God. You're making my head spin. No."

She appeared deflated. "So what's the point?"

For a second Pescoli had forgotten how young she was. "The point is we want to live together."

"Sooo . . . are we going to move to that new place he's building? At the Brady Long estate?" she asked, the wheels turning in her mind. "That place is, like, the biggest in the county, right?"

"Not Santana's portion, but, yes, eventually we'll move into the new house."

"Cool!" She reached for her phone. "Just make sure I get a bigger room than Jeremy does!" As she started to text with her rapid-fire precision, she added, "Tiffany Anderson is going to be *soooo* jealous."

"Well, that's important," Pescoli said before she walked to the window and stared outside. She considered texting Jeremy because he was going to hear what a disaster she'd created, then thought better of it. He'd find out about it when he did. Rotating the kinks from her neck, she decided she needed a long, hot shower. Then she'd go to work again from home.

As long as Verdago was on the loose, she would be obsessed with him. That's just how it worked with her; the closer she came to closing the case, the more all-consuming it became. And this one was close . . . so close.

She could feel it in her bones.

CHAPTER 31

Carnie Tibalt was *sooo* over camping in this pathetic little cabin that barely had running water. What had started out as an adventure, a romantic romp, had ended up being just plain boring. While Maurice left and did whatever it was he did, she was stuck here, in the middle of no-frickin'-where. Worse yet, he had the balls to take her truck all because his loser of a wife wouldn't let him use her SUV.

That Wanda, what a shrew.

Big, fat, self-centered shrew.

Carnie had only met her once, but Maurice had told her all about Wanda and she believed every last word of it. Still, it would have been nice if he had at least filed the papers to finalize that divorce he kept promising.

Oh, well, she did have a fabulous ring, she thought smugly, staring down at her left hand where the clear stone glittered in the light from the fire. It was gorgeous. She smiled and dreamed of a fairy-tale wedding, then as the windows rattled with a blast of cold air, she was brought back to reality. She threw on her coat and grabbed up the lantern so that she could cut and haul in some more firewood. Hopefully, she wouldn't freeze to death.

Outside the back door, she glanced at the woods, dark and foreboding, even with the snow falling and dusting everything. As a little girl she'd thought snow was magical, but now, it seemed little more than a frigid curtain that wouldn't allow her to see beyond her lantern's glow.

Who knew what lurked beneath those hemlocks?

Wolves?

Cougars?

Something worse?

With a furtive glance to the forest, she hurried her pace to the garage, deciding once again she wasn't cut out for this rustic, frontier-like life. From here on in, her idea of roughing it would be at Super Eight motel, sipping drinks by the pool. Forget this snow. Forget the forest. Forget the damned isolation where her cell phone didn't even work unless she was standing out in the middle of the damned lane.

Of course she wasn't supposed to use it, she thought, snagging the hatchet from the inside of the lean-to that serviced as their garage. What a pain. Setting the lantern on the dirt floor, she found some chunks of pine and deftly cut kindling. The sound of the dry wood cracking, though, somehow reminded her of broken bones.

It was probably because of Maurice.

Obviously he was caught up in something illegal and he was an ex-con, so that was a bit of a problem. Hopefully, it was only drugs or burglary . . . he wouldn't say. "You need to stay out of it, honey," he'd told her when she'd asked, and so she'd let it go.

Now, as she swung the stupid hatchet and split kindling and froze her butt out here, she was thinking she'd made a mistake. It wasn't the first time. She'd started saying to Maurice that it was time to move on, that she was bored, that she missed the crew down at the Long Branch, and he'd gotten snappy with her, even once balled his fist.

Man, he'd better *never* hit her, because she wasn't about to put up with that kind of crap. She had once before, with Lenny, and lost a tooth because of it before she'd had him up on charges, so Maurice better mind his p's and q's.

So far, so good, she thought as she hauled the wood inside and stoked the fire as best she could, urging the flames along, blowing on them and watching as they finally crackled and caught.

She was just about to add some more wood when she heard the engine of the old van and her heart soared. He was back! For a minute all her complaints faded and she thought about greeting him at the door in nothing but her boots. Wouldn't that surprise him.

Quickly she stripped down, layer after layer, until she tossed her bra into the pile of her clothes and walked to the center of the living area. The boots were more practical than sexy, but they would have to do, so she posed, tossing her hair over one shoulder, placing a hand on the hip she bent out and with her mouth in a perfect, pouty O that she patterned after Pamela Anderson—well, when she was younger, on *Baywatch*, like around the time she was married to Tommy Lee—and waited.

She heard the sound of footsteps on the porch.

Her heart swelled and a smile teased her lips. Maurice would be so surprised!

The door opened to bang against the wall.

"Hey, baby," she cooed before she saw the rifle. "Wha—??"

Blam!!!

The bullet slammed deep into her brain and she dropped.

Pescoli didn't sleep a wink.

She'd watched the digital display on her clock count off the hours, but while the dogs snored and Bianca holed up in her room, Pescoli thought about the case and tried not to worry about the fact that her son hadn't bothered to return home. Images came to mind, mental images of Verdago at his sentencing threatening the judge, or Grayson's body jerking from the attack upon him, or the ashes in Kathryn Samuels-Piquard's fireplace, or Wanda Verdago's apartment with the woman's mouth opening and closing, her words a blur, a sword running through her son's body . . . She jerked in bed, suddenly fully awake and realizing she'd actually been dozing, hovering at that twilight place at the edge of sleep.

Her head pounded and she felt a general malaise. Tossing and turning, she finally gave up at four-thirty and decided to get on with what promised to be the day from hell.

After letting the confused and yawning dogs outside, she brewed coffee and grabbed one of Bianca's protein bars that tasted about as good as it sounded, then threw on her clothes, made a quick stab at her makeup, and scribbled a note to her daughter and ghost of a son.

"Be good," she warned the dogs in a whisper before peeking into Bianca's room to find her daughter sleeping soundly, her pink duvet wrapped around her like a cocoon.

The house was locked tight, Bianca secure with two dogs to protect her. Pouring hot coffee into a travel mug, she shrugged into her coat and took off.

For some reason, she was jazzed. Maybe it was the caffeine or the lack of sleep, but she was energized and ready to take on the day no matter how it played out, even though she knew it would be a rough shift at the station.

Not long ago, she'd been considered a hero; she and Alvarez having brought several serial killers to justice. But today, and for the rest of the year and into the next, probably, she would be the goat.

"Okay, it's on," she told herself as she pulled into the parking lot just before five. Usually this section of Grizzly Falls with its busy street that cut through some of the county offices was bustling with activity, but at this early hour the sheriff's department was quiet, the few cars in the parking lot covered with two inches of snow, no one on the street.

Spying the paper stand, and inwardly cursing herself for being a masochist, she found the right change and saw, through the glass of the box, her picture front and center. Muttering under her breath, she was able to pick up the early edition of the *Mountain Reporter*.

Tucking the paper under her arm, she made her way inside and spread the newspaper open, reading the long article:

detectives involved in "wild elk" chase.

"Thanks, Manny," she said as she scanned the article that put Alvarez and herself in a very unpleasant light.

No wonder she had sixteen calls on her voice mail already this morning, over half of them from local news stations.

That's what you get for being an idiot and even talking to Douglas.

It was going to be a long day.

Pushing aside her thoughts about what was literally yesterday's news, she painstakingly went over all the evidence on the case, then wrote her report about the events leading up to, and what had actually happened at, Samuels's cabin.

Half expecting a text or a call from Jeremy, she kept an eye on her phone as she would have liked to give him a heads-up about what had happened. After eight, she sent him a text, but still he didn't respond, and she decided he either had the day off or was marked to show up in the afternoon. Hopefully by then some of the backlash from yesterday's botched assignment would have dissipated.

As the morning progressed and the day shift arrived, the familiar noises of the department reached her ears: phones ringing, the fax machine chunking out information, the old heating system rumbling, and the click of Joelle's heels as she arrived. Cell phones buzzed or chirped while the smell of coffee seeped through the offices and feet shuffled or marched in the hallway outside her door. Brett Gage's belly laugh erupted from somewhere near the interrogation rooms, and she couldn't help but wonder if she were the butt of the department's recent jokes.

Now you really are getting paranoid, that inner voice kept reminding her.

She refilled her cup of coffee in the lunchroom and told herself the sidelong glances from the other officers weren't smirks, that the open paper with her picture on the front page wasn't all that unusual. People read the paper every day.

Besides, most of them were too busy with their own workload to worry about her screwup.

"Hey, Pescoli?" Rick Hanson called to her. He was a thin guy with short-cropped red hair, tall enough to have played basketball, and sometimes thick as a brick. He and his partner, Dale Connors, were seated at the table, drinking a cup of coffee and reading the sports page before hitting the road. "I heard you made a big catch yesterday." Hanson was grinning wide, glad for a chance to needle her.

Polishing the lenses of his glasses with a napkin, Connors, who had his partner beat by a good fifty pounds, chuckled. "So what're you serving for New Year's? I hear elk steaks are great."

"Or a roast," Hanson said. "Hey, Pescoli, how about everyone coming over to your place for a roast?"

Connors added, "Of *you*!" as if she hadn't caught the joke.

"Sure. Why not?" She wasn't going to let them get to her.

"Oh, the mighty, how they have fallen," Connors added, sliding his glasses onto the bridge of his nose and smirking. He'd always been a jerk, but she wasn't going to give him the satisfaction of knowing he bugged the crap out of her.

She didn't bother responding, just walked out of the lunchroom doing a slow boil.

"Do you know what time it is?" Wanda Verdago was not pleased to be woken up even though, according to Alvarez's watch, it was after ten in the morning. In the same too-small bathrobe but without makeup, she looked younger and fresher. "I don't know why you're here. I told you everything I know!"

"I just need to clear up a few details," Alvarez assured her.

"Couldn't you have called?"

"I was over here anyway," Alvarez lied and waited while Wanda reluctantly opened the screen door and let her inside an apartment that hadn't changed much since their previous interview. Alvarez purposely hadn't called because she wanted to catch the woman's reaction.

"I read that you and that partner of yours really messed up yesterday, looking for Maurice and coming up with a poacher." She plopped into her spot on the couch again, on the opposite end from an overflowing basket of laundry. "What is it you want to know?"

"It's about Joey Lundeen," Alvarez said, sitting down and watching the big woman stiffen slightly.

For a split second, fear flashed in her eyes, though as quickly as it flared, it vanished. "I didn't know him."

"But you heard he disappeared, right, around fifteen years ago. You were with Maurice then, when he was out of the military."

"We were married," she agreed, frowning at the mention of her husband. "Okay, I know that he and Joey had it out the night before Joey disappeared. The police came nosing around then, too, but they couldn't pin anything on Maurice." The hint of a smile teased her pale lips. She was holding out and proud of whatever it was she was hiding.

"Now that your husband has gone missing and might be involved in some other crimes, the Joey Lundeen disappearance is being looked into again."

"So what?"

"So, if you know anything, this would be the time to let me know."

"And why would I do that?"

"Because it's a crime to withhold evidence. For example, say we find out that Joey didn't just leave the area, that he actually was murdered and you knew something about it, then you would be tried as an accomplice." That maybe stretched the truth a bit, but it had the desired effect. Wanda looked quickly away and fiddled with the "cubic Z" ring that had returned to her left ring finger since Alvarez's last visit.

"It would be a shame if you had to do time for something Maurice did, especially since he's thrown you over for Carnie Tibalt and—"

"I'm still married to him!" Wanda cut in, her face an angry, red pout. "She's nothing to him, just something to play with. He loves me!" she said, hooking a thumb at her chest, where her robe gapped to display her ill-fitting pajamas.

"You've talked to him?"

"No . . . I . . ." She swallowed hard, tears again filling her eyes.

"Well, think about it, Mrs. Verdago. You might believe you're saving him, but what about you? If the situation were reversed and he had to cover for you, would he do it? I don't think so. What's he ever done for you besides lie to you and place a fake diamond on your finger?"

Wanda Verdago blinked and sniffed, her jaw set as Alvarez left her card on the coffee table. "Call me if you change your mind." She took three steps toward the door to let herself out, when Wanda let out an unhappy sob.

"Wait," she called, the waterworks flowing steadily now. "Okay. You're right. I . . . I do have some information. About Joey. About what happened. But I want a lawyer and immunity if I testify. I don't want to set one foot in jail." She shuddered in her tight bathrobe. "I've seen enough episodes of *Law and Order.* I know my rights."

It was one thing to be the butt of the jokes of morons who hadn't bothered growing up, it was quite another to agree with them that she'd made a major screwup.

What had she missed? What, what, what?

Again, Pescoli looked at the maps, and again she went over the information . . . the traffic cam was located at the last major intersection out of town, the road Verdago had been driving on headed into the hills. Because of the time of the photograph—at 3:17 in the morning—she'd just assumed he'd been returning to his hideout. That, as Brewster had so definitely pointed out, was wrong. Settling back in her chair, she eyed the county and state maps.

If not Samuels's place, then where?

He could have broken into any one of hundreds of cabins, summer homes in the area, but that didn't feel right to her. And why was Carnie with him? If he were on a killing spree, would she willingly go along?

The woman had no arrest record, no infractions with the law. So now she's a partner to murder? Or had she been kidnapped? Duped?

Her family had once lived around Grizzly Falls but now was scattered, parents split, mother dead, father remarried and living the Aloha lifestyle in Hawaii. She had a handful of cousins in Washington and Oregon and an uncle in Duluth, Minnesota. No siblings.

So far, none of the calls made to her family by deputies had brought out any information of consequence. More telling, and sad, no one seemed to care much about Carnival's disappearance.

One cousin, Rachelle, had said, "It's kinda too bad about Carnie. She's just not all that bright."

Her father's response was, "I don't know what she's mixed up in, if anything, but I don't worry too much about her. She's like her mother, you know, always lands on her feet."

Only her uncle, Davis Briscoe, had anything of importance to say. "Poor thing never had a chance. Her mother—that was my sister, Lizzie—drank herself to death, and Harvey, well, he just wasn't any good at bein' a dad. He does a whole lot better over on Maui or wherever he is. I tried with Carnie, when I lived there, but, hey, I had to take the job here."

As an afterthought, Pescoli searched titles of property in and around Grizzly Falls for Carnival Tibalt and found nothing. Again. The same went for Harvey and Lizzie, even though she was dead, just on the off chance there had been a slipup, but the search was a bust.

"One last resort," she said, sipping coffee gone cold as she checked out good old Uncle Davis Briscoe and sure enough, he still owned property in Montana, in Pinewood County, in the very hills and off that same road out of town as Vincent Samuels.

"Well, hello," she said softly, her spirits lifting as she once again rechecked the maps.

As she did, she felt that same rush that told her she was on to something. Yesterday it had failed her, however, so she told herself to tread carefully. This time she wouldn't risk more fallout. She would check the place out in broad daylight by herself. From a distance.

Take precautions. If you're right, you'll need backup.

She stopped by Alvarez's office and stuck her head inside, but her partner's neat desk was empty, her chair pushed into the desk, a screen saver rolling over her computer monitor.

Brewster, too, wasn't in, so she called Alvarez and left a voice mail, then bundled up and headed to her Jeep. Alvarez's Subaru wasn't in the lot, which was odd, and Jeremy's truck was MIA, though it could be that he wasn't scheduled to work today; his hours were part-time and flexible. As for Brewster, she really didn't care where he was after the dressing down she'd been subjected to yesterday.

As she climbed into her Jeep, she thought about how nearly a week earlier she'd planned on talking to Grayson about resigning. Now, it sounded like a good idea again, and this time she could shove her resignation under Cort Brewster's pointed better-than-thou nose. She'd marry Santana, take care of her kids until they left the nest, even consider going private, become a partner with O'Keefe, as he was thinking of moving to Grizzly Falls. Starting the engine, she felt a little better. As a private detective she wouldn't have all the rules and regulations and chain of command to worry about.

No more morons like Hanson and Connors. That thought gave her great satisfaction as she tore out of the lot. Gunning the engine to make a light at the intersection, she told herself she had to be patient.

First she had to close this damned case and nail Grayson's assailant.

After that, she could hand in her resignation and tell Cort Brewster exactly where to shove it.

CHAPTER 32

"Wanda Verdago is ready to talk," Alvarez announced. It was late morning by the time she'd returned to the station and had cornered Brewster in his office. Grayson's boxes had been cleared out and now, with all of Brewster's paraphernalia on the shelves and in the bookcases, the room didn't feel like it had ever belonged to Dan Grayson.

Brewster had been reaching for the phone but let it drop. "She knows where her husband is?"

"Not that she's admitting to yet. I talked to her at her apartment, but she wouldn't say much. Not without seeking legal advice."

"Of course."

"But she agreed to come to the station and give a statement about the disappearance of Joey Lundeen, fifteen years ago."

"For the love of Mike," Brewster said, his eyes narrowing a bit. "I always wondered what happened to that two-bit punk."

Alvarez nodded.

"You think it's a homicide?"

"She's not saying until she and her lawyer arrive. They should be here around three. She wants a deal. Immunity."

"Must be serious."

"I'd say so. She seems about ready to roll on her husband, so if she knows anything about the recent attacks, this would be the time to find out."

"I'll talk to the D.A. I'm sure we can work something out." He was sitting up again, reaching for his phone, but she said, "Before you do that, tell me this. You said your brother knew Verdago, and you, too, sort of."

"A long time ago."

"Does he strike you as the kind who would go completely off the rails and plan the kind of attacks that we're dealing with? Well organized. Planned."

"What're you getting at, Alvarez?"

"I don't know. It just doesn't add up to me. Why grab your girl-friend, go on a killing spree, then go to ground? Doesn't follow his pattern."

"Could be one of a dozen reasons. Something ticked him. He was bored with the life of an ex-con and janitor. He has something to prove. Who knows what makes a guy like Verdago tick?"

"Maybe," she said, unconvinced. Alvarez didn't like loose ends and this case, with Verdago at its center, was filled with them.

"So, did Pescoli go with you?" he asked. "I haven't seen her around, but I heard she was in this morning."

"I haven't talked to her." That much wasn't a lie, but she didn't mention the voice mail and text she'd received.

"Well, when you do, keep an eye on her, would you? She's out of control and she dragged you into the muck yesterday." When she opened her mouth to argue, he cut her off, "Don't bother defending her. It's not gonna fly. She's a loose cannon, Alvarez, and if she gets involved in another stunt like that . . ." He must've read something in her face, because he set the phone down and held her gaze. "Oh, fuck. Don't tell me," he said, then abruptly changed his mind. "What the hell's going down now?"

The cabin appeared deserted.

Pescoli, from a position looking down on the graying building, had seen no movement in the windows, though thick curtains cov-ered the glass. No smoke curled from the chimney, however, and though there were tracks in the snow leading to the house and indi-cating that a vehicle had been coming and going over the past sev-eral days, the lean-to that served as a garage was currently empty aside from a stack of cord wood and old refrigerator that had to have been new around 1960.

She studied the place through binoculars. Surrounded by forest, the only access was by vehicle; the single-car lane that wound through the trees was only visible due to the double tracks cutting through seven inches of snow. Whoever had been driving that rig had been gone for a while, it seemed, because the tracks weren't new, a thin layer of snow had accumulated over them.

She'd parked her Jeep in an abandoned sawmill nearly a mile down the county road that serviced this area, then had hiked through the woods alongside that road to find this position, where she'd hidden in the brush, staring down at the cabin. She'd sent a text with her whereabouts to Alvarez, but so far hadn't received any reply. Now her phone was on silent.

She glanced at her watch again. She'd been observing the shack for more than an hour watching the snow fall, but nothing had changed except she'd gotten a whole lot colder and another half an inch of snow had fallen.

Deciding it was now or never, she went for it. Carefully, telling herself she was *not a rogue detective,* her eyes and ears straining, she picked her way from one thicket to the next, zeroing in on the house, spying nothing to indicate that anyone was around. Each window was covered with a thick, unlined material that looked like black burlap and didn't allow for any viewing inside. And each one was locked tight. God Almighty, she hoped her efforts weren't a bust.

At the back of the house there was a rotting wooden stoop protected slightly by an overhang where a rear door with a tiny window cut into it barred her entrance. She tried the knob, as she had in the front, but the door was locked tight. On her tiptoes she looked through the small slice of glass and could see most of the area and kitchen, but nothing more.

She had to get inside.

She looked under a fraying mat and under a forgotten boot brush, but there was no key. Nor was there a key tucked onto the supports of the overhang or on the stoop itself. She made her way to the front door and had no more luck, then looked around.

This was a vacation home.

Unused and nearly abandoned.

Wouldn't there be a key left nearby?

Carnie and Verdago could have it with them.

She thought of breaking in because she knew in her heart that, after his tirade yesterday, Brewster would block any action on her part that wasn't strictly by the book.

About to give up, she walked into the outbuilding that was the garage. Sweeping the beam of her flashlight along the rafters and posts, she found nothing. She even opened the dark refrigerator, which was empty and filthy when she searched inside. Opening the tiny freezer compartment, she found nothing but an ancient, metal ice cube tray, but as she closed the refrigerator door, her flashlight beam caught on a bit of metal in the wall behind the old Frigidaire.

A key.

"Amen," she whispered and only hoped it worked the lock on one of the doors.

The closest was the front door.

No go, she thought, rounding the old building and slipping the key into the back door lock. It turned easily. Her pulse beat hard. This wasn't even close to legal unless she saw something through the window that might be evidence of a crime. Still, she wasn't going to stop and she pushed open the door slowly, tentatively stepping inside where the air was warm, but the smells were off. The lingering smoke was hiding something else, something more sinister.

Using her flashlight, she saw the part of the kitchen table that had been obscured from her view at the window. There were pictures on its grainy top. Head shots of people she recognized, including herself.

Her skin crawled at the thought that she was actually in the whackjob's lair. This was where he'd plotted out the murders of Grayson and the judge, the sicko's base of operations.

Set in the forest with the curtains drawn, the rooms were dark and close, the embers of a fire glowing a weak red from the living area. She took one step toward the front of the house, the beam of her flashlight skating across the dirty linoleum floor to land directly on the unmoving, gray face of a very dead Carnie Tibalt.

Pescoli stifled a scream, but her heart was pounding double time.

The woman, eyes fixed as if she were staring at the ceiling, was nude aside from a pair of boots. A nasty dark hole was visible in her forehead. She took off her glove, reached down, touched her beneath her chin, but found no pulse.

Maurice had killed Carnie?

Leaving the dead body where she'd found it, Pescoli pulled the heavy curtains back just a bit so that it would be believable that she'd seen Carnie before she'd entered. Then, replacing her glove and touching nothing else, Pescoli checked out the other rooms, a freezing bedroom where clothes littered the floor and a bathroom so small she could barely turn around.

Don't mess this up, she told herself as she backed out of the rooms and out the door. She hadn't touched anything other than Carnie's neck, the curtain, and the doorknob, so technically she hadn't compromised the case.

Still, she slid outside and made the call to Alvarez who, thankfully, picked up on the second ring. "It's Pescoli," she said, suddenly cold to the bone. "I found Verdago's hideout. A place owned by Carnie Tibalt's uncle." She rattled off the address at the same time she thought she heard the rumble of an engine.

"We're already on our way," Alvarez said, without explanation.

"Here? You're coming *here*?"

"Yes!"

The engine was sounding nearer, a deep growl. Certainly not Alvarez's Subaru. Then . . . ? "How close are you?" Pescoli asked, her eyes searching the wilderness for a place to hide. Snow was falling hard, but her footprints were still visible. Damn! Quickly, she backed into the surrounding trees.

"We're three, four miles out. We'll be there in five."

"Make it in two," Pescoli snapped out. "Looks like I've got company!" She clicked off just as the white van belonging to Carnie Tibalt rounded a final bend.

Sliding her sidearm from her shoulder holster, she ducked behind a copse of hemlock, enough protection that she could peer through a crack in the branches.

Make the collar. Her inner voice was insistent, telling her she had the drop on him, and her finger tightened over the trigger of her sidearm. But she wanted him alive, to suffer the trial, to spend the rest of his miserable years in prison, to pay for what he'd done to Dan Grayson, Kathryn Samuels-Piquard, and now, Carnie Tibalt.

The engine died and she moved for a better view, a clear shot if she needed it. He'd pulled into the garage. Seconds ticked by and she didn't move, barely breathed, all of her senses trained on that small open area between the garage and the front porch of the cabin.

Come on, bastard, show yourself.

Her jaw was rock hard, her muscles tight and coiled. She could hear the beating of her heart in her eardrums.

Through the snowfall she saw movement as he appeared, dressed in white camouflage, a rifle in one hand, a shifting image in the wintry flakes.

You bastard!

He stopped dead in his tracks, his eyes spying her trail of footprints rimming the house.

Without hesitation he shouldered his weapon and started searching in the shadows.

Training her weapon on him, she yelled. "Police! Drop your weapon, Verdago! Put your hands over your head! Now!"

His head jerked toward the sound of her voice and he fired.

Blam! Blam! Blam!

The trees around her shook.

Ice splintered.

Snow fell in thick, powdery clouds.

Pieces of bark shot from the trunk of the tree she was using for cover. Jesus! She ducked back into the thicket, breathing hard, her heart thundering in her chest. She lost him in the heavy curtain of snow.

He's right here. Has to be.

Frantically, she searched the clearing, then the woods. She tried to focus on his footprints, but the snow was too thick.

He knows where you are, but you can't see him. You're a sitting duck, Pescoli. Move!

"She's in trouble!" Alvarez said.

"She's always in trouble." Behind the wheel of his SUV, Brewster hit the gas. The wipers slapped snow off the windshield, the car radio buzzed, and Alvarez was checking the computer as Brewster drove tensely along this winding road that cut through the mountains. "Call for backup."

"They're on their way."

"Good. Oh, hell!"

The Jeep slid around a corner that he took a little too fast. They fishtailed on the packed snow, the rear of the SUV sliding dangerously near a deep chasm that fell a hundred feet to a stream far below. On the other side of the narrow road, mountains soared, their peaks invisible in the ever-falling snow.

"Son of a bitch," he muttered between teeth that were clamped tight, but he straightened the wheel and the tires grabbed the road again, propelling the Jeep forward as they wound ever closer to the cabin where Maurice Verdago was hiding out. "She's just lucky you figured out where she was."

"It wasn't that hard." Alvarez had pieced together where her partner had gone by the messages she'd left, and now Pescoli had given her the address.

"I warned you about her," he said now. "She's gone rogue. What the hell's wrong with that woman?" He slowed for a second, turning into the long lane leading to the cabin owned by Carnie Tibalt's uncle. "She's a liability to the department and if she hasn't already, she's going to get herself killed." He slid a glance at Alvarez. "She could take you out with her, you know."

She ignored that. "Okay, we're getting close. Should be just over the next rise." There wasn't any time to discuss the pitfalls or pratfalls of Pescoli's professionalism.

Craaack! The blast from a rifle split the silence.

Alvarez sucked in a sharp breath. In her mind's eye she saw her partner, body jerking as an assassin's bullet hit her. "Come on!" Yanking her Glock from its holster, she put her other hand on the door handle just as Brewster careened over the final hillock and hit the brakes.

The SUV slid into a clearing and stopped not forty feet from the tiny cabin's front door. A sniper dressed in snowy camouflage, rifle on his shoulder, took one look their way, then tore away, jogging around the corner of the shack.

"Let's get him!" She was throwing open the door when Brewster placed a hand on her arm.

"Wait for backup. I've got this." Rifle in hand, he took off.

No way! She was out of the Jeep and taking off at a jog through the snow and rounding one side of the house while Brewster secured the other side.

Bang! Bang! Bang!

More shots!

Hang in there, Pescoli, Alvarez prayed as she flattened herself to the side of the building and peered through the curtain of snow to the woods behind.

She spied the killer, setting up, taking aim at a copse of trees. "Pescoli!" Alvarez yelled as a gun went off.

Dashing from one thicket to the next, Pescoli heard her name and turned just in time to see the killer, rifle at his shoulder, the barrel following her path.

In that instant, she knew she was dead.

Blam!

She threw herself forward, diving into a snowbank, landing hard on her shoulder, expecting the sear of a bullet to rip through her flesh.

In that nanosecond before she hit the ground, snow flying, her shoulder screaming, she saw, from the corner of her eye, the killer's body jerk wildly, his rifle flung from his hands as he dropped to the ground.

And standing not fifty yards away, his own rifle tucked against his shoulder, was Cort Brewster.

Just before she passed out she realized the damned sheriff had just saved her life.

CHAPTER 33

It was finally over, Pescoli thought, a week later as she skimmed the umpteenth article about the shoot-out at the mountain cabin. Once again, the reporter lauded the "clear-thinking, quick reflexes, and sharp aim" of Cort Brewster. Intimated in the article was the supposition that should Dan Grayson ever come out of his coma, Brewster would give him a good run in the next election.

Pescoli supposed she should be more grateful to Brewster, and maybe it was a flaw in her character, but she just couldn't muster up much more than a suspicion that he'd done it more for the attention it gave him than because he wanted to save her. She tossed the paper onto one of the lunchroom tables. She was in the office early. Again. Glad to have some time when the sheriff's department was relatively quiet. Her shoulder still hurt from landing so hard during the attack, but nothing was broken, only bruised, tendons and ligaments stretched to their limit but intact. She'd hit her head as well and didn't remember much when she'd awoken in the hospital several hours later. "A more-than-slight concussion" had kept her in the hospital overnight "for observation," but then she'd been pronounced healthy enough to go home and, against doctor's orders and Santana's protests, had gone back to work.

"Am I really going to have to hog-tie you?" Santana had asked and she'd sent him a smile and said, "Kinky. Why not?" So he'd shaken his head and backed off. Grudgingly, she'd worn a sling for nearly a week, then ditched the damned thing because she couldn't stand

her impeded mobility. She'd always been right-handed but hadn't realized how dependent she was on her left until that arm was out of
commission.

But now, physically, she was nearly back to normal. That was, if
she didn't count the twinges and aches that sometimes throbbed
through her shoulder, or the holes in her memory on the day of the
confrontation at the mountain cabin. Like the victim in a serious accident, she just couldn't remember the events around the actual
takedown clearly.

Seeing that the coffeepot was empty once again, she seriously
considered not having a cup, then told herself to be a big girl and
clean up the old grounds packet, swab out the glass carafe, and brew
a new pot. Hell, be a really big girl and make two pots as someone
had left less than a quarter of a cup in the other machine and the
dark liquid was solidifying, turning from sludge to dry on the glass.

Since she was alone in the lunchroom and Joelle wasn't scheduled to arrive for another hour or so, and of the few officers in the
building, no one was likely to come running into the lunchroom
ready to become an instant maid, Pescoli did the honors.

She should be feeling differently.

She should be more satisfied.

She should be experiencing a great relief that not only had Cort
Brewster saved her life, but that Maurice Verdago was dead and
would never kill anyone again.

Still, she felt edgy. Restless. The way she did when a case wouldn't
quite come together. On top of that, work was difficult. The whole
station was different. New Year's had come and gone, and Jeremy
had found a way to get into a few night classes. By necessity, his
hours at the sheriff's department were cut to nearly nothing, which
kinda pissed Jer off, but there was only so much time. Bianca was
back in school and swearing she was "eating like Doug Fallen, the
center of the football team. He's a moose!"

Pescoli wasn't convinced, but had witnessed her daughter plow
into a few of her favorite meals, while picking at others, and she'd
found evidence of some very bad eating habits, candy bar wrappers,
a receipt for a peppermint mocha at the coffee shop, but all of the

evidence she found could have been planted, of course. Her daughter was smart and sly. Though Bianca probably hadn't been that devious, Pescoli wouldn't put it past her.

There it was, her suspicious nature coming to the fore. Whenever she was home at the same time as Bianca, which wasn't that often, she'd kept a close eye on her trips to the bathroom. If she was forcing herself to throw up, it wasn't on Pescoli's watch . . . she hoped.

Now, she rinsed the suds from the carafe, then set it, along with its mate, onto the hot plate of the coffee machine and slapped the premeasured coffee into the baskets before hitting the Brew button and waiting for the first cup, always the hottest and strongest.

Hearing footsteps approach, she caught a glimpse of Connors as he adjusted his pants to rest just below his belly. "Hey, you get promoted?" he asked. Always the funny guy.

"That's right," she said as the coffee drizzled loudly into the carafes. "I'm in charge of the lunchroom now."

"Good. I could use an elk burger!"

"Old news, Connors. Time to come up with some new material." She suspected he'd been the one who had left a ziplock package of meat on her desk earlier in the week. On one side was a crude drawing of an elk, on the other side, a crow.

Yeah, it had been a real laugh.

It would have served the big lug right if she actually had let that meat rot in her desk drawer, then grind some up and drop the meal into his oversized mug when he wasn't looking.

"Kinda boring around here," he said, rocking back on his heels and eyeing the lunch area as he, too, waited for the coffee to fill the pot. The silence between them stretched to the breaking point. "No decorations. No big cases."

"No Christmas cookies," Pescoli reminded him. *The hell with it.* Even if her caseload had slowed, she didn't have time to sit around and shoot the breeze with Connors. After yanking the partially filled pot of "regular," she poured herself half a cup, replaced the pot with a little more force than necessary, and headed out of the lounge area.

God, she was cranky, and as she sipped from her cup and walked down the hallway, she didn't get that same hit from her first sip that she usually did.

She had to face it, she wasn't happy here. Slowing at Brewster's office, she peered through the glass door. The room was locked these days, Brewster not even trusting his own staff. It bothered her. She'd visited Grayson twice in the last week, even felt foolish when she'd touched his hand and told him that they'd nailed his assailant. His condition hadn't changed, and the doctors she'd overheard had been cautiously optimistic, whatever that meant. There was no longer a guard stationed near the doors to ICU, as there was no longer a threat to the sheriff, but that had only made the hospital seem emptier, more sterile, more . . . hopeless.

Pausing at the glass window of Brewster's new office, what she inwardly had dubbed his "throne room," she felt hollow inside over the change in leadership. Brewster had taken to the role of sheriff as quickly as a duck to water, and there were no traces that this space had ever been occupied by Dan Grayson and his trusty black Lab, Sturgis, who, thankfully, Cisco had finally accepted.

Who knew how much longer the dog would be staying with Pescoli and her kids. *And Santana,* she reminded herself. They would all be one big, hopefully happy, family soon. Without even realizing it, she crossed the fingers of her free hand.

"Coffee's done," Connors said as he came up from behind her and, as if he'd realized what an ass he'd been, added, "I mean, if you want a full cup."

She saw his pale reflection in the windows of Brewster's office. "Thanks."

He hesitated, bit the side of his lip, and looked into the office. "Weird, huh?" When she didn't respond, he added, "I mean . . . it's . . . different."

"Mmmm."

In the glass she saw him start to say something, think better of it, then sip his coffee and mosey off.

She lingered a second and was turning away when she noticed the sword. A twin of the one Vincent Samuels had given Winston Piquard, identical to the long-bladed weapon that had graced the wall of the judge's den, her husband, Georges's, bit of war memorabilia and now Brewster's.

She hadn't seen it before, but she attributed its current placement to Cort's wife as right before the press conference about Verdago she'd heard Brewster say to Darla Vale, "Yeah, I finally had to admit that Bess was right, so I've started cleaning out the basement. Found some things I'd forgotten about." Brewster had then gone in front of the cameras and expounded long and loudly about how the citizens of Grizzly Falls would have nothing to fear now that the "reign of terror" caused by Maurice Verdago and his accomplice, Carnival Tibalt, was over.

It seemed a little off somehow, but lately everything did. She'd never quite got her energy level back to where it had been, and the night terrors . . . they still haunted her. Being chased down by Verdago, caught squarely in the sight of his rifle, had only exacerbated her fears.

The truth of the matter was that her confidence was shaken, and she didn't know if she had the edge she'd once honed so carefully. She was more cautious, fearful, and the fact that she still thought she might be being followed, that her paranoia hadn't disappeared with Verdago's death, only confirmed how stressed she was.

Thank God for Brewster's dead-eye aim. He, too, had been a sharpshooter in the military.

And he'd saved her life.

Back in her office, she reminded herself of that very fact as she scooted her chair into her desk and thought that Brewster might be right, she could very well be more of a liability than an asset to the department.

It was time to start a new life with Santana and relieve herself of all the responsibilities, fears, and stress of being a detective with the Pinewood County Sheriff's Department.

Downing the rest of her coffee, she rotated her bad shoulder to loosen it, then started to compose her resignation letter.

Alvarez was bugged.

All of Brewster's preening didn't sit well with her. Grayson was still alive. That was a fact. And though she was glad the case was closed, there were some loose ends that bothered her.

She was at home, dog at her feet, cat slipping in and out of the shelves on the bookcase, O'Keefe rattling around in the kitchen as she double-checked her phone and e-mail for any contact from Tydeus Melville Chilcoate, a computer genius and hacker who was known to be antigovernment and had made it clear that he had no love of the sheriff's department. But stronger than his feelings about the department was his hatred of Cort Brewster, who had, in younger years, pulled him over for speeding and other traffic infractions that Chilcoate had maintained were a "setup" and an "abuse of his rights." She'd met with him in a remote location, her car pointed one way at the old rock quarry, his the other, and they'd made a deal. Chilcoate, in an effort to get back at Brewster, was on board, though, of course, all of her dealings with him were very much on the Q.T. For once, she wasn't going to confide in either Pescoli or O'Keefe. For once, she was going off the rails and not playing by the rules.

So far, Chilcoate hadn't gotten back to her.

"I thought the case was closed," O'Keefe said as he set a cup of herbal tea on the desk next to her laptop. The scents of ginger and lemon filled the air and she inhaled deeply.

"It just seems a little too . . . perfect, for lack of a better word. I just happen to be in Brewster's office when I get the SOS from Pescoli. He then insists on going with me, rather than sending one of the deputies or another detective? And when we get there, he shoots Maurice Verdago dead. The same guy who robbed him of his computer and rifle, then used the .30-06 registered to Brewster in all of his attacks?"

"He'd reported it stolen."

"Around Thanksgiving."

"Sometimes you get lucky."

Glancing up at him, she smiled. His dark hair was rumpled, his jaw unshaven, hints of sleep still tugging at the corners of his eyes. He hadn't bothered getting dressed, still wore only a pair of boxers, so that his abdomen with its compact, hard muscles was visible. His shoulders and arms moved fluidly as he leaned back against the breakfast bar.

"Are you trying to seduce me?" she asked, leaning back in her chair and sipping her tea.

A slow smile spread across his jaw. "Would I do that?"

"Always."

He cocked an eyebrow in invitation. She shook her head and said regretfully, "I've got to be at the office."

"You have to shower. We could—?"

Laughing, she said, "Forget it." God, she loved him. Someday she'd settle down and marry him. This time she wouldn't let him get away, but right now, right this minute, she couldn't, wouldn't, be distracted.

"You know, Verdago's rifle, the one he stole from Brewster, had his prints on it and Brewster's, which is expected, but . . ."

"But what?" he prodded.

"I don't know. It's just the way Brewster seemed to know exactly what Verdago was planning. The man's a decent enough cop, his instincts are usually on target, but this time he was just so damned good. So ahead of the game."

"You think Brewster not only killed Verdago, but somehow he took out the judge and shot at the sheriff?"

"I know what it sounds like, but . . ." She broke off, frustrated, then said, "He also killed his own girlfriend who was wearing nothing but boots and an engagement ring."

"And?"

"It just doesn't make sense." That's what had really gotten the wheels turning in her mind. Carnie's death. It just seemed so far off the rails for Verdago to kill her, even though, according to Wanda Verdago, Maurice had killed Joey Lundeen in a fight. But that murder had been an accident, one punch too hard. Carnie's was a point-blank killing.

But again, Joey Lundeen had died and Maurice had dumped his body high up in the wilderness where it was yet to be found. Maybe it made some kind of sense that Verdago had killed Carnie. Alvarez just didn't see it.

Meanwhile, Brewster had worked with the D.A. for Wanda's immunity. Deputies and volunteers had started scouring that area of the government land, looking for Lundeen, though until the snowpack melted in the spring, nothing much would be found.

If ever.

But it had played well to the press, all the local stations picking up the story, Manny Douglas finding a way to massage yet another story highlighting Brewster onto the front page of the local paper.

"Verdago and his girlfriend could have had a fight. He had a temper," O'Keefe reminded.

"So they get into it, he leaves, comes home, and just shoots her cold?"

"Maybe he had a few drinks?"

She shook her head. "No trace of alcohol in Verdago's body."

"Stranger things have happened."

"Well, maybe they did fight earlier. Who knows. But the way the body was positioned was weird. It was as if she, without hardly anything on, opened the door and got blasted. Right between the eyes. With a rifle."

"The gun Brewster reported stolen," O'Keefe reminded her.

"Was it, though? Why didn't the thieves take that damned sword he's now put in Grayson's office?"

"Sounds like this isn't about Brewster so much as Grayson."

Alvarez turned away. Even to her own ears, her ideas sounded ridiculous. Everything pointed to Verdago. Hadn't they found the pictures of six people he hated on the table? And Cort Brewster's photo as well as Regan Pescoli's had been front and center. She remembered viewing them and feeling a chill, the same chill she'd witnessed in Brewster's eyes.

He'd found the pictures first.

He'd gone into the cabin ahead of her and checked that Carnie Tibalt wasn't cowering inside or lying in wait, armed to the teeth.

"I know," Alvarez said. "This is all just crazy talk. I guess I'm just sick of the way he's lapping up all the attention from the press, even giving private interviews to Manny Douglas and Honey Carlisle at KBTR." She blew across her cup. "It's so . . . not Grayson's style, I guess."

"That's what really gets under your skin."

"Yeah," she admitted, and clicked off the computer. "You know, I've changed my mind." She moved up to him, sliding her arms around his torso. "It looks like I do have time for that shower after all."

* * *

"There's something I want to talk to you about," Jeremy said into Pescoli's ear as she walked out of the quickie mart with her usual supersized diet soda in one hand, her cell phone in the other.

The snow had stopped the night before, the sun rising bright enough this morning to cast a glare off the snow-blanketed street. Juggling her drink and her keys, the cell phone caught between her cheek and shoulder, Pescoli managed to slip on her sunglasses. But the action tweaked her shoulder and she nearly slipped, the soda sloshing onto her jacket as the lid apparently wasn't on as tightly as she'd thought.

Fabulous.

"Damn. So talk already," she said. "No, wait until I get into the car and set this stupid drink in the cup holder."

"Mom—"

"Just a sec, Jer." She slid behind the wheel, replaced the lid of her cup, and staring out the foggy windshield at the customers walking into and out of the convenience store, said, "Okay, now what's going on?"

"It's, uh, something I can't talk to you about over the phone."

"You called me."

"I know. I thought we could meet today sometime."

"You coming into the office? You're scheduled at two, right? That's just a couple of hours from now."

"Yeah, well. I'm not coming in."

"Does the sheriff know?"

"I left a message with Joelle."

"So, why aren't you volunteering? I thought this was what you wanted. Last I hear that's the reason you're taking classes at the community college. You want to be a cop."

He paused and she visualized him chewing on the inside of his cheek, a habit that still came out during times of stress. "I'll tell you about it later."

"Jer?" she said, her latent mom-radar suddenly alert. "Are you okay?"

"I just need to talk to you."

"Okay, sure. When and where?"

"How about at Heidi's house?"

"You want me to meet you at Cort Brewster's home?" She couldn't quite keep the note of horror from her voice.

"Yeah, at four. And don't tell anyone."

"Not even the sheriff?"

"Oh, God, no! Especially not . . . just don't say anything. See you then."

"Jeremy, I don't really want to go—"

He clicked off before she could finish.

She didn't move, just stared blindly through the windshield, her thoughts were centered around her son. Why in the world would he want her to meet him at Heidi's house? Was Heidi going to be there? Four in the afternoon? After she was out of school for the day?

Frantically she called him back and texted, but he wouldn't respond. Nope. He was holding out.

It wasn't like Jeremy to be overly dramatic; that was usually Bianca's department . . . or Heidi's.

A sick feeling started in the pit of her stomach as she considered what could require all this secrecy, and the only reason she could come up with was the horrifying conclusion that Heidi Brewster was pregnant.

CHAPTER 34

Alvarez had been avoiding Pescoli.

Because her partner always had a thing against Brewster and because she wasn't certain exactly how things would play out, she'd kept her suspicions to herself. As she drove through the hills to Chilcoate's place, she didn't miss the irony of it all, that she agreed with Brewster on this one, that Pescoli might go all rogue if she had just the inkling that Alvarez suspected the undersheriff of being involved in the attack on Grayson and the judge.

But why would he do that?

Back to the age-old question: motive. Yes, Brewster was ambitious and, yes, he'd been passed over, probably reaching the acme of his career as undersheriff.

She nearly drove off the road as that thought crossed her mind. *Under*sheriff? Wait . . . what was it Cee-Cee had said about her mother-in-law, Judge Samuels-Piquard? A telephone conversation that Cee-Cee had overheard?

Not on top. I like to be under the sheriff.

Could Cee-Cee have misinterpreted? Could the judge have been talking about Cort Brewster, who was considered a friend of the judge? It wouldn't have been the first time a "friend" had taken to consoling a widow one step too far.

Chilcoate's cabin was as rustic as any she'd seen lately, but larger. Tucked into the mountains, surrounded by forests, his home was built out of rough-hewn logs but was supplied with electricity and running water. She suspected he might have a hidden room somewhere, either in an attic, behind a hidden wall, or in a basement, wherever he did his serious computer hacking.

As far as she knew, he'd never violated any specific laws, but then she didn't know much about him, and preferred to keep it that way.

He was smoking a cigarette on the porch, waiting for her, and she figured she'd tripped some kind of silent alarm on her approach.

"Detective," he said, his eyes full of secrets behind a pair of thick glasses. His untamed, curly hair and beard gave him a slightly sloppy look, a disguise that belied his sharp mind.

"You have something?"

"Did you doubt me?"

"Nope."

"Good. You shouldn't." He took a final drag on his smoke, then led her inside, through a tiny living room complete with a huge, flat-screen TV and a single recliner surrounded by TV trays covered with remote controls for all the equipment plugged into the television, as well as the remains of what looked to be four or five meals on dirty paper plates. Green, Chilcoate clearly was not.

"In here," he said as he stepped into a short hallway and opened the door to a bedroom that had been converted to his office. Inside was a desktop computer, several different laptops in varying sizes, telephones, and radio equipment. As geek-worthy as this place was, it was probably a front, just the tip of the electronic iceberg that was hidden away, where the real sophisticated electronics buzzed, hummed, and collected data she didn't want to think about.

"What have you got?" she asked.

"The judge was pretty clean," he said, "not much dirt to be found. I checked all of her computer logs, phone records, and went deep." Meaning, she assumed, deeper and faster than the department had the time, manpower, or knowledge to plumb. "But she did apparently have a weak spot."

He kicked out a secretary's chair and sat, then nodded to a battered folding chair for Alvarez to occupy.

"And what was that?" she asked.

"Men."

Alvarez lifted a brow.

"Here's the judge's profile, you'll see she went by KC Sam often, or Kitty Sam or even Sammy Cat . . . she played around on a lot of dating sites, some pretty straightforward, a couple a little more . . . personal."

"Kinky?"

"Mmm. But that's not the interesting part. Here's where things take a not-so-aboveboard turn." He brought up a number of e-mails from an address she'd never seen before.

"What're these?"

"Private account. On a different computer," he said, "not any that you found. This one was registered to her husband, and my guess is it's hidden somewhere. A friend's house? A coworker's office? Somewhere no one even knows it's there." He shrugged, as if it were of no consequence. "Here's her most recent paramour."

She saw the e-mail address. "CBer43?"

"I figure it's so most people might think he's a truck driver, but it's really his initials."

"Cort Brewster." The sick feeling that had been with Alvarez ever since starting to question Brewster's motives was back.

"Forty-three must mean something."

"Part of the numbers of his badge," she said, having seen it enough lately.

"Ahh . . . Even if people are trying to hide their ID, they usually make a name out of letters and numbers that they can remember. Want to see what they said?"

"Absolutely."

"They weren't all that clever, though they probably thought they were. This is nothing compared to some of the things I've seen, but here ya go. Over there." He pointed to the computer screen set up in front of Alvarez's chair and the e-mails began to appear. A seemingly endless list of messages claiming love and lust, talking about sexual positions and dates, and the gist of it was that the judge and Brewster were involved in a very hot affair, with the upshot being "Kitty" pressuring "CBer43" to get a divorce.

That, apparently, was her mistake. Cort Brewster wasn't about to trade in his wife and four daughters and half of whatever he had, plus pay alimony and child support, all to become Mr. Judge Samuels-

Piquard. No, Alvarez guessed, he much preferred to be seen as the upstanding family man, elder in the church, and current sheriff of Pinewood County.

As if she'd finally been freed of a suffocating, blinding mask, she saw it all. The driving force behind the attacks. It had nothing to do with Maurice Verdago. The ex-con had only been a pawn.

But why would Verdago go along with Brewster's plan?

She thought of Wanda with her "cubic Z" ring, that Verdago had nearly killed his brother-in-law for skimming company profits, that when he'd gotten out of prison he'd worked as a janitor. It all boiled down to the simple fact that Maurice Verdago never seemed to have enough cash. He was the perfect fit for a hit man.

"Can you hack into bank accounts?" she asked, and Chilcoate looked at her over the tops of his glasses as if she'd asked him if he could walk. "I'm not admitting to that," he said, "but you might want to check a private account at First Credit in Missoula. I'm guessing there might be a series of significant withdrawals. Cash. All under five grand, but totaling twenty-five."

"Thousand? Twenty-five thousand?"

He shrugged and an icy chill ran down her back. Though twenty-five grand was a lot of money, it seemed a paltry amount for the price of a man's life, or a woman's, or both. She thought of Dan Grayson battling for his life, and Judge Samuels-Piquard lying in the snow, and even Carnie Tibalt, dead on the floor of a ramshackle cabin. Had Verdago actually taken the shots to kill the judge and the sheriff? Or had it been Brewster himself who'd used Maurice as a fall guy and then had set him up?

"I'll need this info," she said.

"As long as you don't say where it came from." Chilcoate smiled, showing slightly yellowed teeth. "I love being a part of taking that prick Brewster down."

"Me too," she said.

"It's a fuckin' shame that he got everything he wanted."

Alvarez couldn't agree more, but she was worried, too, because what Brewster had was only temporary. As long as Dan Grayson was alive.

Her blood chilled.

And now there was no guard at Grayson's side.

There was talk that he would be moved from ICU.

He would be vulnerable.

But was it possible? Was Cort Brewster a cold-blooded killer? Had he made one failed attempt on the sheriff's life and was he even now planning a second?

"E-mail me everything and send it from some fake account that only someone like you could untangle," she ordered.

"I don't know if I—"

"Just do it. ASAP. We don't have any time."

Brewster had been out most of the afternoon in meetings, talking to the press again, and, no doubt, planning his official campaign for the next election, so Pescoli knew she'd have no trouble leaving the department without him knowing.

All day long she'd been trying to tell herself that her instincts were off, that just because she didn't like the guy, didn't mean he was a bad cop. So he took over Grayson's office? So what? Maybe his rifle really had been stolen.

He saved your life, Pescoli. You don't like him. Fine. Doesn't mean he's all bad.

But she couldn't shake the feeling that she'd missed something during the investigation, and that it had to do with the acting sheriff. It bothered her, like a sliver that she couldn't quite dislodge from beneath her skin.

When it was nearly four she headed out, bracing herself for the inevitable confrontation with her son and Heidi Brewster. *And maybe good old Cort and Bess. The kids might have already asked him to meet them as well, to break the news.*

Her stomach roiled at the thought and she tasted bile.

As she passed by Joelle at the front desk, she said, "Is Brewster due back today?"

She shook her head. "No." She looked up from the box of red and pink hearts that she was sorting through. For Valentine's Day. *Of course.* "I think he was going into Missoula for a meeting or was it another interview? I guess he didn't really say." She flashed a smile. "I told him he should visit the sheriff and he said he planned to."

"Today?" Pescoli said and felt a niggle of fear.

"Mmm." Studying the hearts, she sighed, then placed a lid on the box. "I've been told by the powers that be that I can't decorate until February." With a can-you-believe-it look at Pescoli, she said, "I don't know about you, but I, for one, think we could use a little ray of sunshine around here. It's just been so darn gloomy."

"Amen," Pescoli said, thinking that it wasn't going to get better any time soon.

Once in her Jeep, she headed for the Brewsters' home, a house she'd only visited once when Bess had hosted a celebration for Cort at the time of his promotion to undersheriff, years earlier. Located on the outskirts of town in a subdivision straight out of the 1970s, the Brewster home was a split-entry, with a garage under the main level and a daylight basement. Like most of the houses on the street, Cort and Bess's was a big box of a house with enough bedrooms for all of the girls when they'd still been living at home. Now, only Heidi was left.

As she rounded the last corner, she spied Jeremy's truck parked near the curb in front of the Brewster's gray house, and she braced herself for the inevitable. Already, alone in her Jeep, she knew what she was going to hear.

"We want to keep the baby."

"We'll get married, Mom, it's gonna be fine."

"I can go to school and work, and Heidi can take care of the baby, maybe even babysit other people's kids for some extra money."

"We've got it all worked out. We're adults now."

But at least Heidi was old enough that Jeremy couldn't be prosecuted for statutory rape. Dear God, how had it all come to this?

She was about to park behind Jeremy's pickup when her phone rang. Alvarez's name popped onto the screen. Half tempted to ignore the call, she was, after all, resigning from the department, she picked up nonetheless. For a little while longer she was still an employee of the PCSD. "Pescoli," she said, slowing her Jeep to a crawl.

"I don't have time to explain." Alvarez sounded breathless. "But I think Grayson's in danger."

"In *more* danger?" she asked, slowing so that she could concentrate. A car was pulling up behind her.

"I think Verdago was set up."

"Verdago?" A bad feeling started deep in her gut.

"Brewster's the mastermind. Listen, I know it sounds crazy, but I've got proof. My worry is that he may want to finish what he started with the sheriff."

"He killed Verdago," she reminded, for the first time that she could remember coming to the man's defense.

"Not to save you. To silence *him*."

"But . . ." As if a bolt of lightning suddenly struck her, she remembered Wanda Verdago referring to her husband's hit list as the "Dirty Half Dozen." Six people. Not seven. When she'd entered Davis Briscoe's cabin, she'd seen six pictures on the table, pictures that included herself, an assistant D.A., a couple of witnesses in Verdago's trial, Grayson, and Brewster. As she eased off the gas, she saw those photographs clearly in her mind's eye. "Sweet Jesus." That part of her brain that had been so blocked suddenly opened, the neurons firing wildly again.

Six pictures. Dirty half dozen. All on the desk. And yet Manny Douglas had received one in the mail.

So the killer must've fouled up and Verdago wouldn't have. He would have focused on those who had done him dirt.

Brewster? With his quick claim to Grayson's office? His need to become sheriff? It seemed so far-fetched.

"I don't know."

"He was crotch-deep in an affair with Judge Samuels-Piquard and she was pressuring him to marry her. He wasn't going to give up his entire life."

"This is your theory."

"I'm getting proof now. My guess is that Brewster used his own key to get into the judge's house; then he cleaned every surface and burned whatever it was in the den fireplace. Probably a calendar or love letters."

Was it possible? The undersheriff? "I don't know," she heard herself say.

"Trust me on this one, Pescoli!"

It could be true, couldn't it? Alvarez was always so careful. It wasn't like her to jump to wild conclusions without facts.

The driver of the car behind her, a low-slung sports model, laid on the horn, then sped around the Jeep, spraying snow and slush as he roared past.

Pescoli barely noticed, so intent was she on the conversation. Through the windshield, she glanced up at Brewster's All-American house in his All-American subdivision. "Has anyone tried to contact Brewster? I'm at his house now."

"*What?* Why?"

"Long story. About Jeremy. He asked me to meet him here."

"Be careful," Alvarez warned. "Brewster seems to be MIA and so far, just you and I know about this. We don't want to tip our hand. He's already trigger-happy."

"Got it. Let me check things out; then I'm on my way. I'll see you soon."

"No, wait. Don't come here. I'm just pulling into the hospital's lot," Alvarez explained. "I called ahead and the staff said Grayson was fine, still resting, but I still thought I'd double-check, see for myself. Once I know he's secure, that Brewster hasn't come by and maybe given him something slow-acting, I'll reinstate a guard. So give me five minutes. If I don't call you, there's trouble. Then alert hospital security and call in the cavalry. Missoula PD would be the closest."

She clicked off and Pescoli, stunned, set her stopwatch. With one eye on the minutes and the second hand counting down, she studied the area. Nothing looked out of place. The house was blanketed in snow, tire tracks in the drive that led to a garage under one half of the house. Footprints were visible on the steps leading to the front door, one set crossing the yard. The biggest prints had originated at Jeremy's truck.

For a second she wondered if Brewster was inside. If he'd gone so completely crazy that he'd kidnap her kid.

Don't get caught up in this. Not yet. Alvarez isn't one to flip out and not think things through. If she says she has evidence, then she probably does.

She was just starting up the steps when the front door of the Brewster's house flew open and Jeremy stepped onto the concrete porch. His face was grave, nearly ashen, his eyes round as if he were shell-shocked.

Oh, God.

Then she spied Heidi, who looked so incredibly small, even frail. Her face was red, tears still visible, her makeup a mess. Placing an arm around her slim shoulders, Jeremy automatically assumed the role of protector.

Pescoli thought she might be sick. "Hi," she said.

"Come inside." Jeremy stepped aside from the door and Heidi started to sob.

"Whatever's going on here, we'll figure it out," she assured them, feeling, for the first time in her life, sorry for Heidi Brewster. She was, after all, just a teenaged girl in trouble.

As she stepped into the landing, where stairs split to go either up or down, Jeremy pulled the door shut. Pictures of the Brewster girls lined the walls, from all ages, as if every school shot of each of Cort's daughters had been framed and mounted.

"We've got a serious problem," Jeremy said, and Pescoli braced herself for the news she expected.

"I figured."

"It's Heidi's dad. The undersheriff."

Heidi was bawling loudly now, her shoulders shaking, tears running freely.

This is about Cort Brewster?

"Show her," he said as Heidi reached into the pocket of her jacket to withdraw her phone. She handed it to Jeremy, who messed with it for a second, then, lips tight against his teeth, turned it around so that Pescoli could see the picture on the phone's tiny screen, a picture of Judge Kathryn Samuels-Piquard, completely naked.

Pescoli's stomach dropped.

"There's more," Jeremy admitted and scrolled through a few

more, enough to show the judge and undersheriff in compromising positions. "And there's a tape."

"They made a sex tape?" Pescoli said, wondering at the stupidity of people. Heidi slid to the bottom step of the upward-leading staircase. Burying her face in her hands, she continued crying softly.

"I . . . I can't believe this," she whispered, hiccups interrupting her. "This . . . this"—she waved at the phone—"will kill Mom."

"She doesn't know?" Pescoli asked, though it was clear her son and Heidi had brought the evidence of Brewster's infidelity to her first.

Sniffing loudly, Heidi looked up at Jeremy. "I should have erased all of it. I found it on a computer in the basement and sent it to my phone and then . . . then it was stolen by that horrible man, that killer, and he was probably blackmailing Dad or something. But then I showed it all to Jeremy and he said I should tell you and . . . and now I think I'm going to be in big trouble." She was gulping for air, winding herself up. Obviously what had been worrying her for weeks had finally come to the surface, probably because of Jeremy's insistence that Heidi tell Pescoli. Worse yet, the girl suspected something more sinister, a suspicion that had probably been growing for days. "Mom's going to be home soon. I don't know what to tell her."

Neither do I, Pescoli thought, but couldn't tell the poor girl that her father was a suspected serial killer. "Look, Jer, why don't you take Heidi to our place. Leave Mrs. Brewster a note." Then she bent down on a knee so she was closer to the girl. "You're going to be okay. And so is your mom."

"And . . . and my dad?"

"We'll see, but he's tough." That much was true. She glanced at the screen once more and looked beyond the subject matter to the backdrop. Wherever the film had been taken, it was unfamiliar territory to Pescoli. "Do you know where this is? Where the pictures were taken?"

Heidi was nodding, her blond head bobbing. "It's at the mountain house."

"You have one?"

"Yeah . . . it was my grandparents'."

"Do you know where it is?" Pescoli asked.

"Sure." She blinked. "Why?"

Just then Pescoli's phone rang and she picked up.

"All clear here," Alvarez said. "Grayson's the same. I've got a guard coming. Now, we just have to find Brewster."

"I think I've got that covered," Pescoli said, and armed with this new information, she was convinced that Verdago, the sap, had been set up.

Cort Brewster was the killer and man, oh, man was he going down.

CHAPTER 35

*T*ick. *Tick. Tick.*

He felt time running out.

There was a chance that Grayson would pull through. After all he'd planned, all the risks he'd taken, all the sacrifices he'd made, the damned sheriff might just make it. He'd been reading up on wounds like Grayson's, which were so often fatal, but sometimes, like in the case of that politician from Arizona, the victims made a nearly full recovery.

He just couldn't let that happen.

Taking a long swallow of his drink, he felt the calming effect of icy vodka running down his throat. In the full-length mirror, he examined his naked reflection. Still muscular. No flab. Just a little gray in his hair and a few wrinkles near his eyes to give a nod to Father Time.

He was sweating from his workout, his muscles warmed, his uniform pressed neatly and hanging on the door. He'd come here, to his hideaway, to settle himself down. The pressures of being sheriff were more than he'd imagined, but he assumed they would ease off and he would calm down once things were settled, once Grayson kicked off and he was totally in control.

He'd covered his tracks, meeting with people in Missoula, playing his part, then before returning to Grizzly Falls, making a last trip to his sanctuary.

It wasn't the same without his beloved pictures, but he had to leave them, wiped clean of prints and DNA, of course, at the cabin where that cretin Verdago had holed up. It had been so easy to coerce him into playing along, the smell of money had always been an enticement to Maurice, in the army, years before, and while he was a private citizen. It didn't hurt that Brewster had figured out that Verdago had iced Joey Lundeen and had used that knowledge as added incentive for the fool to go along with his scheme.

The woman, though, Brewster hadn't counted on her, so he'd had to take her down. What he hadn't expected was that she would open the door dressed as some kind of cheap porn star. He'd felt an exquisite pleasure at pulling the trigger on her, even though inside the cabin he took a major chance with ricochet. But that hadn't happened.

Not with his aim.

She'd dropped the second she'd recognized him, her eyes widening, fear just beginning to show.

He licked his lips at the memory of her quick, horrified expression.

When Brewster had told Verdago to find a hideout, he'd thought the man would have more resources and wouldn't use a cabin owned by his damned girlfriend's family. Nor should he have ever brought her along.

That was the trouble: Maurice always thought with his dick, and that was a sure way to get a man into trouble.

You should know, his brain taunted, and he thought about the tape he'd made with "Kitty." That woman had been a wildcat in bed, unlike his frigid wife who seemed to think that sex was just an act to make babies. Whenever he'd suggested anything a little outside of her comfort zone, she'd started quoting Bible verses against fornication, even though they were married.

It all stemmed from her ultimate humiliation at being two months' pregnant with Jane at their wedding. As if anyone cared.

The upshot had been that while she'd been a horny little hellcat before the nuptials, after their wedding, she'd turned stone cold.

It was her damned fault that he took up with Kathryn after all those years of masturbating in the shower and trying to stay faithful to an ice goddess.

Years of it.

And his life was all too quickly playing out.

Tick. Tick. Tick.

He was about to don his uniform, when he heard it. Far in the distance. A vehicle's engine.

Probably on the road a good two miles away.

And yet.

The engine passed and he decided to finish his drink. Then he'd return to his real life and find a way to ensure Grayson's death. There would be others to dispose of as well, but those would have to be the victims of accidents.

Soon, he thought. Very soon.

Tick. Tick. Tick.

Faster! Faster! Faster!

She couldn't make the miles pass quickly enough. Heart pounding, determination pushing her, Pescoli drove like a madwoman. Passing tractor trailers, cutting corners, speeding through yellow lights, all the while her light bar flashing brightly, she headed into the hills.

Again.

Though she told herself to slow down, she couldn't. She felt time passing, and it seemed to her that every second she wasted was another chance for Brewster to wreak his havoc, either on the sheriff or someone else on his hit list.

How had she been so foolish as to think he was a decent cop, how had her instincts failed her so badly? She'd always been at odds with him, though mainly over their children, but lately, after he'd saved her life, she'd tried like hell to find the good in him while her gut instincts had warned her.

Get over it, she told herself as she started winding her way into the hills. She got the light bar and then managed to get a call into Alvarez, who didn't pick up. Leaving a voice mail, Pescoli kept driving, closer and closer to the cabin.

With a sense of déjà vu, she found the turnoff to Brewster's cabin. Not as isolated as Maurice Verdago's hideout, but not on the main road either. She slowed to view a hand-hewn post of individual signs with arrows and the names of the families who owned recreational homes in the area:

Miller
Snyder
Jamison

And, at the very top, perhaps the oldest sign, the name *Brewster* was chiseled and painted into an ancient piece of wood that had been nailed to the post.

Gotcha, Pescoli thought, her heart racing, adrenaline firing her blood. She parked near the gate of one of the homes, a cabin, that from the lack of prints or tire tread in the snow, looked vacant, then left another message for Alvarez, ending with, "I'm going in."

It didn't matter that she was "a loose cannon" or "a rogue cop." Not anymore. Not when she had Grayson's assassin in her sights.

Clicking off her phone, she turned it to silent mode, then reached for her Glock.

He couldn't waste any more time. As sheriff, he would be missed. As a husband, he would be questioned. As it was, there were holes in his days, holes he couldn't explain, and Bess, somewhere along the line, had suspected he was having an affair. Oh, she'd never guessed the woman involved and had always just hinted around the issue.

"If I didn't know better, Cort, I'd think you were involved with someone," she'd said with a tremulous smile. "Good thing I know you're a strong, Christian man."

That was the problem, he was a man. With needs.

Another time, she'd muttered, "That mistress of yours really has her nails in you, doesn't she?" When he hadn't answered, she'd touched him playfully on the shoulder. "I'm talking about your work, silly. You knew that . . . right?"

Now, he finished his drink and stretched. He couldn't afford a divorce and didn't want one. He just wanted sex. Excitement. And, of course, to be sheriff. Well, maybe a little more than that. In a few years he could see himself entering the political arena . . . first a state senator and then . . . who knew?

He smiled at his ambitions but didn't want to get ahead of himself. Dan Grayson was still alive.

And that was a problem.

* * *

She could see Brewster's cabin through the trees. Lights flickered in the windows, smoke curled from the chimney, his Jeep was parked outside. He hadn't been here too long as the Jeep was wet and dirty, no snow accumulating on its warm hood and roof.

Dusk was settling over the land, so she had a bit of cover. Still, she was careful as she approached, and when she heard the sound of an engine on the road behind her, she smiled inwardly.

She wasn't alone. Alvarez had gotten her message.

Good, she thought, skirting the front of the house to the back exit. Her heart was hammering in her chest, her muscles straining. She thought of booby traps and trip wires, but knew Brewster wasn't that clever or careful. This was his family's recreation home, not the hideout of some antigovernment fanatic. Brewster wouldn't take a risk with his daughters.

She picked her way over the clearing where a dilapidated swing set collected snow, its rusted chains creaking in the wind.

She reached for the door handle and turned.

The cold metal knob twisted in her fingers.

It was now or never.

Running his fingers over the smooth wood of his father's table, he decided he couldn't put it off any longer. He had to leave. His head was a little fuzzy from the drink, but he felt good, pumped, ready to take on the world.

He walked into the bathroom and, humming to himself, he stood over the toilet and peed like a damned stallion, a heavy, strong stream that was as loud as it was steady.

Yeah, he had a few good years left, he thought, walking out of the john.

Regan Pescoli was standing in the middle of his living room, her Glock pointed directly at his head.

If he hadn't just relieved himself, he would have emptied his bladder all over the floor.

His rifle was near the back door. His pistol in his holster.

As if reading his mind, she warned, "Don't even think about it. Put your hands over your head and get on the floor."

Pescoli stared down at the naked man in front of her, coldly furious, partly boggled. She had him dead to rights, but this was *Brewster*.

"For the love of God, Pescoli, let me cover up!" Brewster declared, a look of panic in his eyes. "I don't know what you think you're doing here, what you think you know, but you're wrong. And you're trespassing!"

"I know you killed the judge," she said in a flat voice. "I know you attempted to kill the sheriff, and I'll bet my retirement that you shot and killed Carnie Tibalt."

"What? You've got it all wrong. You've lost your grip! The only person I shot was Verdago, and that's because he was aiming at you!" He looked frantic and embarrassed.

"Bullshit, Brewster. We know you killed them. Even Carnie. That's when you dropped off the pictures, after you dropped her."

"You're crazy!" he sputtered.

"You left the six pictures. Some of them were people you wanted dead. And all of them were ones Verdago wanted to kill. Except you added your picture into the mix, trying to throw us off. One more beyond Verdago's Dirty Half Dozen."

He shook his head violently. "You're not making any sense!"

"You figured that we would think Verdago and Carnie got into a lover's quarrel, so you wouldn't have to plant her picture with the others, but your count was still off. Seven, instead of six. Six people he wanted dead. Not seven. But you didn't know, did you? That the magic number was six"

"I can help you, Regan," he said desperately, ignoring everything she said. "You need help."

"You forgot about sending the picture to Manny Douglas and that's where you made your mistake. Because Verdago had six enemies, not seven. So you screwed yourself with your damned grandstanding. You couldn't resist, could you? Crowing about it! Showing off!"

He blinked rapidly. "I'm innocent!"

"Save it for the judge! Oh, sorry. She's dead, isn't she? You already killed her!"

"You think you're so damn smart," he snarled. "You're a lousy detective, Pescoli."

"Better than you. Always better than you, Brewster. And that's what matters. Put your hands over your head! *Now!* I'm not going to ask again. Get down on the floor, you lying sack of shit, while I cuff you and read you your rights."

"I'll have your fucking badge for this!"

"Hands over your head! Get the hell down!" she yelled, her gun barrel aiming lower, directly at his black heart. She thought about really scaring him and sighting on his nuts, but stayed focused on his chest. She was going to shoot to stop. He wasn't going to get away. "Get down! Cort Brewster, you have the right to remain silent."

"What the fuck! I'm innocent!" he repeated, but his hands shot into the air. He was starting to kneel, when out of the corner of her eye, she caught movement in the window, a bit of blond hair.

Shit!

"Get down, now!" she ordered, but it was too late as the front door of the cabin opened and Heidi Brewster appeared.

"Dad? Oh, God, Dad, I'm so sorry!" She turned red-rimmed eyes on Pescoli. "What are you doing?" she cried.

"Get out, Heidi!" Pescoli ordered as Brewster sprang upward from the hallway, pushing a coffee table into her shins and vaulting toward the back door.

Pain screamed up her shins as Pescoli turned, aiming at Brewster's back.

Heidi screamed, "Dad!" and took off after him, running into Pescoli's sight line, crying and calling to the nude man who threw himself off the porch into the snow.

"Get down, Heidi!" Pescoli ordered.

"You can't kill him! You can't!" she cried. "Just because he had an affair!" She was hysterical now, a drama queen who'd finally found a legitimate stage. Pescoli shoved her aside and took off after him, flying through the back door, following his footsteps around the front of the house to his truck where he stood, still naked, legs braced, rifle at his shoulder.

Pescoli stopped dead in her tracks and saw him smile.

From the open front door, his daughter wailed, "Daddy, please, don't!"

But Brewster, fired on booze and adrenaline, was too far gone.

"Your turn," he snarled at Pescoli. "I've been waiting a long time for this!"

"Drop your weapon, Cort. It's over."

"For you."

"You're really going to kill me in front of your daughter?"

He didn't even flinch and she saw his finger move to pull back the trigger.

Automatically, she dropped and rolled, her gun aimed at him.

Blam!

He pulled the trigger.

She fired back at the same moment, gunfire deafening in the still air.

Her shot went wild, over his head. She aimed again but before she squeezed the trigger, another rifled cracked.

As Heidi screamed, Brewster fell to his knees, blood blooming on his chest, the spit foaming from the corner of his mouth turning red. His eyes were wide and disbelieving as he staggered, firing wildly once more. Then the weapon fell from his hands and he sagged into the snow, flopping forward as his sobbing daughter raced toward him.

"Stay away!" Pescoli yelled, her Glock trained on his still-moving body.

Heidi ignored her. Out of her mind with grief, she ran screaming and crying toward the fallen man who lay groaning and writhing in the snow.

Flinging her body next to his, she was whimpering and crying. "Daddy, oh, Daddy, no, no no." Tenderly, she cradled his head to her body as she rocked back and forth.

In the distance, sirens screamed, but it was too late for Cort Brewster. Spittle, turning red, foamed at the corner of his mouth, and his eyes, though open, were beginning to fix upward, toward the heavens.

"Daddy, please! Don't die! You can't die!" Heidi cried, then looked up to a space behind Pescoli. "You killed him!" she screamed. "You killed my dad!"

Hearing the crunch of a boot in the snow, Pescoli turned to spy her son, shaken and white, standing just five feet behind her. The butt of a rifle was pressed to his shoulder and he still stared through the sight of the damned gun Luke had bought him for Christmas.

EPILOGUE

"So, after all that, you're not going to quit?" Alvarez asked Pescoli a week after Brewster was finally arrested. They were having lunch at Wild Wills at a table with a view of the falls. The place was full, waitresses scurrying from table to table, the clink of flatware and rattle of glasses competing with the buzz of conversation.

"Just cut back some. Work more normal hours, if I can. That's what I promised Santana. And now that Brewster's out of the picture, I think I can make it happen." Pescoli, starved as usual, was half-way through a chili dog while Alvarez picked at a root vegetable salad.

"It's lucky he didn't know about Verdago calling his hit list his Dirty Half Dozen. That's what really got me thinking, when Wanda mentioned it," Alvarez admitted. "Why were there seven pictures, not six? It didn't make sense. Obviously the pictures were Brewster's, but he wanted it to look like they were from Verdago's hit list. Verdago never had any photos. That was all Brewster. He figured he'd just add a couple extra to the mix, and he went to great lengths to find pictures of people *he* wanted dead. Fortunately for him, some of them overlapped with Verdago's list."

Pescoli thought back to Brewster standing naked in the cabin and still trying to convince her how smart he was. "He almost got away with it. His list was only three people who just happened to be on Verdago's list, too: the judge, because she was pressuring him to get a divorce; Grayson, because Brewster wanted his job; and me, because basically he doesn't like me. I'd made mention of thinking about becoming a PI and he couldn't have that. I'd be all over him eventually. My gut always told me that something wasn't right with him. He knew it. And my resignation would never have been enough for him. He wanted me in the ground."

"You're too good an investigator to have out there loose."

"Let's not forget I'm Jeremy's mother."

Alvarez nodded. "He would have kept coming after you."

"Yeah," Pescoli said soberly.

Miraculously, Brewster had survived the attack and was in the hospital, under tight security and awaiting arraignment. Though he'd come out of his coma, he wouldn't be able to walk for a long time, if ever. His spinal cord had been compromised by Jeremy's bullet, which was still lodged in his spine.

The rumor mill had it that his wife was leaving him, and as the scandal erupted about her husband not only being a adulterer, but a murderer as well, she'd taken Heidi and moved out of state to live, at least temporarily, with her sister in San Leandro, California.

Jeremy and Heidi had been in contact, however, though she hadn't forgiven him for shooting her father. Pescoli felt badly for the girl, but hoped beyond hope that she found some surfer dude or other California type to take her mind off of her son and the tragedy in Grizzly Falls.

Jeremy, it seemed, rather than being turned off by the experience, was more determined than ever to become a cop. Come spring term, he was starting school full-time and was still volunteering at the department. He'd also become a bit of a hero over the events at Brewster's cabin, and that led to being hired back at Corky's Gas and Go.

So things were looking up.

Her kids weren't even giving her a lot of grief about moving in with Santana. Both Bianca and Jeremy had grudgingly started sorting through their things as Pescoli had told them she refused to move junk that was only going to somehow multiply and fill the closets in their new place.

The move was a month or two off, but Pescoli, now that she'd made up her mind to marry Santana, wasn't about to put up with any procrastination. Though she still harbored some doubts about her mothering skills, she'd pushed them aside. She could only do the best she could do.

Unfortunately, Dan Grayson hadn't yet awoken. He'd stabilized enough that there was talk of moving him to a neurological facility in Seattle that specialized in brain trauma, but so far, he was still at Northern General in Missoula, so Sturgis would be residing with her family for the foreseeable future.

Cade Grayson had stopped by and offered to take the dog, but Pescoli liked having the black Lab around; he kept Cisco on his tiny toes, so she'd asked to keep him. Since then, she'd also heard that Cade was wrestling with the news that he was the father of eight-year-old twins. With his older brother still so seriously ill, she saw why he hadn't argued with her for the added responsibility of the black Lab.

Which brought Hattie Grayson to mind. "You know that Dan's sister-in-law still thinks her husband was murdered," she mused aloud.

Alvarez said, "Still?"

"She seems to be waffling some, but she called me, asked that I keep the case open."

Alvarez pushed her plate aside. "That case is closed tighter than a coffin lid."

"If I'm not too busy, I might take another look. Bart was Grayson's brother, and if there's any chance she's right . . ."

"When won't you be too busy?" Alvarez asked her. "Besides the job, you do have two kids still and a fiancé. And the promise of shorter hours."

"I know," she said and was tempted to confide in her partner, then thought better of it. Time enough in the future. They finished their lunch and later in the day, true to her word of shortening her hours, Pescoli left the station early. She really couldn't imagine never working here again, for as much as she loved Santana, being a cop was in her blood, as, apparently, it was in her son's.

She drove out of the lot and all the way across town to a pharmacy where she was assured of not running into anyone she knew; then she climbed back into her Jeep and headed home. She knew the kids were out, Jeremy working and Bianca with her newest BFF, Lana, a girl who was on the soccer team and who, if anything, was a little on the stocky side. Though Bianca was still "watching what she ate" to fit in that damned two-piece, at least she was eating.

Pescoli was still monitoring her.

Once she was home, she let the dogs out and threw a ball for Sturgis, so that he ran across the yard, Cisco at his heels, enough times to wear him out. Then she fed them both, changed into her pajamas, and made her way to the bathroom where she unwrapped the home pregnancy kit she'd purchased and read the simple instructions.

"Here we go," she whispered and did everything instructed.

A scant five minutes later, it was confirmed: In less than eight months, she would become a mother once more and the whole cycle of parenthood would start all over again.

Oh, joy.

Lisa Jackson

Devious

It's a holy place – but a depraved killer has made it his playground

When a troubled novice is found garrotted in St Marguerite's cathedral, the first detectives called in are Bentz and Montoya. And Montoya knows who she is – Sister Camille was once his brother's girlfriend. He even knows the prime suspect: Father Frank O'Toole, rumoured to be the father of Camille's unborn child.

The deeper the investigation goes, the eerier it gets. More nuns are dying, brutally slaughtered by someone who seems to know their darkest secrets.

Bentz is sure Father O'Toole is their man. But arresting him is another matter. And there are other suspects, too, including a ruthless murderer who is supposed to have died years ago.

Has the monstrous killer known as Father John returned to New Orleans? Or is the truth even more twisted and terrifying?

HODDER

Lisa Jackson

Running Scared

Fifteen years ago in Boston, Kate Summers made a bargain.

She became the mother of a perfect, beautiful newborn baby, and she promised she would never breathe a word about the adoption to anyone.

Then Daegan O'Rourke arrives in her small Oregon town and strikes up a friendship with Kate and her son Jon. Daegan has his own past to hide – one with shocking ties to hers.

Soon, the past Kate thought she could outrun will explode, unearthing a legacy of lies and treachery and a fury powerful enough to kill.

HODDER